My Rogue, My Ruin

LORDS OF ESSEX

My Rogue, My Ruin

LORDS OF ESSEX

AMALIE HOWARD
&
ANGIE MORGAN

Entangled Publishing, LLC
2614 South Timberline Road
Suite 109
Fort Collins, CO 80525
Visit our website at www.entangledpublishing.com.

Select Historical is an imprint of Entangled Publishing, LLC.

Edited by Alethea Spiridon
Cover design by Erin Dameron-Hill
Cover art from Hot Damn Stock

Manufactured in the United States of America

First Edition November 2016

For the Thelma to my Louise

Chapter One

Essex, England, April 1817

Lady Briannon Findlay was going to die.

She sat back against the squabs inside her father's coach, her eyes locked on the lethal nose of a polished pistol barrel, and half wished she had worn a finer gown for the occasion. As it stood, her body would be found on the side of the road in the most atrocious gray velvet dress known to man. She might have had a fighting chance had she been wearing her breeches. And her pistol. Sadly, she had neither.

"No displays of heroism, please," a voice behind the gun drawled.

All sense of time slowed to a dull stop, and Brynn's breath lodged like a stone in her throat. Beckett, their coachman, stood within the open gap of the carriage door, his white, curled wig gone from his head, exposing a mop of red hair. He was not alone. A man suited in black, with a black mask obscuring most of his face, stood beside the coachman, the barrel of a second pistol tucked into Beckett's ribs. Her heart hammered a brutal staccato in her chest.

"Now that we have that out of the way, shall we begin?" the man said with a slow, breaking smile. His teeth caught the shine of the carriage lantern, and Brynn frowned. The highwayman who had just set upon their carriage on the darkened, private lane running between her family's estate and the neighboring grounds of Worthington Abbey possessed, quite possibly, the finest smile she had ever seen.

What sort of robber *smiled* at his victims? Despite the pistols he held and the fear that gripped her, it was his perplexing mouth she was staring at when her mother, seated on the bench opposite, let out with a bloodcurdling scream. Brynn clapped her gloved hands over her ears as Lady Dinsmore's long-winded screech finally waned and croaked off.

The masked man hadn't flinched. Instead, he vaulted a mocking eyebrow to match the smirk on his lips. "My good woman, have a care for the eardrums of your fellow travelers and refrain from doing that again. I assure you, I do not intend for anyone to lose their hearing tonight—just their valuables."

Brynn lowered her hands at his crisp words, her ears ringing. She was certain she'd misheard, but he nearly sounded like a…a *gentleman*. His diction was as precise as a Shakespearean stage actor, over-enunciating each syllable. No, she had to have been mistaken, deafened by her mother's shriek. The man was a common bandit putting on airs, nothing more. She mustered her courage and stared down at him.

The corner of his mouth curled in an answering grin. He sent a pointed look at the pearls Brynn wore. "Start with those earbobs sitting upon such delicate and privileged ears," he said, the sarcasm in his voice thinly veiled. Her fingers itched to slap the condescending grin from his face, though she kept them firmly at her sides, ever aware of the gun pointed at her family.

Lord Dinsmore had been immobile on the bench beside his wife, glaring at the bandit in confounded shock. Now, as Brynn moved to unclasp her beloved earbobs, he sat forward, nearly coming off the seat altogether. "Who the devil do you think you are, you pestilent son of a—"

"Papa, stop!" Brynn held out her arms to stop him from lunging at the bandit. "He has a weapon."

Lord Dinsmore seemed to see the pistol pointing into the carriage for the first time. He instantly sobered and sat back into his seat. Relieved, Brynn met the appraising eyes of their attacker. The scoundrel was still grinning. He was either mad or extremely cocky. She wondered if it wasn't a little bit of both. Neither of those would bode well for them—an arrogant criminal was dangerous. An insane one, even more so.

Her gaze fell to the pistols again. Even from the carriage she could see the coiled tensile strength in his arms. Beckett was a strapping youth, country born and bred, and he hadn't stood a chance against his assailant. He was a hair taller and wider than the masked man, too. Of course, having a pistol aimed at his chest was likely enough to cow him. She wondered whether Colton, their driver, had suffered a worse fate, and her stomach plummeted. He had been driving them to Worthington Abbey for the Duke of Bradburne's annual ball and had stopped the carriage to remove a fallen tree from the lane. It had been a trap, Brynn realized.

"Where is our driver?" she asked, proud she'd kept a measure of strength in her voice.

"Indisposed at the moment, I'm afraid," the man replied, and if not for the pistols or the mask, or the obvious fact that he was about to rob them, Brynn would have warmed at how concerned he sounded.

No displays of heroism, please. Those words he'd spoken…

"You're the Masked Marauder the newspapers have been writing about," Brynn said, recalling at once the numerous articles printed over the last few months. A man had been waylaying carriages in London and its environs and, according to the articles, the Masked Marauder had an unsettlingly smooth, courteous manner while relieving his victims of their personal items. Apparently, he made the appeal for no displays of heroism at the start of each robbery.

Brynn's mother's deathly frightened expression shifted to fierce disappointment. "Briannon! You know how I feel about you reading your father's newspapers. It isn't appropriate."

"Mama," Brynn said through clenched teeth. "Time and place."

The masked man sighed as her mother's face resumed its prior expression. "That ridiculous name. I'd rather be called a bandit than a marauder. Now, to business, if we may?" He cocked the pistol, and Lady Dinsmore startled, her hands fluttering about her person like a pair of terrified birds. "If you would be so kind as to hand all of your glittery baubles to the rebellious Lady Briannon, and of course, whatever is currently weighing down your money purses, I would be obliged. My lord, please do not overlook your cuff links."

Lord Dinsmore all but exploded. "Now see here, you scurrilous blackguard, if you think I'm going to give you anything more than a sound thrashing, you're—"

"Papa!" Brynn cried, again reaching out to her father as he prepared to leap through the carriage door. "Papa, stop!"

Beckett had scrunched his eyes in preparation for the shot to his heart. The guttering oil lamp inside the carriage showed the purple flush creeping up from her father's starched cravat as he held himself still, abandoning his rash action. He slumped back onto the bench in frustrated silence.

"You should thank your daughter for possessing such rational thought," the masked man commented, amusement coloring his tone. Then, "After you hand her your belongings, that is."

Lord Dinsmore continued to glower at the bandit.

"Papa," Brynn pleaded in a low voice, desperate for his safety. The bandit may have sounded like a gentleman, but Brynn sensed he knew how to use the pistols held so confidently in his grasp and would not hesitate to do so if provoked. A cold sensation slunk down to the base of her spine as his shadowed gaze fell upon her. "Please do as he says."

With relief, she watched as her father reluctantly unfastened his engraved gold cuff links and handed them over, along with the small pouch of sterling he always kept in his waistcoat pocket. He nodded at her mother, and Lady Dinsmore *tutted* and *harrumphed* while shedding a magnificent amethyst necklace and matching bracelets along with several rings. Brynn swallowed, removing her gloves briefly to slip the rings from her own fingers onto the growing pile in her lap. She was relieved the folds of her cloak were still drawn tightly around her, concealing, she hoped, her most treasured possession from view.

"Here," she whispered, shoving a gleaming handful toward the masked man. "You have what you want. Now let Beckett go, and leave us in peace."

"If you could be so kind," he said to her, stepping backward with a mocking incline of his head, "as to step out and place those into my satchel. As you can see, I do not have a free hand at the moment."

"Why, you impertinent blackguard!" her father sputtered.

"You needn't worry, my lord," the man said. "Your daughter's virtue will still be intact. I require only her assistance."

Brynn bristled and blushed. How dare he speak of her virtue so blithely? And in front of her *father* no less, who looked as if he were on the verge of apoplexy.

"Do not worry, Papa. I'll be fine," Brynn said, hiking

her chin and attempting to sound reassuring despite the wild hammering of her heart. Her mother seemed to be swallowing yet another deafening scream, her face turning a stormy sunset color.

Brynn stood, hoping her fear wasn't as transparent as her mother's. The newssheets hadn't said anything about the man being a murderer—or worse. She fervently hoped they had not chosen to edit such sordid details.

Brynn cupped the jewelry and coins in her hands and screwed up her courage. She would *not* allow her legs to tremble and display to this vile criminal how nervous she was…especially not when he was staring at her with such sweeping mockery. Her jaw lifted another notch, fueled by righteous indignation.

"Slowly," the man warned as she climbed out of the carriage. He made no move to offer her assistance. He only continued watching her with that heavy-lidded gaze as she jumped the substantial distance from the coach to the road without the carriage steps. Brynn's knee almost buckled, but she held her ground, cursing him under her breath. *The atrocious toad!* When she looked up, she shot him the most contemptuous look she could manage. "Where is this satchel of yours?"

"At my waist," he replied. Brynn saw it then—a loosely cinched pouch the size of a hand reticule, strung around his hips. It hung in a most shocking way, and Brynn found her attention riveted to *that* region of his body. Instantly mortified, a rush of heat warmed her cheeks. Her eyes jerked away.

"You cannot expect me to—"

"Deposit the jewels? No, my lady, I do not expect it. I require it. Your driver is stirring, and I should hate to inflict another blow to the poor man's head."

She clenched her teeth as a wave of anger stormed through her. He'd struck Colton about the head? He was worse than a toad. He was a heartless degenerate who deserved a noose around his neck and a trapdoor under his feet! Fairly glowering with rage, Brynn stood tall before taking a steady, confident stride toward the masked man. She used her pinkies to widen the mouth of the pouch, considering the cups of her palms were filled to the brim, and let it all slide in. "There. You have everything."

Another slow half smile broke across the man's face, making his eyes glint in the lamplight. They, along with his mouth, were the sole features she could see clearly. The black slip of silk covered his forehead to his upper lip and curved down along the masculine cut of his cheekbones and straight nose to his jaw. If he wasn't such a brigand, she would consider him handsome. Brynn nearly swore at herself—her family had been stopped at gunpoint, and here she was, admiring his features like a besotted idiot with cotton in her head.

The bandit's gaze became appraising as he studied her in turn. "Not everything," he said with a pointed gaze to her neckline. Brynn's hand flew to the strand of pearls just visible from beneath her cloak. The folds must have shifted when she'd jumped from the carriage, exposing them. Of all the rotten luck!

It was the first time she'd ever worn her grandmother's pearls, too. She'd wanted to save the three-tiered necklace and drop earbobs for a special occasion, and while the Bradburne Ball was hardly special, Brynn had felt she needed the beautiful accessories to offset such a drab dress. And they *were* beautiful. Priceless and irreplaceable. The idea of losing them to this ruffian made her blood boil.

"Pearls as lovely as those should not be overlooked," he continued, the gun jerking meaningfully in his fingers. "I'll have them as well."

Brynn's breath hitched, and despair filled her. She had already given him the matching earbobs, and even that had skewered her heart. They were Grandmother's most cherished pieces, given to her by Grandfather on their wedding day. Now this man…this *scoundrel*…was ordering her to just hand them over? She raised her chin, choosing to ignore the deadly weapon trained on her. Some instinct—hopefully not a misguided one—told her he wouldn't shoot. "No."

"No?" His voice held a new, deadly timbre, and Brynn's courage faltered. "My lady, while I admire your… persistence—"

"If you want them, you'll have to take them yourself. I refuse to hand them over willingly," Brynn interrupted before her idiotic display of bravery could desert her.

Perhaps if she could get the masked man to holster one of his pistols, Beckett, or Colton, wherever he was, would have a chance to overpower him. She drew a deep, fortifying breath. Her plan could work. It *could*. And it was all she had at the moment.

A reluctant twitch pulled at the corner of his mouth at her audacity. "Then so I shall." He eyed Beckett. "I am going to release you, good man, but I assure you—my weapon will not waver. Take five steps in reverse and then lay upon the ground. Very still. That's good, and with such energy as well," he praised as Beckett crashed belly down on the dirt lane.

He holstered one of his pistols as Brynn had hoped he would, and then closed the door to the carriage with a deliberate snap, separating her from her parents' view. "Your daughter's life rests in your hands," he warned them through the door, the remaining pistol still trained on her. "Not one move."

The bandit's gaze fell back to Brynn. A deep flush rose in her cheeks as his eyes, glittering in a sudden wash of bright moonlight, perused the length of her person. She practically felt the physical press of them as they slowly roved. No doubt the bandit sought some blazing reaction from her. At least the coach door was closed, sparing her parents from this man's indecency. She would not be able to stop her father from doing something rash this time. Her ears burned as his insolent gaze traced her body from the crown of her head to the tips of her toes. She steeled herself, clenching her teeth so hard it felt like they would shatter. His eyes left her feeling bare, as if they were stripping away her clothing, layer by layer.

The dreadfully unfashionable gray velvet gown had been at her mother's insistence. Its long sleeves and high square bodice, which rested just below her collarbone, was a barrier against any chill. One tiny cough yesterday morning had been enough to send her mama into a fit. Brynn counted herself lucky that Lady Dinsmore hadn't insisted on a woolen shawl for good measure.

Though now, as this bandit all but slid the heavy velvet from her shoulders with his eyes, leaving it in a pool around her ankles, Brynn understood that her frumpy dress hadn't deterred him from imagining what lay underneath.

As his lewd attention lingered over the rise of her breasts, Brynn nearly lost her composure.

"Are you quite finished?" she snapped, resisting the urge to draw the cloak around her body like a shield.

Without answering, the man raised his free hand to his lips. His eyes never left hers as he removed the leather glove finger by finger with his teeth. Brynn frowned, but realized that he would need his fingers to maneuver the delicate latch on the string of pearls.

She tried to make eye contact with Beckett, but the cowering footman had his nose in the dirt. She fought the urge to stamp her foot in disgust. So much for her grand plans to foil the bandit with Beckett's help. It appeared she would have to get out of this on her own. The masked man positioned his body directly in front of hers so that she was pinned between him and the side of the carriage. Almost a full two heads taller than she, Brynn couldn't see anything at all but his broad chest directly in her line of sight.

He pocketed the glove and stepped closer still. Brynn's heart skipped. Obviously, she hadn't quite thought this through. Everything about the man was dangerous. His entire body radiated a leashed strength, from the tense muscles in his neck to the rigid line of his jaw. Brynn wanted to believe he wouldn't hurt her, but she wasn't stupid enough to provoke him more than she already had. She held her breath as he lifted his hand toward her.

"Be still, my lady," he said as if reading her thoughts. "Don't mistake my civility for weakness. While the thought of restraining a lady is distasteful, I will do so if necessary."

Brynn believed he would. However, she'd yet to give this man the satisfaction of seeing her terror and had every intention of persevering with the farce. "Would you please do us both a favor and get on with it?"

She held herself like a statue as his hand neared her body. Men had touched her before—to kiss her hand and guide her into a room or into a conveyance. But this man's fingers, as they brushed her shoulder and the line of her collarbone, seeking the clasp at her nape, did not have that same carefully polite touch. Brynn felt sparks of heat blossom under his fingers, as if they hinted at wanting something more than just the jewels around her neck. They moved at a leisurely pace, indulging in some secret pleasure—one he *wanted* her to know, and one that shortened her breath to pained wisps. Brynn flushed hotly when she imagined the indecent thoughts that must be streaming through his rotten mind.

At least his hands were not coarse. She concentrated on that detail instead, and realized this man was likely not one of the poor farmers who populated the countryside surrounding Ferndale and Worthington Abbey. Her eyes narrowed, taking in other small details she'd missed, like the fact that his well-tailored clothes fit his broad frame handsomely. The material was fine. *Expensive*. Curiosity replaced fear as her earlier thought about his perfect, gentlemanly diction resurfaced.

Who was he, if not a common bandit?

Unconsciously, she leaned closer. So close that she could smell a deep woodsy scent surrounding him. It was pleasant, like cedar and smoke, and it made her stomach feel suddenly weightless—an odd sensation, the kind she sometimes experienced when she rode Apollo over a particularly wide brook.

Her eyes darted up to study him, to see if any other detail might reveal his identity. His hair was an indeterminate color, thanks to his brimmed hat obscuring every last strand. His eyes, which had glinted silver before in the light, now seemed inky and unreadable. Every part of his face seemed hard, except for the soft bow of his lips. For a man, he had extraordinarily defined lips. A deep burn scorched her insides. Why on earth did she keep thinking about this horrible man's lips?

One of the bandit's fingers strayed from the clasp and swirled over the sensitive bare skin at her nape in idle strokes, just above the modest neckline of her dress. She sucked in a sharp breath and tipped closer.

"Have you lost your balance, Lady Briannon?" His voice was light and teasing, making her insides hum as if they were tethered to the sensual resonance of his words. She stiffened and, realizing how close she'd drawn to him, pulled away, horrified. He'd meant to distract her, the beast.

She addressed him with as much disdain as she could summon. "I am simply growing bored with your brutish attempts to undo a basic clasp. Haven't you finished yet? Or do you require a lesson in necklace removal?"

His fingers resumed their work. "I would be interested in whatever lessons you wished to offer. However, I can assure you," he said as the pearls fell away from her neck. "I have more than enough experience in removing all manner of ladylike trinkets."

Brynn heard the suggestive laughter in his voice and grew rigid. "I'm quite sure you do."

He was baiting her. Wanting to embarrass her, perhaps. Which made her only more incensed. The man's fingers caressed the nape of her neck as he drew the rope of pearls away. The Masked Marauder, it seemed, had more than his share of experience charming all measure of gently bred ladies. Brynn's jaw clenched as the pearls, along with her pride, slid from her neck.

Without thinking, she stalled his hand with hers and was shocked at the warm contact of his skin. "Please. You can have everything else but these."

"But these, I want."

She lifted her chin. She wouldn't beg, although her hands tightened on his and wound around the dangling length of the necklace. "I don't think pearls complement your coloring, sir."

His eyes widened at her flippant comment. "Yes, far better suited to frumpy old ladies or" — he eyed her up and down, his fingers slipping around to her wrist — "maids in mourning."

Cursing her repugnant dress, Brynn gritted her teeth. "I am not in mourning! Unhand me at once."

"Release the pearls and I shall."

Her fingers tightened upon his in response. She could not give in to him. It was no longer just about her grandmother's pearls. It was the principle of the thing.

"Do you always get what you want?" she hissed.

"I have a fairly decent record."

Of course he did — manipulating unsuspecting women with his eyes and his words and that sinful mouth. Her fingers clawed into his, refusing to let go, and he had the colossal gall to smile down at her. Brynn had half a mind to lunge for the pistol still held loosely in his grasp and shoot the condescension from his face.

The man's voice cut into her murderous thoughts. "Pearls don't suit you. You need rubies to go with that defiant spirit."

"And you need a necklace of braided rope."

The man laughed out loud at her insult and then lowered his voice as he bent his head, his cheek nearly brushing hers. A strangled gasp caught in her throat, his looming presence doing unreasonable things to her shattered nerves. "That may be, but please don't cause a scene, Lady Briannon. Think of your parents. Are these silly baubles truly worth the neck they rest upon?"

Brynn swallowed, the nearness of him and the rough velvet of his voice weakening her resolve. She raised her gaze to his. "They are worth more than you know," she said softly.

Something flashed in his eyes—compassion, perhaps— but then they hardened with cold purpose. After a long, measured look, the man stepped back, and taking her gloved hand in his, bent over it with an exaggerated flourish. His lips seared a fiery imprint on her knuckles, even through the silk of her gloves. "The starving poor these jewels will feed share those same sentiments," he said. "*Adieu*, my lady. I thank you for your generous contribution."

Generous contribution? Brynn stood in stunned silence, her hand forgotten in midair as the man edged backward with a wicked, yet boyish, grin. He disappeared over the tree trunk blockade and into the night. She stared after him, puzzling over what kind of bandit gave his spoils away to the starving poor. He could be lying, of course.

He isn't lying.

She knew it as well as she knew her own anger, which had not ebbed one bit. Blasted bandit. Now she couldn't even be angry without thinking about some hungry person and feeling guilty as well.

"Briannon, darling?" her mother called in a hushed voice. "Has he gone?"

Brynn turned away from the darkened lane to find Beckett still face down on the dirt. She heaved a sigh, the imprint of the bandit's fingers like a brand upon her neck, and his sultry, teasing smile seared into her memory.

"Yes, Mama," she said as she went to help Beckett up. "Gone like a foul wind."

Chapter Two

The Marquess of Hawksfield, Lord Archer Nathaniel David Croft, pinched the bridge of his nose between his thumb and forefinger, anticipating the beginnings of a headache. He reached for the late copy of the *Times* that Porter had brought along with his formal evening clothes. He'd rather read alone with a cigar and a glass of whiskey than be obligated to attend the ridiculous affair his father, the Duke of Bradburne, was hosting at Worthington Abbey that evening.

As he opened the paper, a handwritten piece of parchment fell from between its pages and settled on the desk. He reached for it, curious. The ink-blotted script was nearly illegible, but within seconds he'd made out the four hastily scrawled words: *I know your secret.*

"Porter," he asked in a controlled voice, folding the scrap quickly. "Who delivered these newssheets?"

His valet frowned. "I did, my lord. Is something amiss?"

"No." Archer crumpled the square into a ball in his fist, his mind racing.

Like any man, he had his secrets. A fair number of them,

in fact. Only one, however, was worthy of such a vaguely threatening note passed in so clandestine a manner. With a brief glance at his valet, Archer considered and dismissed that he had been the one to slip the note within its pages. He trusted Porter, and besides, dozens of hands could have touched the newssheets before him. The note could have been placed by anyone. Or it could have been meant for another member of the house party who had bothered to have their daily paper rerouted to Essex for the duration of their stay. Surely there was a score of men currently under Worthington Abbey's roof with secrets ripe for any ambitious blackmailer.

Archer rolled the wad between his fingers thoughtfully and discarded the second theory. The note had been meant for him. He could feel it. Someone had either guessed his secret or had witnessed something firsthand. Whatever it was, this was a coward's way of making a statement. Outside of tearing apart his entire household to find the culprit, there was nothing he could do but wait to see if further notes made an appearance or if the note's owner decided to make himself known.

Ignoring the unsettled thumping of his pulse, Archer set the paper aside and walked toward the fire in the hearth. He tossed the wadded note into the flames.

"Shall I assist, my lord?" Porter asked.

Archer turned from the blackening parchment and eyed the navy silk breeches his valet was holding up for evaluation. He shook his head once. *Breeches.* He was annoyed he even had to look at them.

"I avoid Almack's for a reason, Porter."

Gentlemen were not allowed inside London's most desirable assembly rooms if they were not wearing the effeminate knee-length contraptions. Archer despised them and was in no mood tonight to bend to tradition. Truly, they looked ridiculous on any man.

He stripped out of his comfortable black buckskin pants, wishing he could simply wear them to his father's ball, which was already well underway downstairs. Not this pair, in particular—the seat had a rather large mud stain from when Morpheus had tossed him from the saddle a quarter hour before. The black gelding had shied and pranced as Archer had led him into the yard at Pierce Cottage. Archer had caught movement in the stand of trees beyond the hay field—a fox, he considered in the moments before Morpheus had reared back and thrown him to the ground.

He indicated the black trousers Porter next held up as acceptable and pulled them out of his valet's hand. "You know I hate to rush you, Porter, but I am already late."

The damned horse. It had bucked and brayed, leaping in great circles as Archer had chased it, swiping for the reins and loudly cursing Brandt Pierce, who stood within the doorway of the cottage, bellowing laughter.

Porter pressed his lips into a thin line, reserving his judgment and his opinions. Once again, Archer appreciated his valet's quiet nature. He could trust that Porter, a stout man with a head of thinning blond hair, would make no inquiries as to where the young Lord Hawksfield had been when he *should* have started greeting guests with Lord Bradburne an hour previous.

Archer would have been only a fashionable half hour late had Brandt helped him stay Morpheus rather than watch in amusement; at least he'd left Archer's gray saddled and ready to ride back to Worthington's stables. As he'd taken off toward the path leading to his estate, keeping his bruised arse raised out of the saddle, Archer had shouted over his shoulder that Brandt was sacked and for him to find new employment. Worthington's stable master had made a rude gesture, and Archer had laughed as he'd disappeared into the wooded path.

"My lord?" Porter said as he brushed the shoulders and back of Archer's tailored swallow-tailed jacket.

"Hmm?" Archer grunted, rushing to fasten his cuff links. His fingers paused for a moment over the tiny sterling silver playing dice. Archer well recalled the day his father had presented them to him in a small box. A man's first pair of cuff links is something to celebrate, the duke had cheered. Though it had been a long time since his father had given him anything else worth treasuring.

Porter cleared his throat. "Might I suggest?" he said, holding out a wide-toothed comb.

Archer inspected his appearance in the mirror—his hair was a disheveled mess, currently studded with short strands of hay and a few leaves. He smiled to himself, running the comb through his hair while Porter turned away and collected the discarded black breeches. Hopefully the old chap assumed Archer had been up in a hayloft with one of the many young debutantes visiting Worthington Abbey. Now *that* was the variety of secret most men of the *ton* had to grapple with.

Archer glanced toward the hearth, at the note that had now disintegrated into ash, and once again, he felt as far apart from his peers as ever.

Ten rushed minutes later, he stood against the stone balustrade along the mezzanine, dressed in immaculate black evening wear and a snowy white cravat. He'd stood in this spot countless occasions before, staring down into the ballroom teeming with his father's primped guests. He could not think of a single time he had enjoyed the experience.

He peered down at the crowd, unable to veil his distaste. It was his own home, and yet he could not have felt more uncomfortable. He tipped his glass of whiskey to his lips and swallowed the fire, enjoying the feel of it burning a path to his stomach. He set the empty glass on the tray of a passing server and ordered another to be brought. He would need all the whiskey he could consume for the next few hours to successfully face the hordes of twittering women, egotistic dandies, and all manner of matchmaking mamas.

"My boy!" The duke's voice boomed from behind him, his hand clapping Archer's shoulder. "You look positively angry! It's a ball. Come, have a drink and a dance."

Archer's father did not descend into Essex often, but whenever he did, he brought the entire London set with him. For the last few weeks, Worthington Abbey had been filled to bursting with at least three dozen of the duke's closest friends and acquaintances. Archer hadn't had a moment's peace or privacy since his own arrival, something his father had ordered after the invitations for the house party had gone out. However, tomorrow afternoon the London elite would be making the journey back to the city, and Archer would have Worthington Abbey all to himself. The way he and his sister, Eloise, both preferred it.

He just needed to come out on the other side of this evening with his bachelor status intact, and then he'd have something to truly celebrate. His title and his fortune—or what was left of it, thanks to his pleasure-seeking father—had landed Archer at the top of the most eligible bachelor list. He supposed his father was also on the list, however the mothers of the *ton* ought to have known by now that Bradburne would not be making another offer of marriage to anyone. It had been twelve years since the duchess's death, and he had never once shown a glimmer of interest in taking another wife. That, at least, was one of his father's actions Archer approved of.

"I'll leave the dancing to you," Archer said, accepting the second glass of whiskey the server had brought with brisk efficiency.

His father laughed. He knew full well the *ton* referred to him as the Dancing Duke, and he didn't mind the silly nickname one bit. Had Archer been given a nickname so emasculating he would have throttled the person, man or woman, who'd contrived it.

His eyes roved the crowded room below, and it was then that Archer noticed the curious lack of dancing. The chatter had an edge of panic to it as well, and there seemed to be a large tangle of guests near the long refreshments table.

"What is it?" Archer asked.

"Oh yes, Lord Dinsmore," Bradburne said, taking a deep sip from his own whiskey glass, which by now had likely been refreshed multiple times.

Archer squared his shoulders as he tried to see through the crowd. "What of him?"

"Claims the Masked Marauder set upon his carriage on the way here, to Worthington Abbey. Can you believe it? Took everything. I've had Heed call for the local constable."

Archer tightened his fingers around the whiskey glass. "Have you? Good," he murmured. The nearest constable was four towns to the south, in Greenbriar, and likely wouldn't show up for another few hours. "No one was hurt, I assume?"

"No, thankfully. That would have surely put a damper on the festivities. And, well, I'm just damn glad no one got shot. Had a brace of pistols, Dinsmore says. Knocked their driver clean unconscious!"

Archer fought a roll of his eyes at his father's first concern. The duke was more worried about his ball than whether people had been hurt in an armed robbery. Archer should not have been surprised by his father's shallowness, but he was. It never failed to antagonize him.

"I suppose I should go down there and express my condolences," Archer said, draining the contents of his glass in one swallow.

His father startled a bit and then clapped him on the shoulder for a second time. "Well done, my boy. I'm glad to hear you're going to do more than stand up here scowling at all of us."

Archer slid an arch glance at his father. The duke's ruddy countenance, portly waist, and fleshy jowls were a testament to his lifestyle. Archer had always been told he resembled his late mother—tall, lean, and dark-haired. The physical differences mattered little, however. When one's father was the Dancing Duke, one was due to be considered just as shallow, if only by proxy and on an entirely different level. Where Lord Bradburne was known as a jovial and hedonistic sort of shallow, Archer was considered an aloof and fractious sort of shallow. It suited him well enough for now. His father drew plenty of attention to himself as it was. For Archer, attention was not something he needed, nor wanted.

Bradburne descended the stairs into the wide, rectangular ballroom and approached Lord and Lady Rochester. Rochester was turned away from his wife as he conversed with a dandified fop whose name Archer was happy not to have remembered. He watched from the top of the mezzanine stairs as his father slipped his hand around Lady Rochester's trim waist. She and Bradburne shared a fleeting glance before he removed his hand and slapped Rochester good-naturedly on the back.

His father may have been five and fifty, but he was far from swearing off his days as a rake. He loved the company of women far too much, sometimes more than he did a hand of cards or a good brandy.

Archer looked away and focused on the area around the refreshments table where his sister stood in reluctant conversation with two young ladies, her face covered by its usual veil. The gauzy layers of dark tulle did well covering the deep scarring that stretched across Eloise's face, inflicted as a result of a tragic fire when she was a child. The same fire that had claimed the duchess's life. That didn't stop his courageous sister from being the kindest, sweetest soul in the room, however. Not that the duke would know. He hardly acknowledged her existence, something that never ceased to infuriate Archer.

Orphaned at birth, Eloise was taken in as a ward by the duke's wife, Archer's mother. His mother had been a saint. Not only for taking in the babe, but for tolerating his father's countless infidelities as well. Before the duchess had died, Eloise lacked for nothing. Though she was illegitimate, there was no doubt of her sire—she and Archer had the same nose, the same chin, and even, oddly enough, the same laugh—and the late duchess had made it clear that Eloise was a member of the family.

Archer stared at her now, and despite her polite demeanor, Eloise's lips, just visible under the base of her veil, were pressed thin with discontent. He wished he could do something to put them both out of their misery. He would make it a point to find her later after doing his duty by making the necessary, and utterly drudging, rounds to greet his father's guests.

He kept his gaze forward and his mouth set tight as he descended the staircase and started across the room. Archer allowed nothing more than small nods of acknowledgment to those women who murmured his name in greeting, and to the men who grumbled it. Encouraging conversation would be a tactical mistake. The debutantes and their mothers all wanted one thing—a title or a fortune. Both were preferable, of course. Archer had the former, though the latter was still a work in progress.

He'd fought to bring his family's fortunes back from the brink of financial ruin, incited by his father's disastrous spending habits, though there would always be women who would forgo the promise of coin to become a marchioness. *His* marchioness. Archer, however, had no intention to marry— not now, and not for anything, not even to save his dwindling finances. He valued his freedom too much, and watching his mother suffer at the hands of his adulterous father had left a foul taste in his mouth when it came to the subject of matrimony.

No one attempted to delay him from reaching his destination. There were benefits to having a surly reputation, and limited interaction with his peers was one of them. The crowd of guests parted for him with apprehensive looks, and within moments he was taking a short bow in front of the three people who lived on the neighboring estate.

The very same people he had just robbed. His *secret*, as it were.

"Lord Hawksfield!" Lady Dinsmore's voice was nearly as shrill as that hair-raising scream of hers had been on the lane between Ferndale and Worthington Abbey, and it made him suddenly wish he could edge back the way he'd come.

Archer had expected the lane would be rife with his father's flashy guests. He'd expected the ladies would be wearing their best jewels. But what he had not expected in the least was to chance upon their neighbor's carriage carrying the enigmatic Lady Briannon, whom he hadn't seen in years. Nor her tempestuous, if foolish, hold on that strand of pearls.

Despite not being his typical target—he much preferred taking wealth from those who flaunted it—Archer had felt only a mild twinge of regret on the lane. The Dinsmores were not lacking in fortune, and the baubles he had taken, including the lady's treasured pearls, would soon be replaced.

"My lady," he replied, his tone low and unfailingly polite as usual. Archer turned to the man at her side. "Lord Dinsmore. My deepest regrets on tonight's misfortune. I hope none of you were injured in any way."

"No, thank heavens," Lord Dinsmore said and, fiddling with his cravat, added, "but the miscreant barely got away from a sound thrashing, that I can assure you."

A number of the other men surrounding Lord Dinsmore

gave rallying replies such as "Here, here!" and "That's the spirit!" Archer fought the twitch of his lips. Tales like this one seemed to become embellished by the minute.

He cleared his throat and took another sip of his whiskey. Altering his voice while on a raid was always a challenge, and it had the tendency to leave behind an irritating tickle. A necessity, however, considering his true baritone tenor was rather noticeable. The one he'd adopted as the Masked Marauder made him sound, according to Brandt, like a jaunty thespian. Archer cringed every time. He didn't enjoy making himself out to sound like a jaunty anything, let alone a *thespian*. But no matter. A glass or three of whiskey seemed to repair his throat well enough.

"I daresay he did," Archer replied to Dinsmore. "He should count himself lucky. The local constable will arrive shortly. If you have a description of the thief to share, I am sure the scoundrel will be brought to swift justice."

"And our belongings returned!" Lady Dinsmore shrilled.

Archer nodded sagely rather than reply. The English sterling Lord Dinsmore had handed over would be distributed before dawn, and the pouch of jewels would be taken into Scotland to a pawnbroker Brandt trusted. Archer had every faith his oldest friend would not part ways with the broker until they had each reached a satisfactory exchange.

Brandt was the only one who knew the truth of things, though the mysterious note, now ash in his fireplace, worried Archer. The note's owner obviously had a purpose. If his secret came to light, the Bradburne legacy would be ruined. Now was not the time to dwell upon such outcomes, however.

He turned his head slightly in Lady Briannon's direction and waited out the awkward moment of silence. Though they had known each other as children, it had been several years since they had met in public. It would be considered rude to speak to the young lady without a proper reintroduction first.

The last thing he wanted to display was a lack of propriety, so he stood there, his neck under his cravat growing warmer by the second. They'd experienced plenty of impropriety with the masked thief, and he wanted to draw no correlations.

Archer had purposefully slipped into that rakish role the last few months whenever he'd donned his black kit and silk mask. The act had been as necessary as his altered voice in order to preserve his identity. However, this evening on the deserted lane, he had actually found himself enjoying it.

Lady Dinsmore must have been truly out of sorts to neglect making the required introduction, however, the Dowager Countess Falthorpe, standing beside Lady Dinsmore, was not as distracted.

"Lord Hawksfield, have you not yet made the acquaintance of Lady Briannon?"

The young woman stood demurely on her mother's opposite side. He'd taken her as a brunette in the gloomy shadows of the wooded lane, but now that she stood underneath the ballroom's chandeliers, he saw that her hair was more coppery gold than brown. The coils piled atop her head and pinned into place shimmered as they caught the light. And she was tiny—slim as a waif. So small he could probably lift her with one hand. She'd seemed taller before, standing up to him on the deserted lane.

"Oh yes!" Lady Dinsmore exclaimed, at last coming to attention. "May I present our daughter, Lady Briannon. She's to make her bow during the upcoming season, you know."

A faint flush colored Briannon's cheeks at her mother's sheer exuberance, but to her credit, she said nothing.

Archer made another short bow, his hands clasped at his back.

"My lady, I hope this evening's earlier events do not keep you from enjoying yourself tonight."

He prepared himself for her tart reply. Perhaps how

the only thing she might enjoy would be to see that masked scallywag strung up by his toes. Yes, he could imagine her saying something so bold.

"Of course, my lord," she said, making a limp curtsy.

He waited for something more, but she had turned her eyes to the marble floor and sealed her prim, though perfectly shaped, lips. Archer frowned. Where was the determined girl who had squared off against him with nothing but pride and spirit backing her?

The distance in her voice threw him, and it seemed to disappoint her mother as well. The countess stumbled into a monologue regarding her daughter's accomplishments, but Archer let the words slide. The fire he'd glimpsed inside Lady Briannon had been extinguished somewhere between the wooded lane and this ballroom. Or perhaps, he thought a bit ruefully, that fire had been stoked only by the appearance of the masked bandit. However, now, with her blowsy dress, pale complexion, and tepid manner, Lady Briannon struck him as bland. Truly, it was a shame.

At last, Lady Dinsmore finished heaping praise on her daughter, whose ear tips had gone a startling shade of red. Briannon must have sensed the torture was ending, for she lifted her gaze from the floor and looked at him through a fringe of deep russet lashes. Her eyes, it turned out, were a sparkling hazel. They fluttered to his in a brief, pained moment before averting again. *Damn it.* He'd been scowling, though he hadn't felt the expression upon his lips until right then. Archer composed it into something less menacing.

"Do you enjoy the quadrille, Lord Hawksfield?" Lady Dinsmore chirped.

Lord Dinsmore had made a stealthy getaway during his wife's lengthy list of Lady Briannon's attributes, as had most of the other men and women surrounding them. The Dowager Falthorpe was the only one remaining. She belted out a laugh that most ladies would not have gotten away with. However, being a wealthy widow of advanced age gave the dowager plenty of room to move.

"Lord Hawksfield enjoys standing still with a glass of punch, if I am correct," she said, still amused.

He indicated his glass. "Whiskey, madam."

"But all young men do so enjoy the quadrille, don't they?" Lady Dinsmore persisted. "Or at least a country dance? Such energy!"

At that wretched moment Archer heard the hired quartet's current selection end, the rustle of sheet music, and then the first familiar strains of a waltz. Lady Dinsmore's indrawn gasp actually pained him.

"What fortune!" she exclaimed.

"Mama!" Lady Briannon hissed. "It is a *waltz*."

It was his father's preferred dance. The waltz brought the body of a female much closer than a quadrille or country dance. Archer did not waltz. He knew the steps, of course. He just didn't care to encourage mothers or their daughters.

He forced what he hoped passed for a smile. "Surely Lady Briannon's dance card is already filled."

"Nonsense! We've just arrived. It would be an honor for you to take the first dance, Lord Hawksfield."

This was a matchmaking mama to be reckoned with, he thought, as she all but shoved her daughter into his arms. He couldn't decline now without being intolerably rude. He set his whiskey on the corner of the refreshments table and extended his arm toward Briannon. Smiling tightly, he wished he could escape to the stables instead for a rousing round of cards with Brandt. The look of unrestrained glee on Lady Dinsmore's countenance was almost too much to take.

"I'd rather not," Briannon said under her breath, softly enough that only Archer would be able to hear.

"We don't want to disappoint Mama, do we?" he

interjected. Her darkened gaze slammed into him, but she slid her gloved palm into his without a ready retort.

She remained close-lipped as they entered the floor, joining the other couples swirling in time with the music. Archer settled his arm around her waist and clasped her hand in his. For all the world, the girl looked as grim as if she was being led to the gallows.

"It isn't as scandalous as all that, Lady Briannon," he murmured. "They are even dancing the waltz at Almack's, or so I'm told."

She said nothing as they moved through the steps, Archer's footwork a little rusty here and there. He truly despised dancing. Apparently, so did the lady holding herself like a block of marble in his arms.

"I see you cannot tear your eyes away from my cravat, Lady Briannon," he said, unable to resist such a prime opportunity to tease. "My valet will be quite pleased to know you approve of his handiwork."

"You look quite well, my lord."

"As do you."

"Thank you, my lord."

Archer bit his tongue and resigned himself to the task at hand. They continued to float around the other dancing couples. Despite the fact that Briannon's body brushed against his time and again, Archer found his attention starting to stray. He didn't even have the distraction of décolletage due to the distastefully prim bodice of her gown. He caught a few glances of surprise, one of which came from his father, whose partner was none other than Lady Rochester. He brought his attention back to the dainty slope of Lady Briannon's forehead and tried to think of something that would engage the timid little mouse.

"Are you often at Ferndale?" he asked.

"Yes, my lord. When we're not in Town."

"How is Lord Northridge?" he pressed, referring to her older brother. He'd crossed paths with the chap over the years. Despite their childhood acquaintance, they had never come to socialize in the same circles. Easy to do, Archer supposed, considering he kept his circle rather small.

From memory, Graham Findlay, the Viscount Northridge, was reputed to be nimble with a sword, fleet with a hand of cards, quick with his temper, and generous with his attentions to the female set. He was first in line to inherit his family's considerable fortune, as well as his father's prestigious title. They had crossed paths in the past, though on those occasions, Archer had found the young viscount to be a little too similar to the duke in his pleasure-seeking. Then again, Northridge's disposition might have changed in recent years. Brandt seemed to always be mentioning that the viscount was at Ferndale. Perhaps he now preferred the quieter life of Essex to the pace of London.

"Graham is well, thank you," Lady Briannon replied, barely above the tenor of the violins. "He has recently completed his final year at Oxford."

Archer was quite sure most young ladies in training to catch a husband would have taken the opportunity to ask if he himself had enjoyed attending university. They would have pretended to have never heard the rumors that he'd been tossed out of Eton for poor marks, or that he'd been suspended from Cambridge for forming an underground boxing club and gaming hell.

Lady Briannon simply stared at his cravat a bit more.

Archer thought back to the exchange with Briannon outside of the earl's carriage, wondering at the dramatic change in her demeanor. He sighed. It seemed she'd been aghast at the thought of losing her jewels, nothing more.

He glanced down his nose and saw Lady Briannon peering up at him.

"What is it?" he asked, his voice harsher than he'd anticipated. Twice now she'd caught him indulging a private thought.

For a moment, he wasn't sure she was going to answer. But then she looked up, her chin—the cut of a diamond, he noted—imperious. Archer also noticed she had a dusting of freckles across the bridge of her nose. She had attempted to cover them up with powder.

"This is as excruciating for me as it is for you," she said.

He forgot the freckles and stared at her. "What did you say?"

"I believe you heard me," she said and then added softly, "my lord."

"What makes you think dancing a waltz with you is excruciating?"

Lady Briannon smiled. The small gesture transformed her entire face. He almost faltered on the next step.

"Because just then you looked as though you had eaten something extremely disagreeable," she answered. "And since you aren't eating at the moment, I assume it is either my dancing or the people in this room."

"Why must it be just one of those two options?" Archer couldn't resist saying.

Lady Briannon's smile widened, revealing a peekaboo dimple in her left cheek. "I'll have you know, I've had the best dancing tutors from Paris. Italy, too. Mama insisted."

Archer shifted his jaw, the spark of humor dying a quick death. He was certain the countess had not spared a single expense on her daughter's "education." Every young lady in the room had a fortune's worth of vain and insubstantial training, all with the objective of snaring a husband. His eyes grazed his sister as she slid along the perimeter of the room, toward an exit, and he stifled a twinge of pity in his gut. Perhaps not all ladies. Although she had received all the necessary education, Eloise had missed her bow due to her disfigurement. She had never let the tragedy twist her, though.

"So you see," Lady Briannon was saying. "I am afraid we have no choice but to lay the blame upon the others."

Archer laughed then, a sound that had more than a few heads turning. He stifled it quickly. He was not known for displays of emotion, and certainly not at the hands of an inexperienced debutante.

He released her and bowed as the music ceased.

"You're correct, it is most definitely the others here. You dance quite capably. Thank you for the dance, Lady Briannon."

She hesitated, as if taken aback by his sincerity. "It was my pleasure, my lord."

He eyed her. The word *pleasure* falling from those full lips made him think of pursuits other than dancing. He knew, however, that such desires were unreasonable. Instead, Archer took a step back, searching for her mother, who had been watching the two of them with unabashed delight. Lady Dinsmore was now engaged in excited conversation with another guest, and he doubted he and Briannon had more than a minute before she made her way back to them. He turned from her and searched for his glass of whiskey, preparing to take his leave. Sadly, the glass had been cleared away.

"Excellent dancing is always a forte for a girl who is about to make her mark on the season," he said. It was a safe, emotionless statement.

"Make my mark," Briannon echoed, then made a sound that sounded suspiciously like a snort. "I'd rather fall from a cliff than—" She broke off, her lips still parted, her expression appalled.

Archer inclined his head, hopeful. "Than what?"

Briannon's mouth closed briefly before she jutted that

pert chin of hers and finished speaking. "Than to be paraded in front of all eligible *ton* like prized horseflesh."

Archer's arched brow went flat, and his lips parted in astonishment. She'd actually met his challenge.

"Come now," he said, ignoring the many pairs of eyes that were riveted to their exchange. Now that that fiery spirit had emerged, he wanted to draw her out even more. "It's not all that bad. Prized horses don't get to wear several gowns a day and jewels on every available appendage, do they?"

Briannon's eyes widened. "Is that truly how you view the women of your acquaintance? As mere fashion plates?"

"Certainly not the most current woman of my acquaintance," he said, thinking to tease her about her dismal gray gown. He'd done so on the wooded lane, and it had spiked a stimulating rise of her temper.

Not this time.

At her stricken gaze, Archer wanted to kick himself. Her mouth tightened, shutters falling over the eyes that had been sparking with amusement mere seconds before.

"Of course, my lord," she said, her cheeks flooding with humiliated color as she gathered her velvet skirt and darted a panicked look to where her mother was approaching through the crush of bodies. "Will you please excuse me?"

Archer stared after her, an apology stalled on the tip of his tongue. His words had been careless and cold. He shouldn't have felt sorry for them. He shouldn't have been feeling guilty at all in regards to Lady Briannon. He'd robbed her carriage and knocked her driver unconscious a mere hour previous. Feeling guilty was not something Archer could afford.

But the young lady was such a contrast of opposites—dull and lifeless one minute and a surprising spitfire the next. Archer remembered the feel of her small, trim body in his arms during the waltz, and for a minute wondered what lay underneath all those unattractive yards of velvet. He shook off the thought. He did not need unnecessary attachments, not with anyone, not even his charming, if puzzling, neighbor.

Lady Briannon had piqued his interest, yes, with her spirit on the lane and her daring statements on a woman's duty. However, beneath that minute spark of intelligence and temper, she would undoubtedly be like all the others in the *ton*. Spoiled, entitled, and insipid.

His tastes simply did not run toward naive debutantes. At the moment, they did not stray further than brief encounters with the sort of women who were perfectly content with remaining near strangers. Becoming involved with any lady of his own set would be madness, especially now that it appeared there was someone close by, hinting that they could expose his secret and bring scandal down upon him.

As much as the *ton* considered him to be ruthless, Archer was not without a conscience. No lady deserved the fate that could befall her should he take her to wife. He drew a grim breath. Not now, and especially not after that bloody note.

Chapter Three

The tip of the foil struck Brynn's chest. The long, thin steel blade bowed from the force of her adversary's thrust, and she muttered a string of curses. Though the mask she wore muted the words, her opponent still heard them.

"My, my, I certainly hope you unleashed that tongue of yours on the Masked Marauder. It would have served the devil right." Brynn's brother, Lord Graham Northridge, or simply Gray as she had always called him, cut a sly grin before poking her white padded vest one last time. "That's four points. One more and I take the match."

Brynn gripped the handle on her fencing foil, her gloved hand sweating from the sparring she and her brother had been doing the last hour in one of Ferndale's attic rooms. Her brother had left London and traveled the short journey to Essex the moment he received word of the armed robbery. She was glad he'd come, though he needn't have. They were all perfectly well and safe now, though she did prefer to have her older brother at Ferndale. Sparring by herself was no fun at all, and besides, having Gray around meant that Mama could divide her focus between both of her children, rather than showering Brynn with all of it.

"As the scoundrel was in possession of a loaded pistol, he received a minor dressing down compared to what you're about to receive," she replied, and before her brother could prepare, Brynn advanced and lunged. Gray's foil came up a beat too late and was unable to deflect her own. The blunted tip struck his shoulder. Gray swore loud enough for the kitchen maids four stories below to hear. "I win, brother."

"Cheating woman," he growled. "You're supposed to warn your opponent of an attack."

Brynn stepped back and spread her arms wide. "Where, pray, is the intelligence in that?"

Gray ripped off his mask. Damp waves of golden hair crashed around his sweaty temples. "It is the honorable thing to do while fencing, Brynn."

She rolled her eyes. Honestly. Men and their honor.

"However," Gray continued, dropping his foil to the dusty, bare, board floor. "In the event of a true fight, I expect you to be *dis*honorable and lunge first."

She smiled, dropping her own foil and pulling up her mask. "Most gentlemen would advise a lady to run and scream."

Gray arched one of his golden brows at her while unfastening his gloves. "Most gentlemen would be wiser than to teach their little sister swordplay. I don't know why I let you talk me into this. Fencing is for men, not girls—and not poorly ones at that."

Poorly! She scowled at him. "You always say that, and yet here you are. Fencing, no less, with a poorly girl!" Brynn said with a grimace, unlacing the ties along the side of her protective vest. "And losing, might I add."

She smiled brightly to cover up the twinge that slid up her back once the fabric released. Her heart was thudding more rapidly than usual, yes, but only because of the exertions of the last hour. Good, healthy, robust exertions.

The corner of her brother's lips twitched, betraying his amusement.

"How are your lungs?" he asked, as if inquiring about a person's lungs was commonplace.

She chucked her padded vest at him, which he easily sidestepped. He had only been teasing her this time. It wasn't always so.

Brynn's lungs might as well have been another member of the family for all the attention they were given. As an infant, Brynn had suffered from all sorts of health ailments surrounding her lungs and heart: a weak pulse, an irregular heartbeat, and the occasional shortness of breath. It had been years since her last bout of pneumonia, however, and she hadn't been short of breath for ages. Last spring, during one of her secret countryside rides with Gray, if she were to be exact. Thank heavens. She detested feeling like an invalid, and it was even worse being treated like one.

Brynn had been cosseted all her life, but she couldn't fault her mother for it—the two babies she'd birthed between Gray and Brynn had both died of the same mysterious respiratory ailments brought on by complications of croup. Brynn had the good fortune to survive and had been smothered ever since.

Mama was the worst of them when it came to fretting over her daughter's health, but Gray did worry. Brynn noticed it in the careful way he'd inspect her whenever they slowed their horses to a walk while riding Ferndale's grounds. It was in the sharp looks he sent her whenever she coughed or wheezed during one of her usual winter colds. Or like now, when he took a furtive glance over his shoulder to assess the coloring of her cheeks.

Brynn caught him and shook her head. "I'm sweaty as a wildebeest, Gray, and not in any danger of fainting. Honestly, stop worrying that I'm going to swoon any second. I'd never hear the end of it, would I?"

He grinned, displaying the dimple in his left cheek that the two of them shared. Brynn had always thought it suited him better than it did her.

"I don't think wildebeests are excessively sweaty creatures," he said.

"Is that what they taught you at Oxford?" she cut back.

"Actually, we studied the elusive pygmy marmoset."

Grinning, she swatted him on the shoulder as they placed their fencing gear in the room's small closet. Her brother liked to tease her, and she liked to pretend it vexed her, when really it was the most wonderful thing in the world.

Brynn shut the door and hoped none of the upstairs maids would be sent on a mission to clean out this part of the attic. If Mama were to hear of fencing gear being discovered in a closet, it would not take her long to ferret out the reason. Gray had been the one who'd taught Brynn to ride, too, and when Mama had learned about *that*, the tongue thrashing had been unforgettable.

Gray made a first inspection of the attic corridor before opening the door wide.

"Our escape route is clear," he said in a dramatic voice that might have rivaled a stage villain. She faltered a moment, remembering the quick, expressive tempo of the masked bandit's voice. Perhaps he was indeed an actor, trained to modify his voice from role to role. She shook her head. It didn't matter now.

They started for the attic stairwell, Brynn's day dress slightly wrinkled from the protective vest she'd been strapped into. She tried to smooth the linen but to no avail.

"Mother said he spoke to you."

Brynn turned to her brother, who had turned completely serious.

"The Masked Marauder," he prompted. "Mother said he

ordered you out of the carriage and then closed the door."
Gray slowed his pace and took her elbow in hand, an ominous
warning in the press of his fingers. "Did he touch you?"

"No, of course not. I was unharmed, I assure you." Brynn
considered her words with care, knowing that if she told him
the truth, Gray would explode. "He was…not at all what I
expected of a bandit."

She recalled the gentle way the masked man's fingers had
skimmed across her exposed nape and the tender skin of her
throat. Yes, his eyes had undressed her with barely concealed
fervor, but even that, she had determined after thinking on it
multiple times, had still been done…well…*gentlemanly*, she
supposed. Though that did not seem the correct word for it.

No common bandit would have such smooth fingers or
polished manners, either. She flushed at the recollection, and
then noticed her brother's eyes darting to the sudden bloom
of color in her cheeks.

"What is it? Are you unwell?"

God help her, she couldn't stop the heat from rushing
across her face, and not even her brother's alarmed
expression could cool the flood. The more she thought about
that atrocious man's fingers, the more flustered she became.
Gray's eyes widened as he grasped her arm.

"Sit," he urged, pulling her to a cream-and-mauve striped
silk bench at the end of the hall. "You're having a spell. I knew
I shouldn't have pushed you so hard."

Brynn could hardly admit to her brother that the cause of
her "spell" was a belated reaction to a stranger's touch. He'd
hunt the man to the ends of the earth if he knew. And truly, it
wasn't as if the masked man had touched her in any unseemly
way—had he? It had all happened so very quickly. Perhaps
she only imagined his fingers lingering on her overheated
skin. Perhaps she had gone over the encounter so many
times she had started to change her memory of what had

actually occurred to what she had *wanted* to occur. Which was ludicrous. Had the scoundrel attempted to slide his fingers through a gap in her modest lace neckline, she would have crushed his instep with her foot.

Brynn took in a labored breath. "I'm fine, Gray. Truly." She flailed around for an acceptable excuse, her eyes scanning the narrow hallway. "These rooms haven't been touched in years. I'm certain it's just the dust."

Gray seemed unconvinced. "Are you sure?"

"I'm sure." To prove her point, Brynn managed a realistic sneeze. She squeezed her brother's hand, watching the lines of anxiety fade from his face. "Please, don't fret over me," she added. "This is the first time I've been able to relax all week, especially after the robbery and Mama trying to marry me off before the season is even underway." Brynn stood up from the bench, her breathing finally returning to normal. "To that awful Marquess of Hawksfield, no less."

"Hawksfield?" Gray's brows snapped together. "Hmm. Mother *would* want you to set your cap at a future duke, but you'd do far better than to marry him."

As they turned down the carpeted steps, the muggy air of the attic cleared, and Brynn breathed easier.

"What do you know of him?" she asked, curious at his cryptic words.

Gray's eyes narrowed in on her as they descended the stairs. "Why do you ask?"

Her brother had always been perceptive. Either that or Brynn had never mastered the ability to sound indifferent when speaking of something that mattered to her.

"Oh, I don't know," she said quickly. "He just seems rather boorish."

"Don't let that fool you. Hawk is a wolf through and through. Values his horses more than he does anything else, including women. Though he's likely as much of a rake as the

Dancing Duke is."

Brynn had actively avoided her neighbor for the remainder of the Bradburne Ball, and in doing so, had unfortunately been required to keep an eye on him as well. She hadn't noticed Hawksfield dancing with any of the ladies in attendance, flirting with them in alcoves, or dashing out onto the terrace "for air" with them. In fact, he spent more time at the side of his sister, Lady Eloise, than he had entertaining his guests.

He certainly hadn't seemed like a rake while dancing with Brynn, either. He hadn't spoken with the kind of smooth elegance and wit she imagined would charm a lady. Why, the bandit had done a better job of acting the seducer than Lord Hawksfield! And that cut about her dress had left her seething and humiliated, while the bandit's barb that she was in mourning had, in retrospect, been slightly humorous.

If Lord Hawksfield was a seducer, he hid the evidence well. However, she couldn't fault him for valuing his horses. They were one of the things she truly valued herself. It got her thinking about Apollo, her chestnut Hanoverian, and how she hadn't taken him out in days.

"Why do they call him that?" Brynn asked as they twisted down the wide stairwell, toward Mama's day room where tea would be underway, no doubt. "Hawk?"

Gray cleared his throat, hesitating as if he'd opened Pandora's box. "Because Hawksfield has a habit of going after what he wants with relentless purpose."

Brynn thought of the marquess's forbidding countenance and unsmiling face. She could see that about him. He did seem ruthless. "You don't like him."

"I don't like him as a match for you."

"Why?"

"Call it male instinct." Gray glowered, his words clipped. He paused, his irritation draining as quickly as it had come.

"And you're right—he is an arrogant boor."

"At last, we agree on something," Brynn said, surprised at his outburst. "He'd leech the very last bit of health from my poor, ailing body." She fanned herself and batted her eyelashes. However, Gray didn't take her joke. Instead his face darkened into a frown as if something else upsetting had just occurred to him.

He paused before they came within hearing distance of the day room, where Mama would be waiting for them.

"You're certain the bastard didn't touch you?" he asked, his voice cast low.

"Lord Hawksfield?" Brynn blurted, shocked at her brother's violent words.

"No, the thief," Gray clarified, keeping the menacing slant of his brows. "But I'll see Hawksfield at the end of my pistol as well if he's been inappropriate."

Brynn frowned, wondering at the thud of her heart. Lord Hawksfield had not been inappropriate, and he'd made it very clear he did not wish to be.

"No, he wasn't. Lord Hawksfield, I mean. And neither was the bandit. He just instructed me to hand over the jewels."

And insert them in a pouch strung around his waist, dangerously close to his trim, shadow-clad hips.

Brynn flushed again and took a deep breath. "Truly, Gray. That was all. Though I should have chucked Grandmother's pearls into the woods rather than give them over."

Gray winced. He knew how special the pearls had been to her. How much she'd loved Grandmother and Grandfather. He held out his arm to her, his face grim. "Whoever he is, I hope he rots in hell."

Brynn, eager to lighten the black mood, linked her arm through his. "Speaking of thieves…what of Lady Cordelia? Rumor has it she's stolen your heart and an engagement is in order."

"Not likely. Unless you want an ice queen for a sister-in-law."

"Gray! That's not a nice thing to say in the least. Lady Cordelia is lovely," Brynn said. *And as frosty as anything*, she silently agreed. That wasn't fair, of course. Cordelia was one of Brynn's friends and had adored Gray since they were children. Despite her exceedingly prim and proper nature, which some could consider cold, she had the pedigree and the wealth to make Gray an excellent match. *Great heavens*. Her thoughts were starting to sound like Mama's.

"If you say so," he muttered.

She inspected her brother with a critical eye. With his blond waves and the classic lines of his nose and jaw, most ladies would consider him handsome. He would have his pick of women when it came time for him to take a wife, though Gray didn't appear at all interested in the prospect of marriage. She smiled, resting her cheek against his sleeve just before they turned the corner into the day room.

"I'm glad you're home, Gray," she murmured. "I've missed you."

"Me too, moppet," he said with a fond smile, rumpling her hair. "Now come on, let's go in before Mother sends a runner from Bow Street to hunt us down."

They were both grinning like a pair of idiots when Gray stepped inside the day room. Mama looked up, her face folding into a frown at the sight of Brynn's flushed cheeks and Gray's amusement.

"Briannon! Why is your gown in such disarray? And your hair! Absolutely dreadful. You two haven't been out riding again, have you?"

Brynn sighed—her mother's eagle eyes missed nothing. She stayed silent as her mother's tirade shifted to her brother. Better him than her. "Graham, how many times must I remind you of your sister's condition?"

Gray bent to kiss his mother's cheek. "Of course, Mama, which is why we went for a light stroll instead."

Brynn bit back a giggle at Gray's bald-faced lie. He winked at her, and Brynn had to duck her head to hide her answering grin.

"Well then," their mother said, all smiles now. "Come sit with your mama and have a spot of tea. Brynn, you can work on your needlepoint."

"While I would love nothing more than the pleasure of your company, Mother, I do have a previous engagement," Gray said, eyes twinkling as he looked to his sister. "And as much as I am in awe of Brynn's talent with a needle, I shall leave you ladies to it."

Brynn wanted to stick out her tongue at him. Her light mood disappeared as Gray took his leave—she'd give anything to be off with her brother somewhere instead of cooped up in this stuffy old room. She sat upon a slipper chair and picked up her embroidery hoop. She stabbed the needle violently through the canvas, feeling the heat of her mother's censorious stare.

"Come now, darling," she said. "Small stitches."

"I loathe needlepoint," Brynn grumbled as she made another precarious stab.

"It is an art, my dear. And an accomplishment for any suitable wife," her mother countered.

"I don't see how small stitches will win a man's heart," Brynn muttered. The needle tip went through the open weave canvas and poked the pad of her thumb. She paused, tossed her hoop and needle, and sucked on her throbbing finger. At least the fencing foils she and Gray had just been using could not injure her in any way.

"Small stitches will win his admiration for your attention to detail and finery," Mama said. Her mother would always have a ready retort. For Brynn to hope that she would ever have the last word when her mother was present was futile.

"Don't frown, Briannon. Your coloring is much too pale for such morose expressions," she went on. "Show some excitement. Yesterday was your first official visit to Worthington Abbey. His Grace looked well, and you know what I've always said, my dear: a girl can't do better—"

"Than to catch a duke. Yes, I remember." Brynn reined in a strong desire to groan. "But, Mama, you cannot seriously entertain the idea that I marry a man twice my age."

Lady Dinsmore's eyes widened and her mouth popped open, her own needlepoint forgotten in her hands. "Marry the duke? Oh, my dear girl, of course not! Everyone knows he isn't in the market for a wife."

Brynn let out a breath and let her shoulders relax. However, her mother wasn't finished. She resumed her stitching, and added, "I should think you would do much better to marry his son. Lord Hawksfield was a capable dancing partner, was he not? And he seemed decidedly interested in you."

Her mother began to rattle off all the reasons it would be a perfect match, but Brynn refused to listen. "Absolutely not, Mama. The man has no manners whatsoever."

Insulting her gown had been the least of it. He'd been unable to mask how distasteful dancing with her had been, what with his constant frown and stiff back and neck.

"You cannot fault the boy for having a country upbringing—and by servants no less!" her mother replied. "It is no wonder he isn't as gentle as the rest of the men of our acquaintance. He simply wants for guidance."

Brynn bit her lip from replying that she'd be more than obliged to guide him—straight into a pond.

Until the evening before, Brynn hadn't set eyes on her neighbor for several years. She'd heard the rumors, though. Of how he'd been raised in Essex after his mother's tragic death, while his father, the duke, had ensconced himself in

London society. How Hawksfield was said to be cold, surly, and humorless, the opposite of his citified, pleasure-seeking father. From his swarthy coloring and unyielding frown, she held no doubt that the rumors of his heathen upbringing were valid. And now, after one silly dance, Mama seemed inclined to chase him down and shove Brynn into his path.

However, her brief interaction with Lord Hawksfield last night had convinced Brynn that the man found her of little interest. He hadn't sought her out for a second dance or even glanced her way after their torturous waltz. No, regardless of her mama's designs, Brynn had failed miserably at hooking Hawksfield as a husband. It was a relieving thought. While she did wish to be successful in finding a husband either this season or the next, she didn't wish to merely *hook* one.

She wanted to respect her intended. She wanted to admire him, and, of course, be admired in return. Was it too much to hope for laughter or companionship in a marriage? The marquess had not struck her as the sort of man who could fill that order. And a girl had to have standards. Brynn wasn't naive enough to dream of a love match, but if her papa had to accept an offer, she'd be damned if she didn't at least *like* the man.

A loud clatter of hooves and the jangle of carriage tack sounded just beyond the day room windows, where the gravel drive rounded a fountain. Perfection. A visitor had arrived to rescue her from this monotony. Her mother peered up at her from over her half-moon spectacles and pursed her lips. "Straighten your back, dear. Whoever it is will not wish to see your shoulders in such a slump."

Brynn did as she was told, though not without a groan. And when a moment later the horse and carriage began to pull away and retreat down the drive, she couldn't contain her disappointment. Apparently a visitor wouldn't be rescuing her after all. A minute hadn't passed before Braxton, their butler, appeared within the doorway and bowed.

"What is it, Braxton?" her mother asked.

"A package, my lady," he said, his eyes shifting to Brynn. "For Lady Briannon."

Victory! Brynn tossed her hoop and needle back into the basket at her feet and stood. Her gaze panned from her mother to Braxton, who held a long, flat case bound in crimson silk ribbon.

"Were you expecting a package, dear?" Mama asked.

"Not at all," Brynn answered, with that warm, peculiar delight that only an unexpected parcel could give.

Mama nodded for Braxton to bring the parcel into the room. Brynn reached for the box, admiring the intricate carvings along its top. The box alone was an exquisite gift, carved from the richest mahogany and inlaid with gold. Brynn's breath caught as she ran her hands along the gilded swirls.

"Is there a note?" she asked.

"No, my lady. Only the instruction to deliver into the hands of Lady Briannon Findlay."

"Did you recognize the carriage or driver?" Mama further inquired.

Braxton canted his head in an apologetic tilt. "No, my lady. Both the driver and the man who presented the parcel were unfamiliar."

The mysterious method of delivery heightened Brynn's anticipation as she loosed the ribbon.

"Thank you, Braxton. That will be all," Mama said, clearly disappointed.

Brynn's suddenly clumsy fingers fumbled with the latch, and as she opened the box, her breath escaped on a silent incredulous exhale. All the feeling in her body drained away as she stared at the contents. Resting inside, on a bed of luxurious cream velvet, was a ruby and diamond necklace.

Each ruby glowed as if on fire, the interspersed diamonds cooling them like ice.

The bandit's words flew into her mind: *You need rubies to go with that defiant spirit.* Rubies. It had to be from him—the masked man. Who else would send rubies without a note? Brynn slammed the lid shut, her shoulders heaving with delayed shock and a wild rush of hot shame.

Her mother jumped. "What is it?" she asked, voice pitched high with concern.

"It's…it's a necklace," Brynn croaked, her throat dry. "A ruby necklace."

Mama tore across the room to where Brynn stood and pried the box from her stiff fingers. She opened the lid and gasped, a hand fluttering to her chest. "Oh *my*. But where is the note? There must be a note!"

"There is no message," Brynn whispered. "Just the necklace."

A breathtaking necklace, worth a thousand times more than the pearls it was no doubt meant to replace. The thought tempered her shock and returned a dash of the anger she'd felt when the bandit had taken her grandmother's necklace. Even such magnificently cut rubies and diamonds could never replace the pearls. Still, Brynn could barely tear her eyes away from them.

Her mother turned to Braxton, who had known to hover outside the doorway to the day room. "Come now, there must have been a note. Braxton?"

He reentered the room, hands clasped behind his back. He had been with their family for ages, and Brynn knew he would not have been so incompetent as to have lost a note somewhere between the front door and the day room.

"There was no note, Mama," Brynn said dully as the butler echoed the same. The bandit wouldn't have been so forthcoming. "What did the carriage look like, Braxton?"

"It was a plain black coach, my lady. Norbert attended the horses and might have gotten a better look at it."

"Fetch me Norbert at once," her mother commanded, returning the box to Brynn and leaving for the front hall.

Brynn could hear her mother questioning the footman, but she knew he hadn't recognized the driver, either. The bandit would never have sent a coach or driver that could be tracked down. She ran her fingers over the rubies and diamonds, each one a carat or more.

What was this, a peace offering? Something more?

Had he *stolen* them? The idea that this necklace might truly belong to another lady made her retract her fingers and slam the lid once more.

Her mother bustled back into the salon and harrumphed. "What kind of gentleman sends a gift of this magnitude and expense to a young lady without so much as a note? It is completely improper," she muttered to herself, taking the box from her daughter yet again. "We will return them the very moment we determine whom they are from. And you will *not* wear these rubies under any circumstance."

"Yes, Mama," Brynn agreed, silently cursing the sheer nerve of the masked man. How dare that dreadful thief? She didn't want anything to do with him or his blasted rubies, no matter how exquisite they were. "I'm going to lie down," she told her mother, casting about for an excuse to leave. "I feel a bit of a headache coming on."

"Of course, dear," her mother said, clearly still distracted as she then thrust the box at Brynn instead of confiscating it as she normally would have done.

Hours later in her bedroom, Brynn still couldn't calm her rattled nerves and flaring temper. Her lady's maid, Lana, kept darting concerned glances in her direction while she warmed the slipper bath with a scalding pitcher of water. Brynn was of no mind to speak, not even to Lana who had, since becoming her maid six months ago, become more friend than servant. She and Brynn had gotten along well from the start, and the fact that they were near the same age helped. Though her mother often sighed at Lana's displays of frankness, Brynn loved them. She depended upon them.

Brynn suspected Lana hadn't been in service for very long. There were moments when she spoke too directly or forgot her place, but Brynn put that down to mere differences between their two cultures. Lana had come to England from Moscow, and while she spoke English fluently, she still had much to learn when it came to English rules. However, Brynn appreciated how Lana never coddled her the way everyone else in the house did.

Brynn eyed her maid, ill-concealed excitement flashing in those transparent green eyes. Lana had no doubt already heard about the mysterious rubies through the ever-reliable flow of servant gossip. She could be trusted with the whole truth, Brynn knew, and she would likely have an edifying opinion on the matter as well. At the very least, confiding in someone would make her breathe easier.

"It's positively romantic, my lady," Lana exclaimed, her eyes round with delight after Brynn had finished telling her the tale. "And rubies, no less!"

"Honestly, Lana, it's not romantic in the least. It's… barbaric. I have no idea who this scoundrel is, and now he feels welcome to send me gifts, which are likely not even his to give."

"A gift is a gift, is it not?"

"Not if it's from a thief."

"Even better," Lana said with a mock swoon as she poured a second ewer of hot water into the bath with a sigh. "Can you imagine what he must have risked to send you such an extravagant gift? It's *terribly* romantic, you must see that. You English have no sense of adventure."

Brynn said nothing as she stepped out of her robe and into the bath. It wasn't a *gift*. It was a message—one meant for her and her alone. She thought about the brush of the man's fingers, his seductive half smile as she'd poured their belongings into the pouch at his waist…and then sank her flushed face under the surface of the warm bathwater. She agreed with her mother, for once, and fully intended to give the rubies back somehow. She'd find a way. Brynn racked her brain as she lingered beneath the water's surface, her skin softening, the fine prickling sensation of the warmth making her shiver.

An idea struck, and she gripped the sides of the tub to thrust herself up, making water slosh over the rim and onto the floor. Could the bandit have been a member of the duke's house party? The idea was an intriguing one. His smooth palms crossed her mind, too. But what titled gentleman would do such a thing? No. The man had to be a criminal who had followed the wealth out of London and into Essex. That was the only explanation. A member of the *ton* stealing from his own was an absurd notion.

Once the water had cooled, Brynn stepped from the bath and into the soft robe Lana held out for her. She sat by the fire and waited for Lana to dry and comb her hair. She didn't have a headache as she'd said to her mother earlier, but she also didn't have the energy to face Gray and Papa over the topic of the mysterious necklace. Lying was never easy, and keeping it hush-hush that she knew who had sent the rubies would be too difficult. "Tell Mama I'm still ill and won't be coming down to dinner. Can you ask Cook to send up a tray instead?"

A few minutes passed while Lana relayed the message to a waiting footman. "What are you going to do with the rubies?" Lana asked when resuming her duty of combing Brynn's long auburn strands.

"Return them, of course." She hoped Lana hadn't noticed

her slight hesitation. Brynn could not put them on. They were a magnificent piece, yes, but a magnificent *stolen* piece.

"Are they very beautiful?"

Brynn tipped her head to the mantel. "They're over there if you want to have a look."

She had been prepared for the *oohs* and *aahs* that came from Lana's mouth as she surveyed the contents of the wooden box. "Fit for a princess," Lana declared. "A queen, even."

"Queen of Newgate," Brynn countered as Lana returned to her place.

"Your secret admirer has exceptional taste."

Her eyes slid to the box. "They *are* beautiful," Brynn said, a wistful note coming through her voice. Lana was right. They were indeed fit for a queen. "But rubies are not uncommon."

"Not like these. I know something rare when I see it," Lana said, something intense flashing in her eyes. "And those, milady, are something incredibly rare. They glow so brightly they seem…alive. I have never seen rubies do that, not even Lady Dinsmore's."

Brynn, too, had never seen rubies shimmer with such rich color. They must have cost a small fortune. Or been taken as her precious pearls had been. Her lips tightened at the thought of their previous owner, now deprived of her lovely jewels. That blackguard had no scruples whatsoever.

"I'll hear no more of it, Lana."

Although they didn't speak anymore of the rubies or the thief, Brynn could see the fanciful smile on Lana's lips. It irritated her to no end, but she loved her maid too much to scold her.

After her dinner, Brynn decided to retire early. She'd had enough of the bandit and his presumptuous rubies. But it was as if he had well and truly insinuated himself into every part of her life, even her dreams. And dreams were ungovernable things.

Fighting a fitful sleep, Brynn woke early, her sleep-deprived mind a riotous jumble of thoughts and emotions. She needed to clear her head, and nothing but a fast, cold ride with Apollo on Ferndale's grounds would accomplish that. Brynn sat up in bed, watching the first streaks of dawn breaking across the tree line. Staying indoors when the sky looked so pink and promising would have been a crime. Her parents wouldn't be awake for hours yet. She dressed herself simply and sneaked out of the house.

Chapter Four

Archer walked silently through the woods near Pierce Cottage. It was early morning, and the trilling of birds was his only company as he tracked the animal that had spooked his horse the evening of the Bradburne Ball. It hadn't been a fox as he'd first suspected, but a wild boar. He and Brandt had spent the next morning tracking it while the house party guests, including a still slightly inebriated Lord Bradburne, had started to leak slowly from the sprawling estate and bleed back toward London. The double rounded hoof indentations in the soft dirt had led Archer and Brandt to the boar's wallowing hole by a stream, but for the last couple of mornings the two had been unsuccessful in finding the beast while it was there, rolling lazily in the muddy banking.

Archer didn't enjoy the hunt. He never had. However, if the boar was coming in close enough to Pierce Cottage to spook the animals or put the tenants of the estate in danger, it had to be taken care of. There were some men, though—like his father and his ilk—who treated the hunt with a disturbing lightheartedness. To these men, the hunt was mere sport.

Something Archer held such distaste for, it had colored his opinion of the men who did enjoy it. Because there were other men who hunted for true purpose. To them, the hunt meant food for themselves and for their families. To them, the hunt included a respect for the quarry that never so much as crossed the minds of those well-heeled sporting men who viewed their kills as trophies.

Archer had been born into the ranks of the first sort of man, but he had been raised by the second. Brandt's father, Montgomery Pierce, the former stable master at Worthington Abbey, had been more of a father to Archer than the Duke of Bradburne had been. It was Montgomery who taught him that though he was noble-born, true nobility came from one's deeds. It was a lesson Archer never forgot, and one that fed his distaste for such privileged men, including his own sire, who lived lives of wanton excess while others at their doorsteps died from hunger and disease. They disgusted him.

As he threaded his way through the forests now, the morning sun not yet having crested the tops of the elms and firs, he was glad to be alone. Brandt had noticed Archer's distraction the last couple of mornings they'd spent tracking together, and though he hadn't yet said a word, Archer knew him well enough to anticipate that he'd have his questions ready today. He could lie to most anyone, but not to Brandt, and he wasn't prepared to tell his oldest friend about the two things that had been weighing on his mind since the ball. First, the anonymous note declaring his secret was known. And second, the utterly irrational and idiotic thing he'd done for Lady Briannon Findlay.

For the first, Brandt would likely call for a cessation of any future raids. Excessively practical, he would insist they hunker down and wait for things to blow over. Something Archer was not in the least disposed to do. And for the second, he would have accused Archer of feeling guilty for the raid on

Dinsmore's carriage. Guilt, however, had nothing to do with the ruby and diamond necklace Archer had sent to Ferndale the afternoon before. He did not regret the robbery, nor the spirited exchanges he'd shared with Briannon both during the robbery and at the ball. He *did* regret insulting her dress and causing her to run off, cheeks burning with humiliation, though neither of those were the reason he'd sent her the rubies.

He sent her the rubies because he was a complete fool.

And because he hadn't spent a single moment since the night of the ball without the memory of her slim neck in the forefront of his mind. Of the warmth of her skin when he'd removed the old-fashioned pearls, her bright, clean linen scent, and the barely contained fire smoldering in her direct glare.

A smile twitched at the corner of his lips as he stepped carefully through the shadowed brush, his bow at the ready, so as not to startle any concealed creatures. He wished he'd been able to see her expression when she opened the box. He grinned into the woods, imagining her perfectly bowed lips parting in soft surprise, furious color rising to her cheeks and ear tips. Archer would have wagered good English coin that she'd even stomped her foot in frustration.

As planned, Brandt had directed his cousin to take the booty from the raid on Dinsmore's carriage up to Scotland's borderlands the day after the house party guests had quit Worthington Abbey. Before departing, Archer had given Brandt another pouch of silver—his own money, not plundered, and set aside for much needed repairs to the pump house. Repairs that would now have to wait. He'd told Brandt to find a ruby necklace fit for a duchess instead. Brandt had pressed one of his dark brows in response but had only nodded at this extra duty.

Archer crouched and ran his gloved fingers over the

muddy swath of bark on a sapling elm. Still wet. The boar had come through here, rubbing against the bark, not long ago. Tracking he enjoyed. Taking down the targeted prey, not so much.

He stood up and shouldered the bow once again. An indistinct rustling jerked his attention in the direction from whence he'd come, and Archer ducked behind a tree. His prey was close. He slid the bow off his arm in a precise, carefully honed movement. He nocked an arrow to the string, pulling it back so that the feathers brushed his cheek, and rounded the tree.

There it was, all five hundred pounds of it, and not a stone's throw from the stream. Archer braced his body against the tree, hunching so he could get a better shot. His thumb twitched on the shaft and released—just as a loud yell cut through the early morning air, startling both him and the beast. The arrow thumped into the wet earth as the beast took off charging into the dense underbrush and toward the sound of the shout. He frowned. Normally, wild animals would run away from potential threats. It had to be defending something. Its young, perhaps.

"Damnation." Archer took off at a fast run. Whoever had screamed would be in danger. The shout had sounded like it had come from near the river. Leaping over some boulders, he skidded through the mud as the icy rushing water came into view. There was no sign of the beast, but he could see someone in the distance, a young boy it appeared, floundering up the steep banking of the rushing river.

"Boy!" he shouted, but the sound of the water took his voice downstream. He swung around as a crashing noise in the woods surrounding him, and the short grunt of a creature that wasn't too far off. His eyes caught movement through the dense trees. The beast was close, *too* close. If the boar felt threatened, it would attack, and that young boy wouldn't have a chance in hell of escaping. Archer was too far away, and he couldn't quite tell if the boar was closer to him or the boy.

He'd take his chances. He scrambled down to the bank in case the boar decided to charge, and Archer had to make a hasty leap into the frigid water. He then started to make his way quickly upstream. As he drew closer to the boy, who was still struggling up the sloped banking, he could hear him shouting a slew of colorful curses that would have made any bawdy sailor proud.

Archer squinted, the rising sun nearly blinding him. The boy slipped, and his hair came loose of its cap. It tumbled in long, sun-scorched tresses down his back, and it was at that moment Archer realized it wasn't a boy at all. His breath wadded up in his throat. It was the earlier object of this thoughts…Lady Briannon herself, climbing the side of the gulch. And wearing men's breeches! He ignored his immediate and visceral response at the shape of her slim thighs in the form-fitting attire, and focused on his brewing anger instead.

What the devil was she thinking?

He bit back a shout, his cooling anger turning to worry at the sight of the raging boar twenty paces ahead of him. It stood at the top of the embankment, directly in her path. She could not see it, not with her chin tucked, and her eyes pinned to the earth at her feet as she continued to climb. Archer nocked another arrow, but with the curve of the river and the interspersed trees and shrubbery, he didn't have a clear shot. He started running and shouting, trying to draw the boar's attention and gesticulating madly for her to stay down.

"Lady Briannon! Stop!"

Briannon's face turned up to see him. Her eyes went round with recognition and then shock, and she started scrambling hard up the gulch as if he posed a greater threat than the wild animal still out of her view.

Archer ran harder, his heels kicking up clumps of dirt, his

boots and clothes soaked from the mist of the river. His ankle twisted as a protruding root nearly made him fall headfirst into the reeds. Righting himself, he ignored the sharp pain and kept her in his sights. He didn't miss the terrified look she threw him over her shoulder. She was running straight into the creature's path, but if she would only stop. Only *listen*. Archer wanted to throttle her almost as much as he wanted to shield her.

Time slowed and came to a standstill as Briannon finished her climb and came face to face with a crazed mother boar defending, Archer could now see, the three piglets behind her. Her mouth froze open with shock—and the sow rushed her with an angry grunt. But what shocked *him* was the way she stood fierce, her back ramrod straight, and then pulled something from the belt tied around those indecent breeches. A cracking shot rang out. The sow crumpled to a dead stop not five yards in front of her.

Archer felt his breath leave his body in a wild rush of astonishment. A pistol. The woman had been carrying a *pistol*. He stared at her, half impressed. The other half, surprisingly aroused.

Briannon, though covered in mud, seemed to be unharmed. The fury he'd felt before returned in full force as he made it to her side in several brisk, painful strides. His ankle throbbed something fierce.

"What the hell are you doing out here?" he demanded, grasping her arm. "Are you injured?"

"Unhand me," she responded, not meeting his eyes. "I am fine. My horse spooked, probably by that beast, and threw me."

"Where is your horse?" Archer asked, searching for anything to distract him from the sight of her covered in dirt. Oddly enough, even with his vast experience with women dressed in sumptuous ball gowns to transparent peignoirs, the sight of Lady Briannon in a mud-splattered white cotton shirt and men's breeches, pistol in hand, made his pulse accelerate and his groin tighten. Archer swore under his breath, furious at his body's unexpected—and unwelcome—response.

"Apollo! Where are you?" Briannon whistled a short note, and within moments a fine-looking Hanoverian trotted out of the bushes. "Oh, you sweet thing," Briannon murmured, dropping her pistol to the ground and running her hands down the horse's flanks, checking for signs of injury. The horse's ears flicked nervously toward Archer, but it dipped its velvet nose into its mistress's palm. Unmindful of her present company, Briannon bent over to check Apollo's hooves. Archer's breath ground to a pained halt as her breeches pulled tight over her backside.

Archer looked away and swallowed hard, focusing on the corpse of the boar she had so luckily dispatched. His brows shot to his hairline as he studied the bullet wound. It was right between the boar's eyes. A precise shot, not a lucky one at all. Once more, she'd surprised him.

He cleared his throat. "Who taught you to shoot?"

"Gray," she said, standing tall but remaining near the horse, as though it were safer there.

"You're a fine shot," he said.

"I wouldn't count it as a victory. Those poor piglets are now motherless."

Briannon turned in the direction of the three piglets, but they had already scattered.

"They are hardy animals," Archer said. "And you should count it as a victory. That animal would have killed you."

She opened her mouth, as if she wanted to argue, but then closed it. Something like defiance flashed across her features. He could see the wheels turning in her head, searching for some suitable excuse as to why she was dressed the way she was. Instead, she eyed him, as if daring him to broach the subject. Briannon crossed her arms over her chest and his eyes darted there, drawn by the movement. She let them slip to her sides, which of course drew his eyes in that direction as well.

"Why are you out here at this ungodly hour?" he asked.

"I could ask you the same thing," she replied. "As well as why you are trespassing on private property."

Archer smiled at her tone and leaned against a nearby tree, easing the weight of his injured ankle for the moment. There it was—the brief glimpse of the woman he'd met in Dinsmore's carriage, not the quiet mouse he'd waltzed with. "Ah, but I believe this tree, right here,"—he slapped the trunk with a rakish grin—"marks the dividing line between my estate and yours. So technically, I'm on my property and you are on yours."

Her eyes narrowed at his teasing before plucking up the tweed cap from where it lay on the ground and tugging it back into place upon her head. She then picked up the spent pistol and tucked it into the narrow, single holster gun belt looped around her waist. "No matter. It's hardly any of your concern why I am out *on my own land*. Go on your way, and I'll be on mine."

His jaw dropped as she wound her fist into the horse's bridle, loosely slung around its neck, and pulled herself deftly up onto the horse's back. She sat astride in a way that made his pulse shorten. "Where is your saddle?" he managed.

She eyed him imperiously. "I don't like them, not that it's any of your business."

"It isn't safe," he ground out, surprised by his sudden irritation.

"I've been riding without a saddle since I was a child," she shot back. "I'm safer without one than I am with one."

"As you were before you got thrown into the river?" Archer couldn't resist taunting.

Her jaw jutted forward, a mutinous look in her eyes. She pressed her lips together, likely to stop herself from uttering something completely inappropriate. Perhaps one of the colorful words she'd been using while attempting to climb out of the gulch.

"And what if you were attacked by the masked bandit—*again*?" he continued. "Or haven't you had enough danger for the time being?"

"I can protect myself," she said.

"What with?" he asked before he thought of the clean hole in the boar's forehead.

Briannon sighed dramatically. "Why, with my knitting needles, of course."

Struck again by her lightning-quick wit, the short bark of laughter left his lips before he could contain it. "Pray, where was your pistol the other night when you were robbed?"

"In my knitting reticule, where all ladies' pistols are kept," came her tart response. "I assure you, if I had my pistol, the outcome of that robbery would have been quite different."

After seeing her shoot the boar with such controlled skill, Archer didn't doubt her expertise for one second. There was always a chance that one of the travelers he waylaid would have a pocket pistol, or perhaps something larger, to fight him with. He knew the risk and accepted it for what it was. But he was certainly relieved Briannon had left her weapon home the night of the Bradburne Ball.

He pushed off the tree and approached the chestnut Hanoverian. Like its owner, it shied away from him. He made a soothing noise under his breath and drew his hand along the horse's nose. Briannon watched him incredulously, her mouth agape. "He's magnificent," he said. *Much like his mistress*, he added silently. "Why do you look surprised?"

"Apollo doesn't like anyone. I'm shocked he didn't bite your hand off."

"Oddly enough, horses seem to like me," he said, rubbing its velvety chin. He glanced at Briannon and grinned. "I'm skilled with all manner of wild creatures."

He was rewarded with a deep flush of color in her cheeks. God, she was so easy to bait. It gave him an odd thrill whenever he made her blush, if only because it prefaced such provoking, if wildly inappropriate, conversation.

However, a mask dipped down over her features, composing her reaction. Ah, yes. There was her ice, falling into place like clockwork.

She bowed as if she was wearing the most elegant of dresses. "I bid you good day, my lord."

"Briannon," he said, grasping the bridle. Her eyes widened at the familiar use of her name.

"Release my horse at once," she said.

His fingers tightened on the reins. "As a gentleman, I cannot in good conscience allow a lady to ride home unescorted in such…*charming* attire. I must insist on escorting you."

He watched her struggle to gather an immediate response, which would have most likely been as salty as the look on her face. She took a deep breath, and though Archer kept his eyes locked with hers, he still enjoyed the heave of her chest.

"Fine," she managed to grind out through clenched teeth. "Where is your horse?"

"I don't have one."

"But you've injured your ankle, and we're miles away from either of our homes. How do you mean to—" Her voice broke off as she took his meaning. "Oh. But it's…well, it's indecent."

As if riding a horse bareback in men's breeches was not.

"Very well. If you wish me to hobble along on my one good ankle…" Archer began with purposeful melodrama, warming to his ploy.

"Of course not," Briannon quickly said, worrying her

bottom lip. It was luscious and full, and Archer had to force his gaze elsewhere as a sudden desire to tug that lip between his own overtook him. "But…but as you've pointed out, I don't have a saddle."

"I don't require one, either," Archer said, enjoying her most fiery blush yet.

What he was suggesting was highly inappropriate, but there was no chance in hell Archer was going to allow her to go riding off alone looking like that. These forests might have been divided between their two estates, but that didn't mean there weren't trespassers from time to time.

"And as far as indecency, I'm sure I don't need to provide you with a lesson on decorum. I think it's safe to say that we are now far past that. Frankly, I am injured. I turned my ankle trying to get to you before that boar. You would be doing me a great service, and I would be in your debt."

Everything inside him warned that this was a terrible idea, but his body buzzed with excitement at the scintillating prospect. "It will be faster. You won't come to any harm, I promise you. Think of it as us waltzing. It will be over before you know it."

Briannon seemed unconvinced, but eventually, she nodded. "Fine. But if you fall off, I am not responsible."

Fall off. If he managed to do something that inept, he had better split his head on a rock and be done with it.

"Agreed."

He pulled himself up behind her rigid body and Briannon turned the reins expertly, the horse cantering toward the thick wood. Archer tried to hold himself away from her, but the minute the horse's natural gait took over, the space between their bodies disappeared. He *was* going to fall off if he didn't hold on to something. It was either going to be her or the horse. Mindful of the situation, he slid his arms below hers and grabbed hold of the reins.

She twisted to see him. "What are you doing?"

"Would you rather I put my hands about your waist?"

If it were possible, her body grew more rigid as she faced forward again. "They are fine where they are."

He almost grinned at the prim comment, but then Briannon clicked at the horse, and they were flying through the woods, jumping fallen logs with ease. She rode with the natural ease of a born athlete, Archer noticed, her movements fluid with those of the horse…and with him. His body rocked in tune with hers as they soared over the jumps, and he fought to keep himself from responding to the seductive motion of her trim hips bracing against his thighs. Archer ground his teeth together, suppressing the immediate carnal response of his body.

"Where did you learn to ride without a saddle?" he asked to distract the train of his thoughts.

"Gray."

It seemed Lord Northridge had taught his little sister all manner of strange pursuits. Distracted by windblown movement across Briannon's slender nape, Archer inspected the scattered strawberry-blond tendrils of her hair that had escaped from her tweed cap. He had an indescribable urge to wind his fingers through the strands, but of course, kept his hands firmly on the reins. Archer eased back on them, Briannon's own hands fisted lightly in the mare's chestnut mane, and their mount slowed. There was no rush to return her to her family just yet.

"May I inquire as to why you chose to dress as a man for this morning ride of yours?" he asked.

She was already sitting as inflexible as a maypole, but right then he felt her stiffen even more.

"I did not think I would meet with anyone."

And riding astride would have been impossible in a skirt, Archer guessed.

"What will your mother say, I wonder, when you return home in your brother's clothes with a man upon your horse?"

He couldn't help himself. Teasing her gave him a strange sense of pleasure. He had never been much of a tease, not with the women he'd known in the past. Those sorts of women did not demand conversation. They demanded money and jewels, and Archer had happily given them from time to time, believing it a much wiser decision than mixing with married, or worse, marriageable, women of his own sphere.

However, Briannon did not react to his goading remark the way he wanted her to. She kept her chin down and her eyes trained on the well-beaten path through a field, just out of the woods.

"She will surely thank you for your assistance," she replied.

"I've done nothing at all. You shot that boar, not I."

She turned her ear toward him, just enough so that he could see the thick fringe of her russet lashes and the gently sloped curve of her cheek. "Please do not say as much. She would murder Gray for teaching me to shoot."

"On the contrary. She would have to admit that your brother had done you a service."

She laughed. "Perhaps. Though not until after Gray's funeral."

Archer smiled. She had a wry sense of humor. This he could appreciate.

The slate rooftops of Ferndale's majestic manor house rose into view. It was far more modern than his own stately home, which had been constructed well over a century before. He meant to make some improvements to Worthington Abbey, once a few of his ships returned to port and the most recent investments he'd made paid out. Investments, he thought as the manor became more visible, that he required to maintain their lifestyles—especially that of his father.

"It is still early," Archer said, aware of the need to protect her reputation despite his earlier teasing. The reason for her agitation was understandable—his mere presence would be compromising. "We may be able to reach the stables without anyone learning of it. I'll borrow a mount to see me home and have it returned before anyone notices it is missing."

"Vickers, our stable master, will notice," Briannon replied.

"Stable masters are not usually prone to gossip."

"Perhaps not at Worthington Abbey," she said under her breath.

No. Not at Worthington Abbey, thanks to Brandt, and for that Archer was beholden. He was now stable master, having taken the position after Montgomery's death two years before. The thought of his passing still made Archer's chest and throat feel tight. It had taken much longer than that for the sharp blade of his own mother's death to dull to something bearable. It was a sort of hollow sensation, like a hand grasping into thin air, reaching for something it couldn't quite touch.

The fire had broken out in one of the many rambling tree houses he and Brandt had built in the Worthington woods when they'd been boys. The duchess had been out on a solitary ride through the fields that morning. It had been pieced together later that she must have spotted the smoke and rushed her mount toward the woods. She'd found the burning tree house, and likely believing her son inside, had climbed the rope ladder to search for him.

Archer had not been inside, though. He didn't know how the fire had started, but by the time servants from the main house arrived, the duchess was dead and a young Eloise, who had arrived minutes before the servants, had been burned severely, attempting to pull her adoptive mother's unconscious body from the tree house.

Archer missed his mother, but the ache had faded with

time. It was Montgomery he still mourned. He only hoped it wouldn't take years for the pain to lessen.

"I wish to apologize, Lady Briannon," he said as he started to direct Apollo toward the grand stables, set kitty-corner to the manor's wide approach. But she stalled his hands, and took the reins, directing the horse in the opposite direction.

"Where are we going?" he asked.

"If you are seen with me dressed in this manner, I won't live down the scandal of it. The gossipmongers' tongues will wag, you will be forced to marry me, and we would make each other miserable for the rest of our lives. I am saving us both from a ghastly union."

He stifled yet another laugh. Briannon turned her head again, this time affording Archer a better view of her profile. The small lobe of her ear was especially tempting, but it was her fine brow, arched in preparation for another dose of his sarcasm, that he paid attention to. "Ghastly?"

Briannon nodded firmly. "Oh, most definitely. I wish for a husband who can smile without looking as if it pains him, and I'm sure you wish for a wife whose wardrobe is more… conventional." She paused. "You were saying something about an apology?"

Archer was torn between incredulity and amusement at her veiled snub, but he conceded to respond. "I made a careless remark at the duke's ball," he said, as she led the way down a small hill that took them once more out of sight of the manor. His fingers skimmed the soft material at her waist, but did not quite grip her body. She pulled the horse to a smart stop in front of a small abandoned cottage covered in tangled vines, green ivy, and new roses, their petals still closed.

"Hmm, a deserted cottage," he said, wanting to turn the tables. "But what of *my* reputation?"

A blush of color spotted her cheeks, but she did not respond to his teasing comment. "You may wait outside while

I change."

He grinned and swung down, and though he regretted the loss of Briannon's body—the spooning press of her legs against his, her straight spine against his stomach and chest— Archer was glad to dismount. He hadn't ridden a horse without a saddle in…well…ever. It hadn't been as comfortable, nor as effortless, as she'd made it seem.

He held his hand up to Briannon to help her dismount as well. She ignored it and, holding on to Apollo's lithe neck, swung herself down with swift competence. The soft, butter-colored buckskin breeches clung to the lines of her thighs and the flare of her backside. They must have belonged to her brother years ago to fit her with such form-fitting accuracy. He could see every curve, leaving very little to the imagination. And yet he did imagine. Her bare skin would be more velvety than that buckskin, he wagered. Warm and yielding.

Briannon disappeared into the house, and he stood outside as she had instructed, waiting the minutes while she changed. Flashes of movement through the windows grabbed his attention. Picturing Lady Briannon nude just behind that single flimsy door made his breath catch. He forced himself to admire her horse instead and then found himself thinking about the way she had ridden him, which led to other, far headier, fantasies.

By the time Briannon emerged, clad in a yellow muslin dress, her hair flowing loosely around her shoulders, Archer was in a cramped state at the heated turn of his thoughts. She appeared nothing like the ragtag hellion from before, and she had, ostensibly, left her pistol in the cottage. But all the same, she managed to look just as appealing, if not more. Her color was heightened, no doubt from having to undress with him standing outside, waiting. It pleased him to think that she had been as bothered by the awareness of his presence as he had hers.

"Yes," she said, resuming their earlier conversation. "You were quite rude at the ball." She rubbed the horse's coat in brisk strokes before tugging on the reins to lead him into a walk beside her. "But I fear you were also correct. As you could see by my attire this morning, I am the furthest thing from a lady's fashion plate."

"I assure you, Briannon," he said, knowing it was too familiar of him to drop her title, and yet not caring. He matched her stride as they walked back the way they had ridden. "Men do not care for fashion plates."

She quit rubbing Apollo's coat and faced him. "What, then, do they care for?"

"In a woman?" Archer asked, a question that pinkened her cheeks. "I can't speak for every man, but I know that fashion plates bore me. Most women do." Watching her carefully, he added, "You are not most women."

Her lips parted under the scrutiny of his gaze. She averted her eyes as they walked into view of the manor house. "You are too bold. Go, and quickly. I don't hear Vickers just yet. Take Apollo." She thrust the reins toward Archer, her short sentences showcasing her flustered state.

She was offering her own horse? Clearly she wanted to be rid of him. He'd said the wrong things, then. So be it. It was at least the truth. Despite the physical discomfort of his perpetual state of half arousal over the last hour, he'd enjoyed their banter and regretted having to part ways. The only person he ever felt at ease with was Brandt. Certainly no women—other than Eloise, of course. Briannon was an anomaly, one that intrigued him.

Archer bowed and eyed the unsaddled mount with an inward groan. "Thank you. I shall have him returned as soon as possible. A good day to you, Lady Briannon." He accepted the reins and pulled himself astride once more.

Archer clicked to Apollo and the stallion took off, full

tilt, back the way they had come. He intended to field dress the boar and bring the beast to Pierce Cottage. It would be a waste to leave the carcass to rot. After, he would see to his already swollen ankle.

He glanced over his shoulder as he rode from the manor. Briannon was no longer behind the stables. The girl was dangerous. Good with a pistol, strong on a horse. Damn fine in breeches. And completely intoxicating. A woman like her could make him forget his purpose and ignore what drove him. He could not risk that. A marriage and family would put an end to this secret part of his life, and it was far too early for that. And especially with the new threat of discovery on the horizon.

Archer hadn't set out to be an outlaw thief. He'd wanted only to help the poor and the sick, as his mother had in her lifetime, and at the tender age of eleven, an epiphany had struck him. It was a year to the day after her tragic death in a fire when the idea of reappropriating his father's wealth had taken root, both as punishment and benefaction. Montgomery had said that a man's deeds were the things that defined him, and Archer would be the one to uphold his mother's legacy.

Archer knew his father would not suffer to continue Lady Bradburne's charitable contributions, even though the duke was the very reason she had been so compelled in the first place. There were few secrets in a manor like Worthington Abbey that a boy could not unearth by listening to servant gossip, and it was not long before Archer learned that when Lady Bradburne had found Eloise's pregnant mother, a maid from another household who had been cast aside, not only by the duke but also her employer, it had been too little too late. The woman had been ill before Eloise had been born and had died shortly after. Archer's mother had taken in his father's bastard daughter as her ward.

At the time, he was also old enough to discern what the

gossip meant and why his mother had been so driven in her tireless work to help the sick and the needy. And the older Eloise became, the more Lady Bradburne had thrown herself into such efforts, as if to atone for a sin she had not committed.

No, the sin was squarely upon his father.

Archer remembered vividly the day he had made his decision. Yet another ostentatious ball at Worthington Abbey had been in full swing, and his father had been distracted with his guests.

Distracted. Always distracted.

That time, however, the duke's disregard had worked in Archer's favor. He'd slipped past his eagle-eyed governess, hoping she would not notice his disappearance from the upper balcony before the next set began.

Tiptoeing into his father's lavish dressing room, he rifled through the duke's belongings and pocketed the first coins he could see: five gold sovereigns. A small fortune. Brandt had told Archer about an orphanage in the neighboring village that very morning. He and Montgomery had helped build a paddock for the orphanage's milk cow. It had been sad, Brandt said, that they had but one milk cow for dozens of children.

Archer knew of the orphanage in question. He'd visited it a few times with his mother. Lady Bradburne had been generous with both her funds and her time, but at the age of eleven, Archer had only a small allowance.

However, he knew where his father kept his own coin.

The duke wouldn't miss the money, not when he lost far more at the betting tables. Even at that age, Archer had been aware of the gossip surrounding his sire. His father's love of gambling, pretty women, and dancing was already as ingrained in Archer as were his mind-numbing lessons of arithmetic and Latin.

Coins in hand, he'd raced out of the rooms and slipped down to the kitchens. He didn't stop until he was at the stables, where Brandt had been finishing his chore of mucking out the stalls.

"Here." Archer had shoved the coins into Brandt's hands. The other boy's eyes had widened. "Take it. I must go or the dragon governess will have my hide."

"Hawk, this will feed that orphanage for months," Brandt said. "Won't you get a thrashing for stealing?"

"I'm not really stealing," he'd answered with a plucky grin. "I'm giving it to the needy. There is a difference."

"Like the ballads of King Richard's Robyn Hode?" Brandt asked. "The outlaw thief who steals from the rich and gives to the poor. Have you heard the songs?" Archer had shaken his head, and Brandt grinned. "Remind me to teach them to you. He was the champion of the poor."

When Archer returned to the ball, a seed had already started to root deep within his belly. As he stared down at all the extravagantly dressed guests through the spindles of the balustrade, he'd thought about the children at the village orphanage with their single milk cow. He thought of the sick his mother had dedicated her last days to helping. She had sworn to Eloise to make up for what had happened to her mother. And Archer would do the same.

A few shillings, or even a few sovereigns, were nothing to his father's friends. They had everything. *He* had everything. All because he was the son of a duke. It had made him angry, though he couldn't quite determine with whom, or what he could possibly do to cure it. But then he'd thought of what Brandt had said in the stables about the champion outlaw, and a fledgling idea had been born—*he* would be their champion. Brandt would help, and his mother would be proud.

Now, as a grown man, Archer doubted Lady Bradburne would have patted him on the back for becoming a thief, nor would Montgomery have approved of his misguided nobility. Both the duchess and the stable master would surely turn in their graves. After all, what Archer was doing wasn't in the least bit noble. He *stole*. But he stole from those who wouldn't miss the little he took—a purse of gold here, a signet ring there—while those on the receiving end would have the chance to eat or buy medicine. Archer didn't condone his actions, but he didn't fault himself, either. If his so-called peers judged him to be a criminal, then so be it. He knew and accepted the risks. One of them being that he might eventually be rooted out.

The anonymous note nagged at him again as he descended into the sloping field. If someone had indeed seen through his disguise, another note was certain to follow. One that would demand a price for silence, he assumed. Archer clenched his fists around the reins, annoyed with himself. Had he somehow, somewhere, let down his guard? Slipped in his performance? The raid on Dinsmore's carriage was a fine example, he supposed. Thinking back, not once had he looked up or down the lane to see whether or not another conveyance or horse and rider approached. He had not thought to listen for unwanted company, either. The only thing he had been able to focus on had been the fascinating surprise of Lady Briannon.

He had made himself vulnerable by being careless. It couldn't happen again. As he directed his borrowed mount toward Worthington Abbey's grounds, Archer decided he would not approach Lady Briannon. Not as a marquess, and not as the masked bandit. She had diverted his attention enough this last week, and others depended on him. She was different from other society women, yes, but she was still one of them. He would not—*could not*—let himself forget that.

Chapter Five

Standing in the dimly lit stables as she saddled Zeus—one of Gray's newer and more high-spirited stallions—Brynn cursed herself yet again for allowing Lord Hawksfield to ride off on her horse earlier that morning. He had sent word that the stallion was favoring his right leg and was being tended. Though she worried for Apollo's condition, she knew Hawksfield was known for his expert horsemanship and love of horses. The stallion would be well taken care of at Worthington Abbey. But Brynn still regretted not making the arrogant man walk or borrow another horse. Like this one, for example, that had already tried to take a bite out of her arm.

She'd spent most of the day fighting a raging headache. And, though she was loath to admit it, thinking about Hawksfield—who was likely the root cause of the pain in her temples. Thankfully, no one had caught her sneaking into the manor that morning, or before, while riding unchaperoned with a man who wore his surly reputation like a badge of honor.

She chewed the corner of her lip, tightening the girth

around Zeus's muscular belly. In private, Hawksfield had seemed nothing like the man Gray and everyone else talked about. He'd even seemed different from how he'd presented himself at the Bradburne Ball. He was solemn, certainly, but he did have a boyish sense of humor when he chose to use it. He was also a surprising flirt.

But he'd cared that she'd been in danger from that boar. She had seen it in his eyes. Eyes that had been like liquid silver in the morning sunlight…serious and somber, but not cold. No, that was where he smiled, she realized. His lips would never betray his humor, but his eyes did.

Brynn shook her head and pursed her lips in exasperation. What was she thinking? Lord Hawksfield was the last man she should be mooning over. Seeing to the chivalrous, if unnecessary, duty of escorting her home had clearly put him out. She'd practically heard him grinding his teeth in annoyance the minute he mounted the horse. Brynn sighed. Really, she had more important things to worry about than Lord Hawksfield's poor temper…or his disingenuous smiling eyes.

For one secret moment, though, Brynn allowed herself to think about what it had felt like to have a man riding behind her on Apollo. The heat of his lean thighs and the bracing power of his chest against her back had been shocking to say the least, but exciting, too. The masculine lines of his hard frame had cradled hers with such intimacy. Warmth flooded her lower abdomen, making her limbs feel utterly useless. On the horse, she'd fought with every bone in her body to keep herself motionless, but now, she wondered what it would have been like if she had just let go—leaned in to him, felt every inch of him clinging to her. Her breath drew to a shuddering, indelicate stop.

Flushing deeply, Brynn banished her unvirtuous thoughts as she finished saddling the horse as quietly as she could. She didn't want to risk waking any of the grooms. Then again, Vickers was more than used to her midnight excursions, and never once had whispers, carried on the lips of a servant, reached Mama or Papa. Vickers could be trusted to turn a blind eye.

She led the horse outside, and pulled herself up onto its back. Zeus pranced nervously beneath her as the moon peeked out from a patch of clouds, riding high in the sky and gilding the surrounding hills with silvery touches. Brynn inhaled deeply and urged the stallion into a canter—a rousing, brisk ride was exactly what she needed.

She'd tossed and turned for hours before deciding she couldn't remain in bed one minute more. Mindful of the hour, she had dressed all in black, piled her hair into a bun, and tucked it under a wide-brimmed hat. At the last moment she had decided to bind a cloth tightly around her breasts. If by chance she came upon someone, they'd think less of a boy being out past midnight than an unchaperoned young woman. Not that she expected to run into anyone else at this ungodly hour, but if she did, Brynn had made sure she could protect herself—her pistol was loaded and tucked into the waistband of her breeches.

Riding Zeus took almost all of her skill and concentration. The horse was certainly faster and less mature than Apollo. It took her a while to get used to his gait and to make him understand that she was in control. Every once in a while, he'd try to get the bit into his mouth, but Brynn was a competent rider and held him firmly in check. It was challenging work but exactly the kind of exertion she had hoped for. She wanted to tire herself out so she wouldn't have to think.

Hanging low over Zeus's neck, they raced like the wind over Ferndale's rolling hills. She felt free and unfettered, the normally stalwart rules of the *ton* as yielding as water or air. It was right at that moment that a bloodcurdling scream cut through the darkness. It made Zeus rear up, nearly tossing Brynn from the saddle. She held on for dear life as he bolted through the woods—*toward* the sound of the scream.

Brynn fought for control as another scream rent the air. It was distinctly female, and it was close. Someone was in trouble. She tightened her hold on Zeus's bridle and dug her thighs into his flanks, soaring over the three-foot estate fence line with ease. She pulled the brim of her hat low and thundered onto the main road where a coach stood at a dead halt in the middle of the lane.

She squinted into the shadowy darkness, the carriage's single lantern hardly bright enough to read a book by, let alone dash decent light over the road. But just then, the crest of the moon better exposed the scene in horrifying detail: a masked man on horseback, his pistol pointed into the open conveyance. A second pistol was trained on the coachman lying in the dirt. Brynn's breath caught on a flood of rage— it was *him*. The bandit. The despicable scoundrel who had tainted her thoughts and toyed with her by sending those blasted rubies!

She didn't stop to think as the man raised his head in her direction. All she could see was his hand, drawing her grandmother's pearls from her neck. All she could feel was defeat and frustration, and by god, the man had robbed her! Pointed his gun at her person!

Brynn pulled her own pistol, took aim, and without a moment's thought or hesitation, fired. Zeus immediately pulled to a stop, and the bandit's mount reared up before bolting into the woods, but she was certain that she had seen him clutch at his thigh before being spirited away. In any case, he was gone for the moment.

She took Zeus abreast the carriage, seeing the two cowering women there. They must have been on their way home from some function. Perhaps the same musicale her parents had attended that evening. Thank heavens this was not *their* carriage. She was quite certain her mother's nerves would not survive another incident.

"Is the man gone, boy?" the older of the two women asked in a shaky voice. Most likely the younger lady's chaperone, Brynn supposed.

"Yes," she answered, holding her tone low. "He's gone, milady."

The younger woman looked like she was about to swoon. Brynn squinted. It was the eldest daughter of Viscount and Viscountess Perth, her neighbors several estates over. "You saved our lives," the young lady said faintly as the older woman held a vial of smelling salts to her charge's nose. "Who knows what that evil man would have done? We are in your debt."

Bobbing her head, Brynn pulled her hat low and called out to the driver, keeping her voice as gravelly as she could manage. "You there, get up and get your mistress to safety."

He hauled himself up and mounted the coach, taking off in a swift cloud of dust. Zeus pawed the earth beneath her as she stared after the coach, watching as it rounded the far end of the lane and disappeared.

The moon had withdrawn again, shrouding the road in shadows and making Brynn's skin prickle stiffly. A coolness had descended, causing her breath to puff like mist. With a sigh, she wheeled Zeus around, stopping at the edge of the road. She'd shot the man, and while she had meant only to wound, what if the bullet had done serious damage? Scourge of mankind or not, if he died, his blood would be on her hands.

"Blast it," she swore and led Zeus into the woods where she'd seen the bandit's horse disappear. It didn't take her long to find both horse and rider, motionless in a nearby glade. The man was slumped over the neck of his mount. Panic struck her like a lance. Was he *dead*?

"Sir?" she called out. There was no response. Her heart sank to her toes.

She inched closer, clicking gently to the bandit's horse so it wouldn't bolt and hoping that Zeus would behave himself. Nearly alongside his mount, she prodded the man with the muzzle of her pistol. An inarticulate groan was his only response, but at least he was alive and she wasn't going to end this foolhardy ride as a cold-blooded murderer.

Brynn had three options: she could leave, knowing in good conscience that she'd found him alive, and hope he wouldn't bleed to death. She could wait until he was conscious enough to fend for himself. Or lastly, she could take him back to Ferndale and call the constable. The last option would see her locked in her chamber for the rest of her foreseeable life. And she wouldn't be able to sleep a wink should she choose the first. No, she'd take her chances right now with the second—and safest—option.

"You there," she prodded harder, and the man groaned again. Her eyes searched for where she'd shot him, but even by the light of the moon filtering through the trees, she couldn't see his leg clearly. His black clothing didn't help. "Wake up!"

The man pushed himself into an upright position, staring woozily at her. Once again, that damned mask obscured his face. But she was sure it was him, and she wished she had brought the rubies so she could throw them at him.

"You shot me," he said in a slightly slurred voice, wrapping his hand into the horse's mane as if fighting to keep himself erect. "In my leg. Could've killed me, boy."

"If I meant to kill you, you'd be dead," Brynn muttered. The bandit groaned and pitched forward. "No, no, no. You need to stay awake."

She clutched at the man's shoulder and nearly toppled off Zeus as his weight slid against her. His head sank into the groove of her neck and shoulder. His clean scent of cedar and smoke struck her again, as it had the first time they'd met. Part of her wanted him to smell, well, like a highwayman should— grimy and unpleasant. She couldn't seem to focus with him smelling so blasted appealing.

Brynn fought a wave of self-disgust as she pushed him off her. She couldn't just leave him here to die. But where could she go? She looked around in a panic. There were trees and more trees, and a road that led south, nearly an hour's coach ride to the village, or north to Worthington Abbey. She was sure that Hawksfield would be anything but thrilled to be roused past midnight from his bed. Or perhaps he wouldn't be asleep if he was anything like his degenerate father as Gray had suggested. The thought made her inexplicably furious.

"Where do you live?" she snapped.

His eyes slanted open. Brynn could tell that he was disoriented, either from the blood loss or perhaps from some low-lying tree branch when his horse had bolted. "Shot me, boy."

"We've already established that. Do you live nearby?"

"Cottage," he gasped and pointed through the woods. "Ten minutes th'way."

She groaned in frustration. The way he was butchering his speech, he wouldn't stay conscious another two minutes, most likely. But it would take far longer than that to get back to Ferndale. Gritting her teeth, she made a decision, and looping his bridle in hers, steered the horses in the direction he'd pointed. She hoped that he wasn't delirious already and giving out flawed instruction.

After about fifteen minutes, she could see a light in the distance through the thicket, and her heart leaped with relief. Tying the horses to a nearby post, she dismounted. She was either insane or entirely too gullible to be escorting a known criminal into a strange cottage. No. She'd take him in and leave immediately.

"Wake up," she said, her eyes on the windows. Only one room appeared to have a fire going, otherwise the place looked asleep. "We're here."

The bandit grunted and half slid, half fell off the horse. Brynn braced herself as he leaned his weight against her, and they hobbled into the cottage. She hoped he truly was as weak as he seemed and not playacting, otherwise more than her reputation would be on the line. She held on to the fact that he still thought her a boy, and ushered him inside. The interior was empty and dim but for a low fire built into the hearth.

The man stumbled to a cot set up by the fire and collapsed on it with a belabored moan. She stared at him for a moment, transfixed by the black scrap of silk that hid his features from view. He was a gentleman; she was sure of it. No common bandit spoke as he did, or looked as he looked. She eyed his trim length, draped halfway on the too-small cot. His boots were scuffed but made from fine leather. The cut of his cloak was tailored, the stitching fine. He was a man of means, and yet he stole. Despite herself, she was intrigued.

It would be so easy to lift the silk and unveil the man behind the mask. Brynn's fingers itched to do just that, but she fisted them tightly at her sides.

Did she truly want to know?

A part of her screamed yes, but another part — the smarter, logical part — urged her to put as much distance between herself and this gentleman bandit as possible. Brynn turned to leave, but his wheezing voice stopped her at the door.

"Boy. Need to clean. Infection…help. Please."

That last word stalled her. *Please*. He should have been cursing at her for shooting him in the first place, but here he was, begging nicely for her assistance.

If she didn't at least bandage the wound to stop the bleeding, he could still die. She exhaled and pressed her head against the worn wood of the door. Why hadn't she stayed in bed? Tossing restlessly until dawn would have been preferable to this madness. But as abominable as the man was, she couldn't walk out the door and rush home. It would be heartless and cold, and for heaven's sake, she had been the one to shoot him!

"Fine," she muttered out loud. She'd patch him up as best she could and *then* leave. Besides, like the ladies in the carriage had been, the bandit seemed to be under the impression that she was indeed a young lad. Which meant she was safe. Somewhat. She hoped.

Brynn pulled the brim of her hat lower, until she was certain the top half of her face at least would be concealed, and then turned around. Blood had drenched his pant leg, turning the black fabric an even darker shade of ink. A small pool of it had already formed on the floor where his injured limb was hanging off the cot.

He rolled his head side to side, appearing delirious. No, she could not abandon the deuced man.

She approached the cot, thinking furiously as to what to do next. She was no healer, and had most certainly never mended a gunshot wound before. First, she supposed she needed to see the actual injury. Brynn touched the blood-soaked trouser leg, thinking she would find the hole made by the bullet. But the man grunted in pain as she poked and tugged, and he made a clumsy swipe of his hand to push her away.

"Off," he groaned. "Take off."

She stared at his masked face, incredulous. His eyes were shut, and the black silk fluttered where it had shifted to cover his lips.

"Off?" she repeated, forgetting to alter her voice. She coughed. "You want me to—"

"And whiskey. O'er there," he panted, his head flopping to the side. Brynn followed the direction of his eyes and saw a ceramic jar in the center of a trestle table.

She rushed for the jug first, her mind still tripping over his suggestion that she remove his trousers. She could not *undress* him! He was the Masked Marauder! A criminal of the worst ilk.

And yet he was still a man who'd been shot. She did need access to the wound, something that would be much easier done without his trousers on. Much easier still had she truly been the boy she was pretending to be. But she wasn't. She was a woman. A lady, at that. She had never dreamed she'd find herself in such an improper and scandalous position.

Well, she'd always craved a good adventure, and here it was. It was her own fault, and she had to face the consequences, no matter how…provoking they were. Brynn's heart drummed while a strange and unexpected grin touched the corner of her lips. Good Lord, she was losing her mind.

"Lie still," she ordered, returning with the whiskey and setting it on the floor beside the cot, far from the pooling blood.

Her fingers shook again as she reached for his waist. *Pretend he's Gray. A brother. Nothing more.* And men wore smalls, didn't they? It wasn't as if he'd be entirely undressed the moment she wriggled his trousers down. At least, that was what she continued to tell herself as she worked the buttons at the front of his trousers. Once the narrow fall came loose, she peeled it down, and her breath stuck like honey in her throat.

An audible sigh parted the quiet at the sight of a pair of white linen smalls. But as she started to wrench the trousers lower on his hips, she couldn't help noticing just how thin the linen was. Dark hair showed through the near-transparent cloth, which was made more see-through in the play of the firelight. And there was no mistaking the explicit swell of his…his…very male body.

Either Brynn's arms grew heavy, or the bandit's trousers had become snagged, because she could no longer tug them lower. And she could not avert her eyes, either. Brynn had never seen anything so…so *foreign*. Or so fascinating.

The clinging linen accentuated the curved shape. It was long—and knowing the little she did about what occurred between a man and a woman in the marriage bed, larger than she expected. Cordelia had told her that her aunt had said that when a man took a woman, it hurt the first time, and that was it. Brynn supposed the *taking* had to do with what lay hidden beneath those flimsy smalls.

Curious, her eyes examined the indecently outlined length, and she felt a frightening rush of heat in her legs. Her pulse shook like the earth in a stampede. Her breasts, even bound as they were, tingled, and something warm and liquid spread through the shivering core of her body. She tore her eyes away and weakly attempted to compose herself. Good heavens, she *was* losing her mind.

The bandit moved and groaned, jerking Brynn out of her lewd distraction. She hurried on with her task, yanking his trousers the rest of the way down. His smalls were cropped a few inches above the knee, and that was where she saw the neat, dark gouge in the muscle of his outer thigh. Not truly a graze, but not a killing shot, either. The wound leaked blood, though a quick inspection told her the bullet had not lodged in his flesh. He would live, but first she would have to make sure it did not become infected.

Brynn pulled the hem of her shirt from the tightly buckled waist of her brother's old trousers and tore off a good portion of it. Wrapping the ragged strip tightly around the man's thigh, just above the shallow wound, she tried not to notice the way his lean corded muscles rippled underneath his skin. And when she reached for the jug of whiskey and poured it over the wound, she also tried not to notice how a splash that landed on his smalls had taken the nearly sheer linen to purely see-through.

She failed on both accounts.

"Oh good Lord," she whispered as a surge of aching warmth pooled low, at the apex of her thighs.

The bandit didn't hear her. He was much too busy hissing and grinding his teeth against the pain, his back arching. As his spine went flat against the cot again, he snagged Brynn's wrist and tugged with surprising strength. She fell forward, the ceramic jug slipping from her hands and landing on the floor with a dull thud. It rolled onto its side, spilling whiskey, but that wasn't her main concern at the moment.

The bandit had pulled her flat against his chest and stomach, bringing his masked face mere inches away from hers. His eyes were still wild and wandering so she could only hope he hadn't yet focused on her face. Would he recognize her, even disguised as she was?

"Release me so I can bandage you," she said, the husky tone of her voice not entirely put on. Goodness, he was virile, even woozy from a shot to his leg. He held her arm like a vise.

"Shot me," he whispered, incredulous.

"Yes, well, what did you expect? You're a highwayman," Brynn replied, attempting to wrench her arm away and pull back to a safer distance.

"No bullets," he breathed.

"Just one, and it barely grazed you," she explained, still wiggling toward freedom.

He finally released her, and she tumbled back, right onto her rump.

The distant whinny of a horse and the steady *clomp clomping* of horse hooves had her up and on her feet again. Someone was coming. One of the bandit's cohorts? Another criminal? What was this place, a hideout? She hadn't stopped to wonder before. There were a number of abandoned cottages and stone ruins scattered throughout the woods of her own estate, and she imagined the neighboring duke's estate as well.

If the bandit and his allies had set up in one of them, she most certainly did not want to be discovered. The Masked Marauder had been shot, and he was weak and clumsy from blood loss, but this new arrival would not be.

Brynn hurried for the door, taking a last glance at the bandit as she whipped it open. He was lying on the cot, his chest rising steadily with each breath. The mask. She'd spent ages ogling the bulge of his masculinity underneath his smalls, and yet she hadn't lifted the slip of black silk to reveal his identity. There was no time now, not that she had any inclination to match a face to the ample…*body part* she'd gotten an eyeful of. If he turned out to be an aristocrat as she suspected, she'd never be at ease in polite society for fear of recognizing the man. She flushed and once again, her knees went inexplicably weak. *Blast it twice on Sundays.*

Brynn rushed outside and swung up onto Zeus's back. It was as if he had been waiting for an opportunity to unleash his boundless energy. She didn't even need to dig in her heels— they were already off, a dark blur through the trees.

. . .

Archer's eyes rolled back in his head. *A boy.* There had been a boy in the cottage with him. He blinked, but as his vision started to settle, saw there was no one there now. His head throbbed with every pounding heartbeat, and confusing snatches of what had happened rushed back toward him. He groaned as he reached for the whiskey jug tipped on its side at the edge of the bed. He took a desperate gulp. The fiery spirits brought him a shot of clarity just as Brandt burst through the door, his eyes widening at the sight of Archer lying half clothed and bloody on his cot.

"Hawk? What the devil happened?" He threw off his coat, rushing forward. "I've been looking for you for hours. One of the footmen said you and the duke had another row. That you stormed out of his study like a man possessed." Brandt crouched by Archer's leg, his hands gently examining the wound. "I heard a shot and thought things had gone south."

"They did." Archer blinked, his gaze slanting down to the faintly oozing but clean bullet wound. Though not life-threatening, it burned like the pits of hell.

Brandt glanced up at him. "You're supposed to tell me when you're going out. Someone put up a fight, I see. I suppose it was bound to happen."

Archer gritted his teeth against the pain and humiliation. But he'd always been honest with Brandt before. "Not the occupants of the carriage. A boy. The cretin showed up on his horse and shot me."

Brandt's eyebrows flew into his hairline. "A boy. Shot you. At this hour."

"That's what I said."

"Losing blood addles the mind. Are you certain it wasn't the coachman or a groom?"

Archer shook his head. Brandt said nothing as he stood to retrieve a strip of clean linen from a trunk. When he returned, he removed the tourniquet that had already been tied tightly around Archer's thigh to staunch the flow of blood. He couldn't quite remember how it got there, but he figured the ripped cloth had come from the boy.

Brandt poured some more whiskey on the wound and, ignoring Archer's coarse outburst, finished the work and bandaged it deftly. "There. You're lucky that it's only a flesh wound, and this mysterious boy didn't have better aim. You'll live." Brandt took a swig from the whiskey jug and offered it to Archer. "Did you ride back here? I didn't see your horse."

He swatted Brandt's hand away when he pressed it to Archer's clammy forehead, nodding as if satisfied that a fever hadn't set in. Archer scowled. He wasn't delirious. At least, he didn't think he was. "Out back. The boy helped me."

"The same boy who shot you brought you here *and* cleaned your wound? I'm surprised he didn't make you breakfast, too. Where is this savior of yours, pray tell?"

"He must have…left."

Archer sighed. It sounded farfetched even to him. But he knew he hadn't imagined it.

"Did he see your face?" Brandt asked, turning serious.

"I don't bloody well know," he groaned, furious with himself and a touch troubled. Coming on the heels of that blasted note claiming to know his secret, the last thing Archer needed was some unknown boy to have taken a peek under his mask.

The boy had been slim in stature, dressed in black with a hat that had obscured his face. No more than fourteen, Archer guessed. He dimly recalled the slim width of the boy's forearm. Maybe younger. He had been fearless. Shooting him, and then returning to save him from probable death. The boy had what Montgomery used to call mettle.

"Let us hope not," his friend murmured, clearly worried. Hell, Brandt didn't even know about the note yet, and Archer again chose to stay quiet about it. He had no proof that it had indeed been meant for him, and no other notes had been forthcoming. Though it lay like a warning prickle in the back of his mind, Archer would not let its rankling presence dictate his course of action.

He closed his eyes as the whiskey dulled his senses—and the pain in the thigh as well. The boy's skin had glowed gold in the firelight. Perhaps it hadn't been a boy at all. Perhaps it had been an angel sent to torment him for his sins. Archer grimaced at the unwelcome thought. He'd returned empty-handed tonight. And there were greater sins in the world than the ones he committed relieving some of the more entitled *ton* of their glutted wealth...like the starving poor and abandoned children, whom his very thievery fed and clothed. Archer ground his jaw and gave in to the exhaustion that crept on the edges of his consciousness.

He'd risk whatever penance his actions brought.

Chapter Six

Given the bizarre circumstances, Brynn had been out far longer than she'd planned. Dawn was already on the horizon when she arrived back at Ferndale, and there was a bustle of activity up at the house near the kitchens. Thankfully, there was no sign of Vickers in or near the stables, so she quickly rubbed down a lathered Zeus and settled him back in his stall with a generous helping of oats.

If only mending the Masked Marauder's injured leg could have been so simple.

She tried to forget leaving him on that cot, his trousers around his shins, but it was impossible. Her mind pulsed with nothing but memories of him stretched out before her, those gauzy linen drawers leaving so little to the imagination. It was utterly disgraceful the way she'd fixated on his muscular thighs and yet hadn't bothered to expose his face.

Grabbing hold of a dusty cloak hanging on a nearby peg, Brynn swore under her breath and poked her head around the doors. The only sounds to be heard were those of the horses nickering behind her. There was a chance she could get back into the manor and up to her room unnoticed, where her dirty, bloodstained attire would feed the fire, hopefully still burning low in the grate.

She drew the large cloak around her and started for the house. Footsteps made her freeze in her tracks, and she flattened herself against the side of the stables, her breath coming in panicked pants. She darted a look at the woods and then one back to the house, and had just made her decision to flee when a deep and decidedly unamused voice halted her escape.

"Going somewhere?"

Brynn turned in slow motion and saw her grim-faced brother. "Why are you looking at me like that?" she breathed out. "So I went for a ride. What of it?"

"Is that so?" Gray said, his arms crossing. "And where, pray tell, is Apollo?" Brynn's heart sank. Of course he would have seen her riding in on Zeus, or if she knew her brother, he would have already noticed that both Zeus and Apollo were missing and had decided to lay in wait to catch her red-handed. She paled at the murderous look on his face. "Zeus isn't properly trained. You could have broken your neck. I will ask you again, Briannon, where is Apollo?"

"Don't you dare take that tone with me, Gray." She bristled at her brother's sharpness, but her bravado deserted her at his thin-lipped expression. "I can explain," she said, the next words tumbling from her mouth without an ounce of grace. "I went for a ride yesterday to clear my head, and came across a boar. Apollo got spooked and threw me. Lord Hawksfield was there. He turned his ankle trying to reach the boar—"

"*Yesterday?* Were you hurt?" Gray interrupted, his voice sharp.

"No," she said, wringing her hands in the lap of the skirt. "I shot it."

"And Hawksfield?"

"He didn't have a horse, and he insisted on escorting me home, considering I was wearing what I usually wear…" She broke off at the thunderous shine in her brother's eyes and gulped. "Considering the way I was dressed, he thought it would be proper to act as my escort. He wasn't pleased about it, either, and well, he'd turned his ankle, as I said…" She was rambling. She always rambled when nervous. "I didn't know what to do, Gray. Leave him there, injured, after he tried to save me? He was a gentleman, I assure you. I changed at the cottage and came straight here. He took Apollo."

"He would have been fine if you had left him," Gray muttered, but Brynn could see him softening. He had a temper, but he usually knew how to subdue it with rational thought. He'd calmed enough to consider the impossibility of the situation. "If anyone had seen either of you, your reputation would be in tatters. And I doubt Hawksfield would care at all."

"No one saw me." She eyed him and drew the cloak from the stables closer around her. Hopefully it shielded the blood spatters and dirt on her clothing. "And, well, last night, I needed to get out. I couldn't sleep, and Zeus was the only one awake. I was perfectly safe, Gray, I assure you." She bit her lip at the lie—no need for Gray to know the particulars of what happened with the bandit. Tatters would be the least of what would be used to describe her reputation should it come to light that she had been in an abandoned cottage with a half-naked man, and a criminal at that. She would be shunned from polite society. An outcast. Her mother's shame would be unimaginable. No, there was no need for *anyone* to know.

Gray's face darkened, but he nodded. "At least you are safe. Count your blessings Mother and Father are both still abed. You best get inside before Lana starts ringing all sorts of bells when she finds your bed empty."

Brynn gave him a slanted look. "Lana has far more sense than to do such a thing."

Gray didn't seem at all appeased. The rigid shape of his shoulders and the downward tilt of his mouth pointed toward his continuing the rest of his brutal setdown. However, he took a deep breath, expelled it, and surprised her.

"Speaking of our neighbor, there are rumors in London." He kept his voice low, as if imparting a confidence. "Bradburne lives an excessive lifestyle, some say to the detriment of his fortune. You have a significant dowry, Brynn, and I wouldn't put it past Hawksfield to try to get his hands on it in order to stock the family coffers."

"Gray!" she cried, though she faltered on what to say next. She wasn't naive as to how marriages worked, and why certain men married certain women and vice versa. Money and titles were coveted. She found it strangely distasteful to think of it *and* Lord Hawksfield in the same breath. Brynn would rather be married off to an untitled pauper than someone as capricious as he. For heaven's sake, she'd choose marriage to the bandit she'd shot over that high-handed man.

She banished the thought as a sudden rush of heat spiraled through her at the recollection of the marauder's utterly virile body. If she were married to him, he would be well within his rights to *take her*, as Cordelia's aunt had put it. At least one form of *taking* seemed to be something the bandit did particularly well. She had to force a breath into her lungs at an unbidden image of him lowering her into their marriage bed and taking something quite different.

"It's not beyond the realm of possibility, that's all I'm saying," Gray went on, holding up his hands in surrender, and absolutely clueless as to the bawdy turn of her thoughts. "And I don't want to see you caught up in some scandal that ends in a marriage to that…that…"

"Scoundrel?" she offered.

He vaulted one of his golden brows. "I would have chosen a slightly less tepid word."

She smiled. His vocabulary did often do his quick temper justice. However, it seemed odd the distaste Gray harbored for their neighbor.

"Is he so very awful? Do not think me too well informed, brother, but are you not known as a scoundrel yourself?" she said, still grinning even as Gray's lips pulled thin with annoyance. Or perhaps it was embarrassment. "And what of the other young men of your acquaintance?" she pressed playfully. "Aren't all men scoundrels in some way?"

"If you have heard that I am on par with Hawksfield, then I would say your information is rather dusty," he replied with a lopsided frown. "And while I know a scoundrel or two, none of the men of my acquaintance are interested in ruining my sister, that I promise."

"You needn't worry, Gray." Stifling her amusement, Brynn was quick to reassure him. "I am in no danger of being caught up in any scandal concerning Lord Hawksfield or being ruined by any man."

Just a half-naked bandit whom she'd shot.

Brynn's mind went to the exquisite ruby necklace in her bedroom that the blackguard had given her, and her heart stuttered. Her early morning ride with the future Duke of Bradburne paled in comparison to the time she'd spent in utterly indecent proximity to that thief. If there were to be any scandals in her future, she'd wager they'd be at the hands of the Masked Marauder, especially if they ever crossed paths again. She would fling the necklace in his face and shoot him again for stealing her grandmother's pearls *and* for bidding her undress him while he was half-conscious. Unwittingly, her hand lifted to her throat as she grinned at the gratifying, if savage, sentiment.

"And what if Hawksfield is the one who sent you that ruby

necklace?" her brother asked. Her startled glance jumped to his.

"He isn't," she answered with conviction. Too much perhaps, because Gray peered at her, his curiosity piqued at her resolute rejection. "Not if their finances are in shambles, as you've said," she added quickly.

"He could have gotten them on credit," Gray mumbled.

Brynn ignored him. "I have to get inside and dress before the decade ends, Gray. We can argue about the mysterious ruby necklace later, although I have it on high authority that Hawksfield wouldn't know the first thing about sending courtly gifts to *any* female, much less something so imaginative. That would require him having an actual personality."

Gray chuckled, shaking his head. "Your tongue is as sharp as a whip, sister. Don't forget, the Gainsbridge affair is tonight," he said over his shoulder, and Brynn cringed. Though desperate to avoid yet another social scene, she'd be expected to go to the annual masquerade since the Earl and Countess of Gainsbridge were dear friends of her parents.

"Blast it," she swore.

Her brother chuckled. "If Mother heard you speaking like that, or found out you were gallivanting around Ferndale in the middle of the night, you'd likely be disowned." He shook his head as if perplexed. "You are the only female I know who would rather shoot a boar than attend a ball."

"I like balls, I just don't like being ogled like a teacake," Brynn muttered. She would much prefer getting to know someone and determining whether they had common interests before being bound together for a lifetime. "You'll be going, won't you?"

He caught up and linked his arm with hers, his teeth flashing. "Why certainly, dear sister. After all, my wonderful, handsome self must attend if I am to set the ladies of the *ton* afire."

Brynn shook her head at his bald-faced lie—she knew her brother would prefer to be locked up in Newgate rather than attend a ball. Of late, Gray seemed to favor the quieter comforts of Ferndale and the local village, despite being a prime target, as the future Earl of Dinsmore, for the mothers and daughters of the *ton*. Just as their neighbors were, the Duke of Bradburne, and his only son, Lord Hawksfield, each of them unattached.

"Liar." Brynn pinched Gray's shoulder, before skipping ahead a few steps out of his reach. "Then again, if you find a bride who loves you as much as you obviously love yourself, you will have made a splendid match."

"That is the plan," he said with an affected flourish and then sighed. "Alas, such perfection like this does not exist, so I fear that it may be a lost cause."

"You are impossible." She skipped forward a few more steps and raised her eyebrow. "Now come on—let us race to the house!"

With the head start, she had decent odds of winning. Until, of course, Gray decided to show off, rushing past her while running backward, a smug smile upon his face. "What did the turtle say to the hare?"

"Not fair!" she panted, still keeping the cloak tightly drawn around her to conceal her bloodied clothing. It was a burden, but she still caught up with him at the side of the house, near the servant's entrance. "You have longer legs than I!"

Brynn collapsed against the brick wall, breathing hard. A sharp pain caught her unawares in the chest. *Oh no.* She clutched her torso and buckled over, a series of dry coughs racking her body. *Not again.* She'd thought the attacks were over. Gone forever. The more she tried to stop them, though, the more violently they came, until she was hunched over wheezing.

"Brynn!" Gray stooped down beside her. She stalled him with a hand as another wave of coughs rendered it impossible for her to speak. He would know, just as she did, that once started, it would be better to let the coughing run its course.

"Fine," she sputtered between coughs. "Be fine… moment."

"Fetch Mrs. Frommer," she heard him say to someone out of her line of sight. "And not a word to anyone, Percival." The stable boy. He could be trusted to keep quiet on the errand to find the housekeeper, though Brynn detested he or Gray, or anyone at all, having to fret over her and her *damnable* weak lungs.

"Of course, milord."

Minutes later, Percival was back with their housekeeper. Brynn could barely see, her eyes watered so. Someone pressed a cup to her lips. Despite being intimately familiar with it, she almost choked at the sour herbal taste. It was the remedy the cook made, which usually eased the affliction, though it tasted like an underripe cherry wrapped in mint leaves. She forced herself to finish it, as she always did, and the herbal tea made its way down her throat, clearing her passages. After a few moments, her breathing, although punctuated by a few persistent coughs, started to return to normal.

"I'm sorry," she said, looking at her brother's anxious face as he tucked a blanket around her. She hated causing that expression, and though she knew it was unfounded, felt guilty for it. "It must have been the early morning air. I took a chill, that's all. I'm fine now."

Gray placed a hand to her cheek. "You are cold as ice. Why didn't you say anything?"

"I don't know," Brynn said, her teeth chattering at the sudden brutal chill in her bones. The truth was she simply hadn't noticed, given the shock of the last few hours. The night's chilly temperatures must have taken hold.

"Come, let's get you inside," Gray said with a frown. Thankfully, he didn't push the matter further.

Mrs. Frommer threw a second woolen blanket over her shoulders and ushered her up the staircase, scattering the servants with a look. Having Gray at her side helped clear their path as well. A few stairwells and corridors later, Gray was ushering Brynn into her rooms and thanking the housekeeper for her confidence before closing the door behind him.

Lana stepped from the attached dressing chamber, the day dress she'd selected for Brynn draped over her arm. She took one look at Brynn—at her wan face and the blanket and dusty old cloak around her shoulders—and dropped the mint green muslin onto the bed. "My lady!"

"I'm fine, Lana, truly."

Brynn's maid cast a glance at Gray, seeking a second opinion no doubt.

"She is not," he replied. "Lana, please ring for a bath to be drawn."

Brynn speared her brother with a glare. She tried not to tremble with cold, but it was a challenge.

"I don't want a bath. I just want to rest." As terrifying as the last few hours had been, they were also somehow… gratifying. It was pure madness. The warm, weighty feeling of exhaustion, paired with the events of the morning, were all driving her toward a very long nap.

"The bath, Lana," Gray insisted. Irritation heated his tone, and though Brynn knew it was his concern for her health, she still saw her maid bristle at the coarse command.

"As you wish, my lord," she said and, with a curt nod, Gray slammed out of the room. "My lady, I should help you out of your—"

Brynn finally cast off the blanket and cloak. They landed heavily on the floor, and Lana's expression grew even more alarmed.

"It's not my blood," she said quickly and her maid blinked her relief, her parted lips sealing again.

Without questioning whose blood it was, Lana stripped off the shirt and breeches. "Shall I put these to be cleaned and mended, my lady?"

Brynn stared at the clothing with rancor. "Burn them, please. And my apologies for my brother," she added. "I fear I have angered him beyond reproach this time."

"There is nothing you could do that would push him to such end, my lady." Lana crossed the room and tugged on the bellpull. "Master Gray cares for your well-being."

As it turned out, a hot bath had been exactly what she had needed to get the remnants of the chill out. After having a late breakfast in bed, Brynn decided to remain where she was and rest. She slept for hours, thanks to the medicinal effects of the tea, and woke only when Lana brought her evening meal.

Brynn sat up and rubbed her eyes. "Is Mama worrying about me yet?"

"I told her ladyship you slept poorly last night," Lana said, setting the tray on the bed beside Brynn. "She blamed the ruby necklace."

Thank heavens for Lana. And, it would seem, for the rubies.

Brynn rubbed her chest as her maid disappeared into the dressing room. The coughing fit had left a slight soreness across her breastbone. She hadn't had an episode like that in years, and she'd started to believe the childhood ailment had been firmly behind her.

It was all that masked criminal's fault! If she hadn't run into him robbing that carriage, she'd have ridden Zeus and returned home. Instead, she'd scuttled around, chilled to the bone, playing nursemaid. She should have left him to rot.

It would have been a waste, though—even for a lady as

inexperienced as she, Brynn knew enough to realize he was an impeccably fine specimen of a man.

Oh for goodness sake, Brynn chided, *get ahold of yourself. He's nothing but a filthy thief who deserves to be given no quarter.*

By the time Brynn enumerated all the ways in which the bandit should be punished, she'd worked herself up into a fine froth. Anything to stop herself from thinking about the lean cut of his legs and the sprinkling of dark hair that had covered them, or worse, the provoking, sinful contour of his masculinity showing through his linen smalls. When he had pulled her against him, her bound breasts had been further flattened against his powerful chest. In such close proximity, Brynn couldn't help remembering his pleasing scent, which set her to reconsidering her theory that he was, in fact, a gentleman.

One who had given her a necklace worth more than any *common* bandit would consider parting with.

Taking the wooden case from the bedside table to her lap, she studied the box for a long moment before lifting the lid to examine the contents. With a swift indrawn breath, she slammed the lid shut. And then opened it again, barely a second later. She sighed, marveling at the perfect cut and color of the jewels. The rubies, a deep crimson with the barest hint of violet, were magnificent. She had to admit that Lana had been correct—the man did have exceptional taste.

A part of Brynn wanted to believe that they were a gift, and not something that had been stolen. Now it seemed that Lana's inane romantic notions were starting to spread. She allowed herself the brief, if reckless, fantasy that the gentleman thief had bought the spectacular gems just for her. The tempting memories of his sculpted lips, his chiseled length, and those uncalloused fingers grazing the slope of her nape slid into her mind. With a gasp, Brynn shook her head in self-disgust.

Could she be any more foolish?

The bandit could be a nobleman, but she would be deceiving herself if she thought him in any way a *gentleman*. Instead of fantasizing about him, she should be trying to find a way to unmask the rogue — as she should have done in that cottage instead of being overcome by immoral urges.

Brynn slid her forefinger across the glittering row of gems, her heart quickening. Perhaps there was a way she could discern the identity of the bandit, if he were indeed a peer of the realm as she suspected. Maybe he'd be in attendance at the Gainsbridge Masquerade. After all, there were still a few families left in Essex before the season drew them back to London. The thought made her heart race into a full gallop.

It's a game, nothing more, she told herself. A game she'd play to determine the identity of the infamous Masked Marauder. Suddenly, the prospect of the Gainsbridge affair became much more appealing than resting in bed with a sore chest and an overactive imagination.

"Lana," she called, after taking a moment to be sure of her decision. Her maid reappeared in the dressing room entrance, her arms piled with Brynn's clothing. "Please let Mama know that I'm well and will attend the ball."

"I am afraid Lady Dinsmore has already left, but your brother is still here."

Brynn suppressed a thrilled smile. It was as if the fates were aligning to her cause. "Wonderful, please pass along that I will be accompanying him."

Lana grinned in delight, and she dropped the clothes into a chair. Something wistful appeared in her eyes for a second but it was quickly shuttered. "Which gown will you wear? The lavender silk?"

"No." Brynn had other plans. She'd show that pompous thief what the opposite of being "in mourning" was. "The silver satin."

Lana's eyes turned into round, shining orbs. "You're going to wear the rubies, aren't you?" she whispered. "Do you think he'll be there? Your gentleman thief?"

Brynn didn't bother to argue that he wasn't *her* anything. Instead, she quirked an eyebrow. "I hope so. Otherwise, it will be a waste of a perfectly lovely dress, wouldn't it?"

Chapter Seven

After Lana had tied her corset to the point of pain and closed the final fastenings of the dress, Brynn looked in the mirror with a critical eye. She wanted everything to be just so—and for the dress to be the perfect foil for the necklace. She squinted at her reflection. Her hair should be up, leaving the slim column of her neck bare. Lana seemed to know this instinctively, and she quickly set about twisting and tucking Brynn's hair into a simple upswept style. She pinned it at the crown with a diamond-encrusted comb, pulling a few tendrils free to frame her face.

"Now for the rubies," Lana said.

As the maid draped the cool jewels across her bare throat, Brynn drew a deep breath and had a brief moment of panic. What if she *did* recognize the thief? And what if he recognized *her*? What then? Brynn discarded the thought. He'd been delirious and had thought her a boy. No, she would be safe. She'd deal with recognizing *him* if the moment presented itself.

"My lady, you have never looked more radiant," Lana

breathed.

"Thank you, Lana, but I expect that's because of the rubies, not me."

Brynn studied herself. The dress itself was stunning, comprised of layers and layers of silvery chiffon and satin with a daringly low bodice—lower than she'd ever worn. She had seen a fashion plate of the dress in Cordelia's *Costume Parisien* earlier in the summer, and she and Cordelia had fawned over it. Brynn had ordered one to be made for her straightaway, but had never thought she'd actually wear the revealing confection. Until now.

The only splash of color was the ruby necklace, the largest gem dipping nearly into the hollow between her breasts and drawing attention to the flushed expanse of her décolletage. Lana deftly fastened the scrap of silver silk she'd fashioned into a fetching demi mask with a handful of white feathers, and the final effect made Brynn's lips part in sublime delight.

Hawksfield won't know what hit him.

Brynn blinked at the unexpected thought. She intended to lure the *bandit*, not Hawksfield. Then again, she was feeling rather daring in this dress. Perhaps she would render Hawksfield speechless for once *and* discover her masked highwayman.

"You are definitely going to set the *ton* on its ear. Perhaps even upside down." Her maid grinned as she helped Brynn down the stairs into the foyer, where Lana held her own middle and spun in a graceful circle, her eyes alight. "Have a dance for me, if you please."

Brynn shook her head at Lana's giddy, if odd, request, and tugged the velvet stole over the neckline of her dress. There was no need for her brother, who was waiting in the carriage, to see the plunging cut of her bodice and insist she return to her room for a more appropriate gown.

"You look lovely, sister," he said as she joined him, his

inspection a mere cursory glance in the shadowy carriage. He nodded to the coachman, and they were off.

"And you look rather dashing," she said. He was immaculately dressed in a black jacket, waistcoat, trousers, and a snowy-white shirt.

Gray didn't respond to her flattery. Instead he eyed her with a serious look. "Are you feeling quite well?"

"Yes, of course. I wouldn't go otherwise."

"You are certain?"

"Yes," she insisted. "Now stop smothering me at once, or I'll tell every lady you dance with tonight how you were afraid of the dark and used to sleep with dolls when you were a boy." She smiled wickedly. "And still do."

"Point taken," he conceded. "But you will tell me if you start to feel unwell."

"Yes, Gray." She smiled at the arrogant command. They sat in companionable silence for most of the ride, until Brynn noticed that Gray wasn't wearing a mask as she was. "Where is your mask?"

"I don't do masks."

"Then everyone will know who I am if we enter together," she said, her face falling. "What's the point of going to a masquerade if you don't wear a mask? You're such a spoilsport, Gray. I won't go in with you, then."

"You can't very well go in there without an escort," he said and sighed. He pulled a black headpiece that looked like a horned devil and tied it into place just as the carriage pulled into the brilliantly lit and crowded Gainsbridge courtyard. "There. Happy?"

Brynn shivered at the fierce mask. She'd expected nothing more than a boring domino. "I think I prefer you without it." She stepped from the carriage, her gloved hand sliding into Gray's.

"This is a huge crush," she said, looking around at all

the people descending from various conveyances. She hadn't imagined the masquerade would be this well attended. The bandit *had* to be here. There was no chance he'd miss an opportunity such as this, not if he truly was one of the *ton* as she suspected. Then again, he had been shot less than twenty-four hours ago. Maybe this was all for naught after all.

"Gainsbridge has clearly spared no expense for this event. I daresay it's larger than last year's," Gray said, turning toward her. "Ready for the hordes?"

"Ready." Brynn let the stole slide from her fingers as they entered the foyer. Gray's eyes landed on the bodice of her dress and his brows shot to his hairline. Brynn stifled a smile at his reaction.

"Where is the *rest* of your dress, Brynn?" he hissed under his breath. "It's…indecent. We are leaving at once."

However, they had already been swept into the throng of guests. Leaving now would be like fighting the current of a river. Brynn laughed, the tinkling sound drawing admiring stares from a nearby group of men. She was glad for the mask—it made her far braver than she would have normally been. She laughed again as he drew her to a nearby alcove. "Gray, this dress is the height of fashion. And we've just arrived. People will notice should we leave now. At least allow me the luxury of one dance."

"Mother is going to kill me. Wait." His eyes narrowed on her throat. "Are those…my god, you're wearing the necklace."

Brynn steadied her shaky nerves. She felt naked and on display with all the attention, but the truth was, it made her feel powerful, too. She lifted her chin and acknowledged a young buck she vaguely recognized. He was nowhere near as tall as the bandit, however.

She chose to ignore Gray's remark about the rubies. "Mama will not kill you, brother dear. She'll worship you for making her daughter the belle of the ball. One dance."

"Fine. One dance," he muttered. "But what were you thinking, wearing those—"

"Don't you look lovely, Lady Briannon!" a soft female voice exclaimed, interrupting her brother's admonishment.

It took Brynn a moment to place the voice, and when she did, Brynn turned to find herself the recipient of a warm smile from Hawksfield's half sister. Her eyes widened in delighted surprise. With a gorgeous plum-feathered mask and matching satin dress, Eloise looked radiant. If not for her familiar voice, Brynn wasn't sure she would have recognized her.

"Forgive me, I know it is a masquerade and we are supposed to guess who is whom," Eloise began. "But I am afraid your hair color is quite distinguishable. And well, Lord Northridge is as tall as my brother."

"I suppose we shall have to behave ourselves now that we've been made known," Brynn said, smiling at Eloise and ignoring the silly trip of her heartbeat at the mention of Hawksfield. "It's so nice to see you here. I missed you at your father's ball. I was rather scattered that evening."

"Of course. I heard about the attack on your carriage. I am so glad none of you were hurt." Eloise smiled, her eyes fairly glittering beneath her mask. She waved a hand. "And I could not miss a masquerade. This is my kind of dance, you see?"

Brynn nodded in understanding, her heart warming with compassion. Everyone would be wearing a mask, not just Eloise. For once, she could pretend that what lay under her mask was as well formed and flawless as any other lady at the ball. Masquerades had an odd way of reinforcing one's courage, as she herself knew. Her fingers brushed the rubies at her neck.

Eloise's childhood accident was no secret, but her sweet temperament more than eclipsed her scarred face. Still, she didn't often attend social functions, and Brynn had seen her only a handful of times over the years. It was sad that she hadn't yet received an offer of marriage, but without the late duchess's backing and her parentage in question, it wasn't surprising.

Brynn gestured to Gray. "You are acquainted with my brother, Viscount Northridge?"

"Of course," Eloise said, a smile in her voice as Gray dipped into a polite bow, pressing a kiss to her gloved hand. "Back from London?"

"Only for a short while to protect my young sister from disgracing herself, it seems," he growled with an ill-concealed glower.

Brynn ignored the barb. "We were just discussing dancing partners, and what it does to a girl's reputation if her brother makes her hold up a column all evening long."

"A thing that I am much aware of." Eloise clapped her hands as if a delightful thought occurred to her. "I have a wonderful idea. We can trade brothers if Lord Northridge will do me the honor, and you must dance with my brother. He has been in a surly mood all evening. Your appearance may yet lighten it." Brynn and Gray wore matching frowns. Brynn guessed that her appearance would do no such thing for Hawksfield, especially not after their encounter in the woods, but Eloise seemed determined. "Yes, let's find that brother of mine and try to convince him, shall we?"

"Convince me of what?" a smooth voice interjected.

The earlier trip of her heart at Hawksfield's name became a thud at the sound of his voice.

"To dance, dear brother," Eloise said, her smile directed over Brynn's shoulder. "If only so your poor sister can dance one set without you running to her eternal rescue."

Both Brynn and Gray turned to see the unsmiling marquess. He was impeccably dressed—a far cry from his disheveled appearance the day before. "Lady Briannon,

Lord Northridge," he said politely, recognizing them as his sister had, despite the masks they wore, though he was not disguised. Hawksfield remained grim-faced as he extended his arm to Brynn, although she could have sworn she saw something like surprised admiration flash in those silver eyes at her ensemble. "May I?"

"At least there are plenty of eyes on the two of you this time," Gray muttered.

"*Gray.*" Brynn flushed, chastising him under her breath, mortified he'd mention her earlier run-in with the marquess. "I'd be honored to dance with Lord Hawksfield. As I am sure you would be with Lady Eloise."

A muscle ticking in his jaw, Gray forced a smile. "Of course." Without another word, he pushed off the faux-Greek pillar, one of many placed around the perimeter of the ballroom, and escorted Eloise onto the floor. Brynn knew he would keep an eye on her throughout the entire set, playing chaperone.

She and her dance partner garnered more than a few stares as Hawksfield led her to the center of the floor, the strains of a new waltz starting. He walked stiffly, and when he drew her close, it was with a slight grimace. "I'm starting to think that the waltz is our dance."

"There is no *our* dance," she said, and with a glance down, frowned and added, "Are you even certain you wish to participate? I do not intend to be rude, but you seem to be favoring your right leg. Are you in pain?"

"My ankle has not quite recovered from our jaunt yesterday, but I assure you, I will not embarrass you, if that is what you fear." His gaze brushed across her face and dipped to the swelling expanse of bare skin above the bodice of the dress before sweeping back up.

She wasn't worried about him embarrassing her before the others here at all. Her concern lay in how flustered that penetrating gaze made her.

A faint curve of his lips hinted toward a smile. "You look beautiful tonight, Lady Briannon."

Something soft and delicate flowered in her chest at the blatant admiration in his eyes, and if it weren't for his expert lead despite his injured ankle, she would have stumbled.

"Thank you, my lord." He looked well, too, Brynn thought, in his finely tailored clothing. The creamy white cravat accentuated not only his unruly dark hair, but the golden color of his skin, which she supposed came from a life spent outdoors. From what little she knew of him, he seemed like the type who wouldn't be satisfied sitting inside, drinking port and growing doughy and rheumy with age. He seemed always to be moving with a restless sort of contained energy.

Brynn's eyes drifted up from his cravat, and she saw him staring at her, an amused expression in those mercurial eyes. She swallowed and realized she'd been lost in thoughts about *him*.

"Where did you go just now?" he asked.

"I beg your pardon?"

"I had made a comment, and all I had for a reply were your eyes upon my neck."

Heat swamped her still aching chest. "Oh, I…thought I saw…a spot of gravy."

Blast! Brynn flushed deeper, certain she now resembled a sickly shade of puce.

Hawksfield frowned, though she could still see a twitch of amusement at the corner of his lips. "How very slovenly of me."

"Oh no, I did not mean at all to—"

"Allow me to try again," he interrupted, no longer hiding his amusement. "I had said, that is a beautiful necklace."

His gaze dropped to the rise of her chest. The sheer gall! He no doubt enjoyed making her uncomfortable.

"Thank you. It was…a gift."

"From a suitor?"

She tightened her gaze. "Of course not."

Admitting she had accepted a gift as exquisite as this from a suitor would have been paramount to declaring she was off the marriage mart. Which, on second thought, didn't seem like such an awful thing right then.

They danced in silence for the next few minutes, Hawksfield's injured ankle making each turn as ossified as a wooden board. The quiet should have made her happy. At least he wasn't baiting her as he seemed to enjoy doing. However, it made her only more uneasy, especially when she twice caught him eyeing the rubies. The necklace had drawn his attention, and for the first time, she wondered if it was because he recognized it. The rubies *were* an exceptional piece. Memorable. Why hadn't she thought of that possibility before? They'd come from the bandit and had most likely been stolen. Oh good Lord. What if the original owner was a lady in attendance tonight?

As they finished the waltz and the marquess escorted her off the floor, Brynn was fairly sweating.

"You look like you might swoon," Hawksfield commented as he led her toward the opposite side of the ballroom where Gray had been dancing, the Greek pillar now surrounded by a bevy of young ladies and their mamas.

"I do not swoon," Brynn said, even as she eyed a pair of nearby doors. They were propped open to a balcony, a gentle breeze wafting inside. Swooning was for ninnies and artful girls, eager for attention. Brynn counted herself above such ploys.

Then again…she *had* chosen to wear the necklace for attention. Though only from one man. It wasn't at all the same. Was it?

She accepted a glass of champagne from a passing server

and took a rather large gulp.

"I apologize. It is just that I have heard something of your condition," Hawksfield said, sipping from his own glass. She cut her eyes from the tempting balcony and hit him with a glare.

"My *what*?"

"No need to be embarrassed." His lips curled up at the corners then. Was he *laughing* at her?

Indignation swelled up her throat and threatened to choke her. "I assure you, I am quite well. Whatever you have heard about my previous health concerns is exactly that— *previous.*"

He lowered his glass and swallowed his champagne, his Adam's apple dipping below the snowy folds of his cravat. *A spot of gravy.* Dear Lord, she was making a mess out of this evening. What had she imagined? That the bandit would actually show up wearing his black silk mask and that he would seek her out for a dance or two? More likely, the true owner of these rubies would spot them, on *her* bosom, and accuse her of thievery. *Oh!* Another rush of heat scorched her chest and neck.

What if that is exactly what the Masked Marauder had planned all along?

"Where is your mask?" she asked abruptly, wishing now that she hadn't been so imprudent. Hawksfield's answer was a slow tented eyebrow. Of course he wouldn't deign to wear one.

"Does the sight of my face bother you so?" he asked. "Perhaps you would rather I place a sack over my head?"

"Don't be absurd. It is a masquerade, and without a disguise you stand out as a spoilsport." Her tone was condescending, and Brynn hated the way it sounded, but she sipped her champagne and faked a bored expression. She'd rather engage in verbal sparring with the likes of him than continue to worry whether some lady in attendance would accuse her of theft.

A shot of embarrassed heat flooded her ears as Hawksfield stared at her for another second, his expression unreadable. He then reached into his trouser pocket and extracted what appeared to be a black slip of silk. Brynn narrowed her eyes on the silk as he shook it out and pulled the demi mask over his face. His gray eyes glittered in the candlelight.

Brynn seemed to tumble forward and then back, her vision shaky as her eyes traced his finely shaped nose beneath the silk, to his unsmiling lips. They flicked past the angular cut of his cheekbones to the silver eyes staring steadily at her.

Why hadn't she seen it before?

Shaking slightly, Brynn gripped the stem of her champagne flute, her fingers surging to her throat and the necklace that lay there like a brand. Her pulse tripped over itself as a million possibilities assaulted her.

It couldn't be…*could* it?

Could *Hawksfield* be the bandit?

The tumultuous fall of her thoughts steamrolled all others, including the fleeting yet torturous one of him *sans* trousers. Her face felt as if it were aflame, and she struggled to compose herself. *If* he were the bandit, why would he rob someone en route to his own ball? Why would he rob anyone at all? His father was a duke for heaven's sake, and he was… Lord Hawksfield—a complete, unimaginative boor.

Brynn shook her head to clear it and set the empty champagne glass on a passing footman's tray. Clearly, the drink was going to her head. The implacable Marquess of Hawksfield would be the absolute last person on earth to lower his esteemed self to rob anyone. He was too poised. Too arrogant. Too stodgy. She frowned at her own swift logic and reconsidered the possibility.

Hawksfield was the right size, and the right age, and had

the right physique. But it could not be him. His precise tones were several shades lower than those spoken by the bandit, whose voice had been sophisticated and educated, yes, but also ostentatious. This peer of the realm was too rigid, too proper, too...*tonnish*. Further, the bandit's tones were higher and more jovial, except when he'd been delirious and his speech slightly slurred. Hawksfield's diction reeked of excessive good breeding. No, the marquess wasn't her man.

However, with that realization, she felt a new emotion cling like a thorn. It prickled and itched, and a moment later she grasped, with a fair amount of alarm, what it was. Blast it all.

Lady Briannon Findlay was well and truly *disappointed*.

Chapter Eight

"You are right," Briannon told him in a bored tone, her eyes averting from his masked visage, likely in search of her brother through the crowd. "Perhaps a sack would be better."

Archer removed the demi mask and stuffed the scrap of silk back into his pocket. She was only being sarcastic, perhaps to insult him the same way he'd done to her about that awful dress she'd worn to the Bradburne Ball, but it still pricked. Deeply. Which infuriated him. So far, he'd counted three men in attendance who could have recognized him as the masked man who had set upon their carriages. Three men who could be the one behind the anonymous note delivered in his copy of the *Times*. And yet, he'd dared put it on. *For her.*

After last night's episode, he'd been loath to attend the masquerade. However, when he heard Briannon would be in attendance, he had made the effort, despite the soreness of his leg. The bullet had gone through, and no infection had set in, thank God, but he'd still had to endure Brandt's mocking.

In truth, Archer was starting to doubt what he'd seen. He *had* lost a lot of blood, and Brandt was right—it could have been a groomsman, perhaps one who had been following the carriage as a precaution to an attack. The newssheets had been making an enormous deal of the Masked Marauder. But why would the groomsman have then taken him to Brandt's cottage? Unless Archer had imagined that, too. Or maybe the man had had a crisis of conscience. It was the reason Archer carried no bullets in his gun during the robberies—he didn't want innocent blood on his hands. He sighed. Archer had gained consciousness with his mask still in place, though he could not be positive the groomsman hadn't been curious and peeked underneath. Discovery was something he could not afford.

Despite that, he had known the odds when he'd donned the silk moments ago, especially so soon after the robbery on Briannon's carriage. A part of him had been hoping, in defiance of reason, that she would recognize him.

The foolish, reckless part of him that had felt flattered she'd worn the rubies was disappointed. Something desperate rose inside of him then: a desire to make her respond, anything to take the bored look off her face, the one that amply conveyed what she thought of the man standing before her.

Archer wanted that man to be the marauder, not the marquess. He wanted her eyes to glow with the tempestuous fire he'd seen on the lane. He wanted her to know exactly who had given her those rubies lying like glowing embers against her breast. They looked as he had expected they would. Dazzling. Seductive. Everything his fevered imagination had conjured and more. Archer wanted to see her in nothing but those rubies. The scintillating thought made his throat—and loins—clench.

He took a desperate swallow of his drink, banishing the provocative thought of Briannon's deliciously naked body from his mind. But Archer knew beyond a shadow of a doubt that she had worn the rubies and that bewitching dress for a reason. She had come here to be the seducer, and he wanted her to know without question that *he* was the man she'd come here to tempt.

"Looking for someone?" he taunted, following the path of her gaze. "A lover perhaps?"

"I beg your pardon?" Briannon's mouth shaped the words, her transparent hazel eyes narrowed with a mixture of emotions. Archer was transfixed at how each one—shock, injury, outrage—made her eyes a shade greener each time, until they were snapping with vivid color.

"Why you vile, ill-mannered—"

Several couples on the dance floor craned their necks to get a better look. Without warning, Archer moved swiftly, taking Briannon by the arm, and led her out the pair of nearby doors to a private balcony.

"Release me," she said. "I wish to return to my brother."

"In a minute," Archer said, keeping a firm grip on her elbow as he steered her farther out of sight, beyond the curious stares. "Briannon—"

She reared back as if his fingers were snakes. "Don't you dare address me in such a familiar matter, you vile—"

"You called me that already," Archer said with a smile. He had no doubt she could be more creative with her insults.

"Don't patronize me. Why have you brought me out here after insulting me so?"

"No lover, then?" Archer's stare fell lower to the daring décolletage of the dress. A becoming flush stole across her skin, her breasts heaving beneath the glittering tier of gems.

"Are you quite finished?"

He stepped toward her, and she took a step backward. Archer wanted nothing more than to provoke her into dropping that fake, haughty stare, and to do so, he had to risk inciting her wrath. "Then whom did you wear this for? This intoxicating dress? Although I can't quite decide whether I prefer you in men's breeches or women's fashions designed to make men lose their fortunes…and their common sense."

Briannon's mouth opened and closed in shocked surprise. He knew he was being vulgar and insulting, but once he had started, Archer couldn't stop himself from goading her. He wanted to punish her for not knowing it was he who had gifted her the rubies, not some stupid fop. He was irrationally jealous of a fictional bandit that he himself had invented. The entire situation was ludicrous, but he continued as if compelled by inner demons he hadn't the slightest control over.

"Or perhaps the answer lies in wearing nothing at all," he said, vaulting a mocking eyebrow. Her slap cracked across his face so sharply that the sound echoed into the night. *Damn.* He hadn't even seen her hand coming. The stinging feel of it seared his cheek and brought him back to reality. Archer stared at her, tears shining in her eyes, and he felt sudden regret. What was he doing, baiting her like an overeager bull straight out of the gates? The minx would drive him to madness if he'd let her—she was absinthe in his blood.

But he ruled his emotions…they did not rule him. Archer drew a deep, calming breath. "My apologies, Lady Briannon," he said in a controlled voice. "Please allow me to escort you back inside."

"I don't want you escorting me anywhere!" Her voice raised into a stifled shriek, the sheen of tears replaced by vitriolic rage. "You're a…you're unspeakable. How dare you insult me in such a manner? No wonder everyone avoids you like the plague!" She backed away, and as if drawn by an attached string, Archer followed the movement. "All the young ladies think you are uncouth and ruthless, and they're right!"

Archer took another involuntary step forward. It eliminated the gap between them. Briannon's hands grasped the stone balustrade that rested against her back. Her eyes grew into wide green orbs at his proximity.

"Are they?" he said softly.

Trapped and unable to flee, she fought, her sharp tongue as effective as any blade. "Yes…it's no wonder you can't find a wife. No respectable woman in her right mind would have you! You're…you are…appalling."

Archer did the one thing he could to silence her tirade. He kissed her.

It was a mistake. The soft contact of her warm lips was his undoing. His mouth slanted on hers, teasing that infuriating lower lip with the point of his tongue as he had wanted to do for days. Tension trembled over her mouth, and he wanted only to release it. To open her to him. But he did not simply want to be the aggressor and make her bend to him—he wanted her to *want* his kiss. He relented slightly, putting a hair's breadth of space between them.

Briannon's hands pressed against his dinner jacket as she stared up at him. Shock clouded her expression, but something else simmered there, too. Archer read it clearly. *Desire.*

He slipped his hand around her waist and drew her closer, capturing both hands between their bodies. Her fingers tightened compulsively, winding into the material as if she knew what was coming…as if she, too, craved it. He could feel her pulse racing, see the fire kindling in her eyes. Here was the response he'd sought all night.

Archer's mouth dipped to brush her cheek with deliberate slowness. "Is this so unspeakable to you?" he said, drawing his free hand down the curve of her jaw. Her skin was pure silk, his fingers skimming the line of her chin and neck, and dropping to where the necklace rested against her heaving chest. "Do you despise me so much that my very touch makes your body shiver with loathing?"

A twinge of regret—for her uncensored words perhaps—crossed her face for a moment. But then she hiked her chin and stared at him with those wide eyes sparking defiance, her lip quivering. She was not afraid of him, he knew. No, this girl was not afraid of anything.

Grasping the rubies in one hand, his knuckles grazed the tops of her breasts. Archer groaned low in his throat at the tantalizing feel of her flesh. God, he had no idea what he was doing. He had vowed to stay away from her, and yet here he was, doing the exact opposite. But once more, Archer couldn't help himself. He wanted to see what else she was hiding, what other passions she kept under strict rein. Archer wanted to lay all her secrets bare.

"Or perhaps you shiver with want, instead," he murmured.

Archer could feel her entire body tremble as his free hand slipped around her nape, tilting her chin up to his. She did not shy away. His eyes met hers, her pulse leaping wildly under his fingers. Despite her innocence, he could see the curiosity blooming in her eyes and feel her heart thudding against his through the layers of superfine and satin. Archer wanted more than anything to satisfy it.

He lowered his lips to hers. It wasn't swift like the first kiss, meant to silence. This one was meant to coax, to seduce. The touch was featherlight, skimming her mouth in leisurely strokes until a soft sigh escaped her lips. As if shocked at her own response, she pressed them shut again. Archer nearly smiled at her sheer obstinacy.

"Kiss me back, Briannon," he murmured against her. "Open for me."

His tongue darted hotly between the seam of her lips, and she gasped. Archer didn't hesitate. He swept into the sweetness of her mouth, exploring the soft interior, until her hands slid up to his throat in an unconscious movement, looping around his neck. The timid acquiescence ignited something deep inside him. Groaning, Archer crushed her to him, flattening her breasts against his chest as he claimed her lips.

He teased her, drawing her tongue into his mouth until she leaned in to him, helpless with the same shaking need that overtook him. An eternity later, he drew away. With a ragged breath, he pressed his forehead to hers. Heaven help him, he couldn't stop touching her. His fingers stroked her cheek, his thumb running across her swollen lips.

Briannon's eyes fluttered shut as his fingers slid lower, down the taut column of her neck to the strand of rubies lying on the swell of those alluring breasts. Her lips parted on a sigh, and he kissed them again, his tongue plunging deep as his thumb slid past the fragile lace edging of her bodice. He expected her to pull away, but she arched against him, moaning into his mouth as the pad of his thumb grazed her nipple. The sensitive skin tightened under his touch, and his groin did the same under a deluge of instant, mind-numbing lust. Archer pulled away, rattled at his own response. He was no greenhorn still wet behind the ears, and yet, one kiss, one small exploration of her breast, had made him feel like a wild and blundering buck.

But hell, he wanted more than this kiss. He wanted to rip open that silk bodice and settle his mouth on the luscious, swollen tips of her breasts. He wanted to torment her with his tongue and teeth and fingers, and hear her whimper with the same lust that tore through him. But he had risked discovery long enough, and putting Lady Briannon's unimpeachable reputation into question would not be wise.

As the moments passed, Briannon remained silent and immobile against him. Although she was flushed, her eyes, so transparent before, were now unreadable. He frowned.

"Briannon?"

"Have you finished?" Her cold tone was at odds with the remnants of passion still flickering across her face. "Please release me and let me pass. I'd like to rejoin my brother."

Surprised, he did as she asked and stepped away. She

held herself ramrod straight and swept past him to the double doors. She paused long enough to throw a backward glance over her shoulder.

For a moment, he thought she was going to ask him to join her, but her voice was low, vibrating with hostility. "If you ever try something like that again, it won't be my brother calling you out. It will be me, Lord Hawksfield, that I promise you."

As the door slammed shut behind her, Archer nearly laughed at her threat. Then he remembered her skill with the boar and sobered. Lady Briannon would make a formidable enemy. *She'd also make a formidable lover.* He returned to the ballroom and took up residence against a nearby pillar, watching as she danced with another young man, refusing so much as to glance his way.

Archer fought the urge to smile. She hadn't run from the ball, or from him, like a frightened fox. She had courage and defiance in spades, choosing to stay and showing him exactly how little his insults and his unwelcome advances had meant to her. Though he continued to question just how unwelcome his kisses had been. She had responded the way he'd wanted, if only for a few scattered heartbeats.

Their eyes met for a scant moment, and he nodded to her. Deep color suffused her cheeks. She was certainly not as unaffected as she was pretending to be. She stared him down across the crowd of dancers, her eyes still sparking with ire. Despite the rumors of her poor health, she showed no indication of weakness at the moment. No, he realized with an odd sense of pride, she held her own, staring him down as if a battlefield yawned between them instead of a ballroom floor. Archer lifted his glass in a silent toast, and she turned her back on him.

Deprived of her company, the evening wore on at a snail's pace. He sipped his third glass of whiskey and noticed Eloise having a wonderful time. It warmed him to see her taking to the floor dance after dance. At one point, their father stood beside her, but she could have been a veritable stranger for all the attention the duke gave her. Beneath the mask, Archer saw the burning snap of her eyes on their father before she'd turned and stalked away. The duke's indifference was still hurtful to her, even after all these years.

He made his way across the crowded ballroom, deftly avoiding as many matchmaking mothers and simpering debutantes as he could, and joined Eloise at the refreshment table. She sipped a glass of punch as a passing footman replaced Archer's empty glass of whiskey with a full one.

"Enjoying yourself?" he asked her.

"Oh yes." Her color was high, and she fairly glowed in the unusually exotic burgundy satin dress she had chosen to wear. Despite her ravaged face hidden beneath the feathered mask, her blond hair cascaded in luxurious curls down her back. Her maid had done an exceptional job tonight, and Archer told her so. Eloise blushed. "You look rather dashing yourself. Did you enjoy your dance with Lady Briannon? She has grown into a lovely young lady, has she not?"

Considering the phantom press of Briannon's mouth was still prickling at his lips, he figured an indirect reply was a safer route to take.

"You are not much older than she. And speaking of dances, I don't see you wanting for partners, either."

"By society's standards, my dear brother, I am an old maid, and she is just making her bow." She eyed him, smiling. "And stop trying to change the subject. Do you find her beautiful or charming? She would make you a good wife."

He lowered his chin in effort to stave off his sister's barrage of questions. "I am not looking for a wife."

Eloise laughed. "Tell that to all the mothers currently planning your wedding at this very moment. Take that one over there," she said, nodding to a matronly woman with two daughters at her sides, neither of whom appeared older than fifteen. Archer scowled. "She has scarcely stopped looking at you since you disappeared onto the balcony with Lady Briannon. If looks could kill when you both returned, the young lady would have met a sad demise indeed."

"The lady should tend to her own business," Archer said, sending a fierce scowl in the direction of the offending mother. "And we did not disappear. Lady Briannon simply needed some air."

"Is that what they're calling it these days?" Eloise teased. Archer did not respond, and she threw him a knowing smile. "I can see from your response that you are not as immune to the lady's charms as you pretend to be. I am sure Lady Dinsmore would be more than ecstatic to have you as a son-in-law. Come now, admit it: Briannon is comely, she is well-bred, and she is heiress to a fortune that most men would die for."

"Then you marry her."

Eloise laughed out loud, and the sound made a smile crack Archer's face in response. "You do say the strangest things. I am not the son of a duke."

"You are the daughter of a duke."

"We both know I am nothing of the sort," she said, a thread of bitterness creeping through. "It will likely kill our father to ever acknowledge me publicly." She shrugged and turned her face away as she tucked her arm in his. Her voice grew strained. "But as long as I have you, nothing else matters. You are my family."

Archer patted her arm, his mouth tight. He said nothing for a moment and then decided to change the subject. Despite her nonchalance, he knew the topic of her status was distressing to her. "Speaking of matrimony, I think Lord Suffield and the Earl of Langlevit are quite taken with you. They have each danced with you a number of times now."

Eloise rolled her eyes. "Are you keeping count?"

"I need to know who to call out in a secluded glen, that's all."

"You may want to wait until you're able to walk without limping," she replied, her gaze dipping to his leg.

It was starting to ache like hell, and apparently he wasn't disguising the injury as well as he'd thought. "Hunting accident," he murmured by way of explanation.

"I don't think you have to worry about calling either of the poor men out anyway. The earl had not officially made my acquaintance, as he has been overseas for some time. I'm sure he will hear the rumors of what lies behind my mask, and that will be that. And Lord Suffield has not yet realized who I am, despite his terrible attempts at flirtation. For now, I am enjoying the moments that I have. When morning comes, all will go back to normal, and I shall be Eloise the Recluse again."

Archer turned to his sister, thinking perhaps he'd see her light words were a protective shield to cover her true hurt. But there was nothing but honesty in her expression.

"Would it be so bad if one of them offered for you?"

"What makes you think one of them hasn't?" She smiled in jest. "I do not wish to be wed, Archer. I am content with my life as it is. We have been through this same argument countless times. I do not have a name—"

"But you have a dowry," Archer interrupted.

Eloise took a deep breath, her blue eyes shining with humor. "One that my generous brother has provided, and one that is enough to compensate for a face no man would want to wake up next to." A stabbing sensation—part guilt, part fury—made him grimace. She placed a hand on his arm, halting his protest. "I hate to be the one to tell you this, but I fear it is I whom you will have to meet in a secluded glen if you persist in trying to marry me off. Now please, go enjoy yourself. Give some young lady a glimmer of hope, and leave me to my enchanted evening."

Archer watched as the handsome young earl approached, and with a bow, whirled his sister off into a dazzling quadrille. A part of him hoped Langlevit wouldn't be as shallow as so many of his counterparts, but deep down, he knew that appearances were everything in the *ton*.

Archer could hear Eloise's tinkling laugh from across the room, and he let out a breath. She was so splendid, and so brave. If only his father would claim her, it would be the tipping point, regardless of her appearance. A title trumped beauty, or lack of it, every time. He glanced around the room. Take Lord Falconshire. He had the face of a boxer on the losing end of a match, but he had a title, and the gorgeous young woman on his arm was testament to Archer's theory.

He took a deep breath. If Langlevit continued to show interest in Eloise even after he saw what lay behind her mask, there was nothing Archer would not do to help the man along toward a proposal. Downing the whiskey in his hand and signaling for another, he strode to his father's side. As always, a throng of admirers and a dozen of his closest friends, including Lord and Lady Rochester, surrounded him.

"Ah, Hawksfield," his father slurred, throwing an arm around Archer's shoulders. "My boy." He chuckled loudly. "He's too good for the rest of us. Won't even wear a mask at a masquerade. You need to let loose, learn how to dance a good Scotch reel with a bonny lass." He winked at Lady Rochester who twittered behind her fan. "Surely we can find one for you."

"I assure you that I am more than capable of filling my own dance card." Archer took a whiskey from the quick servant's tray. "May I speak to you?"

The duke threw back his head and laughed. "Speak your mind, boy, we are all friends here."

"This matter requires some discretion." Archer took his father by the arm. "I insist. It will be only a short stroll on the balcony. You are, if I recall, overly fond of taking the air at these sorts of things."

Secretly he wondered if any illegitimate half brothers or sisters had been conceived on shadowy ballroom balconies or lawns. It would not shock him, if so.

"His Grace has promised me a dance," pouted Countess Mayfield, an aging widow who took pleasure in scandalizing the *ton* by taking lovers half her age. "Will you, dear Hawksfield, be an acceptable substitute as his second?" she asked with a leer.

"Not if I expect to keep my virtue intact," Archer teased with forced good nature. The entire group broke out into raucous laughter, including the countess. "Please excuse us. We will be but a minute. I will return him to you posthaste."

As they arrived on the balcony, and Archer shut the door behind them, his father's jolly mood exploded. "What the devil do you mean by this? We are at a masquerade, son. Enjoy yourself. Be merry. Find a wife."

Archer knew the duke had had more than a few drinks, but he would take the risk for Eloise's sake.

"Your daughter is here, too," Archer said. His father's face immediately went a dark shade of red. Archer did not let that stop him. "It appears that the Earl of Langlevit is quite taken with her. He may even decide to make an offer."

"That is no business of mine."

Archer fought to keep his anger under control. "It *is* your business. Eloise is your blood."

"She is the daughter of a commoner. Nothing more." His father wiped the sweat from his forehead. "She is no more my blood than any child found in the streets."

"Mother didn't think so."

The duke sighed as if the mere thought of his late wife

had sapped his strength. "Your mother's heart was always soft. El...the girl is a ward, no more than that. I cannot claim her, if that is what you are asking."

"I am asking."

"And I am refusing. It shouldn't surprise you, boy. For heaven's sake, I am a duke!"

Archer wanted to shake his father until his teeth rattled, but they were garnering enough curious stares through the paned glass already. He lowered his voice, his rage making his words shake. "Is your title the only thing you think about? Your esteemed place in society? These people you call friends? If they knew the truth about the family finances, do you think they would flock to you as they do?" He jerked a hand toward the massive balcony doors. "Yes, Father, you are a duke without a farthing to his name."

His father stared at him, his mouth a thin, defiant line. They had had this same argument too many times to count. The estates were profitable after Archer's many years of hard-won, and oftentimes risky, investments, yet his father was siphoning money. Archer was well familiar with the reasons. The duke's excessive gambling and lush lifestyle had reached new heights. Add in the parade of weekly mistresses along with the requisite furs, jewels, and gowns, and Archer could practically see the scarlet money trail. Managing his family's capricious incomes and keeping track of his father's expensive proclivities had become a full-time job. It exhausted him, and right now he felt the weight of that all-consuming fatigue turning into something hazardous.

"What would you have me do?" the duke asked. "Stay at home, die an old man in my bed? Waste away?"

"No," Archer said tiredly. "If Mother were alive..." He trailed off, not understanding why he was suddenly attacked by sentiment, or bringing up his mother in the first place. Between Briannon and his sister, he felt on edge and unexpectedly vulnerable.

"If your mother were alive," the duke said, "she would want you to be married and happy. I saw you with that young chit earlier, the Findlay girl. She's a bit thin in the hips, but she'll be able to give you an heir. And her father is rich…rich enough to fill our dwindling coffers, as you say."

"Is that all you think about?" Archer seethed. "Women and money?"

"That, my boy, is what you should be thinking about, instead of driving me mad with these questions regarding an illegitimate ward. Bed a woman—the Findlay girl if you are so inclined. Marry her."

Archer drew his hand through his hair. "I do not want to marry her."

His father grinned and smacked his lips. "It would be asinine to waste such a connection. If you're adamantly against her, well then…perhaps I should have a go. You think she'll have me?" Unmindful of the deadly expression on his son's face, the duke nodded, slurring his words. "That will solve all our problems. Marriage is a damn bore, but I would do it if it meant you'd stop pestering me about finances. Yes, I would. She is a sight in that dress tonight, that she is."

His father turned to peer through the glass panes of the balcony doors, his tongue still licking his lips as if he'd just been presented with a juicy cut of beef. Archer knew what he was looking for, however. No. *Whom* he was looking for. Briannon.

"She would never have you," he said, barely contained fury pulling his voice into a near whisper.

"Of course she would. She's as silly as the rest of these chits, being paraded around the ballroom by their mamas, dreaming of landing a title for a son-in-law." His father clapped him on the shoulder. "Can't do better than a duke, now can they?"

Archer ground his teeth and clenched his fingers around his glass of whiskey. His vision pulsed. He rolled his shoulder and threw off his father's fingers, which had started to dig into the fabric for purchase. The duke was too fogged by all the liquor he'd consumed to be able to hold up his own arm for more than a couple of seconds.

"You're pathetic," Archer said, before starting for the ballroom doors. He stopped, though. Insults had never gone far with the duke in the past. He seemed to care as much about his son's reproaches as he did his "ward," Eloise.

Archer turned back to find his father chuckling as he sipped his whiskey. Just as he'd supposed. The duke had already dismissed his son's disapproval.

"You will stay a far step from Lady Briannon," Archer warned.

Bradburne paused, his glass still at his lips. He finished off his drink in one fell swallow and tipped his glass at Archer. "And you, my boy, will either marry her, or stand aside and say nothing while I attend to the matter. There is no question Lady Dinsmore wants a match with the Bradburne dukedom, and it's immaterial to me whose bed the girl ends up in." His father hopped onto the balls of his feet as if getting ready for a jig. "Though I certainly wouldn't loathe my husbandly duty of getting her with another *legitimate* heir."

Archer stood as rigid as steel, an image taking form in his head. That of a luscious, naked Briannon pinned underneath his gluttonous father. Once there, it burned his imagination as splashes of acid might. Archer held his breath, his disgust for his father so great and vast, everything else—the darkened balcony, the glittering ballroom beyond, the voices of the guests, and the stringed instruments churning out a reel— went quiet. They disappeared. And the only thing Archer could see was the perfect target of his father's jaw.

He tossed his whiskey aside, the glass shattering on

the balcony floor, and struck his target with swift precision. Bradburne's head snapped back, his grunt of surprise muted by another shattering glass of whiskey. Had the duke not been stewed off his arse, he might have been able to right himself despite the blow. However, considering he was indeed well lit, he landed on the balcony stones like a stunned fish. He groaned and writhed, and almost instantly, Archer felt the sickening arrival of remorse.

"You bastard," the duke hissed, attempting to sit up and lift himself from his humiliating position. Archer heard the tinkling of glass, and more shards scraping against the stone floor. His father sucked in a breath and swore again, cradling his hand. Blood, stained black in the moonlight, welled up in his palm.

Good. The pathetic son of a bitch deserved more than a single punch anyhow.

"I'm sure you wish I were," Archer said, reaching for the white cravat at his neck. He yanked at the simple mail coach knot Porter had fussed so earnestly with earlier and unwound the starched linen, tossing the whole thing to his father, still seated on the balcony floor. It landed on his leg. "Had I been born a bastard, you could simply ignore me the way you do Eloise. You certainly wouldn't have me to contend with."

Bradburne snatched up the cravat and wrapped his bleeding hand. "You are no match for me, boy," the duke spat, struggling to stand without slicing himself on the broken glass again.

The balcony doors flew open and a collective gasp of alarm fountained up behind Archer. Lady Rochester and Countess Mayfield rushed past, their voluminous skirts brushing Archer's legs and hips as they parted around him, toward his father.

"What the devil has happened?" Lord Rochester boomed from the doors, and another burst of concerned voices closed in on the balcony.

Archer and Bradburne maintained their locked glare as the ladies twittered over the duke's bleeding hand and the streak of blood dripping from his nose. Countess Mayfield eyed Archer, her lips bowing in curious amusement, while Lady Rochester flat out scowled in his direction.

"The Dancing Duke took a misstep," Archer answered. "I fear he may be out of the game for the rest of the ball. Ladies." He bowed to them before sweeping off the balcony and into the ballroom.

There were more gasps of surprise as he stalked the perimeter of the dance floor with his neck bared to every last delicate eye. Without his cravat, he could no longer remain in attendance. An unexpected boon, he figured, and he set a course for the exit. He kept his focus straight, refusing to search the crowds for a glimpse of Briannon and the dress that had induced his father into scheming his way into her bed. Archer would never allow that to happen. *Never.*

Briannon would never allow it, either. She had rejected Archer's kiss. Why in the world would she accept the likes of Bradburne? Even without having to ask, he knew she wasn't after a title. Or marriage, for that matter. She had told him herself that any union between them would be "ghastly."

Then what was she after? Attention from a dangerous bandit? She'd worn the rubies for him. A thought that made Archer remember how they had rested on the soft curves of her décolletage. And that thought made him think of their kiss. Briannon had, for a good handful of moments, responded to his touch, his kiss, and hell, if she hadn't turned into a winter morning the way she had, he might have lost control of himself. He may have even drawn Briannon down the balcony steps and into the seclusion of Lord Gainsbridge's lawns.

Something he'd just mentally accused his father of doing multiple times with multiple women.

Bloody hypocrite.

Archer fled the ballroom, tensing and releasing the fingers on the hand he'd used to pummel his father. If Archer could strike himself, he'd do so. His father was the lusty, thoughtless bastard, not him, and he'd be wise to remember that. The sodding Duke of Bradburne was exactly the sort of privileged, upper-crust swine Archer took pleasure in relieving of their worldly goods. If the duke had two farthings to rub together, Archer might even attempt to swoop down upon his carriage. Then again, he'd likely recognize his own heir.

He gathered his coat and hat and called for his curricle. His leg ached as if to remind him of his many transgressions. Though Archer longed for some sort of satisfaction tonight, acting as the bandit when his temper was in a furor was not a wise decision. He'd simply return to Worthington Abbey and attempt to douse the fires the masquerade had ignited with a stiff drink and a cold bed.

Chapter Nine

A quarter hour had passed since the Marquess of Hawksfield had stormed out of the Gainsbridge ballroom, and the guests were still humming with excitement. The Duke of Bradburne and his heir had apparently been engaged in fisticuffs on the balcony—the balcony where, just moments before, Hawksfield had swept Brynn into a completely inappropriate, utterly scandalizing, and undeniably shattering kiss. She couldn't believe the liberties he had taken, sliding his thumb against her breast in so wanton a manner or the deeply intoxicating plunge of his tongue. The recollection made her simmer anew.

She stood with her mother and Gray, and a handful of other guests, in a tight circle on the edge of the dance floor. When Gray had met her near a column after she'd come in off the balcony, she'd expected her brother to see the flush of her cheeks and the pulsing of her burning lips. Her breathing had been uneven, and her legs a little untrustworthy. She was certain everyone, especially Gray, could see evidence of sin trailing in her wake. Her lips and breasts burned with the stain of it.

Perhaps a wandering eye had peered through the balcony doors at just the right moment and witnessed the ignominious embrace. If that were the case, the gossip would have already worked its way around the ball. The rumor of a kiss would have happily attached itself to the new scandal of Hawksfield and Bradburne coming to blows. The fact that it hadn't been mentioned once gave Brynn hope. She didn't want a scandal involving the marquess. Her mother would have clucked and crowed and demanded Lord Dinsmore and Gray approach Hawksfield about a proposal.

And what would Brynn do then? Marry the brute? Twice now since meeting again after so many years, he'd been insensitive and vulgar. Yesterday morning in the woods he'd been difficult and brusque, but…warmer. More generous and less prickly. He'd even made Brynn laugh. This evening, however, his whole demeanor had gone back to what it had been at the Bradburne Ball: rigid and fractious.

Until the balcony.

And the mask.

She couldn't get it out of her mind. Brynn listened to the women around her chattering like magpies, condemning Hawksfield for his surly attitude. *He was always such a sulky lad*, the Dowager Monteith had put in no less than four times. Countess Mayfield had fanned herself, chastising him for having the impudence to waltz through the ballroom sans cravat—*as though he were undressing for bed!* All the while, Brynn was thinking only of how familiar those quicksilver eyes staring out at her from behind the silk mask had been. But Hawksfield seemed much taller than the bandit. Then again, last night at least, the bandit had been flat on his back, so she couldn't be sure. She was starting to doubt herself and questioning whether deep down she *wanted* Hawksfield to be the bandit.

When Hawksfield had pulled her to him on the balcony,

and when they'd ridden Apollo, their thighs rubbing against one another, his touch had been scorching, just as the bandit's touch had been as he'd removed her grandmother's pearls and then, that morning in the small cottage in the woods, drawn her across his half-clothed body. But her responses to both didn't mean the marquess and the bandit were one and the same.

Her head spun with the chaos of it all. She didn't know what to think. The bandit had been charming and lively, while Hawksfield was…well…stony.

Not when he's kissing.

Brynn banished the traitorous thought and turned away from Countess Mayfield and Dowager Monteith. She immediately caught her mother scowling at the rubies and concealed her sigh. She was sure to receive a strict dressing down as soon as they all returned to Ferndale. Brynn pushed a smile to her face and pretended to be interested in the dancing. Though she did not look forward to her mother's tirade, she did wish to leave. However, she also did not want to risk chancing upon the marquess on the route home by following too closely in his wake.

Brynn fingered the rubies at her throat. She perused all the masked faces surrounding her, but none of the men seemed to be the right combination. One was the right height, but not the right coloring. One was too old. Another was dark, but stodgy in size. A fourth seemed perfect until she noticed his rather large hooked nose. No, her bandit was not here.

And neither was Lord Hawksfield.

She, like the rest of the crowd, had noted the marquess's rapid departure with curiosity. She recalled the mussed waves of his previously immaculate dark hair and the hard set of his jaw as he'd left the masquerade. He'd been angry, but Hawksfield seemed too austere to engage in such a public display with his father. He was not reputed to be a man given to emotion, unless it was chilling coldness. Except with her. She seemed to inspire nothing but his disapproval.

Or his lust.

His lips had been so warm, so tender. His fingers surprisingly rough as they delved inside her bodice. The small caress had made her cry out, and had he chosen to draw her farther into the shadows of the balcony, or perhaps out onto the lawns, she would have followed. The rugged stroke of his thumb over her nipple had rendered her mindless.

She hadn't been able to speak, and truth was, she hadn't wanted to. Though now, with her thoughts well back in check, Brynn had little doubt that she had been the recipient of a kiss from someone expert in seduction. No doubt his ego had taken a beating when she'd rebuffed him. That would account for his foul mood.

Brynn almost laughed at her inane reasoning. The marquess would never let some foolish girl allow him to drop all social graces. It may have been her first passionate kiss, but clearly, it had not been his. She'd experienced a stolen peck when one of Gray's friends during his days at Eton had paid a visit to Ferndale, but it'd been nothing like Hawksfield's kiss.

For a moment, Brynn imagined whether the bandit would kiss as well. The thought of her mysterious highwayman doing what Hawksfield had done made her blood simmer to dangerous levels. Lord, it was ridiculous how a desperate imagination could eclipse reality, and sanity. *Fancying a criminal?* Brynn fanned herself vigorously and decided that it was time to go home. She'd had far too much champagne, and far too many thoughts about kissing entirely unsuitable men.

She had just turned to her mother when she noticed that Eloise and the earl who had been paying her unquestionable interest all evening were approaching.

"Lady Briannon," Eloise said, proceeding to make the necessary introductions. The Earl of Langlevit found himself in conversation with Brynn's father, and the two young women decided to take a stroll to the refreshments table. "Are you enjoying the masquerade?"

"Yes, it's been a lovely time. And you?"

Eloise flushed. "I am." Her eyes darted to her escort, and Brynn couldn't help following her gaze. The Earl of Langlevit was certainly handsome with his sandy-colored hair and warm amber eyes. Gray had mentioned something about him being stationed overseas and that he had only just returned. They used to be at Eton together, but while Gray had moved on to Oxford, Langlevit had gone into the military. The pair exchanged a glance, and Eloise disappeared behind her fan.

It had been years since she had had more than polite conversation with Eloise, but the girl seemed different this evening. Normally, she hid from high society, preferring the solitude of Worthington Abbey. She wasn't much older than Brynn, only by two or three years, and by no means a spinster. When they were children, she and Brynn had often trailed after their two older brothers, but after the accident and the tragic death of the Duchess of Bradburne, Eloise had withdrawn into herself. Brynn couldn't blame her. She'd seen the damage with her own eyes—the raw burns, the shiny scar tissue, the pronounced dip of her right eye. God had seen fit to spare only the bottom third of her face, leaving her forever changed.

Her body had escaped the worst of it, but Eloise would never be well received by the beau monde, not without whispered comments and pity trailing her every step. Not even the protection of her fierce and intimidating brother could change that. And so she had retreated from society, her appearances at crushes like this one over the years few and far between.

Tonight, though, it seemed as if the flame of life burned anew within her. Brynn told her so.

Eloise laughed, tossing her golden curls. "I do so love dancing. I had forgotten how much I adore it. As it seems, it is a trait I have inherited from my father." Something like contempt thinned her lips before it was eclipsed by a bright smile. "Did you enjoy dancing?"

"Why, yes," Brynn said, grinning back. "Although Lord Filbert gamely attempted to massacre my toes in the last set. Do not tell him so, but he is sorely in need of some lessons."

"And Hawksfield? He is a capable partner, is he not?"

Brynn breathed deeply and kept her voice steady. "Lord Hawksfield is indeed capable." *More than capable.* She remembered the competent glide of his body beside hers in the waltz, and the light press of his hand at her waist. He could sweep any debutante in this room off her feet with a few precise steps and a few well-placed caresses from his expert fingers. Brynn cleared her throat. "Speaking of, he left quite suddenly. Was something amiss with the duke? I heard they... fought."

"Gossip travels faster than a foxhound," Eloise said and then leaned down to confide in her. "Those two are more alike than either of them cares to admit. Stubborn and inflexible to the core. They are always disagreeing about something. Bradburne stumbled and fell. Nothing to fret about, it will all be forgotten by the morn."

Inflexible. It was a word Brynn could understand. She could see it in every line of Hawksfield's demeanor, but the duke? He was always smiling, always jesting. Even now, despite his altercation with the marquess, he was the center of attention with his group of peers. Brynn studied the duke over her fan as Eloise exchanged greetings with the Dowager Monteith. Though he was handsome, his son did not resemble him, except for his nose and well-shaped lips. With their similar coloring, Eloise favored him more than Brynn suspected the duke would care to admit.

Hawksfield looked more like his late mother, whom Brynn remembered as being a charming, willowy brunette who always had a kind word for anyone, from a scullery maid to highborn ladies. She supposed Eloise learned that from her. Kindness, unlike hereditary predisposition, was something that could be taught.

Brynn drew in a sharp breath as her gaze collided with the subject of her focus—the duke himself. He inclined his head slightly, his drink arrested halfway to his lips.

And then he winked at her.

Taken aback, Brynn glanced away, but when she returned her gaze, he was still staring at her with an odd, calculating look on his face. He had never paid much attention to her before. Had Hawksfield said something to him?

To her everlasting dismay, the duke excused himself and cut a path directly toward the refreshments table. Brynn looked around in desperation. Eloise was still in conversation with the dowager, her back to Brynn, and her mother seemed to have disappeared. She had no idea why she was in such a panic. She and her entire family had known the duke for years. But the look in his eyes now gave her pause. It seemed heavy and purposeful. As if he were a hunter and she were the prey…as if he were seeing something he suddenly coveted.

She had to be wrong. He was old enough to be her father! Older than her father, in fact. But as the duke neared, the admiring look in his eye was not to be imagined.

He took her numb hand in his and kissed it. "Lady Briannon, you are as beautiful as a new rose in spring."

"Your Grace," she murmured, curtsying and taking in a gulp of air as her mother materialized out of nowhere. Her mama had a bad habit of appearing in places where she wasn't wanted, but for once, Brynn was exceedingly grateful.

The dowager turned, too, to converse with the duke, and so did his daughter. His mouth tightened, and his eyes grew frosty, and he did not deign to acknowledge Eloise, whose icy demeanor rivaled his for a brief second. Instead, he directed his attention to those who had accompanied Brynn's mother. Eloise smiled and curtsied before allowing the Earl of Langlevit to escort her to the next set.

Bradburne engaged in polite conversation with her mother, but Brynn could feel his eyes fluttering to her décolletage, as if drawn there by the cursed rubies lying so blatantly on the bare expanse of her skin. Resisting the urge to claw the dastardly necklace from her throat, Brynn wished she still had her stole.

The strains of a waltz in the next set started to play, though the music seemed oddly distant. A buzzing in her ears was her first warning. And then she started to feel dizzy. Bradburne turned to her and extended his hand, the other still wrapped in a white winding cloth. The world began to spin, the floor beneath her feet tilting precariously.

"May I?" His stare was confident as though her answer was already a given. He was a duke, after all. No one would say no to a duke.

She licked dry lips. "I…"

Strong hands grasped her arms as the voices faded into an unrecognizable drone. A cool cloth was suddenly being pressed to her head and a glass to her lips. She sipped automatically, and the liquid burned a hot path to her stomach. Brynn coughed, opening dazed eyes that came into contact with a pair of laughing blue ones leaning over her.

"Your Grace," she said. "Please, you do not need—"

The duke grinned. "She is awake!" he pronounced and a wave of cheering ensued. "It's been quite some time since I have caused a young maiden to swoon simply by asking her to dance."

"Still a rake," someone shouted, and the crowd erupted into laughter again.

The duke helped Brynn to her feet, and she swayed unsteadily, managing a sliver of a smile. "If it pleases His Grace, I will retire now. Perhaps I may have the honor of claiming your dance another time."

He bowed, his lips pressing against her hand once more. "I look forward to it with pleasure, Lady Briannon."

Brynn curtsied, trying not to be sick all over the polished floor at his emphasis on the word *pleasure*, and rose to take her leave. Her mother's face expressed astonishment, her father's resignation, while Gray looked as if he'd swallowed an insect the size of a pomegranate. Brynn, however, felt like she needed a scalding bath.

She could feel the duke's eyes on her all the way to the staircase and hear the laughter and raucous comments as he rejoined his friends. She held her head high, walking gracefully up the stairs. As for the rubies and the offending dress, she would chuck both the instant she got home.

"Not one word," she warned Gray as they collected their coats. She wrapped the silver stole around her shoulders. Likely for his own safety, her brother remained quiet as they climbed into the waiting carriages.

If the duke offered for her, her father would be hard-pressed to refuse, and her mother...good Lord, the promise of a coronet would make the age difference between them disappear. Brynn sighed at the coil she had gotten herself into, all because she had dressed to unmask a marauder.

She relaxed into the rocking movement of the carriage and tried not to think about what her future held. Perhaps there was still hope that her mysterious highwayman would appear and whisk her away from it all.

Suddenly the carriage jolted to a stop. Brynn's heart skipped a beat as Gray hopped from the conveyance with a look that said she should stay put. She did. For a moment. If it was indeed the masked man making yet another attack, she would never forgive herself for hiding in a carriage simply because her brother had wanted her to.

Brynn descended the steps. There was no Masked Marauder demanding no displays of heroism. Instead, another conveyance up ahead lay on its side. Brynn's eyes widened, her hands clasped to her mouth. A man leaned against one upturned carriage wheel for support, while another sat upon the edge of the path, his head clasped between his hands. Gray stalled her with a raised hand, but Brynn wasn't to be stopped. She approached the man who was standing, his hands clutching his head. Recognition was swift. It was Earl Maynard, one of her father's oldest friends. "Lord Maynard, what happened here?"

The aging earl cleared his throat and blubbered the words Brynn was dreading...the ones she already knew he would say. "It was the Masked Marauder. He beat Berthold unconscious. Shot my horse! Nearly shot me, too." He turned toward her, and in the light of her footman's torch, Brynn almost vomited.

His face was covered in livid wounds, his eyes puffy, and his mouth split. Blood dampened the white of his cravat. Her gaze returned to the motionless horse in the road, and the strength drained from her body. It was just an animal, but she couldn't stop the shuddering sobs from creeping up in her chest.

Brynn slumped down. The thief she had fantasized about had done this. She had imagined him kissing her, rescuing her. She had dreamed of his touch. Her skin crawled with revulsion and shame.

The rubies weighed unnaturally heavy around her neck as another thought occurred to her: when Hawksfield had left the masquerade he'd been angry. Had she been wrong to dismiss him? *Could* he be the Marauder? Was he capable of such cruelty?

Brynn recalled the chilling look on his face as he'd left, and shivered. But how? It was common knowledge that Hawksfield loved horses, prided them. He'd returned Apollo to Ferndale as promised, groomed, fed, and happy. She could not claim to know the enigmatic Marquess of Hawksfield well, but surely his integrity would never allow him to sink to such callous violence.

No. It was clear now that the masked bandit was nothing more than a lowbrow thief. Cold-blooded and vicious. And she had been a blind, overly romantic fool to ever consider otherwise.

Chapter Ten

Archer reigned in Morpheus as he came upon Pierce Cottage. The two-story stone and timber home and barn were quiet and sleepy in the early Sunday morning light. There was still a chill in the air. Morpheus's hot breath clouded with every pant, but Archer didn't feel the cold. His body had alternated between mild and sweltering heat since hearing the news a half hour before, when Archer's valet had entered his bedroom.

"There has been an incident," Porter had said, causing Archer to sit up and push the fog of sleep away.

His valet, ever efficient, had relayed the attack on Lord Maynard's coach the night before in as few words as possible.

"It is being called the work of the Masked Marauder," Porter had finished. However, Archer had already been up and pulling off his nightclothes to get dressed.

He was wrapping Morpheus's traces around a post when Brandt opened the cottage's front door.

"You look like hell," he greeted with his usual lopsided grin. "How's the leg?"

"Fine," he snapped. He'd been lucky, Archer supposed, that the shot had been so shallow. It was healing at a fast pace, though it still oozed from time to time, especially when he moved too briskly.

Archer stormed past his friend into the warm, familiar front room of Pierce Cottage. Aged oak floorboards, a large stone hearth with a fire in the grate. The long table surrounded by chairs and benches that had been in the same place for as long as Archer could recall. The cookstove sat in a far corner, and when Brandt's mother was alive, it had emitted the finest scents Archer's nose had ever traced. Warm yeasty rolls, butter cookies, roasted chicken, and savory puddings. He knew he was in trouble when his stomach didn't so much as grumble with a single pang of hunger.

He felt ill.

And furious.

Brandt closed the front door and turned to him, his arms crossing over his chest. He was as tall as Archer and as thickly built, but Brandt had a gentleness about him that Archer lacked. It was a grace and tranquility that spoke to the horses in Worthington Abbey's stables, that calmed them and made the animals feel safe and respected. It often calmed Archer as well, though not now.

"What is wrong?" Brandt said, frowning at his ill humor.

By the time Archer had finished relating all he knew thus far, Brandt's arms had come down to his sides, and his hands were flexing in and out of fists.

"You have an apostle, it seems," he said, heading toward the cookstove. He slid on a mitt and lifted a coffeepot.

"A zealot, more like," Archer replied.

He pulled out one of the stick-back chairs at the table and sat, drumming his fingers on the worn wooden tabletop. It was here, at this table, where he'd always felt most welcome. Most at ease.

As a boy, Brandt had spent time at Archer's table, too. The table in the children's nursery, that was, where Archer's tutors had been given the task of teaching the stable master's boy. The duke had not known of this, of course. It had been the duchess to whom Archer had pleaded such a convincing case. She had relented, but had warned them to be quiet about the lessons; if the duke were to hear of them, Brandt would be sent away. Montgomery, Brandt's father and stable master, would be as well.

So their lessons had been discreet, their compliant tutors completely and utterly under the charm of Archer's mother. They likely assumed the second boy was yet another ward of the duke. Sharp-witted and quick-brained, Brandt was a fast learner, keeping pace with Archer and even outdistancing him in some subjects. Despite the social hierarchy separating them, Archer trusted Brandt more than anyone in his own set.

The most intelligent and educated stable master in all of England sat down in a chair across the table from Archer. Brandt sipped his coffee. He hadn't offered any to Archer. Brandt knew if Archer wanted some, he'd have to get up off his privileged arse and get it himself.

Archer didn't think his stomach could handle coffee right then anyhow. He hooked an ankle over his knee. "He killed the bloody horse. Shot it. He beat Maynard and his coachman severely, too."

And Viscount Northridge and Lady Briannon had been the first to come across the unholy scene. He hated that she'd seen the carnage this so-called apostle had left behind. What must she have thought, believing the defenseless beast in the road had been killed by the same man who had waylaid her carriage last week?

"Whomever it was has an obvious taste for violence," he went on, trying to stay focused. "And you can be certain he isn't redistributing the vast wealth of the *ton*, either."

Brandt sat back in his chair. "This is not the Masked Marauder, and people will know it. You've never beaten someone to a pulp, or fired your pistol. Hell, it isn't even loaded with a shot."

"They don't know that," Archer replied. "And though I may announce what I plan to do with their precious coin and gems, how many of them do you think actually believe me? When the news about this reaches London, they'll think that this bloodthirsty thief and I are one and the same. This brigand was no doubt stealing for his own benefit."

Heartless bastard.

Brandt sat forward again, a restless energy coming off him. "Perhaps we should cool our heels a bit. If our zealot is as bloodthirsty as you say, it won't be long before a dead horse becomes a dead peer."

It was a wise suggestion.

"There is something more," Archer said, nodding at his friend and clearing his throat. "I received an anonymous note from someone claiming to know my secret."

Brandt's brows slammed together. "A note?"

"It arrived hidden in my newssheets," Archer said. "It appears that someone is aware of my true identity."

"Do you think they are connected?" Brandt asked, his expression darkening. "The note and the attack?"

"It's possible."

Archer considered the two occurrences—the note and the violent attack on Maynard—and couldn't help but worry that the two were related in some way. It seemed entirely too coincidental to have a zealot marauder *and* an unknown blackmailer appear almost at the same time. There was no way to know, he supposed, yet the malevolence of this imposter rubbed at him. Unlike Archer, he was no gentleman bandit.

Archer sighed, rubbing his temples. He'd known this path would be risky, but there were many who needed him to take that risk. People with no one to turn to. As always, Eloise's mother came to mind. Though the Duke of Bradburne had the means to care for her and their child, he had chosen not to. After he'd taken whatever pleasure he could from her body, she'd been beneath his notice. So had Eloise. Lady Bradburne's feelings of guilt at the woman's death had become Archer's own and, in some small way, redistributing his father's—and the *ton*'s—wealth brought with it some measure of retribution. For Eloise's mother's sake. But he had not expected his alter ego to be usurped by a real criminal… and one whose violence would be attributed to *him*.

After so much time spent funneling the wealth of his peers to hospitals and orphanages, these people needed him… depended on him, even. More precisely, they depended on the generous donations of Viscount Hathaway. Hathaway, one of Archer's false identities, had become a silent benefactor to the poor. At first, small contributions had been made, pilfered from sleights of hand and sweeping wins in the gaming hell he'd started at Cambridge, and then later at other more established gentlemen's clubs where the spoils became far larger.

Soon after that, however, Archer had seized upon the idea to waylay his first carriage. It had been carefully planned, following an obnoxious display at White's led by the bejeweled and pompous Lord Bainley, who had needed to be taught a valuable lesson in humility and divested of some of his fortune. The thrill of the act was undeniable, but it was the subsequent satisfaction of Lord Hathaway's ability to make such large donations that had kept Archer waylaying carriages. Only those deserving of his attentions, of course.

Hathaway had actually been one of his mother's uncle's titles, and not one that could be easily traced back to him. Archer gave as much as he could of his own wealth, but the needs of the poor far outweighed his means. His intentions were benevolent. Those of this follower were clearly not. Outrage fanned higher within him. How dare some overzealous criminal impersonate him?

"Who could it be?" Archer said in an agitated voice. "It has to be someone we know, someone we have used. What of the runner?"

He left that end of the business to Brandt. If the Marquess of Hawksfield approached commoners with a job of running trinkets and jewels to Scotland's border for cash trade, his game would be up in a flash. Brandt, however, had the obscurity that was needed for such a task.

He shook his head firmly. "It's my cousin. I trust him. And he doesn't know about your involvement. If anything, the boy thinks a lower footman is raiding the jewelry boxes of the fine guests that flow in and out of your London and country estates."

Good. That was the theory Archer had hoped the runners would form. Petty theft. Not highway robbery.

"He's new, isn't he? This isn't our first dance. What of the other runners you've employed?" Archer asked.

Brandt's frown deepened as he considered what Archer had asked. Earlier on, they had used less trustworthy people to run the stolen jewels up to Scotland. They had been paid handsomely, and hadn't asked questions, but that didn't mean that they wouldn't get ideas of their own or want a larger piece of the proverbial pie.

"It's possible one of them has started to develop a theory about where those jewels really came from," Brandt said, then sat back in his chair. "Or perhaps that boy you keep talking about from the night before last?"

Archer scowled and waved off the suggestion. "He was half the size of Maynard. And if the lad was a cutthroat, he wouldn't have tried to help me."

"He wouldn't have shot you in the first place."

Archer sighed and nodded. "Fair point."

"He could have been following you for weeks, shot you so you would be out of the way, but didn't want to kill you. He could have accomplices. Perhaps he already knows who you are, which is why he did not remove the mask. And what if he's the one who sent the note?"

Archer schooled his expression to not betray the sudden chaos of his thoughts. It was entirely possible, and it would certainly confirm his earlier suspicion that the anonymous note was linked somehow. "If you're right, this could be a real problem. If it is ever traced back to you or me, and I am somehow blamed for this pretender's actions…" He paused, studying his friend. "There is one thing, though, that we may need to resolve."

"Which is?"

"Lady Briannon Findlay."

Brandt shot him a perplexed look. "The poorly girl from the neighboring estate?"

Archer thought of the time he'd seen Briannon square off against an angry boar, her color high. She hadn't looked so "poorly" then. Neither had she at the masquerade last night in that sin-inducing dress, but servants gossiped, and it would be expected that Brandt, too, would have heard the rumors of her lung ailments over the years.

"One and the same," he replied, his voice brusque. He stood up, restless and eager to clear his throat. He refrained, however. It would make him appear nervous. "She may have recognized me last night at the ball. I can't be sure."

"Recognized you?" Brandt repeated.

"As the bandit who robbed her family," he explained. "I donned the mask last night without thinking—"

"You donned the mask?"

Archer glared at him. "Must you echo my every word? Yes, I put on the mask. She looked at me strangely for a moment as if coming to the correct conclusion before discarding it." Brandt snorted at the frail connective logic, making Archer's glare deepen tenfold. "Nonetheless, we cannot afford to take the chance that she will make good on her guess. She is a clever woman."

"Apologies," Brandt said, still trying to cover his amusement. The man had never gotten riled up about anything before, so his placid reaction didn't throw Archer. In fact, it seemed to calm him. "So hypothetically, what if she did discover your identity? Would she expose you? Go to the authorities? And let us not forget your apostle. He needs to be found."

"I know he does. And, no, I don't know what she'll do." Archer groaned. *Damn it all.* "For now, I will take care of Lady Briannon."

"How?"

He groaned, raking his hands through his dark hair, annoyed by his friend's humor at his expense. "Leave it to me. Surely there's something she wants in return. It won't be the first time I've bought a woman's silence."

The silence he had purchased had been to cover one of his father's flagrant affairs with a woman who happened to be married to an influential man in the House of Lords. The adulterer, now happily ensconced in an Italian country estate, had been more than willing to accept Archer's proposal. He highly doubted Briannon's obedience could be purchased in the same manner. He just hoped to hell he wouldn't be forced to try.

He stopped at the door. "What of the last of the jewels? Was your man able to fetch a good price for them?"

"Yes. They were sold in France a few days ago. I have already sent the proceeds to the three charities and the orphanage you earmarked, donated under the same name, Viscount Hathaway."

Archer nodded. "Excellent."

Brandt took something from a velvet pouch and handed it to Archer. "And these?"

Archer stared at the string of pearls and matching earbobs in his hands. He did not know what had stopped him from sending the costly heirlooms with the rest of the stolen gems, whether it had been the plea in Briannon's voice or the way her eyes had burned with rage-filled tears when he'd divested her of them. He studied the pearls. They—and she—were becoming more trouble than either of them were worth. He stuffed them into his pocket.

"We continue two nights henceforth. The Aberdeen's Ball should have good spoils for the taking. Then I leave for London for the season."

"Hawk," Brandt began. "Do you think that is wise?"

Archer sent him an expressionless look. "Stop any time you wish, but I am going. And may fortune smile upon me that I may meet this pretender face to face."

"That's not it," Brandt said a trifle defensively, though still calm. Still rational. "I have your back, always. We need to be careful now, is all. People are looking for a violent man, not a charming thief. There is a world of difference between the two. Notwithstanding that fact, if anyone were to find out that the true Masked Marauder is really the esteemed Marquess of Hawksfield, future Duke of Bradburne, your family would never live down the scandal."

"And I would be hanged," Archer said drily. "Trust me, I am well aware of the risks to my neck and good name, my friend." He gentled his voice and clapped his longtime friend on the shoulder. "You have nothing to worry about."

As he was about to take his leave, Brandt stopped him at the doorway. "I heard you and your father argued at the masquerade. That it became physical. They said that his hand was bleeding."

Archer froze. "Did they?" His voice was dangerously soft and clipped, offering no further explanation. Brandt was his friend, but there were some things that he did not feel inclined to discuss, especially where his sire and Briannon were concerned.

Brandt was not cowed. "They did."

Archer exhaled and pressed his fingers to the bridge of his nose. "We discussed a matter. He slipped, fell, and cut his hand on his whiskey glass. That is all."

Lying to Brandt, even a white lie such as this, felt like crossing an entire ocean with the stretch of one leg. He didn't know why he bothered to try—he knew the man would see right through him. *Shame*, a cantankerous little voice whispered in answer.

Hell. He shouldn't have hit his father, even if the licentious tippler had deserved it. It'd been an unconscionable act of anger, brought on by the woman who was fast becoming an irritating thorn in his side…his arse, if he was being precise.

"Hawk," Brandt began in a gentle tone, almost like he'd use with his beloved horses. "He is your father, even with all his faults, for better or for worse."

"I know," Archer exploded. "Don't you think I *know*?"

Brandt didn't answer. Instead he set aside his coffee and reached for the ceramic jug that stayed in the center of the table day and night. He poured two fingers of whiskey and offered one to Archer. "Stay awhile. You look like you need a drink."

A handful of hours later, after Archer left Brandt's cottage, he rode his stallion to the property line that divided his estate with Dinsmore's.

He wondered if Briannon would be out for a ride, but then grinned. No doubt it was far too late in the morning to be cavorting around in men's breeches. She preferred early rides when she couldn't be seen. He blinked as something occurred to him in the same moment—could *Briannon* have been the man who had shot him? Archer shook his head, his mind considering and discarding the possibility with swift haste. No, he would have known. He was certain of it. One, she was far smaller than the unknown assailant. And two, he didn't doubt her skill with the pistol, but had it been her disguised as a boy, she would have certainly demanded the return of her precious pearls. And *then* she would have shot him.

Grinning, Archer nudged Morpheus through the thicket of trees near the line that divided their estates, coming to a familiar area that made his gut clench. A long-forgotten pain surfaced, chasing away his humor, as he looked upward. It was still there, along with every emotion he'd thought gone and buried. The stout base of the scorched tree house platform hung haphazardly overhead. Charred bits of lumber awakened memories in him that he wished he could forget—Eloise's face…his mother's horrific death.

At the sight, a savage pain gripped him, making his fingers wind brutally into the leather reins. He could smell the smoke, hear the screams as if he were young again. He had arrived minutes after the servants, but he'd been helpless then, only a boy, and he'd been too late to save her. He had watched as a bawling Eloise had come stumbling down the ladder covered in soot before a burning section of the roof had caved in. There was no sign of his mother, although he could hear a woman keening. It'd taken four grown footmen to hold him down from climbing in after her.

Archer swallowed past the raw lump in his throat as he studied the charred lumber hanging above his head. The tree house didn't have only bad memories tied to it. The summer before the fire, he, Brandt, and Northridge had spent countless hours up there, doing the things they believed grown men did. Northridge had snuck three of his father's cigars for them to hack on. Archer had nicked a bottle of his father's brandy and a deck of cards. Brandt had brought up a pair of dice he'd carved from a block of pinewood.

One night they'd caught the then six-year-old Briannon and an eight-year-old Eloise creeping through the grounds and following them. Briannon had been a wisp of a girl then, but no less fearless than she was now. Northridge had threatened her with all manner of punishments, but she'd stood her ground and refused to be intimidated. Instead of fleeing back to the nursery where they belonged, both girls had spent the evening in the tree house, doing everything their brothers did. They'd even taken sips of the brandy, swallowing with melodramatic gags.

Archer smiled at the memory and shook his head. He should have recognized Briannon's stubborn streak from then. His smile turned to a frown as he recalled Northridge wrapping her in sheepskins that same night so she wouldn't catch her death of cold. Even then, her brother had looked out for her, knowing how easily she could fall ill. That protectiveness hadn't changed, either, Archer thought, recalling Northridge's watchful expression at the ball. It'd been a long time since they played as friends in the tree house. It'd been even longer since he considered anyone other than Brandt a friend. Trust was not something Archer handed out lightly, or often. It had to be hard-earned. And now he was putting his friendship with Brandt in jeopardy because of a woman.

Good god, he'd been such a fool. Donning the blasted mask had been reckless and idiotic, but some part of him had craved for Briannon to look at him the same way she had the highwayman—with open and fervent emotion. Whether it was wonderment or exasperation, it didn't matter. So long as she just *saw* him.

He turned his horse about. Seeking her out now, today, the morning after a ball in which they had danced and strolled on the balcony, would look far too much like paying court. Which would be another foolish move. *Damnation*, he swore under his breath. What was wrong with him? He was normally so level-headed and even-keeled. The woman made him behave like a besotted imbecile. He had to nip this attraction, or whatever lunacy it was, right in the bud and put Lady Briannon firmly out of his mind. *After* ascertaining what she knew, of course.

She would be in London within days and would most definitely be in attendance at the annual Tewksdale Soiree, the first ball of the season. All ladies making their bow attended.

Archer would see Briannon there and, even if it proved a challenge, he would find a private audience with her. Lady Briannon Findlay, it seemed, would have to be dealt with.

Chapter Eleven

More flowers were at Bishop House when Brynn arrived in London. Lilies this time, their drooping petals a girlish pink and white. A dozen of them waited for her in the front parlor of her family's home on the corner of St. James's Square. It was a stately, four-story white-stuccoed mansion that, from the outside, appeared rather severe and block-like. It had been in Brynn's family for generations, and on the inside, Bishop House had been forced into modernity by her mother and layered with elegant touches until it all but reeked of femininity. Perhaps that was why Lady Dinsmore was the one cooing over the lilies, which were dropping orange dust from their long stamens all over the newly polished credenza in the front parlor. The flowers were extremely feminine, and what young maiden didn't enjoy pink?

Brynn. That was who.

Lady Dinsmore ruffled the petals for the third time that morning. "I am all astonishment! I had no idea the duke himself was in the market for a wife!"

Brynn sat upon the edge of the sofa, the teacup in her

hand forgotten. The oolong was likely cold by now, anyway. Her stomach had yet to unclench since the arrival of the first dozen flowers at Ferndale the morning after the Gainsbridge's Masquerade. She'd entered the front sitting room and seen the hothouse flowers, a dozen violet roses, a purple so pale they were nearly a shade of blue. Her heart hadn't known what to do—be still or crash wildly. So it had done both, and her legs and arms had been quivering with confusion by the time she opened and read the accompanying card:

With regret that I did not have the pleasure of a dance with the loveliest lady last evening.

The duke had signed his name for propriety, but Brynn would have known without it. The note had fluttered from her numb fingers, her stomach cramping into horrible knots. The way Bradburne had eyed her the evening before, with unsettling interest, had lingered. And on top of it, the attack on Lord Maynard's carriage, and the sight of his slain horse, had worked more ice under her skin. By the time she'd reached home, Brynn had been shivering uncontrollably. She'd been both exhausted and horrified, and she had gone to bed determined not to think about the marauder.

It had been no surprise when she had failed.

The receipt of the flowers along with the duke's intentions the next morning had been the last straw. She should have stayed home from the masquerade. She should have never worn that blasted dress or those damned rubies. She'd put herself on display, hoping to lure in the bandit that she'd so naively romanticized, and she'd wound up being kissed by a rude, brutish marquess, ogled by a duke more than twice her own age, and then exposed, firsthand, to the violent truth about the bandit. It had shattered her silly dreams.

She should have aimed better the night she'd happened across him robbing Lord Perth's daughter. Either that, or left him to bleed to death instead of acting like a compassionate fool and helping him to safety. He hadn't deserved it.

Brynn refused to think about that horrible criminal for one more second, even if he did have an uncanny resemblance to the Marquess of Hawksfield. She'd already decided it couldn't be him—he would sooner shoot himself than a helpless horse. That said, it didn't stop him from being a loathsome rake. Further, she had worse things to worry about…like the duke's utterly unwelcome suit.

Most girls she knew would die for such attention from someone with so lofty a title, but Brynn felt only the keen desire to disappear to someplace he would not be able to find her. Her mother's breathless delight made it worse.

"I deplore the scent of lilies," Brynn replied to her mother, who had motioned for the maid to tidy up the stamen dust. "They smell like death."

"That is a wretched sentiment, Briannon, and I will not have you stating it again." Lady Dinsmore bustled to the settee next to her daughter, her excitement even able to eclipse her irritation. "The duke himself is completely bewitched by you, dear. Now, I know he isn't terribly young—"

"He is at least five and fifty!"

"But he is extremely respected—"

"They call him the *Dancing* Duke!"

Her mother went on, ignoring her interjections, both of which were impossible to argue, and Lady Dinsmore likely knew it. "—and his lineage is impeccable."

Brynn set down her teacup, splashing cold tea over the brim. "He is a rake of the worst sort, Mama, and you know it."

Everyone knew it, including Hawksfield, who had never, not even while growing up in the country, attempted to conceal the fact that he deplored his own sire.

And then there was Eloise. The poor woman had been willfully ignored by the duke her whole life. The man was infuriating, arrogant, and snobbish, and there was absolutely no chance in Hades that Brynn would ever be induced to marry him.

"All he wants for is a wife to guide him," her mother said, that faraway and scheming look in her eyes as they gazed at the wall behind Brynn's sofa.

"That is exactly what you said about his son, if I recall correctly."

Did her mother truly believe any woman could fix a man's deeply ingrained faults by her mere presence?

Lady Dinsmore lifted her pointed chin and shot her daughter a cool glance. "Well, I haven't seen any floral arrangements sent by the marquess, now have I?"

There was an unexpected twinge in Brynn's stomach, though she couldn't determine what it meant. Disappointment? Of course not. She didn't wish for flowers or flattering notes from Hawksfield. He would never lower himself to beg a woman for her attentions anyhow. And she didn't regret rejecting his lewd kiss.

Even though she *had* thought of it numerous times in the days since the masquerade. At night, mostly, while she lay in bed. Thinking of him.

Oh bother.

Hawksfield was all the things she'd just accused the duke of being: infuriating, arrogant, and snobbish. And yet kissing him had been…it had been tantalizing and urgent. He had pinned her against his chest with the same desperate strength one might use when fighting the pull of an ocean tide. As if he'd feared someone dragging her away from him. She'd tasted his passion. Breathed it. It was an emotion she hadn't thought Hawksfield capable of expressing. Yet, with her, for those brief moments, he had.

Which made her wonder: what else had he been hiding behind his cold and stony facade?

Gray entered the front room with one of the newssheets Lord Dinsmore subscribed to under one arm. He took one look at the lilies on the credenza and scowled.

"Would anyone mind terribly if I were to chuck them straight into the fire?"

Brynn stood up from the sofa, her legs sore from holding them so stiffly. Nerves made her muscles ache and her breathing ragged. But right now, at least, she felt fine. After her fainting spell at the masquerade, Brynn had not been allowed out of the house for a full day.

"Not at all," she answered. "In fact, I will wager that you could not get them all in on your first shot."

"You will not touch them!" their mother screeched, standing up as well and going to the lilies as though to stand guard. She glared at Brynn. "And placing wagers is no proper thing for gently bred girls to be doing."

Gray had worked himself into a froth the morning the violet roses had arrived. He disliked Hawksfield, but he despised Bradburne.

"The man is a toad," Gray said, slapping the paper down on a table by the street side window. "Had you seen the way he looked at her, you would hardly be in such a delirious state. He looked at her as if...as if...she were something to be gobbled up."

"Hush! You know how servants gossip," their mother hissed, looking sideways toward the door to where a footman stood sentry. "Insulting the duke at this phase would be extremely unwise."

A knock on the front door to Bishop House covered up Brynn's reply of, "So would encouraging his suit."

She knew better than to try to sway her mother. She was an ox when it came to certain matters, especially those that concerned marrying off her daughter to the highest, most affluent, and titled bidder. With the duke's attention, she felt more than ever like a prized item on the auction block. Brynn had wanted to enjoy her season, and perhaps meet an eligible bachelor with whom she would have something in common. She had hoped to choose a husband at her own pace. She hadn't imagined things would progress so quickly.

Brynn met her brother by the window while they waited to see who had called upon them. She lowered her eyes to the bold headlines on the newssheet he'd set down. Ladies were not supposed to read the papers for anything more than the gossip columns. However, Brynn made a habit of sneaking the rest of the paper from her father's study, and Gray would often leave them for her underneath her pillow. If Lana found them, she would lay them neatly on the bedside table.

"The day is warming," her brother said casually, even though his finger tapped a lurid headline:

Masked Marauder Strikes Again! Assaults Man, Steals Priceless Heirloom.

Lord Maynard had told her and Gray that night on the road leading from the Gainsbridge estate that the bandit had forced his family's signet ring from his finger. It had graced the fingers of every ancestor for six generations and could never be replaced. The man had been raging between heartbreak and fury.

Brynn shook her head, her body trembling as she recalled the earl's face. He was lucky to be alive. And she…she had been so *presumptuous* with the bandit when her father's carriage had been attacked. It was a miracle he hadn't harmed her. How could her instincts have led her so far astray? The bandit's manner had been poised and unruffled, and while she'd known him capable of striking a man unconscious, as he'd done with Colton, she'd also been certain he was far too highbrow to be a cold-blooded killer. Those eyes of his, much too intelligent and observant.

And then, as he'd lain half delirious in that cottage a few

nights later, his leg bleeding profusely, his trousers around his shins, he'd looked so vulnerable.

Brynn shook her head roughly. What was she thinking? The bloody man killed Maynard's horse, and here she was, reminiscing about his damned eyes and the fact that she'd seen him in his underclothes. The truth was, she'd been too hasty in assuming his genuine nature because of some disgraceful, misplaced attraction. A handsome, well-spoken man apparently could be a savage if he chose to be. Perhaps he simply did not harm women?

She ground her teeth. There she went again, tossing morals that may not exist onto the criminal's shoulders.

Braxton appeared at the entrance to the salon, a black card resting upon a silver tray. "Your ladyship," he intoned with a low bow.

"Thank you, Braxton," her mama said, dismissing him with a nod, her eyes widening at the ducal seal stamped on the outside of the delicate parchment. She quickly opened the note and read the card within. "An invitation from the duke himself for dinner! Tonight!"

"Wonderful," Gray said with an exaggerated eye roll. "Fortunately for me, I have a previous engagement. Not that I wouldn't enjoy watching you deliver your precious daughter like a fatted lamb to His Grace's esteemed table."

"Graham, enough," his mother scolded. Her eyes once more darted to the footman, and she lowered her voice. "If the duke's interest should turn into an offer of marriage, it will be the match of the century. Our Briannon, a duchess!"

She gaped at her mother, the wheels in her head spinning at an alarmingly fast rate. She couldn't conceive of anything worse than being at the duke's residence for a dinner party. And what if his son were there? Brynn's mouth grew dry at the thought of it. "I am busy as well, Mama. I forgot that I was to join Lady Cordelia for…for…"

"Dinner," Gray suggested helpfully. Brynn wanted to kick him.

"There is nothing to be done but cancel, Briannon. I insist. Cordelia will understand. She would agree this is far more important." Her mother tossed a disgruntled look in her daughter's direction. "Come, Briannon, we have much to do. You must look perfect for tonight. The duke's attention must not be diverted for one second." She tapped her fingers thoughtfully. "Nothing you have will do. We must go to Bond Street."

Brynn leaped to her feet. "Mama, you are being unreasonable. You cannot have a dress commissioned in one day, far less a few hours."

"You can when it's for a duke, and one spares no expense. We must find the perfect dress, one fit for a duchess. Do hurry, dear. Braxton," she said in a firm voice. "Ready the carriage immediately. And send Colton ahead."

Brynn's eyes flew to Gray's as their mother swept from the room. "If I am to go, then you must as well."

"Must I?" Gray grinned. "I abhor shopping."

"Not shopping, you lout," Brynn hissed. "To this blasted dinner."

"Careful. If you don't hold your tongue, you'll risk injuring His Grace's delicate sensibilities." He grinned wickedly. "Or mayhap you should. Mother would never live down the scandal."

For a moment, Brynn considered doing just that. It would destroy her mother, and though the woman vexed her, that was one thing Brynn would never do—not even to avoid the prospect of making the worst match in history. She conceded defeat with a sigh and waited for the footman to fetch her coat.

When he arrived, she bade him to fetch her lady's maid. If she had to endure a handful of hours at the modiste with her overbearing mother, she wanted to at least have Lana at her side. One glance at her maid's expression would tell her which fabrics or styles were abominable and which were pleasing. Lana had a clear eye for fashion, her mother having been a modiste in Russia when she was a girl. Brynn trusted her taste implicitly.

"You are truly the most terrible brother in the world," Brynn said, shaking her head at Gray's smirk. "When the time comes for you to be on the marriage block, I shall be sure to remember this."

Gray looked supremely unruffled by her threats. "I look forward to it."

Brynn made one last effort to sway her brother before joining her mother in the waiting carriage. "Gray, honestly—you cannot agree that I should encourage this suit."

Her brother's laughing face sobered. He took her arm, drawing her into the front salon out of view of the hovering servants. "He is a duke, Brynn. He can offer you a life of luxury at the pinnacle of society."

She peered at him in disbelief. Who was this man standing before her? He deplored Bradburne. Hawksfield, as well. Though she didn't know why that mattered, considering Hawksfield was not the one pressing his suit.

"I thought you didn't like him? Or his son?"

"When it comes to marriage, *liking* has nothing to do with anything. Mother is right—in the eyes of the *ton*, it would be a brilliant match."

Brynn exhaled evenly. "What if I don't want a brilliant match?"

"It's what every lady wants, isn't it?" Gray forced a smile. "You'll be a duchess, free to do as you like, free to be happy. This is what you wanted, Brynn."

"Is it?" she blurted out. Happiness and marriage to the duke seemed to be at opposite ends of the spectrum. She wanted conversation and laughter and friendship. He wanted to bed a young bride with a fortune. The thought made her ill.

"I hate to sound like our mother, but you could not do better than a duke," Gray continued. "Even one rumored to be penniless. I'm just relieved it's not Hawksfield."

Brynn's voice softened. "You used to be friends with him."

"As a boy, yes. As a man, he is one from whom I would caution you to keep your distance. The rumors about his ruthlessness are all true."

Brynn thought of the protective way the marquess had watched Eloise. The rumors couldn't *all* be true. Then again, she didn't have the intimate knowledge Gray had gleaned from White's and the many gaming halls frequented by most male members of the *ton*, including Hawksfield.

She came to a stop, her arm still tucked under Gray's. She flung her arms about his neck and held him tight. "Promise me one thing?" she said.

"Anything for you."

"That you will fall in love with the most wonderful woman and not care a whip for propriety and titles and fortunes. This way, at least one of us will have a guarantee of true happiness."

She could not imagine consenting to a betrothal or marriage to Bradburne, but she knew if she refused him, her mother would be injured beyond repair, and Brynn's name would become fodder for the gossip columns.

"I promise," Gray said as Lana hurried into the foyer with her coat and hat in place, one glove on and one off. "Now, go before Mother has an outburst. Give Madame Despain my regards," he said with an irrepressible grin.

Madame Despain was one of the most celebrated dressmakers in London, and the fact that Gray knew her well enough to send his regards spoke volumes about how many ladies he had likely escorted there. Brynn was more than aware that her own brother had the reputation of being a rake himself and was never short of female company. Secretly, she hoped that he would make good on his promise to marry for love, but in their tier of society, such things were a rarity.

Her mother prattled for the entire ride, considering and discarding fabrics and colors and potential necklines and waistlines. Brynn listened halfheartedly, making the appropriate sounds of agreement or disagreement when necessary. However, she spent the majority of the ride staring out the window.

She saw a pair of well-heeled women striding along, arms linked and parasols overhead. They had their heads bowed together as they conversed and smiled. Brynn wasn't wondering what they spoke of. She was wondering if they valued their station in society more than they did true affection. Had either one of them accepted a suit simply because it was *agreeable*? What an emotionless and shallow word that was. She wanted…well, more. She wanted passion. She'd felt the stirrings of it with the marquess, not the duke. How could any woman ever settle for a man who was simply agreeable?

Hawksfield was the furthest thing from it. And his kisses, even more so. She wouldn't use that word to describe any facet of him. Passionate, masterful, driven, yes. Certainly not *agreeable*. But Hawksfield hadn't been the one to send her flowers. Or rubies. Or anything at all. Instead, he'd left her with one kiss, one that still burned her lips, binding her to him more potently than any lilies could ever do. No, he was Hades incarnate, and his gift had been a kiss of pomegranate seeds.

The carriage pulled ahead, leaving the two women on the sidewalk behind, and Brynn surfaced from her train of thoughts. She should have never allowed Hawksfield to kiss her on that balcony. She could have fought. Could have stomped his foot or screamed or bit his lip until it bled. But she hadn't. Like Persephone, she'd devoured those pomegranate seeds willingly.

"Brynn, my dear, are you unwell?" her mama asked, scattering away all thoughts of the marquess and his devastating kiss.

"Not at all," she answered quickly, her tongue dry.

"Good. Which reminds me, do not even think of wiggling out of the duke's dinner with one of your episodes. I shall not believe you if you try."

Blast. She should have thought of that before asserting that she was perfectly well.

Mama had sent Colton on horseback to alert the dressmaker of their arrival, and Madame Despain had gracefully accommodated them. Like her location, Cora Despain had an equally exclusive and dedicated clientele, whom she would not be able to retain if she weren't as amenable to emergencies as she was. A petite and stylish Frenchwoman, she was known for always having the latest fashions from Paris.

Lana stood at her side while her mother spoke with the dressmaker, her hands gesticulating wildly. "From a gentleman bandit to a dancing duke," Lana whispered. "You are setting London on its head, my lady. Look at all these beautiful fabrics. You will be the toast of the town. The belle of the ball. The…the…"

Brynn fought the urge to snort. "Tea at the tea party?"

"Laugh all you want, but any maiden would switch places with you in a heartbeat."

"Including you?" Brynn asked.

Something intense and secretive swept through Lana's eyes before they returned to their usual, open brightness. "Even me, my lady."

Brynn was distracted from asking Lana what that meant when two assistants approached her with armfuls of silks, satin, and lace in a rainbow of colors. Madame Despain flipped through a copy of a book, her lip caught between her teeth, and then pointed to a page. "*Ca y est!* That is it," she exclaimed. "It is the latest style that is sweeping Paris. His Grace will not be able to take his eyes off you, *n'est-ce pas*?"

The dress she was pointing to was a Grecian-style gown that left one shoulder shockingly bare. Brynn frowned. Even from the picture, it seemed far too revealing. She was certain that her mother would select something else. But surprisingly, her mama was nodding. Madame Despain was holding up a buttery fabric that shimmered when it caught the light. Brynn stood still while the lustrous silk was tucked and pinched and pinned all around her. She stared into the tall, framed mirror before her, appreciating the dress as it came together, but dreading having to wear it.

After nearly an hour, Madame Despain finally announced that she was content and would have the dress delivered to Bishop House later that afternoon.

By the time they returned home and she'd had her bath, with Lana fussing over her all the while, Brynn was exhausted. The thought of dinner made her want to weep.

But at half past seven, she slipped into the golden confection, delivered as promised just before sunset, and Lana immediately began preening over the already perfect dress.

Catching sight of herself in the mirrored glass, Brynn sucked in a breath. While not as daring as the silver satin she had worn to the masquerade, the ball gown was unquestionably lovely. It draped over one shoulder and fell in graceful folds to the floor, golden scallops fastened with creamy roses all around the hem. A braided belt hung around her waist, also adorned with tiny rosebuds. In no time at all, Lana had swept Brynn's reddish-blond hair into an updo at the crown with glossy curls cascading down her back.

Lana handed her a matching gold stole and elbow-length

gloves. "You look like a Grecian goddess."

"Dipped in buttercream frosting," Brynn said drily. "Perhaps I should fetch my bow and arrows and channel Artemis."

"You will do nothing of the sort," her mama exclaimed as she bustled into her bedroom. Unabashed pride filled her face. "You look beautiful. Madame Despain has truly outdone herself." She turned to Lana adding, "As have you tonight." Lana flushed, clearly pleased with the compliment.

The carriage ride to the duke's residence on Park Lane was one of the fastest of Brynn's life. Granted, Hadley Gardens was practically a stone's throw from Bishop House, but her nerves had made it seem as if more than just her heart was speeding. Her mother was speaking more rapidly than usual, and her father was blinking and clearing his throat more often. Apparently, they were nervous as well.

There were a number of conveyances surrounding Hadley Gardens, and when Brynn noticed elegant couples emerging from them and approaching the duke's front entrance, she released a long breath. Thank heavens. It was to be a true dinner party then, and not some private affair arranged just for them.

Mama, of course, looked crestfallen as Brynn took her papa's hand and descended from the carriage. Lord Dinsmore squeezed her fingers gently, telling her with his eyes and his unaffected warmth that everything was going to be all right. She believed him, which is why she was only slightly shaking as they were divested of their outer garments and announced by the duke's butler.

"The Earl and Countess of Dinsmore, and Lady Briannon Findlay."

Their names rose up toward the ornate ceilings of an exquisite blue and white salon, where the duke's guests were gathering.

Brynn had never been inside the duke's London residence. She wasn't a stranger to luxury, but this surpassed anything she had ever seen. Her dress was at home among all the gold—threading in the wallpapers, shot through the fabric of every plush chair, dripping from the chandelier overhead and glinting on candelabras placed around the large, rectangular room. Even the paintings gracing its walls captured golden sunsets or sunrises, their gilded frames of the baroque style.

Nearly a dozen various lords and ladies were decked out in their finery and were waiting to be presented to the duke. Brynn recognized a few of the guests, including Lord and Lady Rochester, who were never far from the duke's side, and sipped gratefully on a glass of wine provided by a waiting footman. Her eyes searched the room for the Marquess of Hawksfield, but she could not find him. Fortified, she took another sip. She may be able to endure the evening, after all.

"Good evening, Lord Dinsmore. Lady Dinsmore."

Of course, she could not be so lucky.

Her stomach plummeted at his icy voice behind her. The wine she was in the process of swallowing bobbed back up her throat. Brynn coughed but managed to swallow again and keep it down as she turned.

Hawksfield stood with his hands clasped behind his back, his chin held in an imperious hike. "I am surprised to see so fine a turnout for the duke's impromptu dinner party."

"Impromptu, you say? How merry. The duke is certainly impulsive," Lady Dinsmore chirped.

The compliment sounded hollow and forced. It was how all conversation seemed to be at gatherings like this. People on their best behavior, paying compliments even if they didn't mean them.

Hawksfield broke from his severe posture to take up Brynn's gloved hand. As he bent forward over it, his gaze drifted down the front of her dress. A shiver raced across her skin at his fleeting glance, and the memories of his hand sliding under her bodice at the Gainsbridge Masquerade and his tongue invading her mouth shuttled forward. They retreated swiftly, however, at the distant look in his eyes. He could have been staring at the portrait on the wall behind her for all his aloofness.

"Lady Briannon," he said, brushing his lips across her knuckles. "I notice you've chosen to match the duke's favorite color this evening."

It was not a compliment, and she felt her skin grow heated under the golden silk dress. She should have considered the fact that she would appear like a giant coin. Hopefully not as round, though. Perhaps Mama had thought of it. She'd certainly given her approval swiftly, ignoring the dress's one bared shoulder design.

"It is a coincidence, nothing more," she replied brightly, feeling like a dolt nonetheless. "I do not usually attempt to match the interior decor."

A glint of humor lit his eyes as he straightened his back, but the amusement snuffed out as soon as he stood tall again. She couldn't understand the man. If he wasn't kissing her, then he was insulting her. If he wasn't insulting her, he was treating her with acute disregard. Brynn turned to peer into the crowd, refusing to let his current mood sour hers.

She almost didn't hear it when, his voice pulled low, Hawksfield whispered, "Your beauty casts it, and everyone else here, into the shade."

Brynn snapped her eyes to him, startled by what sounded like a genuine compliment. "Thank you, Lord Hawksfield."

Her mother and father had been drawn into an introduction to a foppish looking man Brynn did not recognize, leaving her at Hawksfield's side for the moment.

They stood without conversing, and yet neither of them moved away. She peered at him while pretending to look around his shoulder at the other guests. He was quite handsome in stylish and superbly tailored dove gray trousers and coat, his pristine white cravat tied in a ballroom knot at his neck. Hawksfield, she was starting to notice, wore formal clothes with a casual sort of elegance, as if full dress were as natural and comfortable as undress. His jacket fit just snug enough over his wide shoulders to display his masculine form, and his trousers encased slim, yet muscular, legs. She turned her gaze away, ashamed of the thoughts making her body uncomfortably warm.

What on earth was the matter with her? She was turning into a complete wanton, first undressing strange men, and now imagining Hawksfield much the same way. That louse of a bandit had ruined her morals. Stained them in some way, especially if she was turning her ribald thoughts to the marquess.

Brynn fought to remind herself that this was the same man who had not only insulted her at the masquerade, but had also manhandled her person. And that kiss…she had to stop thinking of that *damned* kiss. Her instinct was to push him away with some sharp comment, but of course, given he was Bradburne's son, she could not give him a direct cut.

And then a frenzied giggle bubbled in her throat at a horrifying thought: should the duke propose, and should all her morals and pride vanish, inducing her to accept, Hawksfield would be her *stepson*. She choked down the hysterical laugh, drawing a concerned glance.

"Do you spy something amusing, Lady Briannon?"

She stifled her mirth. "Of course not."

Hawksfield accepted a squat glass of whiskey from a passing server. "That is good. It would be a shame if the next Duchess of Bradburne found her future home worthy of laughter."

Brynn blanched then flushed as she watched him take a

cool sip of his drink. The glass of wine in her hand trembled. "I do not understand what you mean."

He smiled into his drink. The cad!

"Come now, Lady Briannon, playing the naive debutante doesn't suit you. My father has been sending you flowers since the Gainsbridge Masquerade. He intends for you, and you are well aware of it."

Of course she had known it, but hearing the words from the marquess's own lips made her go cold.

"It is absurd. We have never conversed. Never danced," she whispered, angling herself away from her parents so Mama could not glance back and read her lips. "He is far too…mature in years."

Now it was Hawksfield stifling his mirth. "He is a duke. Those things do not matter."

"They matter to *me*," she hissed, then remembered her previous realization. "And I do not desire you for a stepson."

The noise level inside the salon rose drastically, and Brynn assumed the duke had joined them. Hawksfield turned to her, leaning slightly too close to her ear. Bradburne's arrival had seemed to capture everyone else's attention. But it was Hawksfield's warm breath on her bared shoulder that captured hers. "Trust me when I say I do not desire you for a stepmother."

He lingered another prolonged moment near her shoulder. This close she could hear him inhale through his nose, as if scenting her skin.

She had no response. The only thing that came to her mind was the well-explored memory of Hawksfield's mouth pressed urgently against hers, the warmth of his tongue tracing her lips, and his hands tensing around her waist and hips, hooking her closer to his body.

Brynn was fairly blushing when the duke finally found them. Bradburne's eyes went first to her breasts, second to her face, then third, to her father.

"Dinsmore!" he boomed, clapping her father on the shoulder as if they were old friends. "Wonderful to see you, old chap." Her mother beamed when the duke kissed her hand and murmured that he could see where her daughter got her beauty.

Brynn's throat closed off as the duke then turned to her. His eyes roved her from head to toe, a satisfied smile touching his lips.

Beside her, she could feel coiled tension emanating from Hawksfield's body. If she wasn't mistaken, the marquess had slid a step closer to her side.

"How good of you to welcome our guests, my boy," the duke said with false brightness. "I did not expect to see you tonight." The change in the marquess had not been lost on him.

"I'm sure you didn't," his son murmured.

The dinner bell rang, and Hawksfield, still made of stone, did not raise his elbow for Brynn to take. The duke pounced, his elbow shooting toward her at alarming speed.

There was nothing to do but accept the invitation to be led to dinner on his arm. Instead of gold, the dining room was a muted bronze theme. The scores of candelabras, chandeliers, and tapered candles cast Brynn's golden dress in sparkling contrast to the bronzed metal sconces, the wood paneling, and burnished copper ceiling.

The duke delivered Brynn to a seat several places down from the head of the table where he would sit. Lord Rochester took the seat to her right, and as the footman behind her was tucking her chair closer to the table, the guest who would be seated to her left glided soundlessly into his chair. She didn't have to look. She could scent the spicy orange and clove of his cologne.

"Are you supposed to be sitting there?" she whispered

to Hawksfield, who had waved away the footman after murmuring to him. The footman dipped into a stiff bow and hurried away to set an additional place.

"Of course not. The duke would like to keep me as far from your side as possible, I would think."

As if on cue, the duke noticed where his son was sitting, and all the jolly humor that usually lit his face fled. He flared his nostrils, and a muscle jumped near one distinguished jowl.

Far down the table, Brynn saw the footman catch the attention of the foppish man her parents had been introduced to, and politely gesture toward a chair. She balked at the marquess's impropriety.

"And why should you like to do otherwise?" she asked, watching as the seats were filled. Her parents were placed across the table, separated by other guests. Mama, however, noted Hawksfield beside Brynn with pursed lips.

"We must speak," he murmured.

"What of?"

Hawksfield canted his head and met her stare, one full dark brow propped up.

Oh. The kiss.

"Certainly not *here*?" she said. It was hardly appropriate dinner conversation, and nearly every ear would be piqued for whatever the marquess had to say.

"No. Elsewhere," he answered.

"I don't think there will be a moment—"

"We will find a moment," he said, his voice so low it was for her ears only. "In private."

She stared at him, ready to refuse, but the soup course was promptly served, and Brynn was nudged into conversation with Lord Rochester. She answered his questions about which balls she planned to attend, but her mind was stuck on the infuriating man to her left. And now, every time her mind landed on the Marquess of Hawksfield, she could think of one thing: that soul-splintering kiss.

The logical side of her knew she shouldn't meet him anywhere in private. After all, there was a distinct possibility that he would kiss her again…or caress her as he had on the balcony. No, she should refuse. Being alone with the marquess would be inviting disaster.

But the other side of her—the scandalous one his kiss had awakened—craved his touch. She longed to feel his mouth against hers, his hands on her skin. Brynn's breath faltered at the scorching memory of his expert fingers delving past her bodice to her breast. Her nipples tightened beneath the silk of her dress at the imagined touch, and Brynn stopped breathing altogether.

There was no denying it—she wanted more.

Chapter Twelve

Despite the lively buzz of conversation at the table, Archer was acutely aware of Briannon sitting beside him—her every inhale, the sleek rustle of silk against her body, the elegant lift of her hands, and the precise movements of her fingers as she tended to the silver cutlery. He'd breathed in her scent before in the salon, and each time she moved, it wafted toward him in subtle, teasing bursts.

He was equally aware of his father's dark mood, undoubtedly caused by Archer's presumptuous rearrangement of the seating. But as soon he had heard of the dinner party, he had ditched his planned evening of cards and whiskey at White's, which had, in reality, been a weak attempt to forget the arrival of a second anonymous note.

It had been among the many calling cards awaiting him and the duke that morning in the silver salver at Hadley Gardens, this one set apart by its odd size—smaller than a typical lady's calling card, and yet larger than the ones men carried in their breast pockets. Also, this card had been sealed and addressed informally to "Hawksfield" in that same scratchy, near illegible script.

Once Archer had slit the envelope and removed the card in the privacy of his own rooms, he'd read four more words, these decidedly threatening: *Your time is up.*

Whomever it was had followed him to London. The knowledge had placed a hard knot in his gut and the intense desire to occupy his thoughts with drink and gambling. Not that either of those things would solve his problems, including the one involving Lady Briannon possibly having recognized him as the bandit. Archer had abandoned White's the moment he'd heard of his father's dinner, knowing it would be far easier to get a private audience with Lady Briannon here than it would at a crowded ball. His father and his preposterous attentions be damned.

Engaged in conversation with Lord Rochester once more, Briannon's body was angled away from his but for her bare shoulder and the ruched fabric lying along her flawless skin. Archer imagined nudging that golden seam aside and exploring the jutting rise of her shoulder blade beneath it. The smooth expanse of skin would no doubt be as perfect as the sample laid bare. He suspected it would taste as good as it looked, and the thought inflamed his senses. His body grew uncomfortably tight, and he shifted in his seat just seconds before Briannon turned her head and focused her attention on him.

"Is your sister not joining us this evening?" she asked.

Archer had barely touched the succulent duck a l'orange on his plate, and at the mention of Eloise, he set his fork down and reached for his glass of wine.

"She isn't in London," he answered.

Lord Rochester, with a mouthful of roast duck, interjected, "I am told the girl has chosen to stay at Worthington Abbey for the season."

"Oh," Briannon said with what sounded like genuine

disappointment. "I am sorry to hear that."

Archer recalled the way Eloise had beamed while dancing with Earl Langlevit at the Gainsbridge's Masquerade, and how the earl had returned the attention in kind. It didn't make sense for Eloise to sit out the season—unless the earl had seen what lay beneath her mask and had cried off, as Archer had suspected would happen.

He had hoped Langlevit would prove himself different from the rest of society. A misguided hope, it seemed. The urge to hunt the earl down and thrash him had Archer strangling the stem of his wineglass. His sister's hurt was his own, and as always, it settled heavy in his chest.

"Speaking of the gaming tables," Rochester was saying, already well into his fourth glass of wine. "What of this bandit tearing through London?"

The subject made Archer freeze. It was certainly not polite conversation for a dinner table, but the participants pounced upon the morsel of gossip with unabashed relish, including the duke himself.

"Poor Lord Maynard," Lady Rochester twittered. "He is still recovering from the shock. I heard the bandit attacked Lady Emiliah, Lord Perth's eldest daughter, too, although she was saved from the scoundrel by an angel in disguise."

"I've heard the girl is prone to exaggeration and hysterics," her husband interjected, his eyes narrowing across the table. "Lord Dinsmore, didn't the terrible fellow attack your coach?"

Dinsmore nodded. "Yes, although no one was injured. It all seemed rather civilized, not at all what happened with Maynard. The thief did exchange words with my daughter."

"He spoke to you?" Archer asked.

Briannon visibly stiffened. She nodded, satisfying the curious faces around the table. "The rogue wanted my grandmother's pearls. I was not amenable at first," she explained. "But he was very persuasive. I did fear for my safety."

"That sounds like a terrifying ordeal," he said.

She blinked, and her stare shifted to her plate, as if she was overcome. "It was."

"The gall of this upstart," the duke spluttered. "He should be hanged."

Archer thought of the way Briannon had stood up to him, her eyes flashing and imperious. She hadn't cowered, not for one instant, not even at the point of a pistol. He couldn't imagine his father appreciating that amazing spirit of hers. If she married him, Archer knew it would be only a matter of time before her unique spark would wither away and die.

"Eh, Hawksfield?"

Archer looked up, realizing Lord Rochester was directing a question at him.

"Did you get the chance to run the hounds this past winter?" Rochester repeated. "I thought the duke's new foxhounds were magnificent, though I didn't see you out on the hunt when I was there."

"No. I had business to attend to," Archer responded.

The duke laughed, derision underscoring his words. "Didn't you know? Hawk finds running the hounds boring and pointless."

"I hunt for game, not for sport," Archer said, rising to his father's challenge. "As a matter of fact, I was tracking a rather large boar roaming between our country estates some days past." Archer sent a sidelong glance to Briannon who fastidiously avoided looking at him.

"Egad, Hawk, how large was the boar?" someone asked.

"A five-hundred-pound beast with piglets to defend." He did not elaborate, and though he could see by Brynn's sharp exhale that she was grateful that he had not, he couldn't resist baiting her. "Do you enjoy the hunt, Lady Briannon?"

"On occasion, my lord, but only at Ferndale," she answered after a moment's hesitation. "I do enjoy a good ride."

The fop whose seat Archer had taken made a noise that sounded like a spluttering croak. "I must say, the thought of a woman in the hunt is as disagreeable to me as women at the gaming tables. Most scandalous. Women have no place there."

"And why is that?" Briannon challenged, drawing every eye at the table, including the alarmed, censorious one of her mother's. "Lord Atherton permits his wife to ride, as do many other nobles. I know for a fact that Mrs. Wilson rode in a hunt two winters past, and no one deemed it a scandal. I, for one, enjoy the hunt."

Lady Rochester and Lady Dinsmore gasped in unison, one with an expression of astonishment and the other one of horror. "Surely *not*?" Lady Rochester said with a look of pure disdain.

Archer fought back a grin, thinking of her in those indecent breeches and her faultless command of Apollo. She could likely outride any number of men he knew in the hunt or otherwise.

Lady Rochester bristled, turning purple. "Mrs. Wilson… is…is…"

Archer could have sworn that Briannon was holding back a laugh at Lady Rochester's choked expression, although she was avoiding looking at her mother, whose face was as sculpted as paned glass.

Aurelia Wilson was a notorious American widow who did as she pleased, when she pleased, including taking and flaunting lovers before the *ton*. She was also one of the best riders he had ever seen mounted, man or woman.

"A complete disgrace," finished Lady Rochester. Her opinion of Briannon appeared to be falling by the second. For a moment, Archer wondered whether Briannon was doing it on purpose and toasted her silently. Then again, it was common knowledge, with the exception of Lord Rochester, that Lady Rochester warmed his father's bed, so it would be natural that she'd see the young woman as competition.

"I seem to recall you on the hunt several years ago, Lady Rochester," Archer said in a mild tone.

Her gaze slid to his and she flushed. "In a *carriage*. It is not the same as a gently reared woman racing astride a horse and jumping all manner of obstacles. Mrs. Wilson is a complete scapegrace who should be shunned by all decent society."

"Forgive me, but I hardly see participation in a hunt as something that warrants being shunned by polite society," Briannon interjected.

"Briannon," Lady Dinsmore hissed.

"I, for one, do not mind women on the hunt," the duke interjected, with a lascivious laugh that made Archer's fists curl. "Women who ride have a certain appeal." The sexual innuendo was blatantly clear, and though Archer found it to be in excruciatingly bad taste, it was his father's table and his father's friends. As such, nervous laughter broke out, and the moment passed.

"Were I to marry again, any duchess of mine shall do as she pleases, including running the hounds or riding any matter of…mount," the duke added, arching a suggestive eyebrow as he smiled down the table at his latest quarry. "Given your love of horses, I have recently acquired a pair of magnificent geldings. Perhaps you would care to see them at some other time, Lady Briannon?"

Though her face remained perfectly composed, Archer noticed Brynn's fingers fisting in the folds of her dress in her lap.

"I should like that very much, Your Grace," she said demurely. Archer saw her clenched hands tremble. When the conversation began to turn yet again, and the duke's attention had been drawn away from Brynn, Archer leaned in toward her. His next words were a hurried whisper. "Second floor parlor, blue door."

She shot him a puzzled glance as Lady Rochester stood and suggested the ladies retire to the drawing room. The footmen came forward, and the men rose to their feet. Before Briannon could move her chair, Archer glanced down, making certain of his own chair leg's placement, and slid back. A harsh ripping sound rent through the room, and heads swiveled in his direction. Briannon caught her breath, her eyes rising to his, but the relief in them far outweighed the dismay at her torn dress.

"My deepest apologies," Archer said, his expression suitably regretful. "The hem of your dress was caught beneath the chair. One of our house maids will have it mended at once."

"Thank you," she said, a footman rushing forward to take her napkin and hold her chair. "Please excuse me, Your Grace," she said. "It appears that I must attend to this small inconvenience." And at her mother's inquisitive stare, added, "I will rejoin the ladies in the drawing room posthaste."

Archer stood as Lady Dinsmore and the rest of the women continued to file from the dining room, Briannon behind them. The footman finally ushered her into the hallway, and Archer slowly followed the crowd of gentlemen filing into the billiards room, attached to the dining room by a pair of pocket doors. He had planned to take his leave as soon as he entered. He flicked an eye over his shoulder and watched Briannon disappear from view. Archer hoped she would heed his directions, though now he was beginning to doubt whether she had even heard him or had perhaps been confused. He tapped his fingers against his thigh and deliberated following now, rather than letting a safe minute pass between both their exits. The opportunity to speak with her in private could not be missed.

He cleared his throat. "Please give my regards to the ladies," he said, standing at the entrance to the billiards room as the rest of his father's guests got settled. "Regrettably, I will not be able to join you. I have an urgent business matter to attend to that requires my immediate departure."

As he turned to leave the room, he couldn't help noticing the scowl on the duke's face. No doubt he suspected something, but he knew his father would never abandon his guests, at least not right at that moment. Archer answered the scowl with one of his own, and by the glances darting between the duke and marquess, the charged interaction was not lost on the other occupants of the room.

Unwilling to waste time engaging in a battle of wills, Archer swung on his heel and left. He turned toward the back of the foyer, and with long, decisive strides caught up to the footman accompanying Briannon. "I will see the lady to the sewing room," he said, dismissing the footman with a curt nod.

Briannon's eyes widened, but she did not say anything as Archer marched them up an elegantly carpeted set of stairs. They made their way down another impeccable hallway decorated with family portraits, and then another, lined with several Roman and Grecian busts, until Archer stopped at the aforementioned room with a blue door. He ushered her into the room, still without uttering a word, and checked to make sure the corridor was deserted before closing the door behind him.

Briannon glanced around the room, her face reflecting her surprise at the lovely floral decor and the subtle feminine touches of delicate rose wallpaper and plush seating. "This was my mother's private sitting room," Archer explained, his voice at last cutting through the silence between them. He glanced around, breathing in the subtle scent of disuse. And honeysuckle. Though closed up and musty, her perfume still somehow lingered in the room. Even after all these years.

"The maids come in once in a great while to dust, but otherwise, it has been left untouched," he said when Briannon remained quiet. "Please sit. I'm certain she had a sewing box in here somewhere."

He moved toward the far end of the room and began rummaging through some drawers in a white linen chest, his side vision tracking Briannon's movements. She walked over to the window bench, her fingers trailing along a neatly stacked bookshelf tucked into the walls beside the windows. He watched her study some of the volumes and then touch the peach-colored cushions on the bench, set just so, as if the duchess were expected to return any moment. The sight of a woman who wasn't his mother standing at the window made his chest feel hollow. It made him wonder what the duchess would have made of the beautiful creature standing within her private sanctuary, currently plumping a lace-trimmed pillow.

Briannon glanced over her shoulder at him, and he shut the linen trunk. "Do you miss her?"

A host of emotions ran through him at the innocent question. Archer settled for a safe, distant answer. "The duchess was mourned by many."

Her eyes fluttered on him for a moment before they fell away, as if she could see right through him and didn't wish to let on. Though he thought of her often, Archer rarely spoke of his mother. For some reason, every time he spoke of her aloud, he felt as if he were giving little pieces of her away. Memories given as gifts that he would never get back. So instead he kept his thoughts to himself. He did miss her. The late duchess had been the sort of person whom people couldn't help being drawn to. She'd had a lightness of spirit and an infectious joy that everyone noticed, especially Archer and Eloise, whom she showered that joy and laughter upon the most. She'd been the light of Worthington Abbey, and the bridge between his father and he. When she died, his father had turned to his lifestyle of flippancy and excess, and Archer had been forced to learn how to run a dukedom.

Archer resumed his search for the mending kit. The risk that one of Brynn's family members, or worse, the duke himself, would come looking for her and stumble upon them was high. He had all the time in the world to think about his late mother, but only a few precious minutes with Briannon.

With a soft exclamation of triumph, he located the silk-pillowed box and strode over to where she was sitting on the peach cushions. She looked entirely too fetching in that golden gown. It managed to look both ethereal and provocative, the bold color complementing her to perfection. It set off the gilded lights in her hair and made her hazel eyes sparkle with the sort of vivacity that reminded him of the late duchess. She would have approved of the young woman now sitting so daintily in her favorite seat. He frowned at the errant thought. He wasn't in the market for a wife, and he certainly didn't want to marry Briannon. He just didn't want his *father* to marry her.

He knelt at her feet and opened the box.

"My lord," Briannon exclaimed. "Where is the maid?"

"In the sewing room most likely, where the footman would have sent her."

"Shouldn't I be there, then?" she asked.

"No need. I can darn just as well as any under maid," he said, sifting through the various threads until he found one that matched the vibrant hue of her dress.

He glanced up to find Briannon's expression loose with shock. "*You* know how to sew?"

The humor sparking in her eyes helped him to brush away the pall of sadness the thoughts of his mother had brought on. "Why is that so surprising? You approve of ladies who hunt, but not of men who know how to wield a needle? That seems somewhat hypocritical, does it not?"

"I did not expect…you of all people…I…"

Archer grinned. "It is eminently satisfying to find you at a loss for words, my lady." He threaded a needle and held together the ripped edges of her dress. "My mother enjoyed needlepoint, and in those spare moments when I was not encumbered by my studies, I spent them in here with her. She was far better company than my father, and I seemed to have had a knack for it." He glanced up with a small smile. Odd. Sharing that memory hadn't felt like giving it away at all.

"I would insist that you let me do it myself, but I fear that I am not as skilled with a needle as you claim to be," she said in an odd, softened voice. "I would likely stitch my skirts to my stockings."

Archer could feel the heat from those delicate stockinged ankles, a hair's breadth from his fingers, and his hands shook as he held the frayed ends of the material together. His fingers ached to peel the delicate silk from her calves, explore the softness of her skin, and venture higher still. He inhaled sharply. The lady's proximity nearly made him forget why he'd purposely torn her dress in the first place. They had little time, and he needed to know what she knew—or suspected—about the bandit. He cleared his throat and focused on making tiny, precise stitches.

"This is quite improper, really," Briannon remarked while he worked, her voice flustered. And yet she did not push his hands away or try to take the needle and thread herself.

"We do seem to find ourselves in these situations," Archer said, biting his tongue in concentration as he put the finishing touches on the nearly invisible seam. "One of these days, we shall not be so lucky to evade the threat of discovery, and then what shall we do?"

"Pledge my hand?" she said with a laugh. "Or one of them, at least."

Archer appreciated her wry sense of self-deprecating humor. He knew she was referring to the duke's attentions. "You would be the toast of the season. A duke and a marquess desperate to win each hand? Mothers of the *ton* have waged wars for less."

Briannon laughed at him, her eyes gleaming with mischief. "Somehow I can hardly see you in the least bit *desperate* to win anyone's hand."

"Why would you say that?" he said, keeping his tone light. "There are many things in this world I yearn for."

Briannon colored and bit her lips. He could see she was shocked at the turn of the conversation and the airy nature of his response—as was he, himself. Archer hoped propriety would not win out.

It didn't.

She grinned wickedly. "Sadly, I have heard that it will be a cold day in Hades before the Marquess of Hawksfield proposes marriage to any debutante."

His eyes met hers. "I have it on unimpeachable authority that the marquess could be swayed by the right maiden."

"Then I would say that your source is mistaken." She laughed. "The marquess in question is, as I've heard, a ruthless and uncompromising man driven by amassing his fortunes and interested in little else beyond that, much less the attentions of some simpering maiden."

His reputation was exactly as he'd molded it to be, it seemed. Why the description fell through him like coins in a well gave him pause. He wrinkled his forehead and turned his eyes back to his task. "What if his attentions were drawn by a fascinating sprite in a golden dress whose skill with a pistol was matched only by her razor-sharp wit?"

Damn. Flirting with her was turning out to be rather intoxicating. He peered at her before tidying a crooked stitch. Her cheeks were like pink rosebuds before bloom.

"That would be surprising indeed," she whispered.

Archer was surprised as well, mostly at himself. He'd brought her here to discuss more pressing things, not flirt. He replaced the needle in the box and stood. "There, done."

"It's perfect," she breathed, inspecting the repair with incredulous eyes. "I did not believe you could do it, sir, but your stitches are near invisible. Madame Despain would applaud."

The French modiste on Bond Street had created this dress? He pictured Briannon standing in the center of a room filled with mirrors and bolts of fabric, stripped down to her underthings as the modiste and her assistants swathed her in this golden silk, and fought to breathe. He wanted to touch the silk against her body, warm it with the palms of his hands.

For the second time that evening, he felt uncomfortably tight in his trousers—which were already tight as it was. He stood, grimacing at the twinge of pain in his injured leg, and regretted kneeling for so long. He backed away from the bench seat, needing distance to clear his fuddled mind.

"Thank you," Archer said. "It is nice to know should I lose interest in the strenuous pursuits of men, I will have something to fall back upon."

"You mock me," Briannon said with a smile at his teasing.

"On the contrary. Now we are even, for I can set a tight stitch and you can ride a horse without a saddle. My dignity has been set to rights."

The flickering movement of her lips burgeoned into a full-fledged smile. "Your dignity?"

"I couldn't walk for hours after I returned to Worthington Abbey upon your stallion. You made it look easy, and I assure you, it was not." He returned the box to the linen case and closed the glass doors. He knew he should remain across the room from her. A good ten paces. At this distance, he could not trace the warmth from her body or the whisper of her perfume. Not the cloying florals most other women wore, but something subtler, earthy, and bright. Like green clipped grass and lemon.

He should have stayed where he was.

He didn't.

Briannon's humor fled her face as he approached her, taking slow, measured steps. The mood shifted from flirtatious to serious with each one. The lightness of their banter evaporated now that he was no longer hindered by the task of mending of her dress. She stared at the door and then at him, her hands twisting together in her lap. "My Lord Hawksfield—"

"My name is Archer," he interrupted and took the seat at the other end of the window bench, again ignoring the accompanying pain at the stretch of his injured thigh.

Her lips parted at the offering of his given name and his intimate position on the seat. "Lord Hawksfield," she insisted, "why did you bring me here?"

"Are you interested in the duke's suit?" he countered.

It was not the question he'd wanted to ask, but bringing up the bandit had to be natural. At this moment, it would be anything but.

"Should the duke make an offer," she said, her eyes drifting to the floor, "it is my duty to do as my father wishes."

He saw her throat bob and her lips pull into a slight grimace, as if she'd just swallowed something distasteful. She was a truly awful liar.

"That's not what I was asking," he said.

She stared at him, no doubt hearing the swift notes of anger in his voice. Her chest rose along with her chin. "Your question is rude, and I do not have to answer it."

A muscle in his jaw ticked in perfect time with his ballooning frustration. "Brynn, what happened between us at the masquerade—"

Her eyes widened at the use of her nickname, but she did not correct him. "Was a mistake."

"Was it?" he countered.

"Yes," she said, her color rising.

"That is a lie." His words were soft, and he watched trepidation play across her expressive face. "Tell me you felt nothing."

A beat passed. She inhaled through her pert little nostrils, as if fortifying herself.

"I felt nothing," she said, but her words sounded hollow. She knew it, too. Her eyes flashed with mortification and then with something darker and fiercer. Something he recognized immediately, because he felt it, too.

She tossed her head, defiant to the last, and attempted to turn the conversation. "Where did you go when you left the masquerade?"

Archer paused at the flicker of surprise in her eyes. As though her own question had startled her. "Home. Why do you ask?"

She lifted her chin a bit higher. "You left around the same time as Lord Maynard. Perhaps you may have seen something."

Here it is—the perfect opportunity. He'd told Brandt he'd discover what Briannon knew of the Masked Marauder and quash it. "Lord Maynard," he echoed carefully, though every muscle in his body tensed.

Briannon met his eyes. "Perhaps you saw someone... suspicious."

"Do you not think I would have come forward with any informative accounts by now?"

The blunt question stumped her, and she cast her eyes down, her teeth buried in her lower lip. She seemed to be staring intently at his knees while thinking. But then she blinked, a small pinch between her brows, and released her lip. She slowly lifted her eyes and met his gaze again. "The bandit was also on your property a few nights previous. He waylaid my carriage."

"Yes, I am aware."

"I spoke to him," she whispered, flushing.

"As you said earlier at dinner. What of it?"

Briannon breathed in sharply. "I looked into his eyes."

Now would be the time to laugh at her. Accuse her of being a silly girl with an overactive imagination. "It seems this bandit affected you, Lady Briannon," he said coolly, standing up from the bench. His wounded leg twitched again. Archer winced, and his hand went to his thigh before he could stop himself.

Briannon witnessed it. "Your leg," she said softly.

"It's nothing," he said tersely. "My ankle is still sore."

She hiked her chin. "So then why is your thigh bleeding?"

He went still, his eyes lowering. A minuscule red stain had blossomed on his gray trousers. The tenuous scab must have split, and the bandage wrapping it must have been too thin to absorb the weeping wound.

There had been an article printed in the *Times* about the attack on Lady Emiliah's carriage. How their rescuer had shot the bandit in the leg. And Archer already knew Briannon's penchant for reading her father's papers.

Quash it. Fix this. He knew what he should do. To protect himself. To protect Brandt. Lord in heaven, how had things turned so bloody complicated?

"A scrape, nothing more," he dismissed, not missing Briannon's odd expression as if something astonishing had occurred to her. "Forget my leg. I'm more interested in your fond memories of the Masked Marauder. His voice, his eyes. One might say you recall them with remarkable ease."

"Fear causes memories to sharpen," she said, though the excuse rang false.

Archer grinned. "You were not afraid."

They were four simple words, and as good as a confession. He'd said them before he could think. Or maybe he'd intended to say them all along. Archer truly didn't know.

Briannon's eyes went round and wide, her back ramrod straight. A rush of color flooded her cheeks. "My god. I'd thought…when you donned the mask and you looked so much like him, but…" Her mouth tightened. "*You* assaulted Lord Maynard and his coachman? And that poor horse." She bristled with confused fear as she stood, her hands trembling. "But…but you love horses. How *could* you?"

The fury he'd felt when he'd learned another man was impersonating him returned with new force. He hated Briannon thinking, for one moment, that he could have been so cruel, so despicably violent. It hurt him, he realized, that her opinion of him would be so low, so *base*, and that alone was the basis for his next words.

"Culling the excess from privileged fops is not the same as beating a man senseless and murdering his horse. What I've done in the past is nothing like what this cowardly pretender is doing for his own gain."

The things he was admitting to could not be undone. He knew this. Knew it was rash. And yet he could not stop himself.

"What you've done in the past," Briannon repeated slowly. "So it *was* you, then, who stopped my coach? Robbed me." Archer swallowed hard and nodded. "But…why?"

Her eyes were disbelieving orbs, fascination and fear warring in their depths.

He had never anticipated the need to explain himself to anyone, or to answer that question. *Why?* He had promised himself and Brandt that he would be meticulous and stealthy, careful and precise. He would take trinkets and coin purses from those who would be able to return home and replace what had been taken, and he would give every last farthing to those who needed it most—men, women, and children, struggling to put food on their tables, coal in their stoves, clothes on their backs, and shoes on their feet.

There was one thing separating the masses from the *ton*: a title. Something that could not be earned by honest, hard work, but by birthright. To see the privileged take what had been handed to them at birth and ignore the other side of London, the side that depressed them because of how dirty and poor it was, infuriated him.

"I do not keep the little I take," he said finally.

"Little?" she scoffed, her voice shaking. "You took my grandmother's pearls. Priceless heirlooms that cannot be replaced. You pointed a pistol at me!" He stepped toward her, and she stepped back, the bench at her calves trapping her. "You are nothing more than a thief and a scoundrel."

"Heirlooms are *things*," he said, the word bitter on his tongue. "Which have since been redistributed to those in need. Widows, orphans, the poor, and the ill. Trust me, they need food more than you or any other heiress need adornment. And my pistols, I'll have you know, were empty."

She opened her mouth and closed it. Archer stared at her flushed face, her chest heaving with the force of her emotion as she weighed his words for truth. The air fairly crackled between them, and she was fighting it. Fighting him and that same raw connection that had formed between them that night on the lane—the spark of sexual desire he'd felt from the very first moment his gaze had crashed into hers. He could see fright in her eyes, but there was something else there, too.

He wanted to kiss her again. He wanted to kiss the fear from her eyes and make them cloud with passion instead. Despite reason, he stepped closer. She inhaled sharply.

"Don't you dare," she said in alarm, throwing her hands between them as if to ward off his approach.

"Dare what?"

"Come any closer. I'll scream." Briannon's eyes darted to the closed door.

"No, you won't," he said gently. "You won't for the same reason that you wore those rubies. And I was right, wasn't I? So better suited to you than dreary pearls."

Her tone dripped condescension. "Did you steal those, too?"

"No. I bought them for you."

He bridged the remaining gap between them, forcing her hands to press into his chest. She fisted them, almost pulling away, but kept them there like a shield. "Please, my lord, move away," she said, her eyes huge. He wanted to drown in them, so clear they looked like pools of honey.

His fingers brushed her cheek, his voice gruffly tender. "I should have bought you topaz to go with those magnificent eyes. They look like molten gold with this dress."

"And when I wear brown, my eyes look like mud, so your money would have been wasted."

Archer smiled at her attempt to diffuse the escalating tension between them. He lowered his voice a notch and ratcheted it back up. "And what if you are wearing nothing at all?"

Briannon's eyes flared with suppressed desire, and he grinned with satisfaction. She could deny their attraction all she wanted, but what he saw there spoke volumes. "Lord Hawksfield, please," she began. "You cannot say such things."

"Archer."

She swallowed, her lip trembling. "Archer—"

The sound of his name on her tongue was a siren song. With a strangled groan, he bent his head, though halted within an inch of her mouth. Archer wanted so badly to kiss her, but he needed her to want it, too. Their breaths met and mingled as he shifted his palm up her spine. Blinking in confusion, her eyes lifted to his, her body straining toward him, and what he saw there made his pulse seize. Deep hunger shone from those rich, tawny eyes, and it was obvious she felt the attraction between them as keenly as he did.

"A moment ago you wanted me to move away," he said quietly. "Do you still wish me to?"

Twin flags of color lit her cheeks, but she closed the gap to graze her lips against his. Their touch was so light he would have thought he'd imagined it if it weren't for the violent reaction of his body. The shock of the intimate contact made his blood race, and his hands shook as he spread his fingers over her shoulders. Drawing her pliant length against his, Archer set his mouth to hers. Her lips were warm and soft, and tasted of lemon and spun sugar.

He plied her mouth further, using every ounce of his experience with the opposite sex to make her melt. He kissed her jaw, the taut column of her throat, and returned to her mouth, sliding his lips between the crease of hers until she opened sweetly for him. He swept in, relishing the swift retreat of her tongue.

Groaning at her shyness and the heated response it elicited in him, he continued to kiss her, reaching deeper, until her tongue made a timid return for one more decadent touch. Her fists wound into the lapels of his dinner jacket. He didn't have to coax her now. Despite her sheltered innocence, the natural passion he had sensed lying just beneath her surface rose ardently to meet his. Archer's arms curved around her, splaying one hand at her back and the other caressing the bare skin at her shoulder as hers hooked around his neck. There was nothing separating the heat of their bodies but a few layers of cloth and silk.

He dropped his lips to her bare shoulder, his tongue tracing a hot path on her skin. It tasted nearly as good as her mouth had. His mouth continued its exploration, tugging on the fabric that covered her breasts. She protested vaguely, a few incoherent words, but when his hand boldly caressed her breast, she gasped and fell silent. Archer couldn't help himself—he'd been consumed by the thought of repeating the act since the Gainsbridge Masquerade. His hand slid past the ruched silk of her bodice, his tongue tracing a hot wet path toward her earlobe. She wore no stays, and the realization enflamed him.

Greedily, Archer sought her warm flesh, cupping her breast as his mouth found hers once more. Briannon's breast swelled against his palm as his thumb rolled across the hard point of her nipple. She moaned into his mouth, and Archer deepened the kiss. The soft, pliant feel of her nearly made him lose hold of himself. He groaned low in his throat, his tongue delving and retreating in imitation of the act he was beginning to crave with desperate longing. God, he couldn't get enough of her—her taste, her scent, her skin. He wanted it all.

Archer broke away, and her eyes sprang open as his aroused body stood flush with hers. Her storm-tossed eyes were wide with shock, her mouth swollen and rosy, and all he wanted was to devour her.

"We have to stop," she said, pushing lightly against him— and then spreading her fingers to touch and explore the breadth of his chest as if she couldn't stop herself.

He couldn't stop touching her, either, sliding his hands against her back, her shoulders, winding in the softness of her hair. "Why?"

"Because…this is…wrong."

"Is that your opinion?" he asked, twisting her curls around his fingers and feeling the weight of the silky mass in his palm. "Or does it belong to the dozens of people downstairs who would judge you should they discover us alone like this?"

Entangled. Entranced. She fit so perfectly against him. Her curves teased the length of his body, creating an exquisite friction.

"But we *could* be discovered," she said. He did not miss how she had not quite answered his question. It was not her opinion, then. She wanted him as much as he wanted her.

"Is that not part of the thrill?" he murmured, with a laughing growl.

"Is that why you're doing this?" she asked, pulling back. "Mere thrill?"

He paused, unthreading his fingers from her hair and lifting his mouth from where it had been nuzzling her temple. Archer gazed down at her and saw raw, honest curiosity in her expression.

"No." His throat closed off as soon as the answer slipped out. Not thrill. Not solely. Kissing Briannon gave him something else, something he couldn't quite articulate. Her innate sensuality, her naive inexperience…they drove him to distraction. Never had some girl fresh from the schoolroom had such a paralyzing effect on him.

"I've wanted to do this again since that night at the masquerade. Kiss you. Touch you. This feels *right*," he continued, his thumb caressing the point of her chin. "Tell me you don't feel the same."

Her lips parted, as if she lacked the strength to keep them pressed shut. When she said nothing, and the tip of her tongue darted out to touch her lower lip in thought, Archer could not resist. He sought her mouth again, sucking the tip of her tongue and holding it firm as he held her against his body. Lost as he was, she moaned and wrapped her palms around his upper arms, clinging to him as tightly as he did her.

A sensual haze engulfed him then, pulling him down and threatening to drown him in the sweetly seductive taste of her. Hell, how was he going to force himself to stop? She wasn't prepared for the wicked things coursing through his mind: his fingers, tugging the golden gown from her shoulders, dropping it into a cloud at her feet. His body covering hers on any surface that would accommodate them. Her moans intensifying as he satisfied their desires in every possible way.

As if Briannon had been able to see his fantasies, she broke the kiss, alarm notching her brow.

"What is it?" he asked.

"There's someone coming," she whispered. "He called your name."

Sure enough, Archer heard the sound of footsteps. A fist rapping on another door down the corridor. *Bloody hell.* With reluctance, he stepped away from Briannon and adjusted his clothing. His groin throbbed, and he hoped she was too distracted and alarmed to notice his arousal. If it was the duke coming down the corridor, or Lord Dinsmore, appearing in the door incontestably tousled—and hard—would only do Brynn's reputation more injury. Damn it, what had he been thinking keeping her up here for so long?

Archer composed himself, opened the door, and let out a gratified breath as a footman rounded a nearby corridor. He stepped out and shut the door softly behind him. "What is it?"

"My apologies, my lord, but I have been searching for you. I understand it is quite late, but the stable master has *strongly* requested your audience. It seems your gray is favoring a leg. I apologize again, my lord, but—"

"It's perfectly fine, do not apologize," he replied, though he couldn't rid the scowl etched upon his face that grew deeper by the second. "Where is he?"

"The kitchens, my lord."

The last thing he wanted to do was to leave Briannon on her own to dwell upon his confession to being the Masked Marauder and to regret their kiss, but he had no choice. Brandt would never disturb him at the residence unless it was urgent. Archer dismissed the footman with a brisk nod. "Tell him I will be down in a moment."

He reentered the room, watching as Briannon rearranged

her mussed hair and fussed over the folds of her dress. Her eyes met his, and his breath caught. She looked thoroughly kissed and so wildly beautiful that it took all his strength not to haul her back into his arms and keep her there. Instead he cleared his throat and willed his body under control.

"I'm needed elsewhere, but please — do not leave. I won't be a moment. You'll stay?"

She hesitated, that delectable mouth of hers slack, her lips likely throbbing as his were. But then she nodded, her agreement soundless, her bright gaze fairly smoldering. Whatever Brandt wanted, it had better be damned important.

Archer closed the door behind him and took several long breaths to cool the ardor in his blood before striding toward the kitchens.

Chapter Thirteen

Brynn stared at the closed door, collapsing onto the window seat with all the grace of an ox. She wasn't in the least bit incapable of speech. She'd wisely chosen to nod for fear of what would come flying out of her mouth.

Oh sweet Lord. It was *him*.

The Marquess of Hawksfield...*Archer*...was the Masked Marauder.

Brynn couldn't reconcile the vivid images of the bandit lying half naked on that cot in the cottage with the autocratic gentleman who'd stood in front of her. She recalled the way Archer had favored his leg and how his hands had touched the injured spot—right where she'd shot him. She closed her eyes, wishing away the disturbing, utterly arousing recollection of his bunched, muscular thighs, and crumpled against the cushions.

Her body felt like it was being held together by the threads of her dress, and nothing much else at all. One touch of his fingers, his lips—oh god, his *tongue*—and she'd been rendered into a useless, brainless, mass of sensuality. His kisses had consumed her, and in the moment, being devoured by him had seemed like a perfectly wonderful way to disappear.

Suddenly breathless, she clenched her fists and turned toward the bookshelves. "Stop it," she hissed to herself.

What did it matter if she'd seen him half naked? He was the Masked Marauder. Lord Hawksfield, the future Duke of Bradburne, was a *highwayman*. She paused. He wasn't the one who had hurt Lord Maynard and his coachman, however. He'd said there was another—the one who had killed the horse—and Brynn believed him. None of that, however, changed the fact that he was a thief and had been stealing from his peers. Whether he gave the spoils to those in need or not, he was not in the right. He was nowhere near the right.

She twisted on the edge of the cushioned seat. The window behind her was draped to block the view of either the street or the side lawns; she didn't know which. Truthfully, she didn't quite know where in Hadley Gardens she was right then. Just that she'd been away from the other dinner guests far too long. She couldn't stay here, waiting for Archer to return as he'd asked. But he'd left it so that she couldn't leave, either, walking around the duke's private residence alone without a servant, and risk getting lost.

Flustered, she paced the room, her feet making little noise on the thick, luxurious carpet. Walking to a dresser on the far side of the room, she stared at herself in the mirror, noticing her swollen lips and flushed, rosy cheeks. She did not look like someone who had left to have her dress mended by a maid—she looked like…like…a woman who had been thoroughly ravished by a lover. She had to make herself look respectable before she set one foot from this room. She patted her face and smoothed the curls of her hair into normalcy. Her fingers trailed to her lips of their own volition. She could feel the phantom press of Archer's still lingering there. God, she didn't want to think about Archer or his blasted mouth, *or* what she already knew lay under those yards of superfine.

Searching for a distraction, her eyes fell on a starched piece of needlepoint still in its wicker frame, lying in a place of honor at the very center of the dresser. A sailboat had been painstakingly sewn along with a name embroidered in bold blue thread—*Archer Nathaniel David Croft*. Her thumb slid along the embroidery hoop as she imagined a dark-haired little boy sitting at his mother's feet, composing this very project. Her heart constricted a little, but Brynn shook herself, placing the hoop back where it belonged. Archer wasn't an innocent little boy. He was nothing but a blackhearted, conniving thief, and she'd do well to remember that.

What on earth was he thinking? A highwayman! If he were to be caught, he would be *hanged*.

"It would serve him right," she muttered before stalking toward the door. He'd stolen her grandmother's pearls and Lord knew how many other jewels that held sentimental value. She bristled at the memory of his mocking tone when she'd called them priceless heirlooms. Just because Brynn had returned home to a jewelry chest filled with other accessories did not mean the pearls would not be missed.

If he so desperately wished to help the poor and needy, why didn't he just dump the money from his own bloody coffers into their palms? It was baffling to even consider. He was a peer of the realm, for heaven's sake. She'd had enough… of him, his demands, and this room. Of her own insufferable weakness where he was concerned.

Brynn cracked open the door to the late duchess's sitting room and listened over her pulse throbbing in her ears. When she was certain the hallway was empty, she darted out, closing the door behind her with a soft click. As her slippers padded along the carpet, she was glad she was wearing silk. Chiffon or taffeta would have made more noise as she snuck down the dimly lit hall.

She thought of the tear in her hem, and the way Archer's surprisingly nimble fingers had gripped the small needle and thread. They were not slender fingers in the least, and they should have been clumsy with the sewing notions. However, he'd been swift and precise, and she'd watched his crown of dark hair bent over her ankles as he worked, with mounting amusement and admiration. The cold and aloof Hawksfield knew how to mend stitches. Seeing him so carefully fixing her hem, even stopping to tidy up a crooked stitch, had made her heart feel bigger in her chest. It had given her the startling urge to reach out and curl his hair around her fingers.

Of course, that had been *before* he'd confessed to being the Masked Marauder. But if Brynn were to be honest with herself, his resemblance to the bandit when he'd donned the mask at the Gainsbridge Masquerade had been far too great to ignore. In fact, if she were being honest, she'd been crestfallen when she'd enumerated the reasons that Archer couldn't be the bandit. She'd been thinking about his kiss for the last week, and, even more ashamedly, hoping to see him again. Archer had been right. She had felt something — for both the bandit and for Archer. Two men who, as it now turned out, were really one man.

She needed to clear her head. Perhaps she could return to the lady's salon, where the women were likely having tea and playing cards, and feign illness. Brynn detested using her breathing affliction as an excuse, but she could not, under any circumstances, risk seeing Archer again tonight.

She had already taken two left turns down connecting hallways so far, and she had the sinking feeling that she was indeed lost in Hadley Gardens.

"Blast," she muttered, turning around and trying to gauge how far back the last turn had been.

A muffled voice had her facing forward again, her heart jumping into her throat. The voice had sounded from farther down the hallway she was currently in. She couldn't be discovered wandering the hallways, especially if the rooms behind these closed doors were bedchambers.

Brynn wavered, indecisive, in the hallway until the voice sounded again, this time louder. It belonged to a man, and whoever it was, he was angry.

She backed up until she came to a cream-colored door with a glass knob. Praying the room was empty, she twisted the knob and opened the door. Darkness met her and, with a breath of relief, Brynn quickly stepped inside and closed the door. Her heart tripped at the threat of discovery.

Brynn kept her hand on the knob, the palm of her other hand pressed against the smooth wood, and her ear turned against the door as well. Perhaps she'd wandered above the billiards room and the shout had been nothing more than a raised voice among the men. But she wanted to be certain no one was coming toward her in the hallway. Her legs were quivering from nerves when she heard a strange thumping noise. Like a table or some other piece of furniture falling onto thick carpet.

Brynn waited, an eternity slipping by though she swore she took only a handful of breaths.

And then, she heard the sound of approaching feet. They were heading away from the previous noises—and directly toward the room where Brynn was hiding, pressed against the door. She held her breath as the sound of swishing skirts rushed past. It was a woman, then. And at that pace, she was in a hurry. Brynn also heard the distinct sound of sniffling, as if the woman were crying.

It seemed as if Brynn had nearly stumbled upon a man and woman having some kind of spat. Whom the man and woman were, would have to remain a mystery, however. She waited another minute before opening the door. The hallway was once again empty, and Brynn decided to backtrack to the previous corridor to avoid coming upon the man who had been shouting before.

Within another minute, she saw a familiar portrait hanging on the wall, and then, miraculously, a stairwell. She descended and immediately heard the echo of voices. Relief was instantaneous. She breathed deeply and forced a smile as she came upon the entrance to the ladies' salon. When she entered, her mother pounced.

"Gracious, Briannon! Where on earth have you been? I'd started to worry your dress was beyond repair."

Several of the other women in attendance all turned from their hands of cards to listen in.

"Not at all, but you know how silk is," Brynn said with a wave of her hand, and attempting to sound exasperated instead of nervous. "So difficult to mend."

Their eyes darted to the neatly mended seam, and she was inordinately thankful that Archer had done such an extraordinary job. Murmurs of agreement put her at ease, and even more so when the women turned back to the card tables and their glasses of sherry.

She glanced around the room as she walked to her mother, seated upon a sofa next to Viscountess Hamilton, a matronly woman who had never bore children and had, instead, a half dozen or more poodles.

"Have Lord and Lady Rochester departed for the evening?" Brynn asked, after settling herself beside her mother and noticing Lady Rochester's absence. She tried not to fidget. Archer could be returning to the duchess's sitting room that very moment, only to find it empty. She wondered if he would come to find her.

The thought of him made her lips tingle and burn.

"Lady Rochester was feeling rather…faint," the viscountess answered with a raised brow.

"She stepped out for a bit of air," her mother supplied.

She didn't scoff as openly as Viscountess Hamilton had, but Brynn could tell her mother didn't believe Lady Rochester's excuse for a moment.

Brynn sat stiffly on the uncomfortable sofa cushion, remembering the sound of a sniffling woman rushing past the room in which she had been hiding. She thought of the deep purple organza gown with its billowing skirts that Lady Rochester was wearing that night and conceded that it certainly could have been her in the hallway.

Perhaps Brynn had simply overheard a lover's quarrel. She breathed a sigh of relief that she had not actually come upon them in the hallway. Then again, had she had the misfortune of witnessing something between Bradburne and his mistress, she would have had something solid to point to for her reasoning behind rejecting the duke's proposal.

The offer would come, she knew. Archer had made that clear enough.

Archer.

The duke's affair with his good friend's wife was minuscule compared to the crimes his son had committed. He hadn't been involved in the waylaying of Lord Maynard's carriage, Brynn was certain of it. Archer had spoken of an imposter, and she wanted to believe him. She did believe him.

Didn't she?

Her head ached with the chaos of her thoughts. He would inherit a dukedom and was a marquess in his own right. Why had he put himself at such risk?

Brynn's good posture slipped, and she let out small sigh. Loud enough for her mother to hear, she hoped.

"Are you quite well, darling?"

Success.

Brynn touched her neck. "A little breathless, that is all."

"Perhaps we should call for the carriage —"

Lady Dinsmore's mouth froze open as a horrible scream

rent the air.

Brynn shot off the sofa. Viscountess Hamilton yelped and spilled her sherry onto the floor while the other ladies at the card tables turned in their seats toward the salon door.

"Help! Good heavens, someone! Help!"

The scream was coming from the grand stairwell that Brynn had just descended.

"Is that Lady Rochester?" her mother asked, standing up with more grace than Brynn had shown. "What in heaven's name has happened?"

The women started at once toward the door, crowding it as all of them attempted to funnel through at once. Brynn stayed near the rear of the confusion, but she could still hear Lady Rochester's next words clear as day.

"The duke! My god, all the blood!"

Chapter Fourteen

By the time Archer met Brandt in the hallway off the kitchens, he was in strict possession of himself once more. He cursed his friend's untimely arrival and thanked him in the same breath. Who knew what would have happened had he and the lady not been disturbed by the arriving footman. Archer had never lost control like that. Certainly never with someone as innocent as she.

Indeed, Lady Briannon was full of surprises.

Now that she knew the truth about him, he had to ascertain whether she would expose him. Archer wasn't above using seduction to get his way. He'd seduce her a thousand times over if it meant guaranteeing her silence.

Perhaps if the duke did offer for her, it would make her more amenable to protecting his family's interests, especially from such a scandal. He clenched his jaw at the sour thought. After what had happened between them, he could never let her marry his father.

But what could he offer her? He didn't want to be married. He didn't want to be saddled with a wife whom he would likely only disappoint in time. What he felt now would be fleeting, like any other passing indiscretion. Once he sated his body with hers, the desire would wane. His own parents' marriage, and how it had unfolded, was testament to that.

Archer did not want to have to live up to anyone's expectations, much less some maiden with stars in her eyes. She would undoubtedly want love and romance, and what did he know of those things? Archer didn't believe in such shallow sentiments anyhow, especially not after seeing what they had done to his mother. And should he end up being tried and punished for his crimes, any wife of his would be left to suffer the backlash. He could not expect someone to pay that price—no matter how stubborn and strong-willed she may be. No. Marriage to the beguiling Lady Briannon was not in the cards.

Taking her to bed was another matter altogether.

He couldn't deny the attraction between them, and neither could she. Archer shook his head, his body aching with a want that only she could appease. He hoped she would still be there when he dealt with Brandt's business. With a flick of his wrist, he signaled for Brandt to follow him down the hallway and through a door that led to the deserted side gardens, away from open windows and providing some modicum of privacy.

"What is it?" he said.

Brandt raised an eyebrow at his rudeness. "Did I interrupt a particularly riveting game of whist?" He eyed him, a knowing grin stretching across his face as he took in Archer's rumpled hair and crooked cravat. "Or was it something more enjoyable…some time in a broom closet, perhaps, with a young wealthy chit looking for a titled fop of a husband?"

It was too close to the truth for Archer. He glared at him and adjusted his cravat. "Did you have something of importance you wished to discuss?"

Brandt's grin widened. He was not afraid of Archer's

posturing in the least. "Cranky, aren't we? Did the debutante in question have too many morals for you? Decided she wanted a betrothal contract before tossing up her skirts?"

"Get on with it before I box your ears for your insolence."

"You could try."

A sliver of a scowl cracked Archer's face, and Brandt relented, handing him a heavy velvet pouch and lowering his voice. "My cousin just returned from Scotland. Here's the money from the last heist. He managed to get a good price for the lot. I've earmarked a portion of it to some of the local village places, and that's what is left."

"Seems like a large amount," Archer said, hefting the weight of the coins in the bag. "None for yourself?"

Brandt shook his head. "I paid the runner, but that's all. It should go to those who need it, and I am not in need."

In all the months they had worked together, Brandt had never taken a single coin for himself, and neither had Archer. He had seen the judgment in Brynn's eyes when she had called him a thief, but he wasn't keeping, and had never kept, any of the spoils. Most of the men he'd robbed would replace their trinkets with new pieces within the week, and the countless lives he had improved were worth the cost.

Speaking of excesses, he frowned at Brandt. "Did the duke commission you to purchase two new geldings for his stables?"

"Yes, a gorgeous snow white pair of Andalusians. They cost a pretty penny, too," Brandt said and then blinked at the look on Archer's face. "He did say to spare no expense."

"And you didn't think to ask me?"

"He is the duke, Hawk. He pays my wages."

"I pay your wages."

Brandt sighed. "What would you have had me do? Tell him that I had to check in with his son? He would have released me on the spot. I got the breeder down to a good price. They're good horses for any stable. Trust me, these two were worth it."

Archer nodded to his friend. He did trust Brandt when it came to assessing horseflesh of any kind. He had a knack with horses and could see traits about them that most others tended to miss. He knew whether a prized foal had a hidden ligament problem or if a mare would be barren.

"You'll have to show these prize mounts to me yourself," Archer said. He tossed him the velvet pouch. "I was invited to a charity dinner for an orphanage in Lambeth badly in need of funds. I declined, of course, but see that it goes to good use there."

Archer glanced back at the house. The lights in the first floor rooms threw long dancing shadows across the manicured shrubs. His eyes wandered up to the second floor, drawn by a light burning in his father's study. He could see shadowy movement behind the drapes and wondered whether the duke had miraculously decided to retire. Odd. His father was always the last to leave a party, even when it was his own.

Archer wished that he had his mother's sitting room window in clear view to see whether Brynn was still there. He shouldn't be this preoccupied with her, but he couldn't help himself. She haunted his every waking moment.

"Is something amiss?" Brandt asked.

He shook his head and stuffed his hands into the pockets of his trousers. He turned to dismiss Brandt and then stopped. "I'm sure you have heard the rumors that the duke is considering taking another wife."

"Yes," Brandt said. "All of London is abuzz with it. Mamas prepping their daughters, dandies closing their suits so that the duke doesn't set his eye on their chosen ladies. Even I, a lowly stable master, have heard the gossip," he said with his usual self-deprecating humor. "I'm sure wagers are being placed at Tattersall's and White's against the maiden he will choose."

"He has already chosen."

"Do tell."

Archer drew a long breath. "Lady Briannon." Her name came out on a sigh.

Brandt's eyes popped. "Lord Dinsmore's daughter? She's but a babe, barely your own number in years."

"She's of marriageable age," he said flatly.

Brandt cleared his throat. "And what of the issue we discussed as it relates to your secret identity? Does the lady know? Were you able to get to the heart of the matter?"

Brandt's choice of words made Archer's chest clench.

The heart of the matter was that he coveted the woman his father was about to offer for.

The heart of the matter was that she knew his deepest secret.

The heart of the matter was that she was in his blood, damn it.

He scrubbed a hand through his hair. "She knows."

Brandt hesitated, rolling onto the balls of his feet and plunging his hands in his pockets. He was not pleased, Archer could tell.

"And?" Brandt asked.

"I will take care of it."

"How?" Brandt prodded. "If she is to be the new duchess, then her loyalty will be with her husband, the duke, not you. How can you trust that she won't reveal what you—what we—have been doing? Do not forget my neck is on the line, too."

"I would never forget it."

Brandt stared at him for a long moment, and when Archer met his look, his friend was shaking his head, understanding dawning in his eyes. "Hawk, say it is not so."

"Say what?"

"Say that you haven't gone and lost your head for your poorly neighbor!" He glanced upward, trying to peer through the windows. "Where is this girl? I haven't seen her for years, but she must be surely some beauty if she can bring a duke and a marquess to their collective knees."

The only words that could fall from Archer's mouth were, "I told you she's not poorly."

"Of all the women," Brandt said in an exasperated voice. "I can find you a woman, if that is what you need. I know the perfect one. Her name is Eden, and she's everything a man could want…for one night."

"That's not what I want."

"Then what *do* you want?"

"Not that, damn it."

Spending one night with a skilled courtesan would have been a satisfactory proposition before. Not now. Archer wanted to have his fill of one woman in particular, and the idea of any other left a bleak, empty feeling in the pit of his stomach.

Brandt's voice sobered as he rested a hand on Archer's sleeve. "Hawk, you are playing with fire. Not everyone thinks as you do, and while you may believe this girl is different, you know as well as I that everyone in the *ton* is the same. She is just like the rest of them, and she will turn you in."

Though Archer knew his friend meant no insult, his words left a mark.

"Lie to her if you must, tell her it was a joke. I can pay people to act as your alibis. No woman is worth stretching your neck over. And if she is meant for the duke, we both know that your father would disown you without so much as blinking, especially if he has found a woman to bear him a new heir."

Brandt's supposition made Archer's entire body feel like it was being swallowed into a hole of despair. The thought of his father lying with Brynn in the efforts of procuring an heir was too much to even think about. He stifled his jealousy, clenching his fists so tightly his knuckles ached.

"I said that I will deal with it, and I will." He turned glacial eyes to Brandt, shrugging off his hand and changing the subject. "What news of the imposter?" His clipped tone indicated the matter of his father's upcoming nuptials and his chosen bride was now closed. Brandt stared at him, his lips a white line, but he knew better than to confront Archer when he was in such a foul mood.

"No leads," Brandt said quietly. "So far it's none of the runners we used."

"Look harder. One of the runners must have confided in someone else. There are too many similarities for this to be a coincidence. I am more worried about this bastard than I am about anyone else revealing who I am."

"Understood."

Brandt turned to leave when a loud, terrified scream came from the house. It sounded like someone was hurt. *A woman.* Archer had already sprinted away in full stride toward the front door when Brandt caught up to him.

"Who was that?" Brandt said.

"I'll find out. Stay here," Archer said over his shoulder and raced up the steps.

He could barely see past the crowd of bodies blocking his view and crowding the foyer. He was looking for only one person. His eyes threaded through, desperate, until the folds of a yellow gown sifted into his vision at the top of the stair. The breath came back to his body in full force, his eyes dragging over her from crown to feet to ensure she was unharmed. She was fine, but when Brynn met his gaze, the emotion he saw there nearly rocked him to his knees. Tears glistened in them. Something terrible had certainly happened.

"Make way," he commanded, and the crowd parted at

once. His eyes surged upward to the top of the landing where Lady Rochester stood in hysterics near Lady Dinsmore and her husband, clutching a handkerchief to her eyes and sobbing uncontrollably. At his glare, the servants scurried back to their posts, and he made his way up the stairs three at a time.

"What happened?" he demanded of her, but the woman couldn't stop blubbering long enough to speak.

"Your father," Lady Dinsmore answered for her, pointing to the study's half-opened door. Her hand trembled, and she too looked as if she was about to swoon. Lord Rochester seemed equally distraught. Had the duke and Lady Rochester finally been caught in a tryst? It would not shock him, however, the fuss seemed too excessive for that. A seed of foreboding took root in his gut.

Had his father passed out from too much drink? Archer frowned, recalling the shadow of a figure he had seen in the study from out in the gardens. He strode forward, pushing the door open fully.

His breath caught and stalled. He was wrong on both counts. The duke lay face up on the pale blue carpet, now stained black by a copious amount of blood. Archer felt his entire body go numb at the sight. A freezing paralysis coiled over his muscles and anchored him to the floor.

"Fetch the doctor," someone said, pushing away the bleak fog that had swamped him. Viscountess Hamilton's voice, he vaguely recognized as he took swift strides toward his father's motionless body.

He was not breathing as far as Archer could see, and a livid raw bruise on his temple was oozing blood. From the amount on the carpet, it didn't seem possible that he could bleed anymore. The wound was deep, as if his temple had collided with something sharp and heavy. Archer's eyes slid to the fallen bronze candelabrum that wasn't in its usual place on the mantel. He didn't have to examine it to know that it would be covered with the duke's blood.

A shout from the entrance drew his attention. "My lord!" He peered around the study door and saw a burly footman holding Brandt at the nape. "I found this man skulking around the gardens, trying to look in the windows."

"Release him," Archer said, pinching the bridge of his nose with his thumb and forefinger as the noise in the foyer rose to deafening heights. The footman was one of Heed's new hires and wouldn't have recognized Brandt. He raised a hand and everyone quieted. "He is the stable master and is here at my request. Unhand him, at once."

He met his friend's stare as Brandt straightened his clothes, a thousand questions in his eyes as they darted from Archer to the sobbing women standing at the door of the study. He shook his head imperceptibly, knowing that Brandt would defy all propriety if he thought Archer was in any pain or trouble.

Archer knew his shock was written all over his face, if the look on Brandt's was any signal. He swallowed past the sudden feeling of sawdust in his throat and returned to his father's supine body. He knelt and placed two fingers at the duke's throat, feeling for a pulse even though the odds said otherwise. Wanting to feel it, in spite of his most recent sentiments regarding his sire.

There was none. His father's eyes stared upward, cold and glassy, his skin already clammy to Archer's touch. He drew his fingers away, trembling just as Lady Dinsmore's had been, and stared at the people pressing into the space at the door. He couldn't speak, couldn't breathe. The Duke of Bradburne was a dissolute wretch and a poor excuse for a father, but that didn't mean that Archer wanted him dead. But someone had. Someone who had been in this very house.

"My lord?" his butler asked as the seconds drew into a torturous minute. Archer's stunned gaze crashed into his.

"It is too late for a doctor," he said in the general direction of his father's guests. "Fetch a constable, Heed," he ordered their butler. "And no one is to leave this house."

Archer's stare returned to his father's inert form, one that had been so full of life such a short time ago. The sight unexpectedly gutted him, and a strangled sound caught in his throat. Archer always imagined he'd celebrate the duke's passing with a *good riddance* and a whiskey toast, but for some reason, it made him think of his mother. The duke had never quite been the same without her. Perhaps in the hereafter, the duchess would take his father in hand once more.

At the thought of his late mother, Archer fought the stinging pain behind his eyes and rocked back onto his heels. She would have mourned. His father was an arrogant ass, but he had not deserved to have his life stolen from him. Archer did not expect to feel so much guilt nor such a savage need for retribution. He didn't move when he felt a delicate hand pressing into his shoulder. He knew Brynn's touch, and it brought him to the surface of the self-reproach threatening to drown him.

His father, the Duke of Bradburne, was dead. Murdered in his own home. A cold, unforgiving rage replaced his remorse. To his last breath, he would find the person responsible.

Chapter Fifteen

After a ragged, sleepless night, Archer woke at the crack of dawn. He stood at the window watching the sun rise over trees and rooftops, taking the sky from bruised purple to dusky gold. His valet had offered him a sleeping draught, but Archer had refused. He did not want anything to dull his wits, not when he had to be present during the questioning for the murder of the Duke of Bradburne.

He heaved a breath and quashed the instant surge of pain in his chest. His father was dead. *Murdered.* Killed in cold blood.

After the constable had left nearing midnight, the dinner guests had been allowed to return to their homes, though they were told to return promptly the following morning. As promised, an inquiry agent had arrived at Hadley Gardens first thing, well before breakfast, to question the staff, and now Archer would listen in while he spoke with each of the duke's guests.

He ran through the faces of the guests in his head for the hundredth time. Lady Rochester had found the duke, with

Lord Rochester not long behind. The motive was there, but neither had it in them to kill their oldest friend. At least he didn't think so. Rochester was a cowardly sort who turned tail at the first sight of confrontation. Then again, festering jealousy and rage could drive a man to do things one would never expect. Had Rochester known of his wife's infidelity and his best friend's betrayal? Could he have been the one to hit the duke in the head—more than once, the constable had ascertained—with the candelabrum?

And Lady Rochester…she could have been jealous of the duke's suit to Lady Briannon and struck out at him in anger, but she knew as well as anyone that Bradburne would not remain faithful to his new wife. It didn't add up. Brynn had been in his mother's sitting room, or at least she should have been. Until she had heard the shouts. He discounted each of the others with a slow exhale. None of them had any reason to kill his father. Viscountess Hamilton could hardly lift a sherry glass much less such a heavy instrument. The duke was two heads taller than her diminutive size—she would have had to stand upon a stool to strike him just so. Even Brynn's parents were far too infatuated with the idea of their daughter winning a duke's hand to be driven to murder the very hand they were courting.

Or perhaps it had been one of the staff. It wasn't unheard of for a servant to feel that he or she had been slighted in some way. Murder was certainly extreme, but none of them could be ruled out. Not even Brandt, he supposed, who had come there at Archer's behest. Suspicion would lay heavy upon him, especially as the footman the night before had said he'd found the stable master trying to look through the windows. But Archer had been with Brandt in the gardens when the duke had been found. Though that didn't account for *when* the duke was killed, he still trusted his friend with his life.

He also couldn't rule out that a thief had slipped in from outside. In an attempt to steal some coin, the thief could have been discovered by the duke. Hadley Gardens was a well-known address. Bradburne, along with any other peer, could be a target for petty crime, especially if there was a dinner underway and guests otherwise occupied. A few pieces of silver along with the duke's rings had been taken, which pointed to the fact that someone had indeed intended to rob the residence. Perhaps his father had just been in the wrong place at the wrong time.

Archer hauled several breaths into his lungs to clear his head. If only he had been in the study instead. He was three times as strong as his aging father, who had likely been well into his cups at the time. He should have been the one to face the attacker. Archer recalled the last bitter look he had exchanged with the duke, and guilt and regret took equal bites out of his conscience. He had faulted the man for many things, but he had never wished him dead. Archer's eyes burned, and without a thought, he smashed his fist into the windowpane.

"My lord!" Porter exclaimed, rushing forward with a towel. Archer glanced down, the pain doing little to assuage what he was doing to himself inside. Shards of glass peppered his knuckles. He stood still as Porter plucked the pieces embedded in his flesh and mopped up the welling blood.

"I am fine," he said. "Leave me."

"But, my lord—"

"I shall manage to dress myself, Porter. Please alert Heed that a new glass panel for the window should be ordered. Thank you."

He dismissed his longtime valet with a short nod and strode to the marble bathroom to soak his throbbing hand in a basin of water. Archer steeled himself, breath by aching breath, a habit born from years of dealing with disappointment and misery. Neither death nor pain was unfamiliar to him. He should not be this derailed. Archer set his jaw. He'd never let himself become vulnerable, yet last night, he had. With Brynn.

He'd opened up to her, and now, every blasted emotion was pushing in where it did not belong. She had dug little cracks into his armor with her beguiling half smiles and witty ripostes, and now here he was, falling to pieces when he should have felt nothing but the cold purpose of finding his father's killer.

Feelings. Bloody goddamned *feelings*.

Swearing beneath his breath, he dressed himself and went downstairs. The inquiry agent was already waiting in the foyer. Heed announced several of the guests from the dinner party were also ensconced in the front salon. "And my sister?" Archer asked.

"No word yet, my lord, but your message should have been delivered several hours ago."

Archer nodded. He had wanted to tell Eloise in person, but he knew gossip traveled fast, and he did not want her to hear it from someone else. One of the grooms had ridden through the night to deliver Archer's handwritten note and return with her response. He wondered how Eloise had taken the news. She'd lost two mothers, and though the duke had hardly been a father to her, he was the only one she had ever known. Emotionally fragile as she was, Archer wanted her by his side in London and not in Essex where she would be alone with her grief.

Dismissing Heed and nodding abruptly to the inquiry agent, a high-ranking officer from Bow Street, Archer turned and led him to the library, set deeper in the house. The man was short and thin with a heavy black mustache. His small, beady eyes seemed to take in everything about him. He carried a small bound book and a pencil. The man inspected him once they arrived in the library, and Archer immediately felt as if he were being weighed and measured. His eyes narrowed, and the man bowed his head discreetly.

"Thank you for your time, Your Grace," the agent said in a nasal voice that rankled his nerves. "I am Mr. Thomson."

It didn't matter that Archer felt an immediate dislike for the man—if he were indeed as good as Bow Street claimed him to be at tracking and apprehending criminals, he would find the duke's killer, and that would be that.

Archer gestured to a large table that had been set up for the agent's use. "Mr. Thomson. I trust this should suit your needs."

"Yes, this should do well, thank you."

Archer sat in silence as the man proceeded to call in and interrogate each of the guests in attendance. As Archer had expected, Lady Rochester could barely speak when she was called upon to enter the library for questioning. Her haggard face pointed to a sleepless night spent crying, and Lord Rochester looked worse than she did.

"Tell me in detail what you saw," Mr. Thomson said.

She swallowed hard, dabbing a handkerchief to red-rimmed eyes. "I…I was on my way to the retiring room when I heard a thud and someone grunting. I walked toward the sound and found the duke lying on the carpet. He wasn't moving." Her voice broke. "There was so much blood. He didn't look like he was breathing."

"Did you see anyone else?"

"No, the hallways were deserted," she sobbed. "I called for help."

Mr. Thomson asked several more questions, ones that didn't seem relevant to the crime, Archer thought, like the length of Lady Rochester's association with the duke. He wrote furiously in his little book, taking copious notes as Lady Rochester spoke. After the Rochesters, Mr. Thomson moved through the rest of the party one by one until at last he came to the Dinsmores. The subject of the expected proposal cropped up almost immediately. Archer eyed Mr. Thomson, surprised the man had already known the gossip.

"Lord and Lady Dinsmore, I have it that the duke was about to offer for your daughter," he said with a glance at Brynn who sat beside her parents. Archer could see that she, too, was unnaturally pale, dark shadows lining her eyes as if she had not slept, either. She clutched a handkerchief in her hand, her fingers tightening as her eyes met Mr. Thomson's.

"Yes, we anticipated an offer," Lady Dinsmore said, her voice tight.

"But no offer was made."

"No."

He looked to Lady Briannon. "How long have you known the duke?"

"Our estates in Essex are joined." Her voice trembled as she answered. "So, I suppose, all my life."

"But you did not wish to be married to the duke." It was not a question. Archer's gaze flew to the man's. Where had he heard of Brynn's feelings on the matter at such short notice? Prattling servants, of course. Anyone could be persuaded to reveal secrets at the right cost.

Brynn cleared her throat, her chin tilting upward. "As you indicated, I had no official offer to consider. My wishes were therefore irrelevant."

"Should there have been an offer made, would you have accepted?" Mr. Thomson asked, his pencil hovering above his notebook.

Archer shifted in his seat. He saw the color rising on the apples of Brynn's cheeks and on the tips of her ears. The flare of her mother's nostrils were difficult to miss as well. No doubt the countess was incensed by the inquiry agent's brazen question.

Brynn, however, kept her head high. "I cannot say. I suspect I would have considered the offer and then given *the duke* my answer."

Mr. Thomson nodded sagely and wrote something in his notepad. "And where were you last evening when the duke was discovered in his study by Lady Rochester?"

Brynn's eyes did not flicker to Archer's. If she had been waiting for him in his mother's sitting room, she would not have an alibi.

"In the ladies' salon," she answered evenly.

"That is correct. We were seated across from Lady Hamilton when we heard that wretched scream," Lady Dinsmore put in.

Archer breathed out with relief. He shouldn't have expected her to stay put in the sitting room, risking a prolonged absence and possible scandal.

Thank heavens she hadn't.

"And before that?" Mr. Thomson flipped back several pages in his notebook, and running a finger along some slanted writing, said, "One of the footmen accounted for Miss Dinsmore's hem being torn during dinner. He said he escorted the young woman to a sewing room where one of the maids would mend the tear."

The alarm flashing in Brynn's eyes mirrored Archer's own, though his was tempered by gratitude to the footman. He could have told Mr. Thomson that Archer had sent him on his merry way, claiming he would show Lady Briannon to the sewing room. Archer would remember to thank the footman in some way.

"That is correct," Brynn replied. He admired her brevity. Rambling would only show how nervous she truly was, and from the color still touching her cheeks and ears, he imagined she was just as nervous as he, if not more so.

"And the maid who attended you," Mr. Thomson continued. "Do you recall her name?"

"Her name?" Lady Dinsmore parroted. "My goodness,

I highly doubt they exchanged more than a few words of pleasantries."

"I am afraid I do not," Brynn said, attaching herself to her mother's genuinely baffled reply.

Mr. Thomson gazed at the lady a beat longer before scribbling in his book again. Archer straightened his back and cleared his throat.

"Do you have any questions for Lord Dinsmore?" Archer asked, eager to draw the agent's attention onto another path. Had he known his scheme to get Brynn alone last evening would be sniffed out by a Bow Street Runner, he would have certainly gone about things differently.

But how could he have foreseen his father's murder? And now every move of every guest last evening would be put under intense scrutiny.

"Yes," Thomson said, shifting his direct gaze to Lord Dinsmore. "I have it that your carriage was set upon by the criminal known as the Masked Marauder two weeks past, on your way to Worthington Abbey."

Archer held his breath as Dinsmore tucked his chin and frowned. "That is correct. We were on our way to the duke's ball. But what does that have to do with what happened last night?"

"And you were in attendance at the Gainsbridge Masquerade, where another carriage was set upon? This time with violent results," Thomson said, ignoring the earl's question.

"Why, yes, but — "

"There were many of our set in attendance at both functions," Archer cut in, apologizing to the earl for his rudeness with a pointed glance. "What of the masked bandit? Do you think he has something to do with this?"

"Anything is possible at this time. I have just one final question for Lady Findlay," the agent replied. "Last evening, did you visit the duke's private rooms?"

Archer stood, knocking back his chair and drawing all eyes in the room. "Mr. Thomson, that is enough. We are done here."

Lord Dinsmore had also risen out of his chair, though a bit slower than Archer. "What do you mean by asking that question, investigator?"

Mr. Thomson stayed seated, displaying nothing but cool indifference to their objections. "I simply must follow the path of every theory that springs to mind, my lord. I will not soften my questions so they suit the whims of my…*betters*." Derision dripped from that last word. "A murder has been committed, and though your *set* may not enjoy this taste of reality, it is still my duty to supply it."

Lord Dinsmore sniffed, clearly taken aback by the agent's tirade. "Well. You can put your theory regarding my daughter to rest, I assure you."

The agent canted his head, acknowledging the statement. He didn't reply, however. Archer watched Thomson's expression as Lady Dinsmore got to her feet, Brynn following more slowly. Stone-faced and observant, the man followed Brynn's movements as she and her parents left the room.

Archer did not look in Brynn's direction even though he could feel her eyes upon him. He waited until the Dinsmores had departed before closing the door behind them and letting his tempered anger loose.

"How is questioning the lady's virtue relevant to your investigation?" he asked, turning back to the agent.

Mr. Thomson smiled, though it did not reach his eyes. "She is a suspect."

The words ignited something in Archer's chest. A hot swelling of desire — of need. The need to protect.

"Lady Briannon Findlay is not a suspect," he growled.

Mr. Thomson did not flinch. "That is for me to decide, and

I have decided that in a case such as this, *everyone* is a suspect, Your Grace."

Archer bit his tongue. The emphasis the man had placed on "everyone" left no doubt that he himself was considered a suspect as well. It was absurd. Christ, he'd been the one to call in Bow Street in the first place!

The agent took a small pocketknife from his coat and began to sharpen the tip of his pencil. "I have a few questions for you, if you don't mind."

Archer walked toward the chair Brynn had been sitting in but decided at the last moment to stand. He moved to the window, overlooking the back lawns.

"Not at all. Ask what you must."

Thomson glanced at the pages in his notebook. "Where were you when the men retired to the billiards room after dinner?"

Though he trained his expression to appear serene, Archer's mind raced. "I had to attend to some matters of urgent business."

"Where? In the house? The duke's study?"

"Of course not. I have my own rooms here."

Though now, he supposed, all the rooms were his. It hit him for the first time. He was no longer a marquess, but a duke.

Hell, he had not wanted the title. Especially not in this way.

"Did you cross paths with the duke?"

The inquiry agent's voice brought the room back into focus. "No. I left to speak in the gardens with the stable master regarding one of my mounts."

Mr. Thomson raised a hand. "You left a dinner party to attend to urgent business, in the gardens with your stable master, regarding a horse. Do I have that right?"

Archer frowned. It did, even to his own ears, sound utterly

suspicious. But he remained stoic. "Yes. And while I was there, I noticed a light in the duke's study."

"Go on. What happened next?"

Archer was beginning to dislike the man's probing, but he held his irritation back. He supposed such thoroughness would help catch the criminal. "We heard the shouts, and I ran inside. I checked the duke's pulse, and there was none."

Archer pulled his timepiece from his pocket. A couple of hours had passed. "I hate to rush you, but I am expecting my sister from Essex shortly. Is there anything else I can answer for you?"

Mr. Thomson eyed him. "Just one more thing. You and your father fought quite publicly several days past. My notes say that it turned physical."

Damnation, where the devil had he heard that? Archer had been present for every interview this morning and not once had the argument from the masquerade been brought up. The inquiry agent had gotten a rather fine head start with the staff, it seemed.

"It was an unfortunate turn of events," Archer said, attempting to put a bland facade on the argument. "Fathers and sons will always have disagreements."

Mr. Thomson nodded. "It was the same with my father. The man was exacting."

Archer didn't respond, nor did he care.

Mr. Thomson's stare centered on Archer as he pulled something from his pocket. "This was found in the pocket of your father's trousers. It is a note, asking the duke to meet *you* in the study."

Archer froze, staring at the crumpled piece of paper.

"The footman who delivered the note to the duke in the billiards room last evening said it was found lying, sealed, on a serving tray in the kitchens."

Archer picked up the piece of paper, the lightweight

linen parchment instantly recognizable. It was indeed his own stationery. Drawn from the stack he kept in the desk in his rooms. One look at the handwriting, however, and his shock turned to fury. It was the same scratchy script that had graced the two previous notes left for Archer. One in Essex, another in the silver salver at Hadley Gardens, and now a third, in the pocket of his father's corpse.

"I did not pen this." Archer dropped the paper. "Or leave it in the kitchen for a footman to deliver, for that matter."

He certainly could not come forward about the other notes, both of which had pointed to a secret. Mr. Thomson was already suspicious as it was.

"I suspected as much," Thomson said, though his words sounded hollow.

The agent gathered his notebook and the forged note and tucked his pencil away while Archer's mind raced. That clever bastard. Whomever it was had intentionally drawn his father from the billiards room and had wanted it to look as if it had been Archer.

"You should get that hand looked at," Mr. Thomson said as he got up and walked to the door. Archer glanced down, still distracted by the note. The gauze bandage he'd wrapped around his wound was spotted with fresh crimson spots.

Archer did not deign to offer a reply. He owed the man no explanation. He followed Thomson to the door and watched with burgeoning unease as Heed escorted the agent toward the front of the house.

It was barely noon, but Archer desperately needed a drink. He left the library and started for the dining room, where the footmen would likely be replacing the white table runner with a long strip of black crepe. Hadley Gardens would be plunged into mourning and paired with the agent's probing questions, a whiskey or two at noon did not sound so unreasonable.

His attention fell on the newssheets, ironed flat and crisp by Heed that morning, lying on the sideboard beside the decanter. He scanned the headlines. Just when he thought things couldn't get any worse—there had been another heinous attack by the Masked Marauder, and this time in town. Yesterday afternoon. It could not be a coincidence.

Archer considered all three of the strange notes again as he entered the dining room, already draped in black. No desperate thief had broken into the townhouse. Someone had wanted the duke in his study, alone. This was no petty crime. This was premeditated murder. And it had to do with Archer's secret identity. Nausea stole over him, and he had to lean against the sideboard.

This was his fault. His father had died because of *him*.

Chapter Sixteen

Brynn had not expected to be back at Madame Despain's so soon. She stood in the center of the back room in a semi-stupor as the modiste's assistants fitted her with a somber dress, appropriate for the duke's funeral.

Her mother and Madame Despain were whispering in the corner, not paying anywhere near as much attention to the fitting as they had the day before when it had been for the golden gown. The whole town was whispering, it seemed. A member of the peerage had been slain in his own home, his guests from that evening all questioned by Bow Street, and the murderer was still at large. Things like this did not happen in London—at least not to the people in Brynn's part of London.

She closed her eyes to the mirror's reflection of the ready-made crepe dress being pinned and tucked by two of Madame Despain's girls. Fashion did not matter. Everyone would be wearing the same color and cut to the upcoming funeral. What did matter, to Brynn at least, were the terrible questions the Bow Street agent had pressed her with earlier that morning.

She closed her eyes as the floor wavered unsteadily.

"What's wrong? Are you feeling unwell?"

Gray touched her hand, his fingers warm in comparison to her icy skin. He had insisted on accompanying them to Bond Street, and Brynn knew it was out of pure concern for her health.

"As I already told you, I am fine," she answered, though her throat was tight and it turned her words into a whisper.

"You were in the same house as a murderer last evening," he said, the pronouncement drawing widened eyes from the two assistants. They were well trained, however, and continued to pin the cuff on the overly long sleeve. "You are not fine."

"Yes, well, I am lucky enough to still be breathing, so I cannot rightfully complain."

He tapped the hat in his hand against his leg, his eyes darting around the space usually reserved for women.

"You should not be in here," Brynn whispered.

There were bolts of lace and satin and silk and, she noticed, an open box of some lacy underthings half wrapped in tissue.

"Do not be ridiculous. I am your brother," he said stiffly. "And besides that, I am furious. Father told me what that inquiry agent insinuated with his questions."

Brynn's stomach soured. Mr. Thomson had certainly seemed suspicious of her. As if he'd known she had been lying about her hem being mended by a maid. All he needed was the account of the maid in question saying she never mended the torn hem, and never saw Brynn in the sewing room at all, and Brynn would be in scalding water.

The inquiry agent would assume she had been skulking around Hadley Gardens on her own. Perhaps sneaking into the duke's study to lie in wait for him.

It was a disaster. She should never have allowed Archer to lead her into his mother's sitting room. Or kneel before her and mend her torn hem. Or kiss her.

"Mr. Thomson was simply doing his job as investigator," she said, attempting to sound as if she could care less.

"That or ignite a scandal," Gray mumbled.

"There you are, my lady," one of the assistants said, placing one last pin. She turned her eyes to Gray, who was still brooding. Brynn sighed.

"Dear brother, this is your cue to exit, as I am about to undress."

He snapped to attention, the girls twittering as he bowed and left to wait at the front of the shop. Brynn smiled, the expression feeling so odd and out of place it almost instantly crashed.

Her mind had been spinning with all the theories the inquiry agent might have been formulating, and as the girls removed her from the black bombazine dress, she couldn't help but get stuck, yet again, on the one that would not leave her alone.

It was not that she herself might be implicated in a murder.

It was that Archer might be.

He had slipped away from the dinner guests as well and then away from her in the sitting room. He had not said to where he was going, but it had to have been urgent. She had felt the overwhelming desire in his kiss. He had been slowly, but effectively, grinding her resistance and hesitation to a fine pulp with every stroke of his tongue and every touch of his hands. As improper as it had been, and as dangerous, Brynn had not been able to stop him. She had not *wanted* to. He'd admitted to being the masked bandit, and the confession had made her confused and furious, even as it had inflamed her every sense. If she were being true to herself, it had always been Archer behind the mask.

Archer was the man she had not been able to stop thinking of. *Archer* was the one she had, in her most private and reprehensible thoughts, imagined drawing her into a kiss. *Archer* was the man she had lost her wits over that night in the forest cottage.

Perhaps that wicked lust had been the reason she'd so quickly believed his assurances that he had not attacked Lord Maynard's carriage or assaulted his coachman.

But where had Archer gone after leaving the sitting room?

As Madame Despain's girls began to dress her again in the deep green day gown she had arrived in, Brynn thought of the muted shout she'd heard while lost in the hall on her way downstairs. It had been a man's voice, and the duke's study had turned out to be rather close to where she had been at that time.

And then there had been the sound of a woman rushing past the room in which Brynn was hiding, the rustling of skirts, and the distinct sound of crying. Whomever it had been, had been upset. Lady Rochester? She had been gone from the salon when Brynn had finally returned. But her screams upon discovering the duke had come at least five minutes later. Had Lady Rochester delayed them because *she* had been the one to kill him, and it had taken her that long to gather her senses?

It was too awful to consider. Brynn felt ashamed even thinking it. But the truth was, someone had done the murder, and the crying woman in the hallway was most definitely a suspect. If only Brynn could tell the inquiry agent about her. But then she'd need to explain what she was doing in that part of the house, and hiding in a room, at that. It would also place her close to the duke's study—and what if Mr. Thomson didn't believe her about the crying woman?

Oh, it was all so disastrous. Her head spun with the chaos of it, making her dizzier and more nauseated than she already had been all morning. By the time the girls had finished lacing and buttoning her, a sharp pain had started in her temple, and her breath was coming short.

Gray and Mama noticed immediately as she entered the front of the shop.

"Oh, my darling!" Her mother swooped over and guided Brynn to a long, padded bench seat by the front window, where a mannequin, draped in a fine Parisian gown and holding a parasol, stood on display.

"It is just a headache," Brynn insisted, thinking it wise to make no mention of the tightness in her chest. Gray took her arm and sat beside her on the bench.

"You never could lie worth a damn," he muttered.

"Graham, your language," Mama hissed with an apologetic glance toward Madame Despain. "Oh, Briannon, this day has been so taxing for us all. We must get you home to rest."

She returned to the modiste's side to finalize the order while Brynn avoided her brother's searching stare. What was he looking for, some sign that she was about to faint? Well, she would not. Gray would never leave her side if she did, and Brynn could not stay in her room wallowing in her worrisome thoughts for the rest of the day. Just the idea of it made the breath in her throat thicker than air should be.

Some fresh air would be nice, even if the day was overcast and cool. Through the front window, ladies in fashionable dress and men in crisp, clean suits walked by. Carts and drays and carriages filled the street, horse hooves clapped the cobbles, and somewhere nearby a traffic whistle blew.

Brynn's eyes traveled past a pair of children on leading strings being held in check by their caretaker, to a solitary man standing beside a street lamp. He had one shoulder against the iron column and both hands in his pockets, as if he had been standing there for quite some time. She narrowed her eyes and inspected his suit. Brown tweed. Not current, nor in the least bit dashing. The mannequin and the wide-skirted Parisian gown blocked her a little from his view, but it was clear that the man was watching Madame Despain's shop.

"You've lost more color," Gray said, standing up and extending his arm. "I'll escort you to the carriage, and do not even think to refuse."

She would have usually made some quip in response, but the man across the street had thoroughly distracted her. If Gray noticed, he likely assumed her silence was due to ill health. As they exited the shop door and stepped onto the sidewalk, the man in the brown tweed took a smooth step behind the lamppost. Had she not spied him from inside the shop, she would have most definitely not noticed his attempt to disappear from view.

He *was* watching her. Who was he, another agent from Bow Street?

Gray helped her into the carriage, her pulse beginning to gallop.

Thomson must truly suspect her. Perhaps he had ordered this man to keep eyes on her, in case she attempted to flee to the Continent as a guilty party might.

Despite the chill early May temperature, Brynn began to grow hot underneath her day dress and cloak.

"I think a rest would be the best thing," she found herself saying to Gray, who frowned from his seat across from her.

"I will ask Cook to prepare one of her draughts," he said.

"No, I just want to sleep," she replied, hoping she was not as poor a liar as Gray had just accused her of being. She wasn't going to sleep at all. No, as soon as she arrived home at Bishop House, she was going to speak to Lana and formulate some kind of plan.

She needed to see Archer, straightaway.

Brynn stared at Lana from under the counterpane. Lana had become her confidante over the past few months, ever since Dowager Countess Langlevit had asked her parents to employ the young woman as a special favor. But could she trust her with such a secretive and delicate expedition? Her mother would have a fit of the vapors and Gray would likely explode if either of them found out she had slipped off to Hadley Gardens. And now that there would be no forthcoming marriage to the late Duke of Bradburne, she had to be careful. Being seen unaccompanied and unchaperoned at Archer's house would invite a whole host of other problems. After all, she had her blasted reputation to consider. For the hundredth time since she was little, Brynn cursed the fact that she had been born a girl. Boys simply weren't saddled with propriety and modesty as much as girls were. They could come and go as they pleased, caring not a whit for *reputation*.

Still, reputation or not, she had to see Archer.

"Lana," she began in a low voice. "I must ask you to do something for me. Something that could get us both into a lot of trouble, but I can't see any other way around it."

Lana moved to the side of the bed, her face concerned. "What is the matter, my lady?" She set the draught Cook had prepared on the bedside table, and Brynn's eyes fluttered to the contraption already standing at the side of her bed. A length of Indian rubber tubing ran between a glass container at one end, which Lana was about to fill with the special draught, and a cloth face shield at the other. Her father had consigned the device to be built at the advice from the *ton*'s leading physician, who swore by its lung healing properties. The device had helped to clear her throat when her passages had become blocked as a child and reduced the severity of her infections. But now, she was struck by a brilliant idea.

"I need you to be me," Brynn said and then clarified what she meant. "Pretend to be me. Lie in bed and wear the mask—it will cover your whole face. We can put a cap over your hair."

It would be the only thing to give them away—Lana's hair was glossy and dark, while Brynn's was decidedly not.

Lana frowned, her dark eyes narrowing. "Why would you need me to do this?"

"I need to go somewhere, and Mama will kill me if I leave the house."

"Lord Northridge cannot take you?"

"No," Brynn said hastily. "He cannot know."

Lana's frown deepened. For once, Brynn wished that she would simply listen as a servant should. Then again, if Lana were any ordinary servant, she would go immediately to Brynn's mother.

"Please, Lana, I need your help."

The plea seemed to soften her maid's pinched reaction. "Where will you go?"

Brynn gritted her teeth. She had no choice but to tell Lana the truth, for she would see right through any lie. It was one of the things she loved to hate about her. Lana was sharp and clever, and earning her trust had not been accomplished by telling her lies. She drew a deep breath. "I am going to see Lord Hawksfield."

Lana sat on the edge of Brynn's bed, her disbelief plain.

"Surely that isn't wise. There was a man here questioning the servants all day. He asked me many things."

Alarm shivered along Brynn's veins. "What did you tell him?"

"The usual," Lana said. "That I came here from Russia eight months ago, worked for the Countess Langlevit shortly before receiving a position here, and now I am your lady's maid. And that you are a sickly girl who needs constant attention and looking after."

Brynn's tension drained away at Lana's words and the

teasing smile on her face. Lana was quick on the uptake. She would never betray her mistress, Brynn knew. What she didn't know was whether Lana would agree to do this one thing for her. "So will you help me?"

"Should Mrs. Frommer learn of this, I will lose my position."

Brynn exhaled, knowing Lana was right.

"I understand," she said, her plan quickly unraveling around her. She would never wish Lana to suffer for her actions.

"However," Lana added, her brow rising. "Mrs. Frommer is rather busy today interviewing a few girls for the second laundress position."

Hope renewed, Brynn took Lana's hands in hers. "We won't get caught. All you must do is go downstairs and alert my mother that you will be sitting with me for some time while I rest, and that I don't wish to be disturbed. And tell the kitchen to withhold my luncheon tray. Then come back up here and settle into bed with the mask, just in case."

Brynn hoped it would be enough.

"Be swift about it then," Lana said with a glance at the breathing tube. "Lord knows what will happen to me, breathing in that appalling concoction."

Brynn grinned at Lana's near aristocratic diction and, throwing decorum to the wind, flung her arms around her. She supposed Lana's command of language stemmed from listening to the ladies of the Russian aristocracy in her mother's dress shop. "Don't worry," she told her. "It's only vinegar, camphor, cinnamon, and some other aromatic herbs."

Lana helped Brynn dress in a simple navy day dress and began tucking her hair into a bun at her nape.

"Thank you for doing this," she whispered.

"Don't get caught," Lana said, draping a gray cloak over her shoulders. "The things I do for you. Worse than my own sister."

Brynn turned to her. "You have a sister?"

"Yes," Lana said quietly before giving the cloak a final sweep of her hands. She clearly did not wish to speak of her, Brynn determined.

She tightened the cloak and pulled the hood over her head, and recalled something else Lana had said. "You did claim that we English had no sense of adventure. Am I proving you wrong now?"

"I was talking about dancing, not secretly meeting a lover."

"He's not my lover!" Brynn cried, though her entire body fired at the thought.

"He should be, if you're going through all this trouble." Lana's response was soft, but Brynn still heard it as her maid cracked open the door to leave and do as her mistress had asked. Her limbs felt like water, and her breathing had tripled its normal pace.

She shook her head, forcing into submission her utterly sinful thoughts regarding Archer as a lover. The hallway was deserted, and she slipped down it before darting toward a narrow staircase at the side of the house. She descended without being seen and raced out a little-used back door leading to the mews, where she could escape with the least amount of notice.

Pulling her hood low, she hailed a passing hackney as she had once seen Gray do, and gave directions to a few townhouses down from Archer's residence. The ride was quick, and after Brynn stepped onto the curb, she walked swiftly down the street toward Hadley Gardens.

She did not go up the front steps of the residence, but instead, slipped around to the back. She was taking a risk attempting to see Archer without a proper chaperone and without being announced, but she couldn't take the chance that he, too, was being watched by Thomson or his men. As she rounded a neatly clipped hedge, she almost jumped out of her skin at the sight of the person walking along the mews, and heading straight for her.

"Eloise!" Brynn exclaimed in breathless surprise.

"Lady Briannon." The girl's eyes widened behind the sheer veil she wore. "I did not expect you."

Brynn took Eloise's hand and led her out of sight of the house to a nearby garden bench. She had not thought Eloise would arrive from Essex so soon, but her brother must have sent for her immediately.

"What are you doing back here?" Eloise asked, glancing around. "Is Lady Dinsmore with you as well?"

Brynn shook her head. "I…I came alone." She paused, her face flushing. Her presence here, instead of at the proper entrance, had to appear strange. Perhaps suspicious.

She took in Eloise's red eyes and wan complexion as they settled on the garden bench, the marble cold beneath them. She gave Eloise's hand a squeeze. "I am so sorry for your loss."

Eloise nodded, lifting a handkerchief behind her veil as she sniffled. "You must be aware of how it was between us…but he was my father. I can't imagine someone attacking him. Everyone adored him." Brynn heard her sobbing some more, her red-tipped nose visible, even through the veil's lacy pattern. Brynn shifted closer and patted her lightly on the back.

"There, there," she soothed, rubbing her shoulders. It had been so long since she and Eloise had considered each other friends. But that wasn't the only reason Brynn felt awkward consoling her right now. She'd been caught approaching the kitchen entrance to Hadley Gardens like an intruder. Archer's sister was not so naive, or dejected, as to overlook that.

"Thank you," Eloise sniffed. "I'm sorry I'm blubbering all over you, but it has been so much to take in. I haven't talked to anyone about it. Archer has been occupied since I arrived." She raised tear-dampened eyes to Brynn. "I heard that you were here last evening."

"Yes. I was in the salon…when it happened."

Eloise took a long, shaky breath and pushed the lacy veil up and over the deep-plum-colored silk flowers adorning the brim of her hat. Outwardly, Brynn did not flinch—she knew better than to react to Eloise's disfigurement in so heartless a way. It did not change, however, the way her stomach tightened at the sight of the scars inflicted so many years ago.

"Archer is with that investigator, Mr. Thomson, again," Eloise whispered. "He said it could have been anyone. Someone at the dinner, or a robbery. They are looking at all avenues. Even that Masked Marauder character."

Brynn choked on a breath. "What do you mean?"

"Haven't you seen the paper?" Eloise asked. "There was an attack near Oxford Street. Mr. Thomson said that the marauder cannot be ruled out."

Brynn was surprised Gray hadn't mentioned anything that morning, though perhaps he had been more concerned over her well-being than worrying her with news.

"But the Masked Marauder…he has never robbed someone in their own home. He…well, as I have *heard*, he sets upon carriages."

Eloise shrugged. "Perhaps the criminal has found there is more secrecy in invading homes. This is London, after all, with fewer opportunities for a carriage robbery that would go unseen."

"That makes sense," Brynn murmured. Her mind raced, considering and discarding multiple scenarios. She believed Archer when he'd told her that there was an impersonator. First, the false bandit struck in Essex while Archer was there, and now here, in London after Archer's arrival in town. Was the impersonator following in Archer's footsteps, then? Or was he, as she had surmised initially, another member of the peerage, coming to London for the season? The whole idea seemed preposterous, but then again, *Archer*—a pinnacle of the beau monde—had confessed to doing some marauding of his own.

Brynn didn't quite know what the false bandit's presence in town might have to do with the duke's murder, but she couldn't get past the coincidence. Though why would he invade Hadley Gardens and kill the duke? Unless…unless he knew who Archer was. Her heart flew into her throat, her tangled thoughts suddenly ironed out. It was a possibility she couldn't discount.

"I hope they catch him, whomever he is," she said, distracted by the terrible notion.

"I do as well, of course," Eloise said. She took her hand from Brynn's and laced her fingers together in her lap. "So. Are you going to tell me why you were attempting to enter the house through the kitchens?"

Brynn shifted on the marble bench. "Oh. Well, it's a little…complicated, and I know it's…not exactly proper, however…"

She had no idea how to continue. There really was no excuse, and her plan had been hasty to begin with. Desperate. Which she no doubt appeared to be right then.

"You are here to see my brother," Eloise whispered.

"Of course not, I—"

Eloise took her hand again and, as Brynn had moments before, gave it a squeeze of reassurance. "How silly of me. You came to visit *me*, didn't you?"

Brynn looked into her eyes, ready to apologize and confess, but what she saw silenced her. Eloise was biting back a smile, her eyebrows, one of which had a track of scar tissue cutting through, were raised in amusement.

"Come, let me see you in." She stood, bringing Brynn to

her feet as well. "Of course, I feel terribly exhausted from my journey. Would you mind if my brother hosted you for tea instead?"

Eloise started for one of the back terraces instead of the kitchens.

"That would be very kind of you," Brynn said, relieved she hadn't been made to admit the scandalous truth.

Arm in arm with Archer's sister, she waltzed into Hadley Gardens' ballroom. In the quiet, their slippered feet echoed off the vaulted ceilings. Brynn had not seen the ballroom on her visit the evening before, but she found it strange that the terrace doors would be left unlocked and unattended, especially after the events of last night.

"Let us see if Archer has finished his business," Eloise said as she led them from the ballroom and into a hallway. "I cannot say enough how nice it is to see a friendly face, Briannon, in the midst of all this awful tragedy."

Brynn smiled, overwhelmed at her kindness. "I feel quite the same."

The door to the library where Mr. Thomson had questioned everyone earlier was closed. Eloise raised her hand to knock, but an outburst from inside the room made her pause.

"Pray tell, how is that a motive for murder?" Brynn recognized Archer's rumbling voice immediately.

She glanced at Eloise with wide eyes. Eavesdropping was highly improper, but the girl seemed as disinclined to move as Brynn was.

"At the Gainsbridge Masquerade, you were overheard arguing about Lady Briannon. Marriage was mentioned. Close friends of the late duke's suggested that you both desired the hand of the lady in question."

"*Close friends,*" Archer repeated, his mocking words dripping with acid. "Lord and Lady Rochester? Lady

Mayfield, perhaps? An intelligent man would not take their word as gospel, Thomson."

"You were angry with your father for showing interest in Lady Briannon," Mr. Thomson hedged.

"Do not be absurd. I had much to be angry with my father for, but the flowers and simpering looks he showered upon Lady Briannon were of no concern to me."

Brynn winced. That hurt, and unexpectedly, too. Why on earth would he have kissed her those two times if he did not care a whit whether she married his father or not?

"You were absent for a length of time last evening after dinner concluded," Thomson said, his voice rising to match Archer's.

"I told you where I was, and whom I was with," Archer ground out.

"Yes, you did," Thomson replied. "However, it appears Lady Briannon did not quite tell me the truth of *her* whereabouts. She never went to the sewing room to have her dress mended."

Brynn stifled a horrified gasp, and Eloise's eyes found hers. She put a gloved finger to her lips.

It took Archer a moment to respond, and when he did, his attempt at sounding careless was strained. "What are you about?"

The agent did not hesitate. "I believe one of two things happened. You went to the kitchens to leave a note summoning the duke to his study, while the lady slipped off to the study for her own rendezvous with the duke. You arrived, surprised to find her, and shortly after, the duke arrived as well. There was an argument. The duke was killed."

Archer's rejoinder was instant, and deadly soft. "You are treading dangerous waters, Thomson."

"Or," the agent went on. "You were in the gardens as you claim. Lady Briannon went to the study, summoned for the duke using that note and your name, and upon his arrival—"

"Say another word, and I will remove you bodily from that chair."

"My apologies, Your Grace," Thomson said. "But it is my job to consider all avenues. And Lady Briannon lied."

Eloise tugged on Brynn's sleeve, her eyes wide with apprehension. "Is what he says true?" she whispered into Brynn's ear, but Brynn was in shock—she *had* lied. Brynn drew Eloise several paces away from the library's closed door.

"Hawksfield mended my dress," she whispered in a choked voice. "We were in another room. Alone."

The shock barely settled on Eloise's face before a flicker of something sharper, like excitement, lit her eyes. She quickly replaced it with a rueful, sympathetic smile. "As I recall, my brother did have a talent for the needle."

If her help in the garden was any indication, Brynn knew Eloise would not judge her, not now. She swallowed hard, desperate tears springing to her eyes. "I couldn't tell Thomson the truth. My reputation would have been compromised beyond repair. And now he suspects me. And…your brother."

"This is indeed catastrophic," Eloise continued, her voice low. She took a deep breath and grasped Brynn's shoulders. "The only thing that would save you and Archer is the announcement of an engagement. Go in there and say that my brother was proposing to you."

Brynn felt the breath leave her body in a violent sweep at the outrageous suggestion. Announce an engagement, just like that? Without speaking to Archer first and without receiving an actual offer? Her fingers went numb. She considered herself bold at times, but not *that* bold. "I cannot."

"I saw the way you looked at each other at the masquerade. I know you have feelings for him. Otherwise, why would you care so much to come here and further compromise your reputation in the process? Admit it, you care. And nothing would please me more than to have you as a sister-in-law. We are nearly sisters already, aren't we?"

"But Hawksfield and I *aren't* engaged," Brynn said. "He was never even planning to press his suit."

Just his body and his mouth against my own, she thought to herself.

"The inquiry agent needn't know that," Eloise replied.

Brynn stared at her, at a loss for words to argue with her logic. "I don't see how this will help."

"If you were busy becoming engaged, neither of you could have been killing the duke, and that would account for both your whereabouts," she replied, whispering even lower as Archer and Thomson continued their back and forth inside the library. But Brynn wasn't paying attention to their words any longer. All she could hear were Eloise's: announce an engagement. To *Archer*.

"I… Hawksfield does not wish to be married," she said.

"Briannon, please. It doesn't mean you must carry through with it. You could cry off once the true murderer has been found. But right now, you are the only one who can clear away any suspicion Mr. Thomson harbors regarding my brother, especially if he was with *you* when my father was killed. Please," she said, her grip on Brynn's shoulders constricting. "Please, I can't lose the only family I have left."

Brynn's heart raced. What Eloise was suggesting made sense—an engagement would certainly diffuse Thomson's theory. But that wasn't what made her consider such a flimsy and mortifying plan—it was the simple fact that if Archer were under suspicion, it wouldn't be long before Mr. Thomson and the rest of Bow Street dug deeper and found evidence that could implicate Archer as the Masked Marauder.

Thomson had already made mention that morning of the marauder's most recent attacks, and even aligned them with the new duke's movements. A carriage waylaid on the way to

Worthington Abbey's Ball. Another carriage attacked after Archer had left the masquerade. Brynn recalled hearing about a third in the country before Archer returned to London, and just last night, another carriage stopped on a side street and robbed by the increasingly hostile criminal.

Thomson had seemed to be sniffing around a connection between the marauder and the duke, and what if he continued to align the other highwayman attacks with Archer's whereabouts? The way he'd spoken earlier that morning, about a need to bring the peerage down several notches so they may taste the reality of justice, stuck in the forefront of her mind. If he got so much as an inkling regarding Archer's secret, he would set on it like a rabid dog.

He would revel in the scandal that exposing Archer would cause. Poor Eloise could barely show her face in polite society as it was—a scandal like that would ruin her. Brynn's own honor, and her family's, could also be thrown into question if Thomson continued to suspect her. And if Archer were to go to the gallows…as infuriating as the man was, the thought of him being hanged was simply too much to bear.

Brynn took a deep breath, turned to Eloise, and nodded. "I'll do it," she said before her courage could desert her, and tiptoed back to the library door. Eloise shot her a grateful and encouraging look. Neither did much to calm her pounding heart and quivering legs. Or quiet the voice in her head that kept telling her how foolhardy this was.

"Thank you," Eloise mouthed.

Brynn nodded again and swung open the door before her mind could register that she'd taken complete leave of her senses.

"What *is* the nature of your relationship with Lady Briannon?" Mr. Thomson was asking.

"Darling, we are going to be late," she said loudly, and then pressed a hand to her lips in mock surprise as both heads swiveled toward her. She lowered her hand immediately when she saw it tremble. "I am so sorry. I didn't realize that you were still occupied."

To Archer's credit, his face remained inscrutable, although she could see a muscle twitching in his jaw—the only sign of any outward reaction to her sudden uninvited appearance. His eyes flashed a silver storm, but Brynn noted only how utterly exhausted he looked. Dark shadows congregated beneath his eyes, making his face look drawn and haunted. Despite his brutish kisses and the unexpected and confusing desire she felt for him each time, Brynn couldn't quell the immediate surge of compassion that filled her breast.

Eloise swept in behind her, and Archer's eyes flicked to his sister. They lightened a bit, Brynn noticed, but remained suspicious.

She, too, feigned surprise. "I thought Mr. Thomson had left, and I told Lady Briannon as much. I am deeply sorry, brother."

Brynn smiled as brightly as she could manage, and walked to Archer even though he was glowering at her. Her heart was tripping over itself, and she was sure her feet would follow suit, but they held steady, surprising her. Once she'd reached his side, she slid her clammy hand into his cold one. Archer stiffened, though she doubted the agent had observed it. Just in case, Brynn beamed an excessive smile for Mr. Thomson's benefit.

The man's face puckered into a frown as he took in Brynn and Archer's linked hands.

"Mr. Thomson, I am afraid I have not been quite honest with you," she began. The agent pinned her with a look of dawning victory. She nearly felt the need to apologize for being about to disappoint him.

"You see, I did not have my hem mended by a maid last evening—"

Archer took his hand from hers and turned to step in front of her. "Do not say anything more."

Brynn stepped aside so she could see the agent again and avoided Archer's eyes. "The truth is—"

"*Briannon,*" he growled, but she gathered one last shot of nerve and spoke over his voice, loudly enough for any servant passing in the hall to hear.

"We are engaged to be married. His Grace and I. As of last night."

Archer's entire body tensed like a coiled spring, and this time Mr. Thomson most certainly witnessed it. She could not look at Archer, though she could feel the astonished weight of his gaze upon her cheek.

"We met after dinner," Brynn went on, preferring to watch the inquiry agent's slowly narrowing stare than to risk a glance up at Archer. She would never be able to finish the lie if she did.

"We were alone when he proposed, and…well, I accepted, of course, and I know we should have rejoined the others straightaway, however—"

Thomson's cheeks flared red, and Brynn could no longer even look at him. Her good sense was returning, and it was sorely disappointed in her. Not for lying about the proposal, exactly, but for admitting to the improper rendezvous and planting a lurid picture in Mr. Thomson's astute mind. A picture that was, in all likelihood, entirely too factual for her comfort.

She flushed, her eyes catching on Eloise, who took her cue and rushed forward. "Isn't it lovely news? I have hoped to have Lady Briannon as a sister-in-law ever since we were children playing in our gardens."

Archer had not moved a muscle. He continued to stand with his back to Thomson, his eyes boring into the crown of Brynn's head.

"My father would have been happy," Eloise went on. "Despite the rumors of his own suit, he wanted only for his son's happiness." She reached for her handkerchief again, dabbing at the tears welling in her eyes. She had kept the veil up, Brynn noticed, and as Mr. Thomson glanced at her, he seemed to grow more agitated and uncomfortable.

"I am sorry for deceiving you," Brynn said. "But as you may have already determined, it was a delicate situation this morning, what with my parents present and the announcement of our engagement not yet made. We could not say anything last night…not with how the evening ended."

Mr. Thomson's eyebrow rose in disbelieving surprise. He shifted his attention to Archer's back. "Is this true, Your Grace?"

Archer held his statuesque stance, and Brynn noticed his hands were clenched into white-knuckled fists.

For a long, agonizing moment Archer withheld his answer. She feared the worst—that he would spin around and declare it all a lie. That he would make her look like a fool and out her as a desperate deceiver. Could he have been so utterly repulsed by her bold and ridiculous tale—all in an attempt to help *him*? Her insides twisted, flashing hot and cold, until she thought she might see black stars cross her vision.

But then she felt his hand slip back into hers. It grounded her, his palm a shade warmer this time. "You dare question the lady's integrity?" Archer's voice was terse but resonant. His grip tightened to a near stranglehold as he turned to face Mr. Thomson, giving his back to Brynn now. She forced herself to breathe in a normal manner. "Of course it is true."

Mr. Thomson cleared his throat. "Then why did you not say—"

"I am a gentleman. Risking the reputation of my betrothed simply to make nice with you is far beneath my character," Archer said, his hand still encasing hers. "Really, I took you for a somewhat intelligent man, Thomson."

Mr. Thomson nodded and wrote something in his little notebook. "I'm afraid I have taken up too much of your time today, Your Grace. May I be the first to congratulate you on your forthcoming nuptials. I will be in touch should anything arise."

"Please, allow me to show you out," Eloise said, glancing at her brother with a faint frown. "I'll return shortly."

Brynn didn't exhale until Eloise and Mr. Thomson had disappeared from view and their footsteps had faded down the hallway, toward the front door.

Finally, Archer's grip relaxed. He dropped her hand the way a scullery maid might drop a dead mouse. She took a few steps away while shaking out her numbed fingers, a sudden desire for self-preservation falling over her. Archer still had his back to her. She had yet to look into his eyes since announcing their engagement to the inquiry agent, but she sensed bridled anger emanating from his broad frame.

My god. What on earth have I done?

Brynn checked the library door, but Eloise had not returned. Nor would she, Brynn imagined, if the girl was wise. Brynn, too, wanted nothing more than to slink away toward the door without Archer turning to see her escape.

She held her place by a silk slipper chair. She had too much dignity to go slinking out of rooms.

"I can imagine what you must be thinking," she began, needing to say something. Anything other than this silence and tension, building into something ugly and solid.

The wall of his back dissolved as he turned to face her. With a shaky breath, Brynn raised her eyes to his and braced herself for the onslaught of his anger.

Her preparation wasn't enough.

The driving pressure of Archer's stare pushed her back a step. Her legs hit the slipper chair and, without an ounce of grace, she plopped onto the cushion.

"You cannot begin to imagine what it is I am thinking," he said, his voice lower than a growl. It sounded like thunder, trapped in a glass jar.

In that moment, Brynn could think only one thing—she had made a terrible, *terrible* mistake.

Chapter Seventeen

Archer stared at the tempestuous beauty before him, watching her chin hike an inch as she fought to stare him down. He struggled to control his rapidly swelling anger, along with another sharper sensation spreading through him at the welcome sight of her.

Brynn's color was high, her chest falling and rising with each shallow breath. She had yet to remove her cloak and hat, and he wondered at Heed's lack of duty.

Unless she had not entered through the front door and crossed Heed's path.

Archer narrowed his gaze, but his mind was too occupied at the moment to consider anything other than the startling lie Brynn had just spouted off to Thomson and Eloise.

What that lie was currently doing to him confused and infuriated in equal measure. Archer ground his teeth and curled his lip in response to the overwhelming union of anticipation and panic.

Brynn's eyes fluttered wider at his expression. The girl had to be terrified, and yet she refused to cower. Archer admired that about her—that fiery stubbornness that had made her stand up to him when he'd taken her coach along Worthington Abbey's tree-darkened lane. It was the same emotion now making her back ramrod straight and her eyes spark with defiance.

God, he wanted to take her into his arms and crush her body to his. He wanted to feel her resistance melt under his touch.

He also wanted to put her over his knee.

Archer resorted to walking to the side mantel to pour himself a liberal drink. He glanced over his shoulder when he spoke. "I must have addled your brain last night. I recall kisses, my lady, while you seem to recall a proposal."

Shame flashed over her features before it was replaced by a detached smile. "Do not be obtuse. It was only a ploy to focus Mr. Thomson elsewhere. I overheard what he was saying."

"You overheard," he repeated. He peered at her once more from over his shoulder and saw her wither slightly beneath his glare.

She took a deep breath and fell into a whisper. "I didn't mean to eavesdrop if that is what you are thinking. I overheard a small part of the conversation, nothing more. His theories about what occurred last night. He was intent on placing one or both of us in the duke's study."

"He cannot arrest either of us when all he has are *theories*," Archer cut in, his hand trembling with frustration. He set the glass down without taking a sip. "What are you doing here, Lady Briannon?"

He heard her take a breath at his excessive politeness as if to calm her simmering temper. "I was followed earlier, to Madame Despain's on Bond Street."

He faced her then, a frown drawing his brows together. "Are you certain?"

She nodded. "And so when I heard Mr. Thomson suggesting that we both had something to do with the duke's murder, well…we both required an alibi, and you must admit, it is—at least in part—the truth." She finished in a rush, as if she had to get out the words before Archer interrupted her.

Someone had been trailing Brynn? Spying on her? Not Thomson, but perhaps one of his informants. Some street urchin he paid to track a suspect and deliver anything of interest. The idea that some stranger was following her took his anger to a new height.

He turned and picked up his drink, needing it more than before. "It was a reckless and rash decision, Brynn. I was five seconds from tossing him out into the street."

"He would have come back, and perhaps next time, with something more than a theory."

"Something more?" He faced her again. "Explain."

She started to work the clasps of her cloak at her neck, clearly feeling the same increased warmth in the room. "Mr. Thomson," she paused, eyeing the library door. He watched with hooded eyes as she padded over to the door and closed it. Then, continuing in barely a whisper, "Mr. Thomson is one of Bow Street's finest, and he has a thorn in his side regarding the peerage. If he delves any further into the connections he's already been drawing between the Masked Marauder and your whereabouts, don't you think he will ferret out what you have been doing all this time?"

The short burst of frustrated anger surprised Archer. His hand stalled in midair, his drink arrested halfway to his lips. "He is reaching. I have been meticulous."

If possible, the ire in her eyes rose until they ignited with repressed fury. "Oh, this is hopeless! You make it impossible to help you."

"If lying about a betrothal was your idea of helping, I do not want to know how you might plan to injure."

Brynn came toward him, her skirts swishing loudly as she approached. "Have you no sense at all? The marauder is all anyone in London can think and talk about. The duke's murder, the items missing from his person and study, they are going to be connected to the bandit! And Thomson is positively frothing at the mouth to capture him. You and your bloody secret activities are going to get you hanged!"

Archer was taken aback at her tirade, although he kept his face carefully composed. Few men ever dared stand up to him as she was doing now, and certainly no women. Then again, Brynn was not most women. He recalled expressing the same sentiments to her in Essex. Her eyes sparked and her mouth trembled as she berated him. He had never met such a passionate creature, and Archer felt an indescribable urge to match that passion. To kiss her senseless.

"It is my neck, my lady," he said instead, taking another sip of his whiskey. "And I have every intention of keeping it at its current length."

"Yes, well, if a false betrothal keeps Bow Street from suspecting me of murder, it is a price I will gladly pay. I thought, for a man of your intelligence, you would have appreciated the merit in it as well."

She had not yet managed to undo the clasp of her cloak, and had, every few seconds, removed her hands from their task to wave them about in the air. Right then, she was working the clasp again, and once more, unsuccessfully.

"I have put my reputation, my honor, on the line by coming here," she muttered. "I have lied to an investigator. *Twice.* I have…I have…what are you doing?"

Archer had placed his drink down and taken several purposeful steps toward her.

"Stay where you are," she warned.

Archer didn't listen. He crossed the distance between them while Brynn glanced around, as if searching for ways to escape his approach. He felt like a wolf prowling closer to its prey, and it was a heady sensation.

Archer stared down at her, trying to stifle the sudden realization that she had done much the same to him. Only, instead of a wolf, Brynn had been a fox, nicely and cleverly trapping him.

He had no choice but to go along with this farce now, or risk looking like a liar to Thomson. And as stunned as he'd been when she had burst in here before, unannounced, he'd also known denying her claims or disagreeing with the lady would have been unforgivably offensive. So now here he was—engaged to a virtual innocent via an offer of marriage he had not extended.

Well and truly ensnared.

Archer cursed under his breath. It was a damn sticky turn of events. He had to hand it to her, though—she was either a brilliant schemer, or she had the luck of the devil himself. He couldn't extricate himself if he tried, not without damaging her reputation and dragging more attention to himself in the process.

He was willing to bet Brynn knew it, as well.

Archer reached for her cloak clasps. She jerked away, but his hands were faster. They closed around the buttons.

"What are you doing?"

"Helping you out of your cloak," he replied, slipping the first of the four clasps free. "Something Heed would have done had you entered my home through the front door and not, where? The kitchens?"

She lifted her chin again, holding still this time, though more out of annoyance than gratitude.

"The ballroom," she answered. "Eloise saw me in."

She glanced toward the doors, the very ones she had closed. Hoping for Eloise's return, he was sure. His sister would not come, though. Instinct would keep her away.

Archer worked the next three buttons quickly and then walked behind Brynn to pull the cloak from her shoulders. As the velvet slid away, her clean, fresh spring scent hit him. The confusion and irritation of the last several minutes cleared, and all he could focus on was the exposed skin along the slope of her neck. Her sunset gold hair had been coiled up high, a few loose tendrils left to tickle the tops of her shoulders. Archer came back to stand in front of her.

"Thank you," she whispered and began to step away.

His hand moved of its own volition, capturing her fingers with his. She stilled with a small, sharp breath as he raised her hand. Before she could speak, he gently tugged the tip of one gloved finger. The dark gray silk slipped like butter, loosening around her other fingers. He pinched the tip of another finger and tugged again. He wanted to see her hands. Wanted to slide his palm against hers.

Her chest heaved. "Please, sir, this is highly—"

"*Sir?*" Archer echoed. He wouldn't let himself be swayed by her guileless innocence. It had to be an act. Enough women had thrown themselves at him over the years for him to recognize chicanery when it was being flaunted in his face. No one could be as innocent as she pretended to be and manage to arouse this kind of inebriating lust inside him. *No one.*

"This is hardly a proper time or place," Brynn said, her breath coming shorter as he finished sliding her silk glove from her hand. He laid it upon the closest surface—the back of a chair—and lifted her bared hand to his mouth, turning it palm up at the last moment.

He watched her closely as he pressed his lips to the inside of her wrist. Her eyes stared in shocked wonder at his mouth as it caressed the petal-soft skin there. Her lips parted as he touched his tongue to her pulse, but the intake of breath he heard was not one of revulsion.

"My lord, you cannot," she protested, but there was none

of her usual strength behind the half-formed command.

"Can't a man kiss his betrothed?" he asked.

Or at least sample what he'd been inadvertently coerced into.

"You may not." She stepped backward, pulling her hand from his as if sensing the leashed anger that snaked beneath the surface of his outwardly calm exterior.

He followed her movement, keeping a thin amount of space between them. A hot rush of color bloomed in her cheeks as she shifted one more desperate look to the door. Archer advanced, and she retreated again, until she had backed up against the wall. A smile tugged at the corner of his lips at the irony of it.

"Tell me, my lady, how does it feel to be trapped?"

"Whatever do you mean? I have not trapped you in any way." Brynn's flush deepened, and Archer almost smiled—she truly was a magnificent actress.

"If that is the game you want to play," he said, drawing ever closer. "I am willing to match it."

Her lip trembled. "Lord Hawksfield…Your Grace, you must not…we mustn't. You cannot."

"Cannot what?" He braced his hands against the wall at either side of her head.

"Look at me like that," she said.

"And how is that?"

She raised limpid eyes to his, making him want to eliminate the remaining space and the pretense between them. "Like you want indecent things."

She licked her lips, drawing his gaze there.

"So sweet," he murmured, trailing his hand along her downy cheek. His thumb tugged her full lower lip, and her eyelids grew heavy. "Or are you just a woman in search of a prize and a title?"

She blinked, alert again. "I beg your par—"

He silenced her with his lips, claiming her open mouth with his.

Brynn's entire body went slack, but not with desire. With indignation. He could see it in the flash of her eyes, and her sudden, controlled lack of response. It infuriated him, but he released her mouth. They stood in charged silence, her breaths coming in short, frantic bursts as she stared at him.

"I do not desire a title," she said in a clipped tone. "And you would be the last thing I would consider a prize."

Archer's thumb grazed her smooth chin. "Is that so?"

"Yes."

His knuckles reached forward to skim the underside of her chin and the velvet column of her throat, his voice a murmur. "You could have fooled me."

Oddly, Brynn made no move to extricate herself from his embrace, but instead continued to regard him with a measured, assessing glance, as though trying to separate his cruel words from his tender touch. It felt like she could see right through him, and her thoughtful perusal made Archer want to kiss her again.

Giving in to the desire, he bent his head slowly, allowing her the time to pull away if she so chose. However, other than a sharp intake of breath, Brynn did not move. She met the tentative pressure of his kiss, and within moments, he found himself being seduced by the sweet warmth of her mouth. With infinite care, he plied her with expert and confident nudges, tracing his tongue along the seam of her lips. When she gave in, it was with a sigh and a shy moan that traveled through his blood and instantly made him tight with desire.

Brynn was soft and responsive under his mouth and hands, and she tasted like the sun shining through rain. How easy it would be to give himself over to the lust coming to a head inside him. It would take little effort to block out the rest of the world and simply let their mutual attraction run its course. His feverish thirst to bury himself deep inside her until he found release was as appalling as it was arousing, so much so that his lips and tongue could hardly keep pace with his lewd fantasies. And yes, as she had said, they were indecent.

They involved the lady, the boundary of her skirts removed, every inch of her bared to him and spread out upon his bed like a feast. Brynn drove him senseless, moaning in his arms as if she, too, craved the release that only one thing could bring. But his bed was not here. All they had was a carpeted floor. And not nearly enough privacy.

Bracing one hand on the wall, his body pressed against hers, his other hand slid up her side. The feel of her was utterly drugging, and it had tossed his senses—and reason—to the wind. His palm skimmed up the fine wool dress, and without a moment's hesitation, he cupped her breast boldly through the material. She leaned into his hand with a whimper as his tongue continued to tease hers in a torturous rhythm.

Archer's mouth slanted on hers with relentless urgency as he succumbed to the need building deep in his core. She was not immune, either. Brynn trembled against him, her body coming alive in his embrace. Moaning against his lips, her hands slid around his neck, anchoring herself to him. With a muffled growl, Archer drew her closer, lost in a dizzying haze of passion, though a small, logical voice within him warned that he was going too far.

Just one more sweet taste, he thought, *and I will stop*.

Archer drew his mouth across her cheek to her ear, sucking the velvet lobe into his mouth. Her head fell back, and his lips found her throat, his hands roving in restless hunger over her body. He caressed the length of her spine before returning to graze her flat stomach. His hands drifted upward to tug on the square neckline of her dress, drawing down one sleeve from her shoulder and baring a breast to his greedy gaze.

She was even more perfect than he had imagined—her skin like cream, petal soft, and tipped by a rosy nipple. He lowered his head and closed his mouth over the silken point. She gasped against him, her fingers tangling in his hair. Archer fought for control, nearly as lost as she was. The voice inside his head warned that he was taking advantage of her innocence, but he could not slow down; could not help himself, especially not when Brynn was so pliant in his arms, bewitched by the same sensual spell ensnaring him.

His tongue swirled around the tip of her breast, and then he suckled it deep. Baring the second with an easy tug on the gown's neckline, Archer licked and nudged his way across the fragrant valley to lavish the same attention on her other breast. He wanted to make her moan his name. Damn, she was perfect. Her breasts were everything he had fantasized and more—full, lissome, and delectable.

Drawing her to him, he sought her lips again, consuming her sweetness with the hunger of a deprived man. His tongue reached deep and withdrew in an explicit rhythm, and Archer crushed her hips to his. He ground the bulging evidence of his arousal against her.

Brynn's eyes snapped wide at the intimate contact. Something flared in them, and she pushed wildly against his chest. Had he frightened her with his ardor? Archer inched his hips away, watching as her eyes dropped for one fleeting look before skittering away, a fiery blush suffusing her already heated cheeks. He grinned at her sudden shyness. If he had his way, there would be no barriers between them, least of all clothing.

But in a moment of delayed clarity, he knew he should stop before his sister returned from seeing Thomson out and Briannon's dignity was irretrievably shattered. Reluctantly, he tugged her bodice back in place. He pressed a swift kiss to her mouth, his tongue sweeping in for one last sweet taste. With a groan, he pulled away from her as she opened bemused, stunned eyes the color of stormy jade.

"You are full of surprises, my lady," he remarked, straightening his back and putting a sliver of space between their bodies. Brynn inhaled sharply, looking as if she'd just been doused with a bucket of icy water.

She did not respond. The only thing that broke the electric silence between them was the soft cadence of her breathing. She licked her lips, the action unconsciously seductive. Archer couldn't help himself. He bent his head toward her, only to be stopped by the push of her hands against his chest. She turned her lips away, her voice a mortified whisper. "Please, you have to stop. Lady Eloise will be back at any moment."

"We are engaged, are we not?" he said, inexplicably irritated at having started this in the library instead of in his rooms. He nudged her chin back toward him. "And Eloise has seen enough closed doors to know what they mean."

She froze at his overtly suggestive words, her face flaming again. "You are not a gentleman," she whispered in an accusatory tone.

"I never claimed to be."

Her eyes flared, flashing fire for a moment before lowering. If looks could kill, he would be floating in the Serpentine. Before Archer could guess her intent, she ducked beneath his outstretched arm and walked briskly to the door. He frowned at her tight-lipped expression, confused by her swift change in demeanor.

"I am certain that His Grace has been behind more than enough closed doors," she said in a mocking tone. "I, however, have not. And I beg you to find it within yourself not to dishonor either of us any further than I already have by coming here. I bid you good evening."

Archer should have let her go and be done with it. But the glimmer of shocked hurt in her eyes made him hesitate. He had thought her a schemer, but now doubt leached through him. Despite his own accusations, he couldn't believe she was "out to catch a duke." If that were the case, she would have fallen at his father's feet as every other title seeker had for the past decade, regardless of his advanced age. But *why* had she gone to such lengths, then? Unless she truly had come here and stormed into Thomson's interrogation out of some selfless, if inane, desire to save him.

He scrubbed his hand over his cheek, a bedlam of emotions raging through him. He'd been more than angry that he had been caught in her ruse, but the intensity of what they had just shared had been as staggering to him as it had been to her. His blood still raced from the heat of it. And now, the truth was, he didn't want her to leave. Not like this.

"Please, don't go," he said quietly.

He watched her hand stall on the doorknob, her body shaking. Her lip trembled as her eyes lifted to his. Her face flushed with embarrassment, and he wanted nothing more than to pull her back into his arms and kiss away the hurt he'd put there. Archer felt like a fool for letting his guard down whenever Brynn entered his presence. She made him forget himself, forget his detachment, forget that the only female company he sought was to warm his bed, nothing more. The woman made him consider dangerous things, and the ludicrous engagement was the most dangerous of all. She had risked much coming here unescorted and admitting to being alone with him last night. As it stood, she was caught in this diversion as much as he was. If she doubted herself and called off the betrothal now, it would not bode well for either of them.

He cleared his throat. "I do not intend to dishonor you, Brynn, and let me assure you, you have done nothing more than impress me." Her fingers clenched on the doorknob. She was fighting him—he could see it. "It may have been rash coming in here and saying what you did, but it was also bold. It is also done, so let us discuss it rationally."

He took a deep breath and said the words he never thought he'd say. "If this betrothal is the course we must pursue, then there are some things that we need to speak about." He held up his hands in surrender. "I promise to keep my distance, if that helps you make your decision."

She met his eyes evenly, and Archer almost grinned at her display of pride. He didn't, however. She would likely view it as condescension on his part. God, she was beautiful when she was angry.

"I don't have much longer before I am discovered missing from Bishop House."

Archer strode to the door and signaled to a waiting footman. "Please ring for Lady Eloise. And bring two glasses of sherry for the ladies."

He took a seat on the sofa and invited Brynn to do the same. The sherry arrived before Eloise.

"I do not wish to be married," he said bluntly as soon as the footman left.

"You've made that abundantly clear," she replied.

He nodded. "But neither of us can deny that there is something between us."

"If you say so."

He stared at Brynn, a lingering, slow look that swept from the top of her head to her breasts to the hands that rested neatly folded in her lap.

"I do."

She blushed fiercely, but set her lips and stared him down with her frostiest glare. "That is neither here nor there. Physical attraction has nothing to do with anything. It is lust, nothing more." She didn't even flinch at the vulgarity of her language. If she was trying to shock him, it would take more than a few choice words. He took a sip of his drink, his gaze mocking. She tore her eyes away. "And if you touch me again, you'll be lucky if you escape this *situation* with your neck unscathed, I promise you."

Eloise entered, her apprehensive gaze drifting between the two of them like a frightened bird. Archer was quick to put her at ease with a gentle smile. He noticed that Brynn did the same, patting the empty seat beside her as she hastily composed herself.

"Thank you, Eloise, for joining us," he said. "I will be brief. Neither Lady Briannon nor I wish to be married. However, it appears that this charade has become a necessity."

"Brother—"

"Hear me out," he said in a businesslike tone. "Despite my reluctance, I will agree to this engagement for now, at least so that we can focus on finding the real killer, which means we will have to post banns and have an official announcement in the papers. I doubt my father will care if we break tradition to hunt down a murderer considering how much he loathed mourning. We shall be forced to see this farce through to the end if we are to be successful."

"This farce is as much an inconvenience for me as it is for you," Brynn glowered. He stared at her, but said nothing. Lady Briannon was turning out to be unlike any other woman he had ever known—infuriating and maddening to the point of distraction.

"And we must plan an engagement ball," Eloise was saying, her voice meek as if sensing his black mood. Archer stared at her grimly, but nodded. A ball was a natural event to follow such an announcement, despite the late duke's death and society's expectations.

"Will you not go into mourning?" Brynn asked wide-eyed.

"It was not the duke's wish," he replied mildly. "My father was...unorthodox."

"I am happy to begin the preparations," Eloise added.

"May I suggest a masquerade?"

"It is *de rigueur* this season," Brynn said with a smile, her tone holding none of the anger it had moments before — anger he knew was directed solely at him. Archer couldn't help noticing his sister's grateful look. They both knew that she would enjoy the ball more if she wasn't the only one covering her face.

"Lovely," Eloise said. "We could always say you fell in love at a masquerade. The Gainsbridge one…if anyone asks, I mean…" She trailed off in uncomfortable silence.

Archer frowned. His sister was an incurable romantic, but there would be no talk of love. Marriages in the *ton* occurred for reasons of convenience, just as this one would. However, instead of a title or a fortune, the matter of convenience happened to be his neck.

"Let's not get ahead of ourselves," he said. "Anything else?"

"You will need to speak with my father," Brynn said. "Although he will be the least of our problems. In the wake of the late duke's death, I fear that an announcement of our betrothal will draw more attention than necessary."

Archer nodded again. "I will attend to your father as soon as possible. As far as attention goes, that would have happened regardless. I have been particularly vocal in my desire not to wed, but should I be interrogated on the matter, I shall simply say that it was my late father's wish."

"And the killer?" Brynn asked.

"Leave that to me. I do have some suspicions of my own, which I will investigate."

"Do you think it was the Masked Marauder?" Eloise asked in a small voice. "I have heard that he is in London."

Archer and Brynn exchanged a swift glance.

"It bears looking into," Archer said. "But we must be vigilant. It could be anyone, and we don't know that the duke was the target. The target could have been me, and the duke was simply in the wrong place at the wrong time."

"Why would it have been you?" Eloise asked, frowning, and Archer realized that he had almost slipped up.

"His Grace has also been particularly vocal in his efforts to find the masked bandit, particularly after the attack on Lord Maynard," Brynn interjected. "Perhaps the killer simply wanted to put an end to a possible threat."

"That makes sense." Eloise's face scrunched up, her hands trembling. "What if he comes back? To finish what he intended to do?"

The imposter had put that terror in his sister's eyes. It made Archer want to catch the bastard even more. "He won't have another chance. You are safe here."

"Promise me you will be careful. I can't lose you, too."

Archer reassured her with a fond smile. "I promise."

"I should be getting back," Brynn said. "Before my absence ruins any chance of this scheme being launched."

"Allow me to escort you home," Archer said, standing. "I will attend to your father, if possible, at the same time just in case he is questioned by an overexcited Thomson."

"I'd rather return alone and prepare myself. Perhaps you can arrive in time for dinner."

Archer nodded, watching the two women leave the room. It would be better if he called upon Brynn as a gentleman, instead of returning her home in some sly, scandalous fashion. He couldn't help feeling that his life suddenly seemed as if it were no longer his. On the other hand, he wanted her, and she wanted him. He curled his fingers around his glass, his body tightening at the memory of her dewy skin and how it had tasted. He was glad that the glass was thick crystal or it would have shattered in his hand.

Disgust and lust spiraled through him like twin demons. He lifted his drink and drained the contents, silently toasting his last few hours of uncomplicated freedom.

Chapter Eighteen

Brynn was already at Hadley Gardens when the guests started to arrive. She waited in a guest room on the second floor, perhaps even the one she had dipped into that awful night one week prior. She listened now as muffled voices drifted from the foyer.

"This is never going to work," she muttered.

Lana stood behind her, placing the last of the pins in Brynn's upswept hair. The set of four had been delivered to Bishop House the day before from the exclusive Rundell and Bridge, jewelers to the crown. Inside the box, the hairpins had been nestled on a bed of lapis blue silk, each one topped with a diamond-crusted bird, the wings on all four in a different position.

The accompanying note had brought a sad smile to Brynn's lips.

Make certain you do not fly away before the ball.

Archer must have known how desperately she wished to fly away, and that had made her smile. But knowing that he, too, likely wanted to fly away had brought on a wave of sadness. It underscored the pretense. Deep down, Brynn knew that his gifts and little notes were all part of a show for her parents and brother. For anyone who might be watching closely.

It had been a whirlwind of a week, starting with a funeral and now ending with an engagement ball. Even another attack on a side street off Piccadilly by the Masked Marauder had not dampened the *ton*'s excitement swirling around the new Duke of Bradburne. That attack had left the driver of the carriage with a broken arm and the lady riding within, not a peer but a member of the gentry, scandalized. The papers had run the story saying she had been riding alone and that the bandit had "handled her person" with all the care of "a wild boar." It seemed that the imposter was growing bolder and more vicious with each attack.

"Don't fret, my lady," Lana whispered, closing the box from Rundell and Bridge and primping Brynn's hair once more. "It *is* going to work."

She had told Lana everything—except for the truth about Archer being the masked bandit—and like always, Brynn had not felt judged by her in the least. Brynn had wanted to tell Gray the truth, as well, but his reaction to the marriage banns the day after Thomson's questioning had stopped her from confiding. He hadn't been at all pleased by the turn of events.

"He's not good enough for you," Gray had stated flatly. "How could you possibly accept him?"

"I know it's difficult to understand," she'd tried to explain, the rest of her excuse still unformed.

"It's not difficult at all. He is now a duke, is he not?" Gray had replied, his gaze searching hers and looking disappointed in what they saw. "I know what I told you. That a duke could offer you luxury at the pinnacle of society... I just never thought you would be so shallow as to take it."

The accusation had been gutting, but she couldn't fault

him for thinking it. Nor could she confess it was a sham. She knew that Gray was simply concerned for her well-being, but his response had hurt. Brynn hated remembering the aghast look on his face and had attempted all week to forget it by focusing on the plans for the engagement ball. The season had barely gotten underway, and already the prized bull—the new, young and handsome Duke of Bradburne—had been whisked off the marriage mart. Everyone, it seemed, had so easily forgotten his reputation as the brooding and ruthless Marquess of Hawksfield. The cold, unsmiling recluse had been touched by tragedy and now love, and along with his new title, had a new following of admirers.

The announcement of their betrothal had created a flurry of activity as she had expected, with invitations to every possible social event appearing on their doorsteps. They had had to decline more than they could accept out of respect for the late duke, but it seemed everyone wanted to celebrate their forthcoming nuptials in spite of the rumble of disapproval that Archer and Eloise weren't honoring the usual mourning period. Between planning her own ball and with turning away a constant stream of visitors and well-wishers, Brynn was already overwhelmed.

It made the farce all the more horrible to bear. Because Archer had not changed in the least. Like a proper doting fiancé, he sent her jewelry and flowers, and he smiled whenever he was in the same room as Brynn's mother and father, but that same distant chill was present whenever someone wasn't looking. He didn't attempt to hide it from her, no. He blasted her with that wintry expression nearly every time they saw each other, as if she were the scheming mastermind of some hideous plot to trap him into marriage. Brynn fumed. He'd be the last person on earth she'd choose, even if his touch made her forget herself.

For the most part, he'd kept his distance as promised, and

thankfully, they had not been alone since that afternoon in the library, when Archer had peeled off her glove and kissed her wrist…when he had trapped her against the wall and thrust his hips against hers, divulging his arousal. She'd imagined, all too vividly, of course, what she'd glimpsed by the firelight of that small forest cottage.

The memory of his searing kisses in the library and his touch made her weak-kneed. His kiss—his *mouth*—had branded her to the bone. No man had ever made her feel the way he did, as if her entire body lay at the center of the sun. Even now, her lips tingled. Brynn's breath came in quick spurts, shame flooding her cheeks with hot, violent color.

"Do you feel ill, my lady?" Lana asked with a concerned look, rousing Brynn from her disturbing thoughts.

"No. It's a little warm, that's all," she said, fanning herself vigorously.

"Well, you look lovely with some color in your cheeks," Lana commented.

Brynn grimaced. If Lana only knew what had caused her to flush so, she would be shocked. She stood up from the vanity and felt the dress she wore pull on her shoulders as if it had been made of lead and not layers of deep green satin with a black lace overlay. The square-cut bodice hung low, and wide bell sleeves trimmed in black lace edging extended down to her wrists. Tapered in at her waist and falling in graceful folds to the floor, the gown was exquisitely made. She should have felt beautiful wearing it, but Brynn felt only hollow.

"I feel like such a fraud," she said, her gloved fingers touching her neck where a necklace of priceless and gorgeously set diamonds rested. "As if I am not here at all." She sighed and adjusted the stunning tiered necklace at her throat.

"Well, I can see you, and you are lovely," Lana replied. Then, after studying her with a critical eye, her lower lip caught between her teeth, she said, "The rubies would go so well with this gown. Much better than those diamonds, I think."

Brynn stared at her maid. Lana certainly had proven to have an eye for turning out the perfect pairing of gowns and jewels, but sometimes Brynn caught a hint of something else—Lana spoke as if she were personally familiar with such adornments, which made little sense, Brynn knew. She'd have to agree with her in this instance, though. She would have chosen the rubies over the diamonds herself. They made her feel bold and confident, and she needed that feeling tonight more than ever before.

And Archer had given them to her.

He had given them to her with far more honesty than he had these ridiculous heirloom diamonds. The necklace itself felt like an immense jeweled shackle, unlike the rubies that he had sent her under another guise. It was as if Archer were two different people—the aloof duke with a stone heart and the bandit rogue with a velvet touch. And she seemed to be trapped directly between them. It still did not feel real, and with every passing day, the confession he'd made to her felt more and more distant. They could not discuss it, of course, until they were alone again.

And being alone with him had its dangers.

"The diamonds are truly stunning, though, my lady," Lana said. She had been tiptoeing around Brynn all week, especially after Brynn's quarrel with Gray. She must have guessed how awful it was for her to not be able to confide in Gray…how much it was tearing her apart to keep secrets from him.

"They're too much, and you know it," Brynn replied, catching a look from Lana in the mirror. She was smothering her grin and trying to hide behind Brynn's frame.

They were Archer's grandmother's diamonds, and there were plenty of people among tonight's guests who would remember the spectacular necklace. They were, after all, quite…unforgettable. But they weren't hers—they were the belongings of the past Bradburne duchesses, a role that she was now expected to step into. Brynn swallowed, her hand fluttering to her side. The diamonds winked in the light, and their icy color made her miss the fiery rubies all the more.

Lana squeezed her shoulders, bare thanks to the low cut of her gown. "It's time," she whispered. Brynn's entire body felt numb all over, and Lana shot her a fierce look. "Hold your head high, my mother always used to say. Don't let them see what you do not give them permission to see." She smiled at Brynn's blank expression and tilted up her chin so that her profile became instantly regal. "Like so. You are to become a duchess. Let them see the duchess."

Brynn frowned at Lana's unexpected and thoroughly profound advice, but couldn't dwell on it, as she was ushered from the room in a swish of skirts. Archer and her parents would already be downstairs, mingling with the first wash of guests, and Brynn was expected to make a grand entrance before too long a time had passed.

She walked through the hallways until she came to the set of Palladian stairs that led into the ballroom. She stopped at the top of the stairs and drew a strangled breath, glancing down. The ballroom had been transformed into a magical paradise. Guests wearing gowns of every imaginable color twirled on the dance floor with their equally impeccably dressed partners. Thousands of shimmering candles in gleaming chandeliers cast the ballroom in an ethereal glow, while bouquets of fresh flowers dotted the room and dewy rose petals littered the floor.

She exhaled. This was it.

Lana handed her a stunning jade and obsidian Venetian mask, and mouthed *be the duchess* once more. Brynn nodded, her gloved fingers resting along the cool marble of the balustrade. She tilted her chin as Lana had demonstrated and took the first step.

Heads in the ballroom below swiveled upward as she descended. Her eyes sought those of her family at its base—her mother's proud ones, her father's already misty ones, Gray's accusatory ones—before searching for those belonging to her unwilling fiancé.

Archer's back was to her. He appeared to be in conversation with a young man she recognized behind his demi mask as the handsome Earl of Langlevit, and Brynn was inordinately grateful for the reprieve. Her breath calmed, and she relaxed her death grip on the curving handrail. As she descended, conversation in the room slowed and stilled, and as the earl inclined his head in an admiring bow, Archer finally turned.

She stood frozen on the last step, her emotions swelling in her chest. The sight of Archer took her breath away. He was not wearing a mask, which made her smile. It was so like him to go against convention. Dressed in immaculate superfine, his midnight-blue tailored evening clothes fit his broad frame superbly. The snowy white cloth of his cravat and shirt contrasted sharply with the tanned skin at his throat. But it was his eyes that held Brynn immobile. They glinted with unmistakable possessiveness, claiming ownership with a single sweeping glance that made her treasonous body tremble from head to toe. She steeled herself—it was an act, she knew.

To everyone else in the room, the duke appeared to be gazing at his bride-to-be in fond, proud appreciation. But Brynn knew better. Only she could see the layer of ice that lay behind those eyes. *It is all a pretense,* she reminded herself. Remembering Lana's words, she jutted her chin and pushed a radiant smile to her lips.

As if a spell was broken, Archer strode swiftly to her side and offered her his arm. She placed a gloved hand upon it, and cheers broke throughout the ballroom. Brynn's breath caught as he bent his head toward her, a waft of his spicy cologne tickling her nose. Even if it were an act, the full dazzling force of his charm made her legs feel unsound. She peered at him from behind the mask she held aloft inches from her face, wondering for the hundredth time what she had gotten herself into. "You look lovely tonight, Lady Briannon, but I am sure you are aware of that fact."

"Thank you, Your Grace," she murmured as they strolled around the ballroom, accepting congratulations and bidding greetings to close family and friends. Her mama hugged her, her face already streaked with tears, and her father looked like he was on the verge of the same. She searched for Gray, but he had disappeared. Although his absence made her heart ache, she determined to find him later. Her brother would have to get used to the idea or risk embarrassing them both. He was truly too stubborn and protective for his own good, but Gray had to trust that she was a grown woman capable of making her own decisions, especially where matters of the heart were concerned.

Brynn almost gasped at her own gaffe. This charade was nowhere near a matter of the heart. It was a business agreement, nothing more.

Guests raised their glasses in toasts to their future health and happiness, interspersed with sadder ones that expressed how tragic it was that the late duke could not be here. Archer took them all in stride with unfailing courtesy.

Eloise approached and greeted Lord and Lady Dinsmore before turning to her. "Lady Briannon, you light up the room with your presence."

"As do you." Brynn smiled and embraced her friend. Eloise's color was high, no doubt due to the Earl of Langlevit, who couldn't seem to take his eyes off her. She was radiant in a silver dress that shimmered with every movement. A sheer white silk mask covered her face with glittering sequined plumes wound into her hair. She fairly sparkled. "You've outdone yourself, Eloise," Brynn told her, waving a hand at the whimsical and elegant decor. "This is truly magnificent."

Eloise leaned in, pride in her handiwork evident. "I meant what I said about wanting you for a sister. I wouldn't have gone through this much effort otherwise." Brynn's stomach clenched at the thread of hope in her voice. But Eloise's hope was a fruitless one, as was hers. This ball was as real as Archer's proposal.

She darted a glance up to the implacable man at her side who was in conversation with Viscount Carlisle, and exhaled. His face could be chiseled from the same marble as the elegant staircase. A smile was fixed on his lips, but it did not touch his eyes. Those remained detached and indifferent as if he wanted to be anywhere but here. Brynn had to remind herself that this was an inconvenience to him. *She* was an inconvenience to him. The awareness of that made her feel small and acutely insignificant.

After a moment, Archer signaled to the musicians to begin, and he led her out for the first waltz of the night. His hand slid around her waist, resting like a brand against her back, and Brynn trembled. She stared at his neck cloth, her feet automatically taking the steps. "Damn it, look at me," he hissed. "At least pretend that you want to be here."

Her eyes met his, fury sparking at his unprovoked attack. Her fingers tightened on his sleeve. "As you've done thus far?" she snapped back.

She gazed over Archer's shoulder and finally saw her brother. He stood on the periphery watching them with ill-concealed misgiving. He, too, was not wearing a mask. For Gray's sake, she pasted a bright smile on her lips.

"Happy now?" she muttered to the man leading her with effortless and expert ease. A muscle ticked in his jaw as if he weren't in the least bit *happy*. But then again, neither was she.

They finished the set in silence, tension stretching between them despite the matching painted smiles on their faces. She scanned the room, noticing that her parents were deep in conversation with the Rochesters. Gray was once more noticeably absent. He was avoiding her, she knew.

Bowing stiffly, Archer escorted her to the refreshment table and handed her a glass of champagne. Several loud rounds of toasts ensued as Brynn drained the contents of the glass. It did nothing to calm her rattled nerves. She plucked another off a tray and did the same. Her face hurt from smiling so much, and she felt dizzy, laughter and conversation slamming into her on all sides. Suddenly, the room seemed to shrink, and she wanted nothing more than to escape.

"Please excuse me," she said weakly. Archer's eyes fell on her. "I won't be a minute."

As she turned to leave for the nearest retiring room, her palms grew clammy, and it felt as if the soles of her feet were sticking into the floor. She could hardly lift them. Her legs were like iron posts, and a huge weight pressed down into the center of her chest. The whole room started to spin, closing in on her, a noose around her neck. Brynn's breath caught like a vise in her throat. *Oh no. Not here. Not now.* Hot white stars popped in her vision, and she cursed her stupid, pathetic lungs. Her numb fingers reached for Archer's arm, struggling to keep her balance. She couldn't breathe.

"Brynn?" Strong fingers grasped her shoulders, cradled her chin. Archer's voice seemed terribly far away, and his eyes even more so. Soon they both faded, and the only thing she could see was darkness.

• • •

Archer knew the instant that something was wrong. One

minute she was exchanging pleasantries beside him, and the next she was stumbling away, her skin ashen. He'd caught her before she could collapse, and now Briannon hung in his arms like a ragdoll. Not caring a whit for respectability, he scooped her up and strode to one of the adjoining salons. A path cleared for him, the music beginning to grind to a halt.

"Poor thing, she is overcome…"

"It is to be expected. It's far too soon after the duke's death…"

"She always was a sickly girl, was she not?"

Archer nodded for the musicians to continue to the next set, and as the strains of a vigorous quadrille began to play, those closest to them moved toward the dance floor and chatter resumed.

Brynn lay like a dead weight in his arms, her labored breaths shallow. Eloise would know what to do. He searched for his sister, but she was halfway across the ballroom and smiling up at Langlevit. The earl had drawn Archer aside earlier and asked for a meeting to discuss his intentions, and he didn't want to disturb his sister now. Archer's gaze fell on, and just as quickly discarded, Lady Dinsmore—he did not want that scene, either.

He glanced at Heed, already standing at attention in the salon's entrance. "Summon Dr. Hargrove immediately. Show him in the minute he arrives, and make sure we are not disturbed by anyone else. And send for her maid at once."

"Yes, Your Grace."

He slammed the heavy French doors behind him and set his bride-to-be on a chaise lounge. Fetching her some water, he held the glass to her lips and spun around as someone pushed open the door.

"Forgive me, my lord, I am Lana, Lady Briannon's maid." Without waiting for his response, the girl rushed to Brynn's side, nearly shoving him out of the way. He rocked back onto his haunches and watched her take charge, pulling a cool compress from the pocket of her dress and pressing it to her lady's face. She smiled reassuringly at him.

"Her lungs need a little help from time to time," she explained. "It won't take a minute. No need to worry."

Archer cleared his throat, relief pouring through him. "Does this happen often?"

"No, Your Grace, but she has been under more stress of late." Her gaze darted to his, and Archer flinched at the tiny note of accusation in her voice. He set his jaw, instead of reprimanding the servant as he should have, and poured himself a stiff brandy. It was his fault that Brynn had collapsed. Self-disgust surged within him.

Lana straightened her mistress's gown and tucked a tendril of hair back into place as Brynn's breathing leveled and grew more even. "There now," she murmured. "Easy, my lady."

After a few more moments of breathing in the aromatic compress, Brynn's eyelids fluttered. Archer opened the door and spoke a few curt words to the waiting footman. "Do not let anyone past this door," he said, before striding into the crowded ballroom. On his way to Briannon's parents, a dozen concerned guests who had witnessed Lady Briannon's near collapse waylaid him. He forced a smile to his face and reassured them that the lady was fine.

"Lord Dinsmore," Archer addressed Brynn's father, keeping his voice low. "Everything is well, but Briannon needed to take some air. The heat in the ballroom caused her to swoon. Her maid is with her at the moment, and there is no cause for alarm. I have sent for Dr. Hargrove as a precaution." Archer knew he was being duplicitous, but the last thing he wanted was for Lady Dinsmore to cause a scene, and from the look on Lord Dinsmore's face, he was arriving at the same conclusion. He nodded, and Archer made his way back to the salon.

When he entered, Brynn was in a seated position and

sipping a glass of water. Her maid had removed her gloves and was fanning her gently. A hint of color was coming back into her cheeks. She dismissed the maid with a grateful look, and the girl curtsied and stepped several paces away.

"I am so sorry," Brynn began, her hands twisting nervously in her lap. "My attacks are not as frequent as they used to be but do tend to come on rather suddenly."

"No, I am the one who should apologize," he said. He could feel the maid's curious gaze center on him, but he did not dismiss her. He could tell that her presence soothed Brynn, and that was more important than his privacy. "This has all happened so fast, and I didn't stop to think of the effect it would have on you." He sat beside her and noticed she had taken off his grandmother's diamond necklace. She flushed, her eyes darting to the pile of jewels atop the side table.

"They were rather heavy," she whispered, her hand lifting to her throat. Archer's gaze followed the movement, and his own breath caught at the bare expanse of creamy flesh swelling there. He cursed himself in the same moment—she was ill, and all he could do was think of her breasts and divesting her of that dress. The effect she had on him was unimaginable. A wan smile lit her face. "I much prefer rubies, as you know."

Archer's glance darted to the maid, who had suddenly busied herself at the far end of the room, opening the doors leading out onto the terrace. Fresh night air blew into the room and cooled the back of his neck. "I shall endeavor to remember that," he said softly. He took the slight softening in her manner toward him as an invitation. "Brynn, I know that this has been difficult for you, and tonight was no exception. I apologize for whatever part I have had in that." He slid his fingers between hers. "Regardless of how we came to be here, we are in this together. So I beg you to forgive me. Shall we restart this unfortunate evening?"

"I should like that very much."

He raised her ungloved hand to his lips and stared into her green-flecked eyes. "You are a vision tonight, Lady Briannon. Any man would be honored to have you at his side."

"Thank you," she said, warming to their game. "You—"

The door flew open, crashing into the wall behind it and interrupting her sentence. Her brother stormed into the room. Archer could tell that Northridge was already well into his cups, if only from the reek of whiskey that accompanied him. He looked utterly disheveled with his cravat nearly undone and his face mottled. "Where is she?"

Heed bustled into the room behind him, his face apologetic. "I apologize, Your Grace. He would not be deterred."

"Fine, Heed," Archer said in a clipped voice, his eyes never leaving Northridge. "Leave us."

As Heed closed the doors, Brynn half rose out of her seat but sank back down, her breathing once more agitated. Archer stood, but before he could take one more step toward him, the maid had crossed the room, positioning herself between them and Northridge. "She is upset enough, my lord."

Northridge's eyes flicked to his sister. "Get out of my way, Lana," he slurred. "Or I will remove you bodily, so help me."

"I will not allow you to make her worse," she said, throwing her hands onto her hips like she was addressing a misbehaving lad. Archer's eyebrow flicked up a notch at the girl's courage.

Northridge hesitated, his hands clenching at his side. "I am not here to endanger my sister," he gritted out. "Now let me pass."

"You are drunk."

"And you forget your place."

"Do I?" A silent battle of wills ensued that had Archer frowning. Perhaps the Dinsmores were more lenient with their servants than he was.

"Lana, please," Brynn interjected weakly as if she, too, could see the angry sparks flying between them. "Wait outside."

The maid shot her mistress a concerned glance, but did as she was told, her lips compressed into a tight, furious line. She raked Lord Northridge with a disparaging stare worthy of any highborn lady as she stalked past him.

Brynn turned to her brother. "Gray, I know you're upset, but this is not the time or the place."

"It is the perfect time," he countered, his words crashing together.

"You're foxed," she said, eyes widening. "His Grace and I—"

"His *Grace*," Northridge mocked. "The man has looked down his nose at all of us for years, preferring to spend his time in a stable than in his own house." He eyed Archer, who stood motionless, his body tightly leashed. A muscle jerked in his cheek at the man's insults. "It was a surprise to everyone at large that his father claimed him out of all his other bastards."

"That is enough!" Brynn gasped, her eyes flying to Archer's.

"I won't give you the thrashing you deserve," Archer said in a dangerously quiet voice. "If only out of respect for your sister, soon to be my wife. I will offer you the chance to leave of your own free will."

"Your *wife*," Northridge echoed, spit flying from his mouth. He swayed. "What did you do to get her to agree to your proposal?" He choked on his words, and Brynn's fingers flew to her mouth. "She would never marry you. Did you compromise her honor? Did you?"

"Gray! Stop this. He did no such thing." But her scruples betrayed her. She flushed guiltily, which seemed to make her brother's drunken temper skyrocket.

"Name your second, you bastard." Northridge took a swing at Archer and missed as Archer sidestepped him, grabbing him by the scruff of his collar.

Without a word, he stalked to the end of the room toward

the open terrace doors and tossed the younger gentleman out. Glancing over his shoulder at Brynn, Archer smiled reassuringly and closed the doors behind him. Once out of her earshot, however, he drew a ragged breath, fighting the inclination to beat Northridge to within an inch of his life. The man sought only to protect his sister. In truth, Archer would have done the same if their positions were reversed. "Go home. You're drunk, and you're making a scene."

"I demand satisfaction," Northridge shouted, his hair falling into his face as he fought to regain his balance. His voice echoed in the deserted gardens. Archer hoped no amorous couple was out taking a stroll just then. "Do you hear me, *Hawk*? At the point of a pistol. You forced my sister into this. She is obviously terrified of you. So terrified that she nearly fainted in your arms at the thought of sealing this betrothal. Don't you think she knows that you were questioned for the late duke's murder? Everyone knows that you are no gentleman."

"Enough," Archer said, trying to control his mounting fury. "Or you will have exactly what you want. I assure you, I am an excellent shot, and where will that leave your beloved sister? Without a brother?"

"Without a bastard of a husband." But the words were said without any real force behind them. Northridge's eyes drifted to the doors and peered through the glass panels, to where Brynn still stood, her face distraught.

"I assure you my parentage is as unsullied as yours," Archer said in a gentler tone, not missing the flash of regret that swept Northridge's face. "You may dislike me, but I am still marrying your sister. And unless you are truly willing to die to stop this wedding, I suggest you return to Bishop House and sleep it off. This is what she wants. What we both want."

"You will only hurt her," Northridge whispered. "Everyone knows of your proclivities—you could never be faithful. It would break her, and she doesn't deserve that." He hiccupped, his fingers clutching the iron railings behind him as his bluster abruptly faded.

Sodding hypocrite, Archer thought. *His* proclivities? As if Northridge was an innocent and hadn't had his own share of dalliances and more dependable mistresses. Archer had heard whisperings, unproven of course, of illicit rumors involving Northridge, a well-heeled courtesan, and a scandalous sum of money two years before. But nothing more had ever come of it. Perhaps that was the very reason he so despised Archer. Perhaps he thought he knew, based on his own actions, what it was his sister was facing down. A man she couldn't trust.

Northridge slumped against the railings, and Archer took pity on him. "She deserves a chance to be happy," Northridge muttered.

Archer swallowed and ran a hand through his hair, the anger draining from him like an outgoing tide. "You are right. She does."

The two men stared at each other in silence; the common thread between them was the woman peering at them through the glass panes. Something unfamiliar and deeply protective unfurled inside Archer at the sight of her. He had always known that Brynn was different. Despite her temper, she had a purity of spirit that only one other woman had ever possessed—his mother. It was a rare gift, and Archer knew that as surely as he knew his own name. She had come into his life with the ferocity of a summer storm, and fake betrothal or not, he had no intention of hurting her.

"I'll do everything in my power to ensure it."

At the quiet vow, the tension seemed to slip from Northridge's shoulders. "Brynn's heart is special. I want your word as a gentleman that you promise to do right by her."

Archer nodded and reached down a hand to his almost brother-in-law. "You have it."

Chapter Nineteen

Archer pinched the bridge of his nose as the coach rattled over the streets toward St. James's Square. It was an ungodly hour. Not even noon. Most of Bishop House would still be abed. Lord Northridge was likely out cold, his head pounding from the copious amount of alcohol he'd consumed last night.

Archer had every intention of waking the bloody fool up with a fist to the jaw.

That morning's copy of the *Times* lay crumpled on his lap. The paper had likely been delivered to Lord Dinsmore's home as well, but Archer wanted it in his possession when he approached Northridge. He wanted to press it into his future brother-in-law's face and pummel the drunken lout with it until he cowered.

Archer blamed himself, too. He should have been more careful. Someone *had* been in the gardens last evening and had tipped off the press. At the time, he had been thinking only of protecting Brynn by taking Northridge outside onto the terrace. He should have known that journalists from the *Times* or the *Gazette* would be lurking around, attempting to write a piece about the engagement or some part of the ball. He cursed himself for the hundredth time. Those who reported on the doings of the *ton* were like rabid dogs, and now that they had scented blood, it would be near impossible to deter them.

His fury at a lurid new headline about the latest attack from the now notorious Masked Marauder in Leicester Square had been eclipsed by the society pages. Archer had read the first few sentences of the gossip piece an hour before, as he'd taken his first sip of black tea. He'd promptly spit it out all over his desk and the edges of the newssheet. He looked at it now, and the words still stabbed his gut.

Scandal is afoot! From the mouth of her own brother, the lovely Lady B is terrified of becoming duchess to a murder suspect! Is she being forced into marriage? Lord N certainly seems to believe so.

Everything Brynn had sacrificed—everything they had both sacrificed—to protect each other from Bow Street's eagle eyes was now at risk.

The moment the coach stopped, Archer leaped from his seat and out the door without waiting for the set of steps to be set in place by his groomsman. The moment Thomson read this column—if he hadn't already—he would be back at Hadley Gardens and Bishop House, sniffing around just like before. The man probably had barely believed this ridiculous false betrothal to begin with.

And now that Archer and Brandt had spent the last week planning ways to trap and capture the man impersonating the Masked Marauder, he most certainly did not need Thomson's beady, inquiring eyes pinned on him.

Their butler, Braxton, opened the door shortly after Archer pounded on it. He stepped aside to allow him in, and Archer entered the foyer.

"Your Grace," Braxton said, dipping into a bow.

"I am here to see Lord Northridge." His eyes traveled up the red-carpeted steps to the second floor. The house was still and quiet, as he had expected.

"His lordship is not present." Braxton's reply took Archer by surprise. He'd figured the brat would be sleeping in and nursing his hangover. "He has taken the air to clear his head."

Finely put, Archer thought, his scowl still locked into place even though the wind had been sucked from his sails.

Now what?

"I would like him to call at Hadley Gardens as soon as he returns," Archer said, not bothering to leave his card or hear their butler's reply before starting back for the door.

A voice from the top of the stairwell stopped him.

"Your Grace?"

He turned and saw Brynn on the second floor landing, her hand upon the banister. She looked soft and sleepy, her pale blue day dress extraordinarily simple compared to the luxurious gown she'd worn last night. Her hair was up, though not severely.

"My lady," he murmured, stepping away from the front door and closer to the bottom of the stairwell.

She licked her lips and started down, her eyes coasting back up to the hallway behind her. Checking, he was certain, for any signal of her mother or father's presence.

"Braxton, please call for tea in the morning room," she said, but before the man could bow, Archer put up his hand.

"No, thank you, I won't be here long."

Braxton looked to his mistress, who nodded. He finished his bow and retreated into the back of the house, out of sight.

Archer stepped closer to the bottom step, where Brynn had just arrived. "We need to speak. Uninterrupted."

It had been a full week since they had last done as much. A full week since their encounter in the library at Hadley Gardens, though Archer had relived it in his mind every hour of every day.

Her body softening under his touch, her dress and chemise slipping from her shoulders to expose her lush, full, rosy-tipped breast. She'd moaned insensibly when he'd filled his palm with her flesh, when he'd suckled her and then kissed her breathless. Archer felt his loins tightening in an immediate and visceral response.

What was it about this girl that made him lose his senses so?

Brynn hesitated before nodding once more and leading him down the hallway, in the direction Braxton had just disappeared. She put a finger to her lips, indicating that he should remain quiet. Those lips, so pink and full, made him mad with desire. As he followed her into a room that was decidedly not a morning room, a host of indecent imaginings flooded his mind. His eyes fell to the gentle sway of her hips.

He wanted his hands on them.

He wanted her lips on his.

He wanted those lips on parts of his body ladies did not generally acknowledge. Damn it, but he wanted to finish what he had started days ago, his body still caught in an uncomfortable and unfulfilled state.

Archer attempted to compose himself as she shut the door behind them. "We won't be bothered here," she said.

The room was cramped, stuffed with floor-to-ceiling bookshelves piled with texts, a long, low velvet sofa in front of a fireless hearth, a desk in the corner with a reading lamp and slim leather chair.

"This is not your father's study," he said. It was far too feminine, and there was no wet bar. A shame. Archer could use a drink even at this hour of the morning, if only to give his hands and mouth something to do that did not involve defiling Lady Briannon's body.

Brynn walked to the center of the room, before the

hearth. "No. It is my own room," she said, lifting one shoulder as if to apologize. "No one else wanted it. The single window doesn't give much light."

Archer glanced toward the window, draped in layers of white lace and gauze, completely obscuring the view outdoors. He walked deeper into the room. He didn't fail to notice how Brynn wavered back a few steps. It was as if she wanted to keep a good five-foot buffer between them. It was probably the best course of action. Any closer and he would be able to reach for her. He couldn't trust himself.

The thought of his hands on her body reminded him of what he *did* hold right then.

He held up the *Times*.

Brynn saw it, her chest rising with a long, full breath. "I read it this morning," she said in a rush. "It seems your imposter is hell-bent on terrorizing the peerage."

"I'm not concerned with the Masked Marauder at present, Brynn," he said in a controlled voice. "I'm more concerned about my *terrified* fiancée."

She nodded, exhaling silently. "I saw that also. It's why Gray is out for a ride. He's furious with himself."

"As he should be." Archer tossed the paper onto the cushion of the sofa.

"He was inebriated and angry, and…well, I know he didn't intend to say all the things he did." The way she spoke reminded him too much of his mother, and how she had consistently defended her husband's actions. Even when they had involved days of delirious parties and countless women warming his bed. Archer blinked, his fury taking fresh root.

"He was a fool."

Brynn threw up her arms. "He doesn't know the truth! All he sees is a rushed betrothal, and he knows me too well to overlook how…how nervous I am."

It struck him then what she was admitting. The defiant

wit, the displays of temper, and that iron chin of hers…all bravado. All a shield.

Archer held his tongue and stared at her. Standing there, she looked so small in that dress. Small and delicate, whereas last evening, when she had stepped into the ballroom, she had been a grand, glittering jewel. Last evening, in that gorgeous gown, the entire ball had revolved around her, as it had been meant to do.

Despite his resolve to be aloof, he'd wanted to peel her out of that gown, layer after silken layer, right there on the dance floor, with everyone watching. Here, in this small study of hers, he wanted to do the very same thing. Perhaps even more than before, now that the dress she wore would not be as complicated to relieve her of. The light and airy day dress was the fashion for women, Archer knew, the cut of it a shapeless billowing length of linen, though tight and laced around the breasts. The fit was perfectly proper for women with small or modest bosoms.

On women such as Brynn, however, it was as tantalizing as a nightdress. The tops of her breasts swelled into view, the ribbon along the scooped neckline accentuating her shapely figure. It would be an easy thing to strip away. He wanted her bared to him again. He longed for the sight of her. For the warmth of her skin against his. Archer took an involuntary step forward.

The tension in the room solidified a thousandfold.

"Why are you nervous?" he asked, desire pulling his voice lower in his throat.

Her eyes flashed. She was an innocent when it came to men, but that did not mean she was naive. No, the spots of color on her cheeks told him she knew what emotion gripped him.

Want.

"You should be as well," she said, a touch breathless.

"I am," he admitted, though it had nothing to do with Thomson's inquisitive eyes, his father's murderer still on the loose, or the threat of being discovered as the Masked Marauder.

He was nervous because he had not wanted a woman with this sort of mindless intensity for a long time. Perhaps ever. The women he had pursued in the past had all given themselves with a willingness he had appreciated—at the time. They were women. They were pleasurable. But it had never been anything more. Never a challenge. Never so damn complicated. Never so inexplicably *exciting*.

Archer went around the arm of the sofa toward her, forgetting the newssheet he'd tossed down, and with it, his anger and concern. If his life had taught him anything at all, it was to savor the small things. Beyond this room, there were troubles enough; troubles that had kept him and Briannon from speaking privately all week. Who knew when they would next get a chance to be alone like this.

"What…" she blurted out, following his strides across the small room with alarmed eyes. "What are you nervous about? Mr. Thomson?"

"I don't wish to think about him. Or speak of him."

Brynn stood at the desk, her backside leaning against the edge, her palms flat on the desk's top. She squirmed as he drew closer, but she did not try to dodge him the way she had in the library at Hadley Gardens.

She had not been immune to him, and though she may never admit it, Archer knew she wanted to feel his touch again. He could see it in the darkening shadows of her eyes, and in the accelerated rise and fall of her bosom.

"Then…why are you nervous?" She was more than breathless now, those hazel eyes of hers wide and searching. They matched his steady gaze as he stopped directly before her, so close he could feel the heat of her body and see the throb of her pulse in her neck.

He breathed in and leaned closer. The woman intoxicated him with merely her scent, so clean and perfect and fresh.

"Because I am about to ruin you, Lady Briannon, and this time, none of it will be an act."

. . .

Brynn couldn't breathe. She couldn't move, either, not with Archer's body practically pressing hers against the desk at her back. He had given her plenty of time to skitter about the study as he'd prowled closer, but she had stayed put. If he intended to intimidate her with his height and those broad shoulders that blocked her sight of the door, well, it would not work.

You're lying to yourself.

He did intimidate her, but not because of the storm clouds she'd seen in his eyes as he'd stood in the foyer with Braxton. It had nothing to do with his anger over the gossip column or her brother's wretched behavior from the night before, or even her hasty lie that had started this whole charade in the first place.

He intimidated her because he made her feel things she knew were wrong. Things that were base and wicked. He made her feel weak and ravished and completely and utterly reckless. It was not like her at all.

And yet she liked how it felt. How *he* felt.

She wet her lips and tried to speak in a coherent fashion. "You have already taken liberties, or do you not recall?"

His hands braced the desk on either side of her hips. His forearms brushed along her dress, an item of clothing that began to grow curiously warm.

"I recall," he said, drawing so close his mouth touched her ear. His breath tickled over her skin. "Fondly and often."

"Your Grace—"

"My name is Archer."

"Archer—"

"You feel it, too," he murmured in her ear. His hands were still on the desk, and not touching any part of her body. "The wanting. I tasted it on your tongue. I felt it on your flesh when I touched you. I heard it when my mouth made you moan. I see it now."

Brynn took a shaky breath at his purposefully seductive words. The memory of baring herself to him, of her breast filling his palm, was closer than it had been all week. And yes, she had thought of it many, *many* times.

"We are not betrothed," she whispered, his musky male scent invading her nostrils and threatening to steal away all thought and reason.

"On the contrary," he said, his lips skating over the delicate curve of her ear, and making butterflies take flight in her chest. "I believe our engagement ball was last night."

His hands stayed where they were, gripping the edge of the desk. She turned away from his mouth and glanced at them; his knuckles were white from holding the desk so tightly.

"That does not make this right," she said.

"Tell me you don't want me to touch you again." She straightened her head, and his mouth was at her ear once more, teasing her with its warmth. "Tell me you find me repulsive."

Oddly enough, it didn't sound like an arrogant challenge. It was almost as if he did want her to tell him those things. She stole another glance down at his hand at her side. It continued to grip the desk like it was his lifeline.

"Tell me, Briannon," he whispered. "Tell me to leave, and I will."

She turned her face up to his and, for the first time, saw

the crusade he was waging inside of himself. He *did* want her to tell him to leave. It would be the sane thing to do. The wise thing. All she had to do was open her mouth and repeat his command. *Leave.* One word, that was all it would take. He would sweep out of her study and back to Hadley Gardens, and she would be safe from ruination. She would be safe from *him*.

She closed her eyes in sublime rapture, her voice a tortured whisper. "I don't want you to leave."

A low groan built in the bottom of his throat. The tension blossomed between them, raw and powerful…and incredibly fragile. It held Brynn captive. "Then say yes," he said. "Tell me I may touch you."

Brynn arched toward him in a semi-trance, her eyes sweeping open. She swallowed hard, and her mouth shaped the words he was begging her to say. "Yes. Touch me."

The words were wanton and vulgar, and yet she could not feel ashamed of them. They were honest. She wanted his hands on her again. She'd wanted it every moment of this last week. And right now, she could hardly say no, not with him looking at her the way he was, plying her with his heavy-lidded eyes and his tantalizingly close body. Brynn was acutely aware of how attractive he was—the smooth wings of his eyebrows, the sensual curve of his mouth, the sharp planes of his cheekbones. His eyes glittered with restrained passion. She licked suddenly dry lips.

The desk shook as he continued to grasp it. "Where? Tell me where to touch you."

She blushed at his bidding. To know where she wanted his hands was one thing, but to tell him where he could put them…she couldn't do it.

"I don't know," she managed to say.

He lowered his mouth to hers, but continued to speak, his lips brushing against hers in featherlight nudges. "If you cannot be more specific, I have my own ideas in mind."

Finally, his hands came off the desk, but they still did not caress her—at least not her body. His fingers trailed down the linen of her dress, bunching the fabric so that the hem was starting to rise above her ankles.

Then her calves.

Then her knees.

Brynn gasped as his hot fingers slipped underneath her skirt and skimmed her thigh. She wore a pair of thin cotton drawers, but she could still feel the heat of his palm as it rounded to the back of her thigh—and hiked her leg up so that her foot left the floor. She gasped, shock and desire filling her in frantic beats.

Desire won out as Archer stepped closer, tucking himself flush against her body. He brought her raised leg around his hip and hinged it there, her skirt tossed up around her knee. She felt him—*all* of him—and it stole away any shred of decency she had left.

He stared boldly into her eyes, daring her to look away or to blush at the bulging ridge of his desire pressing so intimately into the soft, yielding parts of her. But Brynn held his gaze, her breath coming in small, shallow huffs, her body feeling as if it were melting at the point where their bodies intersected. God help her, she wanted more.

A hint of a smile curved his perfect lips, so close to hers; all Brynn had to do was move forward an inch in order to claim them.

So she did.

Her bold but tentative kiss surprised him. She felt the squeeze of his hand on her thigh in response, and then heard another low groan in his throat, felt it reverberate through her. His tongue pushed past her closed lips with less tenderness this time. He stroked inside, while his hand… Brynn inhaled sharply when she realized where his hand, buried under her skirts, was traveling.

His fingers reached the waistband of her drawers and tugged, pulling the undergarment lower around her hips.

"Archer—" she gasped.

"I told you I had my own ideas," he replied before capturing her lips again.

His flattened hand scooped underneath the waistband of her drawers and slid along her bare skin, curving around her buttock until he had it firmly in his palm. He kneaded her flesh, his fingertips stroking lower and inward, closer to the heart of her.

Brynn could not bring herself to twist away from his mouth in order to stop him. She was lost to the trembling sensations pulsing in the pit of her stomach. His lips were on hers, plying her with slow, sensual kisses, and with every push and pull of their mouths and tongues, the further away the rest of the room, the rest of the house and world became.

It was only she and Archer, his hands and mouth possessing her utterly. But as his hand swept over the top of her thigh and tugged her drawers a little lower, she stiffened. She parted her lashes to see if the door remained shut, a small voice in her head begging her to see reason and sense. The door wasn't locked. Anyone could walk in.

"No one is there, Brynn. You are safe." Archer had pulled from their kiss long enough to counsel her and now returned to her mouth, his teeth gently nipping her lower lip. She sighed into the kiss, her tongue touching his and retreating shyly. Archer coaxed it back as his fingers brushed lower.

"Don't be afraid. I won't hurt you," he whispered as his hand finally settled over the most private part of her. She caught her breath, her body again turning rigid at the shocking contact of his palm.

"I don't think I—"

One of his strong fingers slipped between her legs, dipping

into her most secret place. The rest of Brynn's sentence dissolved into a hushed moan. She froze against him, clamping her legs together, a pulsing sensation streaking through her.

"Don't, darling." His lips moved against hers as he spoke. "Trust me, Brynn."

She nodded as he caressed her, parting her thighs, his palm brushing past the soft thatch of curls. Archer drew his finger along her sensitive flesh, the feathery stroking making her giddy with longing. "I'll stop if you ask," he murmured against her. "But tell me you want my touch, and I promise you will feel nothing but pleasure."

Brynn knew he was telling the truth. He would stop— *if* she insisted he do so. But his promise felt too divine, too glorious to deny. And his words, the sound of his whispered voice, his breath hot in her ear, made her more inflamed than his hands did. Filled with unfathomable yearnings, Brynn parted her lips.

"Yes. *Yes.*"

With a groan of relief, Archer slid his finger deeply into her. Brynn gasped at the sudden pressure, her eyes going wide. His finger stroked and teased, filling her for a moment, but then drew out. She had just gathered a breath when he sank into her again. Her pulse hitched at the gathering tension between her thighs, a stunned moan escaping her lips.

"You consume my thoughts," he whispered in her ear, his teeth taking the lobe and tugging it gently. "Day. And night."

He nipped across her jawline to find her mouth, sucking her lower lip in between his. He flicked it lazily with the tip of his tongue, while his thumb skillfully teased the delicate bud at the apex of her thighs, building a hot, swollen pressure inside of her. As he stroked into her again, a second finger joined the first, and she arched her back, straining to get closer to him. The sensations coming to life between her legs and rippling through her body were so maddening that she cried out with the sinful pleasure of it.

"What have you done to me?" she whispered. "Archer, I can't…"

"Soon, sweet." His mouth took hers in a ravenous kiss. His tongue mimicked the sensuous slide of his fingers, driving her into a near frenzy.

With shameless greed, Brynn closed her eyes and instinctively thrust her hips against his hand. She almost sobbed at the relentless urgency of his fingers as liquid fire raced unheeded along her limbs, building and building.

"I've wanted to touch you like this since that night on the lane to Worthington Abbey," he said, his expert strokes bringing her higher on that swell of hot pleasure. It threatened to incinerate her. "You were so beautiful in the moonlight, so fearless. Had we been alone, I would have taken you then."

Had her head not been thrown back in pure ecstasy, her ability to speak utterly lost, she would have told him how she had felt the attraction, too, and how every night since she had drifted to sleep with shamefully erotic dreams of him. Dreams just like this reality. Only she had never imagined it could feel this sensual and frustrating at the same time. It wasn't just her body reaching for him, wanting more of his touch, it felt like her soul was craving him as well. Pleasured with one breath, unfulfilled with the next.

Archer's fingers quickened, teasing and toying. His thumb rubbed the little nub at her entrance until her body strained against him. "Please," she begged, not knowing in the least what she was pleading for.

"You're intoxicating." He nipped her bottom lip with his teeth before laving it with his tongue. "I want to drink you, Brynn. Consume you. I want to taste every warm, wet part of your body."

Brynn moaned at the picture he'd just painted. *Every* part of her body? Did men do such things? He smiled as if knowing her thoughts.

"You're imagining how it will feel when I take you with my mouth instead of my hand," he whispered.

"You…your…" was all Brynn could gasp with the sweet burden inside her swelling high and hot.

"Yes. Like this," he murmured before driving his tongue inside her mouth. He curled it around hers, tugging and stroking, promising her something she had never before fathomed.

Brynn could no longer breathe, and surprisingly, she found she didn't need air. Just his sliding tongue and plunging fingers, and with Archer's rapid breathing hot in her throat, pleasure broke through her. She cried out at the shockwaves of bliss and then whimpered as she rode Archer's hand shamelessly, thrusting to claim the last ebbs of satisfaction.

As they flattened out inside of her, she exhaled. She felt as if her body had splintered into a thousand hot fragments that were now slowly piecing themselves back together. She'd never experienced anything so shattering in her life.

Archer kissed her softly, removing his hand from the damp crux of her body and pulling her drawers back into place. Her leg, rid of all muscle and strength, fell from his hip, and Archer smiled knowingly as he straightened her skirts. She breathed heavily, though for once, being breathless felt absolutely divine.

"I cannot believe I allowed you to do that," she whispered after a long moment.

Archer parted his lips to reply, his raffish grin promising a witty—and lewd—reply, but a knock on the study's door smothered his grin and sent him whipping around and away from the desk. Brynn pushed off the desk and lunged toward one wall of bookshelves, a trembling hand reaching to her hair to smooth whatever damage had been done to it.

"Enter," she said in a voice far more composed than she

felt.

Braxton cracked the study door to find Archer near the hearth and Brynn at the shelves. If he sensed anything amiss, his emotionless face did not betray it.

"Lord Northridge has returned, my lady, if His Grace still wishes for an audience."

Archer turned from the hearth, his shoulders squared, his back straight as an arrow. "Thank you, but I have other business to attend to. I will see Lord Northridge at another time."

Braxton bowed and retreated, though Brynn noticed he did not close the door all the way.

She let out a shaky breath, watching as Archer strode slowly across the room. At the door he paused and turned to face her. His sultry stare was gone, but she was glad to see his more familiar cold and distant expression had not replaced it. Instead, Archer looked at her with a kind of searching wonder. The same way he had the night before when she had arrived in the ballroom.

"I must leave," he said, the abrupt words not matching the deeply possessive glint in those storm-swept eyes.

"Of course." What else could she say? She could still hardly breathe from the last few minutes of relentless pleasure his hands and whispered seductions had brought her.

After another awkward pause, Archer lowered himself into the deepest bow she had yet seen him make, and took his leave.

Exhaling slowly, Brynn stood at the bookshelves, her legs still weak and her core still throbbing from his ministrations. Sanity and reason came back in a slow, inexorable rush. Hot shame was swift to follow. Good god, what had she *done*?

Chapter Twenty

"Hawk," Stephen Kensington, the Earl of Thorndale, said with a lazy smile, "at least leave some of our money on the table if you're not in the game. That's the ninth hand you've won, yet you are a thousand miles away."

Archer drew the pile of chips from the middle of the gaming table toward the already significant stack lying in front of him. Despite his social elevation to the Duke of Bradburne, the nickname among those who knew him had stuck. Thorndale was one of the few men he tolerated—liked even—amongst his peers. He had always struck him as a fastidious but generous man. Archer knew for a fact that he had donated a large part of his own fortune to build a new wing for a struggling hospital on the outskirts of London, an act largely due to his new wife, whose father was a local physician. Thorndale was one of the few not targeted by the true Masked Marauder.

Archer collected his cards for the next round, checking the single one lying face down beneath the king in front of him. An ace. A natural. He pushed a handful of chips toward the large pile as the others did the same. "Lady Luck is with me tonight, it seems."

"Luck of the devil, you mean," Marcus Bainley muttered sourly. Archer shot the young man a level look but did not respond. Of the five other men at the card table, Bainley was the youngest. The son and heir of the aging Marquess of Bromley, he was a society dandy with a reputation for gambling, profligacy, and gossip. With a massive fortune at his disposal, he cared nothing for expense and flaunted his money with the delicacy of an elephant in a tearoom. Which was why he'd been the Masked Marauder's first victim. Archer couldn't fathom how Bainley was such a favorite within the upper crust of London society. He made a mental note to divest the fop of more of his coin at a future date.

The other three men he knew only by association. Helmford Monti was a handsome Italian ambassador with a penchant for whiskey and women. He and Archer's father had had a lot in common. The Duke of Bassford was an elderly man who spent so much time at the tables that he was rumored to have his own suite of rooms in the upper level apartments of the club, despite having several properties in London and multiple sprawling country estates. His fifth wife was younger than his oldest son and heir. Unbeknownst to him, Archer had stripped the lecherous old bastard of a significant sum in Cheshire the previous autumn during hunting season.

The last player, Viktor Zakorov, was a man Archer had never met before but had disliked from the start. Thorndale had introduced him as some important Russian diplomat. Something about the man seemed slippery. His austere face hid secrets, and Archer had enough experience with those to know that Viktor Zakorov was not who he seemed. Archer didn't mind taking his money, however.

He had never been fond of gambling, but tonight he

had made an exception. White's, the exclusive gentlemen's gaming club to which he had belonged since his days at Cambridge, was crowded, and Archer was grateful for that fact. He glanced around at the sumptuous decor. Sparkling chandeliers, plush, deep blue velvet carpets, and rich mahogany furniture surrounded by priceless paintings gave off a feel of unsurpassed luxury. For many men of the *ton*, it was a well-cherished home away from home. They ate and drank their fill in the supper rooms and moved on to play a relaxed hand of *vingt-et-un* or bet entire fortunes on a roll of the dice in the game rooms until the wee hours of the morning. Though the club was designed exclusively for males, there was no shortage of female company should such diversions be required.

The soft hum of voices and the constant sweep of cards kept Archer's innermost thoughts at bay. He wanted nothing more than to be distracted by anything other than the three things plaguing him—his father's killer, exposing the impersonator, and deflowering the lovely Lady Briannon, the last of which kept him in an uncomfortable state of perpetual arousal. Normally, Archer would find a suitable companion with whom he'd engage in a meaningless dalliance, but he knew that only one woman could sate the raw ache within him.

Her natural, artless sensuality drove him to distraction. Earlier that morning in her study, Brynn had opened to him, trusting him as she had never trusted any other. Despite the sweet torment of his own unfulfilled desire, he would gladly repeat the act endless times just to savor the delighted surprise in her eyes as her body found its release.

Archer knew they were flirting with disaster. They weren't truly engaged, and to continue on as if they were was simply inviting destruction upon both their heads. But he couldn't help himself when he was around her. He became a besotted fool.

He also knew that he was being selfish. Archer had every intention of breaking the engagement once the duke's killer—and the man impersonating the bandit—was found. They were one and the same, Archer was certain of it. The handwriting on all three of the notes was unmistakably the same. When he found the killer, he would find the impersonator as well, and then Archer would set the marauder's reputation to rights.

Brynn may now know the truth of the crimes he'd committed, and to what purpose, but she would not stand aside and be complicit while he continued his mission—the single-minded duty that had driven and satisfied him for years. But for the first time Archer could remember, he desired something for himself, something far more satisfying than the gratification of repurposing the *ton's* wealth. He wanted Briannon Findlay. But where would that leave her? If he did what he truly wanted to do, she would be ruined for any other man.

A surge of wild jealousy ripped through him at the thought of Brynn's naked body wrapped in the arms of anyone else. He shoved the unexpected emotion away with a low growl. He had never let a woman get under his skin the way she had. And it wasn't just about losing himself in her. Archer enjoyed their verbal sparring. He liked hearing her real thoughts as they flew, unedited, from her tongue. He liked seeing her upon a horse and watching her across a dinner table. He especially liked knowing she belonged to him.

"She doesn't," he muttered to himself. She was not his, not truly.

"She doesn't what?" Thorndale said with an elegantly raised eyebrow. "Something on your mind, Hawk? A special someone, perhaps? Care to elaborate?"

"No, I do not." He frowned fiercely and signaled to a hovering server to refill his drink, ignoring the knowing smile on Thorndale's face.

"Don't worry, my friend," he said, toasting him. "This is the easy part. Wait until the wedding nears. The insanity has only just begun. Have you set a date yet?"

"No," he snapped.

"His Grace is to be married?" Viktor asked, his thick accent distorting his words.

Thorndale tucked a cheroot between his lips and lit it, clearly enjoying Archer's plight. "It was announced only this week, and to the lovely Lady Briannon Findlay no less." His eyes brightened. "Speaking of, here is the lady's brother himself. Northridge, wonderful to see you, old chap," Thorndale said and gestured to the last open seat at their table. "I see you are back for another sound whipping." At Archer's raised eyebrow, Thorndale grinned wolfishly. "Northridge made the mistake of coming here before your engagement ball last night. I doubt he will remember much of it, other than leaving with sadly empty pockets."

Archer looked up and nodded a curt greeting to Brynn's brother. He hadn't quite forgiven the young man's foolish outburst the night past, but what was done was done. Northridge looked wan and worse for wear, although he still cut an impeccable figure in his dapper evening clothes.

His grin was sheepish. "Thank you for the offer, but I think I'll favor the dice tables tonight."

Perhaps it was Northridge's arrival or the fact that seeing him made him think of his sister, but Archer lost the next hand. And the next four after that. He was just about to throw it in and take his leave when he realized Bainley had asked him a question.

"Rumors abounded that you would never marry, Bradburne. Why the change of heart? Or is it your change of fortune?"

Bradburne. No one had called him by his father's title

until now, and it hung like a pall in the air. His name had always been Hawksfield, and hearing his father's name applied to him now, alongside the young man's sly, baiting question, made him thirst for a fight.

Archer did not respond in the way Bainley expected. Calling him out would only draw more attention to himself, and after the unfortunate article in the *Times*, he didn't need any more of that.

He lounged back in his chair and tossed a few more chips onto the pile in the center. "Why, the love of a good woman could induce the devil himself to court a lady."

"So it's love, then?"

"I don't know," Archer said smoothly. "Is that what the rumors are saying?"

The men at the table broke out in laughter, and Bainley turned red. Archer hadn't insulted him by calling him a gossip to his face, but the underlying insult was there just the same. Bainley stood, darting a seething look in Archer's direction, collected his remaining chips, and left without a word.

Thorndale won the next hand and smiled in satisfaction. "It's about time."

"Hawk," a man's voice said. "May I join you?"

Archer looked around to see Brandt standing there. His longtime friend was immaculately dressed in a moss green coat with gold buttons and gray pantaloons. It had been a game of theirs early on to pass Brandt off as a gentleman in the *ton*, inventing outlandish double identities for him, particularly during the season, but they hadn't done it for some time.

It had amused them to no end that no one ever recognized Brandt. The privileged had a way of behaving as if their servants were invisible. Archer nodded to the proprietor of the establishment who had escorted Brandt to their table, vouching for the newcomer's arrival. Though Brandt was not a member, Archer knew the owner would not risk alienating the new Duke of Bradburne.

Archer hid his surprise. Perhaps Brandt had simply wanted a change of scene. "Mr. Brockston," he said casually. "When did you get back into town?"

"Just today." Brandt's bored response could rival any English peacock's. "Sorry I missed your engagement ball. I heard it was the crush of the season."

Brandt endured the other men's curious stares. An invitation to Hawk's engagement would only mean that he was a close friend of the duke's. Archer nodded for him to take Bainley's vacant seat. Brandt placed a stack of chips on the green felt of the table as Archer introduced him to the other players. "Mr. Brockston is a friend of mine from Essex. He is in the export business and manages some of my international investments. He travels frequently, so he is not often in town."

Brandt settled in like a natural, and play resumed for another hour with Thorndale and Brandt taking most of the hands. Archer was forced to concede that his luck had run out. Or perhaps he wasn't focused enough. Brandt's arrival had made him more inclined to stay, but he was considering asking his friend to retire with him to Hadley Gardens and take on the better part of a bottle of aged brandy when a whispered comment at the table beside them stopped him cold.

"Dowager Viscountess Hamilton was attacked…"

He turned and saw Lord Everton holding the men at his table transfixed with the news. "She was attacked?" Archer interrupted. "Where?"

The young lord was eager to share the gossip. "In her home. By the Masked Marauder. Last night. She was beaten severely."

Archer frowned, exchanging a swift glance with Brandt.

Viscountess Hamilton had pleaded illness and had not been at the engagement ball.

"What kind of animal would attack an old lady?" Thorndale said, disgust coating his words.

"How is she?" Archer said.

"Recovering, but Dr. Hargrove says that she is lucky to be alive. My mother is the viscountess's cousin."

"This scoundrel has to be stopped," Bassford growled. "He attacked my carriage several months ago. No one was hurt, thank goodness, but it appears he is becoming more vicious in his attacks. Lady Hamilton is ancient."

No one remarked that she and the late duke were the same age, but the news certainly dampened the previously jovial atmosphere in the club. Cards lay forgotten on the tables as conversation grew agitated with everyone weighing in on the identity of the bandit, his burgeoning list of crimes, and his newfound passion for violence. Archer felt sick to his stomach.

"Any more news on the duke's killer, Hawk?" Thorndale asked. "Do they think it's this masked bandit?"

Archer shook his head. "Bow Street has their suspects, including him."

"But no leads?" Monti asked, watching him with interested black eyes.

For a moment, something in the man's tone bothered Archer, and he wondered whether Monti or someone else here could be the imposter. It was certainly plausible.

His body grew rigid. He met Brandt's stare and knew that he had arrived at the same deduction. Perhaps that would explain the stable master's presence here. He had come to scope out possible suspects. Archer felt something take hold of his body as his gaze perused the room, meeting familiar and unfamiliar faces in turn. Could someone here know his secret?

The dark downturn of the conversation along with his luck made Archer signal a footman to call for his carriage. He made his excuses and left, silently beckoning for Brandt to follow him at a later juncture.

As he entered the foyer at Hadley Gardens ten minutes later, an annoyed-looking Heed met him. "What is it?" Archer asked him, frowning.

But before Heed could answer, a familiar gaunt figure strode from the adjoining parlor.

Thomson.

Archer's eyes immediately fell to the bloodstained linen dangling from the inquiry agent's hand. He didn't have to look at the delicate embroidery in the corner to see his initials stitched there. He knew his own cravat when he saw it. Despite the shot of worry that arced through him, Archer's expression gave away nothing as Thomson smiled, his eyes glittering with veiled triumph.

"I believe this belongs to you."

It was an unfashionable hour for a stroll or drive through Hyde Park, but Archer was there, nonetheless. There would be a number of carriages tooling along the park lanes past dark, and they would be ripe for the picking. There were at least two balls occurring that night that Archer knew of, invitations to which he had received and politely declined. Enduring hours in a stuffy ballroom, while wearing a starched suit and cravat, could not hold a candle to the freedom Archer felt where he stood now, within a stand of woods near the border of Kensington Gardens. He wore his black buckskin trousers and Hessians, a long black greatcoat, and his mask, of course—a guise he had not worn for weeks.

It had been too long since his last outing. The jumping

nerves in his arms and legs and the insistent clench of his gut were proof.

"We should not be here," Brandt whispered from the trees behind Archer.

"Come now, Mr. Brockston, where is your sense of adventure?" he murmured in response.

Brandt snorted. "Playing a gentleman and riding the coattails of your influence at White's earlier was adventure enough for me. Although I have yet to change out of these over-starched garments."

Archer breathed in the early spring air, tracing the dank bite of the Serpentine's stagnant water. The trees had bloomed with new foliage weeks ago. They sheltered Brandt and him well, especially in the darkness.

"I needed to get out," Archer explained. "Especially after dealing with that hound from Bow Street."

Thomson's visit at Hadley Gardens had lasted over an hour, during which the zealous inquiry agent brandished the bloodied cravat bearing Archer's monogram, which had been found inside Viscountess Hamilton's burgled home.

Archer, sitting in his chair at his desk, his fingers laced over his stomach, had explained with forced calm that he had given the cravat to the late duke to staunch the blood flow from a gash on his palm at the Gainsbridge's Masquerade. The duke had not seen fit to return the length of linen, stained and ruined as it was.

He'd also denied dropping the damned thing while robbing Lady Hamilton's home and beating her senseless. Thomson had not been so stupid as to formally accuse him of the despicable act, but there was no question in Archer's mind the man was digging to pin both the duke's murder and the bandit's crimes on his head.

That wasn't what had driven Archer into a foul temper, though. What had was the fact that the imposter had left the bloodied cravat behind on purpose in an attempt to implicate Archer. Which meant the imposter had taken the cravat some time ago. The duke would have most likely tossed the ruined linen to Heed or his valet, Porter, after the Gainsbridge affair. If that was the case, the imposter must have been inside Worthington Abbey, where he'd formulated a future use for the cravat. Who the devil was he? A servant? Or had he sneaked into the duke's home unseen?

"That Bow Street hound is precisely why we should have stayed put at Hadley Gardens," Brandt replied. "You are breaking your own rules, Hawk."

Archer paced a small swath of ground between two trees. "I'm simply restless."

Waylaying a carriage and taking away a nice purse to be delivered to one of the parish churches, perhaps near Seven Dials or Whitechapel, would settle him. Besides, when he took a carriage tonight—a single carriage, no need to get cocky— he would ask the occupants to relay a message: that the real Masked Marauder does not steal for his own benefit, but for that of the poor. The real Masked Marauder does not harm women or slaughter defenseless animals.

Archer would like to wake up tomorrow morning to a bold headline like *that* in the newssheets.

"It is poor timing, and you know it," Brandt said.

"You did not have to come. I made that perfectly clear."

In fact, he'd ordered Brandt to await his return in the stables. There were only a handful of servants assigned there, but Archer did not want to risk being seen by any of them when he returned from his outing. He'd rather his staff have no reason to believe he'd left his rooms at any point during the evening. He'd gone so far as to climb from his own window and descend the trellis into the gardens and out to the curb, where Brandt waited with two rented mounts from a nearby livery. His departure had been degrading enough as it was; he didn't want it to have all been for naught.

"Someone needs to look after your reckless arse," Brandt murmured as the telltale sound of rattling tack and carriage wheels sounded down the lane.

Archer let out a pent-up breath as the squall of tension within him released. He knew what to do and how to do it, and damn it if he wasn't going to give the Masked Marauder his reputation back.

Before the imposter started on his rampage, the bandit had had a mysterious air about him, but no one had truly feared him. At the card table at White's that afternoon, he'd heard pure revulsion in the voices of the men who had, before, shrugged off the masked bandit as a petty criminal unworthy of their concern. Some part of him desperately wanted to defend his alter ego's honor.

"Be careful," Brandt whispered as Archer's muscles tensed and released, ready to spring.

"Yes, Mother."

He jumped out of the stand of trees and into the darkened lane. The approaching carriage had two lanterns near the driver's bench, and they threw off enough light for Archer to see the boxy shape of a brougham, pulled by one horse. The interior would fit two passengers at the most, and a single driver. Perhaps a groomsman at the back.

Archer relaxed even more. How many times had he waylaid such a carriage? Countless, and here in the woodsy area of the park, he could have just as well been in Essex again.

As the driver's figure, outlined by the coach lamps, came into view, Archer readied his pistol. The weapon was not loaded and never had it been for any of his outings. He knew enough about weaponry to know the dangers of a shot accidentally going off and maiming, or killing, a man. He would never endanger anyone's life, which made the imposter's actions that much more infuriating.

The driver finally drew close enough to spot Archer standing in the center of the road. He spoke to his horse, pulling back on the reins and bringing the brougham to a halt. Once the jangling of the tack quit, Archer delivered his greeting in the silky voice he reserved for the bandit: "No displays of heroism, please." To which he expected the driver to hold up his hands in surrender, just as the others, for the most part, had always done.

This driver, however, bucked tradition.

He threw down the reins to his horse and stood from the driver's bench. As he descended from the bench, Archer took in the shape of him. Well over six feet and possessing the breadth of an ox, the driver looked like a bear clad in fine livery.

"Stay where you are, my friend," Archer advised, the smooth cadence of his voice faltering.

"I ain't your friend," the driver said, though to Archer's ears it sounded less like a voice and more like a handful of stones being ground to dust.

The driver reached into the footboards of the bench and drew something out.

"No one need risk injury tonight," Archer said, the pulse in his throat beginning to throb. "I simply require the valuables of your patrons."

The driver advanced while a female voice inside the brougham called out, asking why they had stopped. Archer fixed his eyes on the flintlock pistol the driver carried in his hand.

This is going all wrong.

For the first time since he'd started this whole charade, he doubted the sense of it all. No one had ever challenged him—a dangerous masked highwayman. Nobility didn't generally rise to the fight. They cowered. They spluttered and complained, but they always shrank away from Archer, from his masked face and the threat of injury. And hired help… well they certainly did not get paid handsomely enough to risk life and limb for their masters.

"Lawrence?" The clipped female voice called, clearer this time.

The door to the carriage opened, distracting Archer's attention from the approaching giant. His eyes stuck to the lady as she popped her head out and turned to see what was amiss. *Hell.* He recognized her as one of Brynn's friends, Lady Cordelia Vandermere.

Without a moment's hesitation, the chit screamed. The high, bloodcurdling pitch slammed into his ears and echoed through the park. Her driver, Lawrence, did the exact opposite of what Archer expected him to do: instead of turning and rushing to his mistress's side, he raised his pistol and charged at full speed.

Archer flipped his useless pistol in his hand and brought the butt across the driver's hand, knocking the man's unfired weapon aside. The shot didn't go off, not even when the pistol hit the lane. The driver tackled Archer to the gravel. He had at least ten stone on Archer, if not more, but he used the beast's own momentum against him, tossing the driver overhead and onto the lane.

The marginal victory did not last long.

Archer barely made it to his feet when the driver successfully set upon him again, bringing him to the ground. Almost instantly, however, the driver's weight was taken from his back, and Archer heard the grunts of another, the sounds of knuckles on flesh. He spun around to find Brandt pummeling the driver with his fists, and then taking a hook to the nose in return.

Lady Cordelia's screams for help were getting farther and farther away, but as Archer pulled the driver off Brandt, the sounds of shouting men drew alarmingly close.

The driver tossed Archer off and dove to the ground. Even in the darkness, and with the silk mask tugged askew and half blinding him, Archer knew the man was lunging for the dropped pistol. Before he could take a breath or even think to run, a pair of hands shoved hard against his chest, knocking him aside.

The report of the pistol split through Archer's ears as he hit the gravel lane. He tore off the mask and with his vision restored, saw Brandt on the ground where he had just been standing.

"No!" He rushed to his friend and bent over him. "You bloody fool!"

He received a groan in answer and a rough shove against his arm. "Go," Brandt rasped in pain. "Get out of here, there are others coming."

The driver was already running toward the sounds of the men's voices, shouting, "Here! Over here, the masked bastard is here!"

Archer tried to pull Brandt to his feet, but the rasp of pain turned into a grating growl. "I'm shot, damn you! Leave me here and *go*."

"There is no chance in hell—"

"I cannot walk. *Go*, Archer. The sodding driver knows *I'm* not the bandit. I'm still dressed as Brockston. I'll think of something. Get out of here!"

Brandt shoved him away once again, and this time Archer got up. "You'd better be a damned good liar and get yourself out of this. Or else I *will* come forward."

And with that, Archer turned. He hated leaving his friend there, but he knew he wouldn't be able to help Brandt if they were *both* in prison. With a growl of frustrated rage, he fled.

Chapter Twenty-One

Brynn stared helplessly at her betrothed sitting slumped and defeated in the chair behind the massive desk. Archer was knee-deep in a bottle of whiskey and seemed intent on drowning himself in the rest of it. She had come to Hadley Gardens the minute she had heard the news that a man had been arrested in conjunction with the Masked Marauder and tied to an attack the night before. She had not, however, known that it was Brandt, Archer's friend and stable master. It did not surprise her that Archer still considered the man a friend, despite the differences in their social standings. They had been childhood friends in Essex, and Brynn knew that Archer valued Brandt's unswerving loyalty. And vice versa.

Enough to try to save his liege's neck, it seemed.

She had gotten part of the story from Cordelia, and the rest in broken bits and pieces from Archer, and was still trying to make sense of it. Why Archer had felt compelled to don his mask and waylay a coach on a darkened side street, Brynn had no idea. Perhaps it had been to show that the *true* Masked Marauder was not a killer. Regardless of his intent, it had not gone well. Because of the imposter, the driver had been armed and had not bowed to Archer's requests. And Brandt had been shot. In the aftermath, a discarded mask had been found next to Brandt. He had attempted to tell the constable that he had arrived on the scene only after hearing the commotion. Unable to prove his identity, however, they did not believe him and arrested him on sight.

"It's my fault," Archer muttered, raking a hand through his disheveled hair and reaching for his empty glass.

Brynn strode forward and removed the glass along with the bottle. "You've had enough."

He eyed her as if doubting she was really there. "Why are you here?" he slurred. "Come to celebrate your freedom?"

"My freedom?"

"From our engagement. Haven't you heard? I am a suspect. Found my bloody cravat and now they think I killed my father, for real this time. Thomson's grasping for straws, and I am one of them."

She glared at him and crossed the room to close the study door before returning to his side. "I am well aware of that, Archer. You need to collect your wits and figure a way out of this. This imposter is targeting you. Come now, you don't strike me as the sort of man who simply gives up, which is what you are doing by drinking yourself into a stupor."

He grasped her wrist as she leaned over him. "Why are you doing this?"

She flushed, his touch igniting a fire underneath her skin. "You know why."

His haunted dark gray eyes searched hers, and Brynn couldn't help herself. She brushed a curling lock of dark hair back from his brow. Her fingers stroked his skin with soft, gentle touches. He closed his eyes and leaned against her palm. Somehow the pleasure the intimate gesture gave her rivaled the pleasure his kisses usually did, and something profoundly delicate blossomed in her heart. "You should separate yourself from me before this gets any worse."

Her hand slid to his chin, and she grasped it firmly, twisting his face toward hers. "Regardless of what future lies between us, I care about what happens to you, and I won't abandon you now. Pull yourself together and fight, damn it." She didn't care about her language. She wanted to make him react, but her provoking words only made him shrug.

"What would you have me do?"

Brynn eyed his unshaven face, thinking how vulnerable and unbearably handsome he looked with the dark shadow along his jawline and without his usual arrogant smirk. "Have a bath for one, and sober up." She opened the study door and told the footman there to summon Heed. The butler arrived within seconds.

"Heed, please have the duke's valet prepare a bath." The man bowed without a word at her unorthodox command, though Brynn swore she could see a slight softening in his eyes. It was clear that Archer's servants adored him, including Heed, whose impervious demeanor never wavered. "Thank you, Heed. Oh, and please ask the cook to prepare something simple for His Grace once he has finished."

"My lady."

Archer got up and stumbled past her, on his way to the door. "Already giving my staff orders, I see."

Brynn ignored the comment and paced in the study after he had left. There had to be a way out of this calamity… something they hadn't yet thought of. Brandt's possibility of bail had been revoked in the interests of public safety, and Thomson and his cronies were on a witch hunt. They were no longer interested in finding the true killer, which meant that task must fall to those who still cared…a number that she could count on one hand.

Even if Archer weren't implicated, Thomson would do

everything in his power to tie the stable master to Archer once his identity was confirmed. Archer had told her of the bloody cravat, but anyone could have planted the item. Archer's alibi was solid—he was at his own engagement ball when the attack on poor Lady Hamilton occurred. But Brandt had not been.

Thomson was relentless, and she was certain he was wily enough to fabricate gossamer links between the evidence at hand and what had actually happened. Brynn also wagered he was not above using the newspapers to drive the public into a frenzy.

She thought about confiding in Gray and then shook her head. No, Gray would not understand. He would lock her up in Bishop House or ship her back off to Essex without a qualm. He would be concerned only for her safety and what might happen if she were attacked.

At the thought, Brynn suddenly had an epiphany. She frowned, turning the idea over in her mind. It was a long shot, but it could work. She needed only to convince Archer of its soundness.

She glanced at the ornate grandfather clock at the far end of the study. Archer would be gone for an hour or more, so Brynn settled herself into a comfortable armchair to wait and leaf through a book from one of the well-stocked shelves. She read the words, but they disappeared from her memory, it seemed, moments later. She was far too distracted by the idea she'd formed.

She was halfway through the book when the study door opened and Archer walked back in. His eyes looked more lucid, and the defeat in them was gone. Freshly shaven with his hair still wet, and clad in only a white chamois shirt and tan breeches with shiny Hessians, he looked utterly desirable.

"Feel better?" she asked, a trifle breathless.

"Yes, thank you. Brynn—" His words were interrupted

as Heed announced himself, opening the door to escort the waiting footman in with a large tray. Brynn nodded to the desk, and the footman set it down, uncovering the dishes and laying out the silverware. She smiled her thanks to Heed and noted with surprise that his lips actually drew up at the corners before he bowed stiffly and left the room.

"What's this?" Archer asked, even though she knew he had heard the exchange with Heed.

"You need to get something in your stomach *other* than drink."

As Archer sipped some of the broth, Brynn took a deep breath. It was now or never. "The Kensington Ball is two days hence. We should plan to go." He frowned at her, and she rushed to get the rest of her thoughts out before she lost her nerve. "I will wear the Bradburne diamonds and make every effort for it to be known in all the ladies' circles, no matter how vulgar such boasting may appear. If our bandit is indeed a gentleman, this will be a prize not to be missed. We will lure this imposter to us and clear Brandt's name."

Archer stared at her, a muscle starting to tick in his jaw, his eyes going glacial. "Absolutely not. I won't have you risking your neck for mine."

"It is our only chance," she argued. "We will leave separately, and you will follow the coach. Once he attacks, you will be able to catch him."

"No."

"You needn't worry for my safety. I will have my pistol with me, and as you are well aware, my marksmanship is excellent." She said the last with a smile, one that faded at the violent look on his face.

"*No.*" Archer rose in slow motion and walked to where she stood on the other side of the desk. She stared up at him, refusing to give up on her plan as they faced each other nose to nose. Her breathing hitched at his nearness and the clean scent of his freshly scrubbed skin.

"No," he said more gently. Archer leaned down as if he meant to kiss her, but a moment before their lips touched, he turned away to return to his seat. Brynn felt bereft of him, her body utterly desolate at the loss. He met her eyes, his voice a pained rasp. "The imposter has a tendency toward violence. I couldn't bear it if anything happened to you."

His whispered words made her heart clench. Archer *did* care about her. She had wondered after he had touched her so intimately; Brynn was new to navigating the waters of seduction, but not naive. She had no illusions that the duke loved her, though she also knew he wouldn't be so adamantly against her plan if he didn't care for her a little. That tiny knowledge gave her a boost of much-needed confidence.

"That's it, then, we are agreed."

"We are not."

"Archer."

"I forbid it."

She smiled at him, despite the low warning in his voice. "We are not yet married, my dear duke, and as such, I do not require your permission, nor am I forced to obey your wishes. Should we escape the gallows and agree to swear by our marriage vows, I will endeavor to be your *ever* obedient wife. But until then, my will is my own."

She almost laughed at his look of shocked incredulity. "Now eat. I shall take myself for a stroll where I will declare to all and sundry my intention to wear the Bradburne diamonds to the Kensington crush. Wish me luck."

Impulsively, she walked around to the side of the desk and placed a swift kiss atop his head, not noticing the hand that snaked around her waist until she tried to step away. Brynn swore under her breath. She should have left, but she couldn't bring herself to do it without touching him just once. Unable to move with his hand clamped around her, they stared at each other in charged silence. Brynn could see the turmoil in his eyes, and, without thinking, she leaned down and sealed her lips to his.

Archer reacted after a half beat of frozen surprise, sweeping her into his lap and claiming her mouth with desperate urgency. His tongue dueled with hers as she dug her fingers into the soft linen of his shirt and pushed her breasts tight to his chest. She was as greedy for him as he was for her. The interior of his mouth tasted faintly of whiskey and mint. The combination was intoxicating, and she clung to him, unable to get enough.

What was it about this man that made her want wildly indecent things?

All it took was the press of his lips and the reckless thrust of his tongue, and Brynn found herself ready to capitulate to anything. He made her weak, and yet, in his arms, she'd never felt more powerful.

After a long interlude, Archer lifted his head and stared at her in baffled wonderment. "What am I going to do with you? You are infuriating, maddening, impulsive, and so damned stubborn it takes my breath away. I cannot deter you from this foolhardy plan?"

Brynn stared at his face, her heart in her eyes. "No," she said softly. "You cannot."

"Why?"

Her answer was the same as the one she had given him before, although this time her voice trembled with the force of the emotion behind it. "You know why."

Archer may not love her, but Brynn knew that what she felt for this man was unlike anything she had ever felt before. It was all-consuming, exhilarating, *terrifying*, and it filled her body and her heart to bursting. She didn't know if it was love, but she did know that if anything happened to him, her life would be forever altered. She couldn't imagine seeing him punished for crimes he did not commit. Brynn would do whatever she could to prevent that from happening.

Archer didn't speak as he pulled her toward him, cradling her head in the hollow where his shoulder met his chest. She fit perfectly, her body molding itself to his. Brynn didn't speak, either, but she could feel their heartbeats aligning, and that felt more perfect than any words ever could.

Brynn stood in the front sitting room at Bishop House and smoothed her gloved hands over the layers of the emerald green chiffon. The gown she'd chosen for the Kensington Ball was a favorite among all her dresses and gowns for the season, and she'd wanted to save it for a truly special evening. She hadn't imagined that such an evening would include catching a thief and a killer.

Braxton had just announced the arrival of the duke, and her palms were fairly sweating.

This was it. There could be no turning back now.

Her parents had declined the invitation to the Kensington Ball in favor of another that they had previously accepted and had already left for that affair. Unfortunately, Gray had been charged with escorting Brynn to the Kensingtons' and representing the Dinsmore name, which had left Brynn scrambling to concoct a diversion to keep her brother occupied until *after* she'd left for the ball—alone. Of course, Archer would be trailing her on horseback, so she would not truly be alone. It would seem that way to only the imposter, should he have heard the rumors that the Bradburne diamonds were out and about for the evening.

She took a deep breath and glanced at herself in the beveled glass. Her hair had been twisted into a loose chignon with a few strands left free to fall in heavy ringlets down her back. The style displayed the Bradburne diamonds to perfection. The ostentatious gems glistened at her throat, the last tier falling into the hollow of her breasts.

Mary, one of the undermaids, had outdone herself with the elegant hairstyle. Lana had not been at Bishop House when Brynn had started to prepare for the ball, and for good reason. She had whispered a desire to travel to the ball alone, without alerting or alarming Gray, and Lana had promised that she would see to it. So far, her maid had been true to her word. Brynn had not seen hide nor hair of her brother or her maid since late morning.

Brynn, too, had played her part well and had flaunted her intent to wear the priceless necklace yesterday at a tea hosted by Cordelia and her mother. Not one invited lady had declined, including Archer's sister, which meant the tearoom in Lady Vandermere's home on Grosvenor Square had been overwhelmed with women, young and old, all of whom sat agog while Cordelia accounted her lurid tale of the attack on her carriage in Hyde Park.

Brynn had sipped her oolong while sitting beside Eloise, listening to Cordelia's timorous voice but thinking of Archer and his friend Brandt, instead. All eyes had been on Cordelia, her teacup shaking in her hand until she had finally needed to set it down. However, Brynn still felt as if she were hiding in plain sight, and that at any moment, one of the ladies would look at her and just somehow *know*. Of course, no one did. No one yet knew who the man arrested in Hyde Park was—he had purportedly not given his identity and was being held in Newgate. Brynn imagined he was being questioned heavily by Thomson. She didn't want to consider what more was happening to Archer's trusted friend inside that abominable stone fortress, though she imagined Archer had been able to think of nothing else.

Despite cringing inside at how shallow she appeared,

Brynn had found a way to bring up the Bradburne diamonds and her plans to wear them to the Kensington Ball. Most of the younger ladies had simpered along with her, but she had seen vaulted brows from some of the more experienced ladies of the *ton* and had felt the sting of their contempt. Eloise had not said a word, though she had been more reserved for the rest of the afternoon. Granted, discussing fashion and diamonds so soon after Cordelia's harrowing tale had been gauche, but she could not waste time caring about what anyone thought of her.

"I can do this," she whispered to herself in the glass.

Braxton stepped into the sitting room and announced the duke. Brynn turned from the mirror and caught her breath as Archer filled the entrance. As he strode farther into the room, she felt the strangest reaction: her palms grew even more hot and damp, and yet the nerves churning her stomach instantly settled.

Having him here put her at ease, even if she wasn't completely comfortable being left alone with him as Braxton took his leave. It didn't make any sense, and yet there it was.

He stared at her, a slow, appreciative grin lifting the corners of his mouth.

"Well, you've done it. No thief worth his salt will be able to resist that display."

His eyes glittered as they took in the diamonds and the expanse of décolletage they rested upon. The skin there grew warmer under his gaze, and Brynn, without thought, touched the tips of her fingers to the lowest tier of jewels.

Archer's breathing hitched and his jaw shifted as he followed her movement. "You take my breath away."

She flushed at the amorous look in his eyes as they devoured her, sweeping to her breasts and then back to her face. She lowered her hand. "Thank you, my lord."

He was clad in raven-black attire from head to toe with

the exception of his shirt and cravat. Brynn hadn't thought it possible that he could be any more attractive, but he had somehow managed it.

He lowered his voice and came closer to her. "It's not too late to change your mind."

"I won't lie," she admitted. "I am terrified this plan of mine will succeed in drawing the imposter out. But your friend in Newgate must be even more terrified than I."

Archer grimaced and cut his eyes from her. "You don't know Brandt. He doesn't scare easily. Still, he will not be there much longer."

No, she did not know Archer's friend well at all. However, she had come to know *Archer*, though she didn't know how or when, exactly. "You plan to turn yourself in."

He wouldn't look at her as he crossed the room in the opposite direction of her, toward a divan near the hearth. The fire was small in the grate, and it threw weak light over his figure. He stood with his back to her, the fingers of his right hand twisting the duke's signet ring upon the third finger on his left hand.

"I will not allow him to rot in that filthy hole. And if Thomson recognizes him as the man my footmen dragged in at Hadley Gardens the night of my father's murder…"

He didn't finish. He didn't need to. Brynn could suddenly feel how tenuous the whole situation was. The tightrope Archer had been walking the last few days. She felt a surge of empathy and wished she could do more to lessen his burden.

"You care for him," she said as she walked toward the hearth. He continued to stare into the flames.

"He is a brother to me," he replied, still twisting his signet ring. He was always so cool and unflappable, and this nervous twitch of his was the first bit of vulnerability he'd shown her.

Brynn wanted to reach for him. To take his restless hands and hold them firmly in her own. The urge was so keen it left an ache in her.

"I haven't changed my mind about tonight," she said. "Catching the imposter is the only way through this."

He turned his ear toward her but stayed facing the hearth. "There is another option."

Brynn gave in to her craving and settled her hands lightly on the broad width of his back. "Even if you were to turn yourself in, the imposter would still be out there. The robberies will continue, and he'll keep harming people. We are the only ones who know he is not the true bandit. We must stop him, Archer. I know you don't want to allow Brandt to rot in Newgate, but I won't allow *you* to be escorted to the gallows."

He lifted his head at her touch and stopped twisting his ring. His body went rigid under her hands, his ribs expanding with a held breath.

"Only a coward would let another man take the fall for his own crimes. I am many things, but a coward is not one of them."

Brynn swept her hands up to where his shoulders widened, curving her palms around each muscled one. He was so big and strong. She wanted to cling to him, if only to stop him from marching to Bow Street and turning himself in to Thomson.

"But you have not committed the crimes worthy of hanging—the imposter is the violent one, not you."

There was a difference between the two bandits, as clear as the divide between night and day.

Archer laughed. "I am a highwayman, Brynn, and last I knew, that was crime enough, worthy of the noose."

She let go of his shoulders and circled around to stand before him. "You do not keep what you take. You give it to the poor—"

"The magistrate would not give a damn about that."

"*I* give a damn!"

She sealed her lips the moment the curse was out. The man made her want to swoon and swear in equal measure. Archer's tensed shoulders softened. Firelight reflected in his eyes as he cupped her cheek, his gloved hand sliding like silk against her skin.

She gathered a breath and held it.

"I mean, I…I care. I don't want anything to happen to you or your friend. Not when you were only trying to do some good," she said, adding, "as misdirected as it was."

His mouth quirked into a half grin before falling somber once again. "Why do you care? I've been a beast to you."

Brynn shook her head. Archer's fingers raked lower, down the slope of her neck. She didn't know how to answer. *Why?* It was a fine question. One she wasn't quite certain how to answer.

Honestly, when Archer had confessed his darkest secret— that he was the Masked Marauder—she had felt a slap of repulsion. Explaining what he did with the items he stole had allayed that feeling, though only slightly. She'd wondered at his endgame. Did he not think he would ever get caught? What kind of fool acted so recklessly, without a care for his own title and lands?

At some point, without even realizing it, the answers had struck her: a man who did these things was a man who cared deeply and passionately—a man who was willing to risk himself and everything he had in order to make a difference in the only way he knew how. If Archer's father hadn't sunk the Bradburne dukedom's finances to such depths, Archer would have given everything to his cause. A cause Brynn found herself caring for—simply because he did.

She had heard whisperings from the Countess of Thorndale at Cordelia's tea about several mysterious and large donations that had been received for the new children's hospital on the outskirts of London. Brynn suspected the donations had been from Archer and, even though thievery was wrong, she had to admire his skewed sense of nobility.

Archer stroked the nape of her neck, his fingers threading through her loose ringlets. Brynn's lids fluttered shut at the delicate sensation.

"I suppose I've come to understand what you intended to do. And you aren't a beast," she whispered, a delectable shiver unfurling deep in her stomach. "Not when you touch me like this."

He scraped his fingers around her nape and tensed them. "I am a wolf, and you know it."

She opened her eyes and found he'd angled his head lower. Instead of alarm, Brynn felt anticipation.

"Well, perhaps you are," she said, her eyes on his mouth. "But wolf or not, I don't want anything to happen to you."

His expression pinched. "You have your pistol in your reticule?"

She pulled back at the question, the mention of her pistol jarring. His grasp at the back of her neck wouldn't let her go far.

"If we must carry out this plan, I need to know you will shoot the bastard if anything goes wrong." He tugged her closer, until the tips of their noses brushed together. "I need to know you will be safe."

Brynn nodded, beset by the intensity of his request, of his stare and the possessive hand clutching at her nape. It was as if he never wanted to release her.

"I promise," she said. Before she could take another breath, Archer kissed her, the pressure of his mouth just as demanding as his request for her to use her pistol well.

He parted her lips with his tongue, and stole inside with savage need. He'd called himself a wolf, and this kiss had a dangerous edge. But she knew in her heart that he wasn't trying to be a beast. He clung to her, devouring her with his kiss, because he was afraid. He wanted to shield her from harm, and tonight he feared he wouldn't be able to do so. That knowledge, she knew, was gutting him.

Brynn opened to him, allowing him to sink deeper, closer. How had she learned so much about this man? To know the distinctions between his kisses, and what each one meant underneath their passionate surface, frightened her.

I know him as I never thought I would, she thought as his hands traveled down the back of her gown and over her rump, crushing her against his body.

I love *him as I never thought I would.*

Heat and shock flared inside Brynn's chest, and she gasped against his mouth. Archer pulled back.

"What is it?" he asked, concern leaping in his gaze.

"I just…I think we should get on with things. Before I lose my nerve," she answered, her eyes falling away. He took a deep breath and nodded upon releasing her.

"And I mine," he said. "I'll leave through the front door and have my driver take the carriage to King Street. I have a mount waiting for me there. I'll double back and wait for your conveyance to pull away from Bishop House. I'll follow you at a close distance."

"How will I know you?" she asked, eyeing his attire. He would stick out sorely as he was and would most definitely have thought to bring something to cloak himself with.

"I'll be wearing a greatcoat and a hat with plumage," he answered with a quick peck to the tip of her nose. "I'll look positively dandy."

Brynn tried to smile, but her fractured nerves were doing strange things to her facial muscles.

"Relax," he told her. "The imposter may well spring upon you after the ball. If at all."

He left her at the hearth and strode into the foyer. Once

Brynn heard the door close behind him, she met Braxton in the sitting room entrance. "Call for my carriage," she instructed, and with a bow, he left to see it done.

The next several minutes waiting were tortuous. She left Bishop House only when she knew Archer had been given plenty of time to exit his carriage and take up his waiting mount then come back and watch for her departure. Braxton helped Brynn up into her waiting coach and closed the door behind her with a short bow.

When they pulled away from the curb a moment later, Brynn felt as if she might be ill. Archer was correct, of course. The ball would go on into the small hours of morning, and that would be an ideal time for the imposter to pounce. If he planned to at all. If he did have a connection to Archer and the late duke, he may very well avoid Brynn altogether. Suddenly she felt silly for believing she could draw him out by wearing the diamonds. They were too well-known a piece, and if he pawned them, they would no doubt be recognized.

She sat against the back cushions and let out a breath. Archer was behind her somewhere on the street and for nothing at all. He'd have to return to his carriage on King Street and then be late for the ball. What a waste.

With that thought, Brynn's coach came to a stop. The Kensingtons' home was still another ten minutes away, so they could not have already arrived. She sat forward, biting the inside of her cheek, and listened.

There wasn't a sound, except for the distant clop of horse hooves and normal street noises. Muted, though. As if the carriage had drawn off the main road.

"Beckett?" she called to her driver.

"Sorry, my lady," came his answer. "There was a section of road closed off, and I needed to make a—"

His sentence ended with a grunt, and the whole coach rocked violently.

Something was happening up in the driver's box, and Brynn knew exactly what it was.

She grabbed her reticule and felt around inside for her pistol. Deuce it, she should have had the thing ready! The cool metal grip hit her palm, and she pulled out the lady's pistol, aiming the short barrel at the door, the tasseled curtain over the window shaking as the coach made its final rocks.

Beckett had not made another sound, and with a surge of self-disgust, Brynn realized she hadn't thought of any risk to him the bandit may pose. If anything happened to Beckett, she would never forgive herself. Without thought or plan, she opened the coach door with her free hand. Lifting the hem of her voluminous skirts, she jumped the two feet to the ground. Her shins ached on impact, but she turned immediately for the bench—and came face to face with a masked man.

Brynn raised her pistol, but even with Archer's demand to shoot still fresh in her mind, could not pull the trigger.

The masked man was tall and broad like Archer, but not in a fit or regal way. He wore the same sort of guise Archer had that night on the lane to Worthington Abbey, but his black mask hid a rounder face, his posture was slovenly, and he'd chosen a black cape rather than a greatcoat. He also did not have the smooth, gentlemanly manner Archer had possessed, even while demanding coin and jewels.

"No displays of heroism please," he said in a mocking voice. "Hand them over."

The diamonds.

Her half-cocked plan had worked.

"No," Brynn managed to say, her finger numb on the trigger.

He took a step forward, and she saw he held a pistol in his own hand. Beckett looked like he was laid out in the driver's bench.

"We both know you won't shoot me," the man said.

"I, however, will," came a steady voice behind Brynn.

Archer. Thank God. Still, she didn't lower her weapon.

The imposter didn't startle, she noticed, and that gave her pause.

"Your weapon isn't loaded. It never is," he stated. Brynn held her breath. Archer had admitted as much weeks before in his mother's salon.

"It is tonight. Who are you?" Archer asked.

They were on a quiet side street, stuck between lampposts set twenty or so yards apart. She saw figures ahead, passing under the lamplight, but they had not seemed to notice the waylaid carriage in the center of the street. Either that, or they had and had decided to look the other way.

"A person no one cares to notice," the man said with detectable amusement. As if what he'd said had been funny.

"Drop your pistol," Brynn said, her wrist shaking from the tension up and down her raised arm.

"Give me the diamonds," was his reply.

"Brynn, step aside," Archer said, his voice deadly calm.

She did, moving closer to the coach.

"Now, you lecherous bastard, I suggest you—"

Archer's sentence was cut off, just as Beckett's had been, with a grunt and the sound of a commotion behind her.

Brynn made the mistake of spinning around to see what had happened to him. Her eyes had barely taken in the sight of Archer, unmoving on the ground with a hooded figure standing over his body, when a hand clamped over her mouth. The imposter's arm hooked her waist and sealed her body against his, pinning her arms to her sides. He squeezed her wrist until a sharp pain cracked through the small bones, forcing her to drop the pistol. Her muted screams filled his palm instead of echoing out to passersby as she thrashed.

She did have one weapon left, however, and by all that was holy, she would use it.

Brynn opened her mouth and bared her teeth, biting into the meaty flesh just under his thumb. It tasted like salted cod and dirt, but she continued to clamp her jaw until the man released her with a howl. She stumbled away and tried to run to Archer and the shorter, hooded man, but the imposter grabbed her arm, pulled her to a stop, and spun her to face him.

She saw a hand flying at her head. Felt an agonizing blow to her cheek and nose that rattled everything in her skull.

And then nothing more.

Chapter Twenty-Two

Archer's eyes creaked open and then closed once again at the excruciating pain pulsating through his head. He blinked gingerly as waves of nausea followed. It took him a full minute to get his bearings, and then awareness came rushing back. En route to the Kensingtons', their plan had worked. He'd had the masked imposter at the end of his pistol, but some unseen assailant had attacked him from behind. A blow to his head.

Oh god.

Brynn.

His eyes searched for her in the darkness and settled on a dim shape at the far side of the room. The emerald silk dress lay like a shroud around her, but he could see the slight rise and fall of her shoulders. She was still alive. He exhaled, relief swamping him. If that bastard and his accomplice had hurt her, they wouldn't have lived to see the light of day.

He blinked again, his eyes adjusting to the shadows of the room. The smell of horses and dung permeated the air. They were in a mews, but where, he did not know.

Forcing himself to think clearly, he assessed the situation.

His hands were bound behind his back and something filthy was pulled tight across his mouth. A damp and sticky wetness coated the skin of his brow and made his eyelids heavy. Archer knew it was blood, even though he could not feel the sting of an injury. He could smell its rusty and metallic odor. What he didn't know was how bad the wound was, and whether or not he could free himself and rescue Brynn before their unknown assailant came back. For now, they seemed to be alone.

Archer took in his surroundings, looking for weapons or anything sharp that he could use to loosen the ties around his wrists. If they were in a mews, then where were the grooms? Someone should be here. But there were no sounds except for the gentle nicker of horses in the neighboring stalls. His head still felt cottony, and his tongue pushed against the disgusting rag in his mouth as he attempted to swallow.

He assumed that they were still in London, but there were hundreds of carriage houses to choose from. His eyes narrowed on the rows of tack. Archer frowned, his stare traveling in reverse to stop on a familiar saddle, polished to a burnished shine.

His own saddle.

At least, it looked like his. Was this Hadley Gardens? As he squinted around the stall another time, his befuddled senses clearing, he was certain it was. His relief was short-lived as he realized why the carriage house was empty. No one *was* here. This was one of the few nights during the week the grooms were off. Normally Brandt would be hanging about, but, of course, he was stuck facing a nightmare of his own in a dank cell. And if Archer didn't free himself and Brynn, his friend would stay there for the rest of his days.

Archer renewed his struggles, scooting backward until he came to a center post. He pushed through the rabid throbbing of his skull and sawed at his ropes using the post's splintered edge. Once he felt them loosening, he increased his efforts.

"Archer?" Brynn's voice was muffled, and he realized her mouth was also bound.

"Here," he managed, limited by the gag, watching as she pulled herself into a sitting position.

Her hands were tied, as well, but lay on her lap instead of behind her. Having adjusted to the dim light, he saw a trickle of blood under her nose and a flowering purple bruise on the side of her temple. Archer's fists clenched, and his earlier vow to beat their assailants into a fine mash returned. She lifted her hands to tug the dirty brown cloth from between her lips.

"Where are we?" she asked.

"Hadley Gardens, I think." He hoped she could understand his muffled words.

"Are you hurt?" she asked and then gasped as her eyes, too, adjusted to the gloom. "You're bleeding."

"A scratch."

His tongue pushed against the soiled scrap pressing into his mouth, the foul taste of it making him heave. "Can you… shout for help?" he choked past it.

Brynn nodded and did as he asked, opening her mouth and yelling out, "Is anyone there? Hello? Help us! We're in here!"

"We'll have none of that, if you please, my lady."

They both stilled as the heavy wooden door pushed open. The same man from earlier entered the stall holding a pistol, and this time he wore no mask. Archer frowned, fighting to recall his face. He could not always recall names, but faces he never forgot. There was no recognition, though. He was certain he had never seen this man before tonight.

The man was tall and swarthy and dressed in the midnight garb of the Masked Marauder, with the exception of the mask. Archer glanced to the door, but no one else entered. The second man, the one who had come up behind Archer and knocked him senseless, had to be here somewhere. He needed to remain alert and focused. His life depended on it, as did Brynn's. And Brandt's, he supposed, who would take the fall for everything, should this cretin get away. A lethal calm descended upon him as he assessed their assailant.

The killer's clothes were of decent quality, which marked him as a man of some means, and he seemed well-groomed. But Archer had never seen him before, certainly not in any of his social circles. He grunted against the rag, and the man approached, keeping his weapon trained right at Archer's heart.

"Have something to say, Your Grace?" Stooping low, the man loosened the tie, pulling it out of Archer's mouth. "Sorry about this, but we couldn't have you attracting attention, could we?"

Archer wanted to leap to his feet and meet the man face-to-face, but if he moved, he would lose the splintered edge of the post. He continued to saw the ropes, hoping he appeared to be only struggling with discomfort. The ropes were slowly loosening, the twisted hemp coming apart strand by strand.

"Who are you?" he asked.

"Someone who has benefited handsomely at your expense, it seems."

"You are a cold-blooded criminal," Archer seethed, not rising to the man's bait.

The man slanted an eyebrow. "If I have to be."

Said without an ounce of remorse. Reasoning with such a man would be pointless, but he had to keep him talking — and distracted.

"Why are you doing this?"

"For the riches, of course."

Archer tugged on his bonds until the skin at his wrists rubbed raw. His hands were already slick with blood, but it wouldn't take much more for him to get loose. "I can pay. Release us, and you will have all the riches you desire. I give you my word."

To his surprise, the man laughed, the sound echoing off the wooden rafters. "I am already well compensated, and you are meant to serve a much better purpose. After all, Bow Street already considers you a suspect. We are simply facilitating your arrest."

Archer's eyes narrowed. The man knew a lot, but it was to be expected. He wouldn't have been able to find out about Archer if he wasn't meticulous by nature. "Where is your friend?" he asked casually. "The one who hit me?"

"Around. Making sure we remain undisturbed."

The man smiled, shooting a lascivious glance toward Brynn, who had stayed silent. For the first time, Archer felt a prickle of fear pool deep in his belly. Not for himself, but for her.

"Touch the lady, and it will be the last thing you do," he snarled.

"And how, pray tell, will you come to her defense?" the man taunted.

Archer's breath stalled as the man turned toward Brynn and dragged her up like a ragdoll against him. She gasped at the cruel latch of his hand on her arm but made no other sound. "I like this dress on you," the imposter told her. "Though I think I'd like it better on the floor."

Archer once again battled the urge to get to his feet and charge the bastard. His bonds were almost loose, and now he redoubled his efforts, sliding his hands against each other in slow, deliberate movements. He used his own blood to help lubricate against the coarse rope. The pain kept him focused. That, and thinking in vicious detail what he was going to do to that piece of filth once he was loose.

Brynn turned her face away, keeping her eyes on Archer. He could see the sheen of tears in them, but she held her chin erect. *Valiant as ever*, Archer thought, his chest tight with pride and fury. She wouldn't cave or grovel, not to this beast of a man.

The man's hands fluttered toward the ostentatious display of diamonds attached to her throat and removed the clasp, the backs of his knuckles brushing deliberately against Brynn's breasts in the process. Archer's jaw clenched, regretting he'd ever agreed to this damned plan. He'd put her at risk and hadn't been able to protect her. He watched as the impersonator pocketed the jewels, his hand sliding down Brynn's rib cage and around to her rear. Archer would kill him. Of that he was absolutely certain.

Brynn struggled wildly, kicking up with her legs, not even stopping when he pressed the point of the pistol into her side.

The man grinned at her as he fended off a knee aimed toward his groin and turned in slow motion to point the pistol at Archer.

"One more move, lovely, and I shoot your betrothed. You can make this nice and quick, or long and painful. It's your choice."

Brynn froze, her body going limp. Shutters descended over her eyes as the man ripped the chiffon dress from bosom to waist. Archer tore at his restraints with single-minded purpose. He stared helplessly at her, rage and agony eating at him. She was the only woman he had ever cared for, and he could do nothing to protect her as the bastard dipped his head to her exposed body, his fingers fumbling at the laces on her stays. Silent tears tracked her face, her bottom lip trembling with fear.

With Herculean strength, Archer ripped one wrist from the rope shackle. He forced himself to move slowly, controlling his bloodlust long enough to meet Brynn's gaze. He needed her out of the way. As he waved his free hand low at his side, her eyes sparked with understanding. He set his jaw, adrenaline surging through his body like an uncaged beast. She inhaled sharply and flung her bound hands up toward the man's throat, catching him in the soft part of his lower esophagus.

"You bloody bitch," he coughed, raising the gun as he stumbled backward from Brynn's strike.

But the movement was no match for Archer's savage burst of speed as he sprung to his feet and dove forward. With a guttural growl, he tackled him to the ground, the impersonator's pistol flying into the air and disappearing behind a bale of hay. The man had a stone on him in weight, but he was no contest for the demonic wrath possessing Archer. Blinded by cold fury and purpose, he straddled the man's body, his fists flying like battering rams, crunching into bone, teeth, and tissue until the man's face was an unrecognizable bloody pulp. After an eternity, Archer staggered back. He turned sharply in search for Brynn, his knuckles aching. She threw herself into his arms, and he hugged her body to his as he hauled burning breaths into his lungs.

"Are you hurt?" he gasped, kissing her hair, her face, her eyes, while being careful of the ragged bruise on her cheek.

"No," she whispered.

Archer turned to find a knife from one of the tack shelves and snapped the bonds at her wrists. "Let's go," he said to her, but Brynn's eyes were wide and terrified as she focused on something—or someone—just beyond his left shoulder.

He turned, and in disbelief, saw the man he'd just pummeled unconscious standing. His face was swollen and drenched in blood, but the hand holding the short pistol he had recovered from the hay did not waver. The man's bloody mouth puckered into a smile, and his finger tightened on the trigger. Archer shoved Brynn behind him, and as a shot exploded into the silence, he braced for the pain.

None came.

He opened his eyes just as the man's body fell to the

ground in a thump, a bloody hole gaping at his breast. Archer whipped around, his mind a tumult of relief and confusion. A whimpering Eloise stood in the doorway, smoke rising from the muzzle of the gun in her hands. He couldn't believe what he was seeing. His sister had just shot a man. Saved their lives. He wanted to go to her and take the weapon from her shaking hands. But he couldn't move. His legs refused to step away from Brynn's side. With shattered gratitude, Archer nodded to Eloise and pulled Brynn to him as she collapsed sobbing against his jacket.

"It's over now," he whispered against her hair.

Eloise slumped against the door, breathing hard, her hand falling to her side. Archer met her eyes, thankful for once that he hadn't insisted she accompany them to the Kensington Ball. If she hadn't been here, he shuddered to think of what would have happened. She must have heard a commotion in the mews, though he didn't know how or when. It didn't matter—she had come. But they were not entirely free from threat yet. He motioned her to come closer, putting a finger against his lips.

"What's the matter?" she whispered.

"There is a second man."

Her eyes widened as she handed him the spent gun. "I don't know how to reload," she began, her entire body shivering in delayed shock. She and Brynn clutched each other as Brynn whispered her fevered thanks. "You saved us," she said.

"I was only lucky that I was able to help." Eloise touched the bruise on Brynn's temple, wincing in sympathy. "We should have that looked at. You may be concussed."

His sister was correct, and perhaps he himself was as well. But they had a more immediate urgency.

"I need to get you both somewhere safe," Archer said. "But first, Eloise—how did you know that we were in trouble?"

"I thought I heard someone shouting," Eloise explained, her voice trembling. "I knew the grooms were off, and it sounded like the shouts had come from here. So I sneaked into Father's study and took that pistol out of the gun case."

Archer's eyes narrowed on the still-smoking gun she had given him. He frowned, studying the shiny embossed twin barrels. He had never seen the intricate bone-handled butt before, and he was familiar with every pistol and rifle in the late duke's gun case. He'd shot them all at one point or another. His frown deepened as he studied the finely etched designs on the handle. This gun was decidedly not his father's. The slope of the handle had been cut to fit a much smaller hand.

His blood slowed in his veins as a sticky realization took hold. His eyes met his sister's, and the fragility in them winked away, replaced by a ruthless, calculated determination. He shook his head as if his own eyes were deceiving him.

"I see the game is up," Eloise commented, the shift in her voice going from pleading and frail, to strong and cold. Her very appearance transformed before his eyes. In truth, he did not recognize her.

Archer blinked in disbelief as his sister backed away from them, a second pistol appearing out of her cloak. She pointed it right at his head, a smile crossing her lips.

Betrayal speared him like a pointed lance. "Eloise, no."

"You are far too clever, brother. I should have been more careful with my words. Then again, I suppose it is so much more gratifying this way, isn't it?"

"Eloise," Brynn whispered, her eyes stuck fast on the second pistol. "What are you doing?"

But his sister didn't have to answer. Archer already knew. "*You're* the second man," he said slowly. "The other assailant."

She nodded, satisfaction glinting in her icy stare. Suddenly his delicate, physically and emotionally scarred sister didn't seem so shocked or weak or frail. Her hands were no longer shaking. She was in utter control. "Drop your weapons, Archer."

He did as she asked, if only because he sensed, with her brutally swift and seamless transformation, that she was far more dangerous than the other man had been. "Why are you doing this?"

Another rapid shift swept over her, Eloise's unveiled face contorting into something demented and violent. She'd never looked at him this way before, and it chilled Archer to his very core. "Because you deserve to die, you arrogant filth. You should have died in that fire, not your mother. It was meant for you." Archer stared at her, saying nothing despite the hot burst of pain flaring along his veins and burrowing into his chest.

"*Meant* for me?" he repeated. The fire had been an *accident*. At least...that was what it had been determined to have been. "You set the fire?"

She sighed, but her answer was clear in the annoyed look she sent him. As if he was a fool. As if he should have figured it out ages ago.

His mother's death had been an accident...but only because she had died in Archer's place. His sister was insane, he concluded, the sinking awareness wringing his heart and stomach together in anguish. His *sister* was the threat. His *sister* wanted him dead. *Them* dead. He felt Brynn clinging to his side, her breath coming in a choppy rhythm. He was not Eloise's sole target anymore. Which meant he had to proceed carefully—and stall for time.

"And the duke?" he asked, attempting to keep his voice flat.

"Oh, I killed him, too," she said in a bored tone. "That was unfortunate, but honestly, I'm glad for it now. The man rutted everything that moved and had the nerve to punish *me* for it. Do you know what it's like being born a bastard and despised every day of your life? No, of course you don't. You, after all, are *legitimate*." Her words were bitter, the sneer on her lips more so, but she shrugged. "I think he suspected about the fire, but he didn't have the guts, until that night in his study, to confront me about it." She smiled. "The look on his face when I told him was priceless. So yes, I killed him. After all, I didn't want him ruining all my beautifully laid plans. I did you a favor, Archer. I did us both a favor."

He ignored the blinding ache that spiraled through him at her confession and struggled to keep his face unmoved. "And the Masked Marauder?"

She responded in a mocking tone. "I made it my business to know everything going on at Worthington Abbey. I found your mask; followed you to Pierce Cottage. It wasn't hard to put two and two together and work out what you and that bastard of a stable master were doing. It's fitting that he will rot in prison, is it not? I've never liked him, always at your side like an insect. Even *he* thought he was better than me."

"You sent the notes," Archer concluded dully.

"Of course I did. I took great pleasure in watching the great Archer Croft cringing at the threat of being unmasked." Her lip curled. "You're nothing but a common thief."

"He is not," Brynn blurted. "He does not keep what he takes."

"And that excuses the crime?" Eloise laughed, the hollow sound making Archer's skin rankle. "Oh, I know of the demons that drive my brother, and his desire to right a situation that can never be fixed. The duke killed my mother, you see. Left her to rot and die like the commoner she was. She didn't have the means to save herself, which was why Lady Bradburne took me in. Out of guilt. And likewise, my dear brother steals from his peers because of his own sorry *guilt*." She smiled.

"He loathes being born into privilege. Scorns it, even, while the rest of us grovel for crumbs of approval."

"I am not my father," Archer returned quietly.

"I suppose that's one good thing that could be said for you," Eloise said, eyeing him. "You think your skewed sense of nobility in feeding the hungry and saving the sick makes up for his sins?"

Archer stared back, though not in a confrontational manner. He was not familiar with this unpredictable, volatile Eloise, and the wrong look or response could work against them. "No, but at least it's something."

"Something worth hanging for?"

Archer's jaw tightened at the underlying thread of menace in her tone. Was that her plan, then? To out him to the authorities? "If that is the price I must pay, then yes."

"Then you are more foolish than I ever gave you credit for." His sister's gaze shifted to Brynn. "Light that candle over there, will you please, Lady Briannon?" Archer felt Brynn stiffen at his side, and Eloise's eyes hardened at her hesitation. "Do it. I warn you that I am not as softhearted, or as stupid, as that dead brute lying beside you."

Brynn lit the candle and moved back to stand at Archer's side, her body trembling as she grasped the torn edges of her bodice. He wanted so much to take hold of her hand, but he knew without a doubt, Eloise meant every word she said, and that she was more than capable of killing in cold blood. How had he not seen this hatred, this seething resentment before? How had he been so blind all these years? He couldn't dwell on it, however. Once more, he needed to find a way out of this deadlock and get Brynn to safety. He could deal with his sister's betrayal after.

"You see," Eloise continued, "my plan was to frame you for the duke's murder. Poor Barnstead here was more than happy to earn his keep. He kept what he stole and altered your secret persona into something more despicable. I *was* going to let you hang, but this is so much better. Instead, I shall pin him as the criminal who hurt so many people and murdered my father, as well as my brother and his beautiful fiancée, all of whom are survived by poor, helpless Eloise."

"You plan to *kill* us?" Brynn gasped.

"Oh yes, my sweet girl. So tragic." She spread her palms with dramatic flair. "Attacked by the Masked Marauder who was lured by the prize of the Bradburne jewels." She nodded at Brynn. "Nice tactic, by the way. It really was a perfect ploy." She tapped her chin thoughtfully. "There was a struggle, the bandit was shot, but a candle tipped over, setting the place on fire." She eyed Archer, malice dripping from her words. "And you will die as you were meant to all those years ago."

Something settled inside Archer at his sister's words. A new determination. He didn't know what would happen to him in the end, but he did know, without a moment's doubt, that he would die before allowing one more injury to befall Lady Briannon Findlay.

"Why, Eloise? We are friends," Brynn whispered.

"We were never friends," Eloise spat. "You looked down on me like everyone else. And with a face like this, who wouldn't? What were my chances for happiness? Of making a decent match?"

"But what about Langlevit?" Brynn asked. "He cares for you. I've seen—"

"Shut up, or God help me, I'll make you!" Eloise's words, though doused in acid, cracked.

Suddenly, Archer saw his opportunity. He shook his head. "She doesn't care about the earl, Brynn. After all, my mother loved her, too, and she threw that away. She doesn't care about love, nor any of the people who love her."

Naked pain slashed Eloise's face. "She loved her precious son more. I couldn't stop her from going into a burning tree house to look for you, could I? She died because of you. She was the one person who treated me with compassion, and you took her away from me."

Destabilize her. Distract her. It was all he had to do before he made his move.

"No, Eloise, she died because of you. You set the fire. You killed her."

"Shut up!" she screamed. "Or I will drop your precious love like a fly." Archer deliberately pressed Brynn behind him, but Eloise only laughed madly. She raised the gun — and froze. A hand holding a pistol appeared in the horse stall entrance where she stood. An arm, and then a body, quickly followed it.

Brynn's brother, Northridge, pressed the muzzle of his pistol to Eloise's temple. "I'll take that, thank you."

Archer felt Brynn's soft exhale against his back. "Gray, how did you find us?" she cried out.

Northridge's eyes flicked to his sister. "Lana told me everything, and Hadley Gardens was my first stop to find you when I heard the shot," he replied grimly, relieving Eloise of her gun though he could not stop her from whirling out of his grasp. She dove behind a wooden saddle stand.

"Don't hurt her," Archer ordered while Northridge kept his weapon trained on her. "Get Brynn out of here. I will take care of it."

Brynn rushed to her brother's side, clutching at him as Northridge wrapped his cloak around her shoulders. "I have Lana in the carriage outside. Come."

"No. Archer," Brynn said, her worried eyes leaping back to him. "I won't leave you."

He went to her, his need to have her gone from this wretched horse stall warring with his desire to keep her safely at his side. She would be safe with Northridge, though. Archer trusted that. "It's over, love; she can't hurt anyone now." He kissed her swiftly on the temple and nodded to her brother.

Archer took Northridge's pistol and waited until they had left before addressing his sister, still hunched behind the saddle stand. "Eloise, it is finished."

She stood, and the madness in her eyes had not snuffed out. If anything, it had flared. The light from the candle threw long shadows on her cheeks, making her scars there seem even more gruesome. Even after having stood at the end of her gun, after hearing her merciless plans to do away with him and the one woman he'd ever truly cared for, Archer felt a twinge of pity. The fire had burned scars on her face, but it had burned worse ones into her soul. Eloise was so consumed by hate that she would give up a chance at happiness and love just to punish him. Archer didn't know if he could forgive her, or whether she would be able to forgive herself, but he knew that he had to try.

"We can work this out," he said softly.

"Work what out, brother? You have a pistol pointed at me, and I have nothing."

Despite his better judgment, Archer tossed the loaded weapon to the stall floor. Her eyes follow the movement and then leveled on him as if trying to see inside his heart. He would not shoot her. He could not. His sister needed help, and he would do anything to see it done. "Better?" he asked, inching closer to where she stood, eying him nervously. "Eloise, please listen to me. Langlevit wants you. He has already approached me."

Her fingers clutched the folds of her dress. "Don't say that to me," she cried in a broken whisper.

"He wants your hand in marriage. You have a chance to be happy."

"And what of you? Will you forgive what I have done?"

Archer stared at his sister and felt only deep, driving pity. Unloved and unwanted, she had twisted herself into something broken and bitter. But Archer knew that despite all her machinations, his mother's death *had* been an accident. Eloise had loved her desperately. Her jealousy against him had been fortified and fed by his father's indifference. Archer swallowed hard. "I can only promise that I will try."

They stood in silence, separated by the wooden saddle stand. He could almost reach for her, but he didn't want to startle her. He kept his arms and body relaxed. Emotions clashed in her eyes—the promise of happiness that lay just beyond her grasp and the desolation of what she had done, drawing her down into its depths.

"No, Archer, I don't deserve to be happy." She raised a shaking hand.

It wasn't empty.

Archer recognized Brynn's lady's pistol trained on his chest. He froze as Eloise knocked over the nearby candle with a flick of her wrist. Hungry flames sprouted along the dried hay at her feet and licked at the hem of her dress. "This ends now, the way it was meant to."

Brynn is safe. It was all he could think of as he saw the fire spreading at his sister's back and traveling into the space between them.

"Don't do this," he said, his voice hoarse, his mind racing forward to calculate how to reach Eloise without being engulfed in flames. As it was, the exit to the stall would be closed off to him within seconds. "It's not too late."

"It was too late the moment I killed the only person who loved me." She smiled at him through her tears and through the flames, and for a moment, Archer had a glimpse of the old Eloise. The girl he had grown up with. Had loved and protected and cared for. It was as if all her scars had disappeared, and she was a young girl once more. Her eyes were light and clear and finally, *finally*, filled with remorse. "I am sorry."

It was then that Archer realized that she was no longer pointing the gun at him. Instead, she had turned it toward her own chest. He lurched forward, but his feet touched a wall of fire, and he jerked back, the flames singeing his trousers. "No, Eloise!"

"Don't think too badly of me, brother," she whispered.

And then she pulled the trigger.

Chapter Twenty-Three

It made little sense that people would spend summers in town instead of out in the country, Archer thought as his horse trotted along the dirt lane, undulating through two fields of new spring grass. The blades were so pale they neared chartreuse. Essex's air was clean and fresh, and by midsummer it would be scented by fields of wildflowers, hay, and meadowsweet. He breathed it in, his hold on his reins loose, his posture unusually relaxed. London was sticky, dusty, and smelly, and right then, it was also a hotbed of gossip revolving around the events that had unfolded in the mews behind Hadley Gardens two weeks past.

So much so that his removal of the marriage banns from the *Times* had barely garnered a reaction. Archer had cited the postponement of the nuptials on the pretext of his entering mourning for his sister, but he knew deep down it was what Brynn wanted. It was what she *deserved*.

Now that Eloise—and the imposter—was dead, there was no need for the farce to continue. They had each known, should the imposter be outed, that there would be no wedding. That Archer would continue with his life, and Brynn with hers. Their agreement was over. He pushed the thought of her from his mind with brusque finality.

Archer was relieved to be gone from London for the remainder of the season. He would be more relieved when he did not wake every morning with the memories of his father's and sister's deaths already front and center in his mind. In time, the pain that accompanied those memories would pass. The clench of his stomach and the ache in his heart wouldn't be so all-consuming. He knew this from experience, of course. It had taken him years to heal after his mother's death, though now that he knew the truth—that the fire that killed his mother had been set purposely by Eloise, her intent aimed at his death, not his mother's—all the pain he'd thought he'd finally buried churned back to the surface.

He needed time alone at Worthington Abbey to come to terms with all the things Eloise had revealed in her final minutes. Everything had unfolded so quickly that when the authorities had arrived at Hadley Gardens and inquired what had happened, Archer had not felt guilty in the least for lying. Preserving his sister's memory and honor had been his foremost goal, and thankfully Brynn, her lady's maid, Lana, and Northridge had gone along with the story Archer had quickly concocted:

The Masked Marauder had set upon the carriage taking Lord Northridge, Lady Briannon, and her lady's maid to the Kensington Ball, and Archer had simply chanced upon the attack. They had all been forced back to the Hadley Gardens mews for safekeeping while the bandit scoured the main home for the loot he'd had to leave behind on his last visit—the visit where he had beaten and killed the Duke of Bradburne. Eloise had interrupted the bandit in the mews, and she had been shot. Northridge had wrestled free of his restraints, gotten ahold of the bandit's second pistol, and had shot the bandit, though not before a lit candle had set the stable on fire.

That story had been the one printed on the front page of every major newspaper in the city. It was the one that had run like wildfire through the *ton*. And it was the one Archer wished were true. The truth was ugly and complex, and much more difficult to understand. He doubted he ever would. Archer also owed Northridge a debt that could never be repaid, not over any lifetime. His quick thinking and unflinching courage had saved Brynn. Had saved *him*.

As the rooftops of Worthington Abbey came into view, Archer gave his mount a nudge. He wanted to get home and start with the tasks that needed seeing to. Clearing out his father's and sister's rooms would hurt, but it was better done straightaway rather than let it hang over him like a shroud. He had sent his staff ahead, and things should be well underway.

A horse and rider sat in the middle of the lane up ahead, just before the twin pillars that marked the entrance drive to the abbey. He knew the slouch of the rider's shoulders, the low pulled brim of his hat, and, more recently, the stiff hold of his right leg.

"I've been sitting here for an hour," Brandt called. "Your lack of sympathy for my injury stings, Hawk."

Archer withheld the grin fighting to bow his lips. He hadn't seen Brandt since his release from Newgate the morning after the mews fire. Thomson had nothing on Brandt worthy of facing the magistrate to begin with, and now with the "Masked Marauder" dead, there had been no point in keeping him imprisoned. Brandt had sent a message to Hadley Gardens saying he was free, but that it would be best to keep a safe distance from Archer for a little while at least.

The sight of him now was a sorely needed balm. Archer wouldn't let on, of course.

"One pistol wound to the thigh and three days in the

Stone Jug has made you quite an old hen, my friend," Archer said, reining in his mount.

"If that isn't the pot calling the kettle black. You whined like an old lady over yours, if I recall." Brandt laughed, tipping back his head and shaking it. "Remind me to never take a bullet for you again."

They sat atop their mounts in silence for a few moments, the good humor evaporating like morning mist.

Brandt squinted against the sun. "I read the *Times*."

Archer shifted uncomfortably. He'd ridden straight through since London, and his body ached from the hours of travel, but he'd welcomed the distraction. This variety of pain was preferable to the kind he could not cure.

"Do you want to tell me what really happened?" Brandt asked.

"Not particularly," he answered. But he directed his horse through the pillared gates and recounted everything he knew anyway. Brandt deserved nothing but the truth, and he may well provide some fresh insight. Archer could use it.

Unable to approach the main house just yet, he rode with Brandt to Pierce Cottage. Once they'd worked together to rub down and water their mounts, Archer had finished the true version of events. He'd kept emotion out of it, but laying it bare made everything he'd buried deep inside ache.

Brandt hung their saddles and tack without a word while Archer waited. He crossed his arms, nerves jumping, as his friend finished stabling the two horses. If he hadn't known Brandt so well, he'd have been growling with impatience. But Archer knew he was only carefully choosing his reply to everything he had just heard.

"You are a good brother," Brandt finally said, leaning against the frame of the stable doors. He crossed his arms and ankles and stared into the paddock, the ground still muddy and puddled in spots where the spring rains had not yet dried up.

"Did you hear a word I said?" Archer asked.

He had not expected an ounce of praise, that was for certain.

"You made certain Eloise's character remained unblemished and unknown by those who did not love or care for her the way you did."

Archer frowned, averting his eyes to the bales of hay stacked in the back of the stables. He had not allowed tears since the night Eloise had taken her own life. They threatened to brim now, however.

"Archer," Brandt said in a way that made it clear he'd noticed. "You know as well as I that there cannot be great hatred without some fragment of love burning there to fuel it."

Archer leaned against the opposite stable door jamb and faced Brandt.

"I believe Eloise hated herself, not you. She needed someone to bear the brunt of that hatred, because she could not accept it upon herself," Brandt said. "I think she just chose the strongest person she knew."

Archer swore under his breath. Strong? He didn't feel it in the least. "How the devil do I get on from this? Every time I think of her and what she suffered…the lies she told to me, to everyone…"

He couldn't finish. For the past two weeks he'd been searching his memory for the hints he had overlooked of her hatred for him. The only thing he could determine for certain was that she had been a superb actress.

Brandt stepped forward and clapped him on the shoulder before turning for the cottage. "You get on like we all do— put one foot in front of the other, then the next." He paused, looking back. "I saw the second notice in the *Times*, too, the one postponing your wedding."

Archer stayed where he was and slammed the back of his head upon the weathered wood. He did not want to remember that announcement, even though it had been a necessity. Thinking of Brynn and remembering her touch, her lips, and the desire she stirred within him had been his only source of comfort these last wearisome weeks. And yet, thoughts of her had worn on him as well.

"Have you seen her?" Brandt called from where he'd limped to the cottage's front door.

Archer turned to follow him. "Who?"

"Don't be obtuse. I heard one of the house staff saying Ferndale was being readied for Lord Dinsmore and his family. They thought to take a break from London for a time, as well."

Ensconced in the country for the summer, it would be a place where her parents would not have to weather any direct embarrassment from the broken betrothal. He stepped into the cottage, shaking his head. It had to be done.

He'd never intended to marry at all. The act had simply been a necessity, and it had been easy to stomach, considering the girl knew the game. And she'd been one hell of an ally. Everything about Briannon had impressed him—her courage, her humor, her indomitable nature. She was everything any man could ever want. But Archer did not deserve her, this he knew. He couldn't bear the thought of disappointing her, of crushing that incredible spirit of hers. What if he turned out to be like the late duke, just as her own brother had feared?

"You are frowning," Brandt commented.

"Canceling the banns was the right thing to do. My reputation would ruin her good name."

Brandt didn't make a reply, though the crinkled forehead and frown spoke it for him. He didn't believe Archer.

"So what will you do with your time then, Your Grace?" he asked instead, dipping into a cartoonish bow. His wound must have pained him because he hissed and straightened his back without putting weight on his right leg.

"You deserved that," Archer muttered. "And I will fill my time easily enough."

"The Marauder is dead?"

Brandt's question had nothing at all to do with the man Eloise had shot. His name had turned out to be Mr. Gregory Barnstead, the third son of a late baron from somewhere up in Cumbria. Barnstead had come to London with the little inheritance he'd been afforded upon his father's death and had gambled it away within a week at a gaming hell.

All of London had determined the man had been desperate and had resorted to becoming a highwayman to make a living. He'd been bred from the gentry, and perhaps that was why he'd been polite — at first. He must have become desperate, the papers had opined, and had taken out his anger and frustration upon his victims.

Archer, however, figured Eloise had found the wretched cad and had offered him a fine sum for his assistance. What Barnstead had said, about being someone no one cared to notice, made sense if he was a bitter third son of a baron.

No, what Brandt meant to ask was if *Archer's* marauder was dead.

"I do not know," he answered honestly, trying to sort through the mess of his thoughts. "It's all I have. It's all I've ever been able to offer to anyone."

"That's hogwash and you know it," Brandt said. "You're afraid to give up the Marauder, Hawk. You've been using that identity as a shield for so long you've forgotten how to exist without it."

Brandt's words hit with barbed accuracy. *Damn him.*

"I should go," Archer said. Not that he wanted to. Pierce Cottage, at least, felt as comforting as a home ought to.

But it was time.

Archer went for the door.

"They are said to be arriving today, you know."

Brandt said it to his back, and yet the words hit low in Archer's stomach. "Don't."

"You love her. Admit it."

Archer grasped the doorknob and pulled it wide, the warm spring afternoon gusting into his face. *She* smelled this way—fresh and clean and with the barest hint of moss. The memory of her scent was enough to unhinge him. The girl had gotten under his skin and deep into his senses. But none of that mattered now.

"What if I turn out to be a bastard like my father was? What if I love her now, want her *now*, but the feelings fade with time?"

"So you do love her."

Archer clenched his fists, despair filling him. "Did you not hear the rest of what I said? What if one day the feeling ends? What if I can't explain it or stop it from ending?" He ran a frustrated hand through his hair, gritty from road dust. "I can't stand the idea of hurting her. Of disappointing her."

Brynn had given so much of herself to him. She'd risked her life pulling that stunt with the Bradburne diamonds, and when Archer had been forced, bound and gagged, to watch Barnstead put his hands all over her, he'd wanted to murder the impersonator and then flog himself for being the one who put her in danger to begin with.

Archer wanted to wrap her in his arms and fight off the rest of the world. He'd indulged a vision of her for these last few weeks, of her buried under the blankets of his bed in Worthington Abbey, deep in slumber, her silky curls strewn over his pillow. There, beside him, he would keep her safe. He would cherish her and ravish her in equal measure. He would do everything he could to make her smile and laugh. To make her happy in every possible way—just as he had promised her brother.

I love her.

"You're right," Brandt said, interrupting the sudden awareness that had wriggled into Archer's head. "You would disappoint her. You're certainly not good enough for her. Especially as the Masked Marauder with your heart under lock and key."

Archer turned and eyed his stable master. "What?"

"You'd make all sorts of mistakes, I wager."

He crossed his arms and stared at Brandt, guessing his game. "Would I?"

"You'd cheat, that's for certain. You'd lie to her, too. About everything. Including your marauding ways." Archer held his tongue as his friend went on. "Not to mention, the way you'd stop admiring her. But why wouldn't you? She's going to become a boring ninny. They all do."

She would not, Archer thought to himself, half annoyed by Brandt's teasing. But it had made him pause. Lying to Brynn, cheating with other women…he could not envision it.

Those were the things his father had done. But had the duke ever felt for Archer's mother the way Archer felt for Brynn? Had he ever loved her with a force that felt utterly unstoppable? A force that made him feel full to bursting, so just the idea of losing her was enough to make him feel empty, bereft of any purpose or joy?

Just as he felt now.

Not even the idea of continuing his raids as the Masked Marauder could fill that gaping void. It would not be enough to fill him, he knew. It would be nowhere near enough to make him happy.

There was only one person who could give him that, and she could never be a part of such a dangerous and secret life. He didn't *want* her to be a part of it. Hell, he didn't want that life any more at all.

He wanted only her.

"The Marauder is dead," Archer said, and repeated it more firmly as the decision took root. "He's dead. It's over, Brandt."

Now that he held control of the dukedom's finances, he would be able to begin repairing the damage that had been done. His investments, as risky and vulgar as they might seem to other members of the peerage, would turn a profit. He would soon be able to help those who truly needed it without living the dangerous double life of a highwayman.

Brandt nodded before stoking the fire in the cookstove, trying unsuccessfully to hide his grin. "I'm relieved to hear it. I'm weary of saving your arse."

"You could have been killed," Archer said, all seriousness. "I was selfish and stupid, and I will never put anyone else I care about in danger like that again."

Brandt put on a pot of water to boil. "Apology accepted. Though, I wouldn't reject an additional offer to pay my tab at the village tavern."

Archer laughed. "You'll sink me before I'm afloat again."

He rested his hands on the back of a chair at the long supper table, a sense of peace descending upon him. Pulling out the nearby chair, he felt too restless to sit and turned back for the door. He'd feel restless until he stepped inside Worthington Abbey as its master for the first time.

Until he entered its grand foyer and felt how completely and utterly alone he was there. Then again, with Briannon he would never be alone. Unlike his father, he knew he could be a worthy husband. He also knew he'd do whatever it took to make himself worthy of her.

"So," Brandt said with a knowing laugh as if he could see right through him, "when are you planning to tell the lady of your intentions?"

His answer must have been written all over his face

because Brandt grinned and clapped him on the back.

"Go get her, Hawk," he said.

He knew he must.

Archer left the cottage with a fire under his heels.

Chapter Twenty-Four

The evening sun descended beyond the rolling hills of Ferndale, spreading rose-tinged fingers across the meadows and dusting the countryside with a golden sheen. A few dark clouds threatened on the horizon, but they only added to the beauty of the burgeoning twilight.

Brynn tore her eyes from the windows and watched as the footmen cleared the last of the dinner plates, her gaze locking with her mother's fraught one across the ornately set dining table. Though it was only a quiet family dinner, Brynn longed to escape to the solitude of her chambers—and from the fretful eye of her mother. Lady Dinsmore had taken it to heart that both of her offspring had been in mortal danger, which had propelled her motherly devotion to new heights.

Surprisingly, she had taken the postponement of the banns well. The reasoning—that the new duke was far too consumed by grief over the deaths of his father and sister— was beyond reproach. However, that did not stop her from treating Brynn as if she were made of eggshells, about to crack at the slightest pressure. As such, Brynn's health had been the subject for most of the dinner conversation, despite Gray's Herculean efforts to steer it elsewhere. Brynn swallowed her sigh of exasperation at her mother's suddenly acute stare.

On cue, Lady Dinsmore's eyes narrowed. "You look quite pale, dear. Are you about to have a spell?"

Brynn stifled a sigh along with the tart response that she was weary only from all the smothering. "Mama, for the thousandth time, I am fine. My lungs are *fine*. I am not sick or in any immediate danger of becoming sick. I am pale because I have not been outside in days, and *that* is because you are convinced I will collapse at the slightest puff of wind."

Her veiled sarcasm was entirely lost on the countess, however. Lady Dinsmore *tut-tutted*. "No, no, there's a distinct quiver in your voice. You need to get some rest." She signaled to one of the hovering footmen. "Summon her maid at once. Lady Briannon wishes to retire."

She felt her face grow hot, and an irrepressible need to be taken for her word, to be trusted and undisputed, drove her to her feet.

"I do not," Brynn snapped. "*Enough*, Mama. Please." She gentled her voice, seeing her mother's displeasure and forestalling the forthcoming explosion. "I love you, but I am not a child who needs to be put to bed. I am a grown woman, and I need a reprieve from this constant mothering. I am going out."

"The hour is late, Briannon!" Lady Dinsmore gasped and turned to her husband. "Herbert, do something! She'll catch her death."

As her father grappled for a reply, dabbing a napkin at the corners of his mouth in order to stall for time, Brynn walked around the table and leaned down to press a kiss to her mother's furrowed brow. "No, Mama, the fresh evening breeze will do me a world of good, trust me." She smiled at her father and brother who were both staring at her with identical expressions of astonishment as they, too, stood. "Papa, Gray, please excuse me. I need some air."

"Bravo," Gray mouthed to her, his hands mimicking a clap as she swept past him.

Leaning against the paneled wall of the outer room, Brynn closed her eyes and took in a slow breath, pressing her palms to her trembling middle. Inside the dining room, she could hear her father attempting to pacify her aggrieved mother, but Brynn didn't care to intervene. Or apologize. She'd shot a marauder, endured a kidnapping, and escaped a killer, all without collapsing. If she'd learned anything at all from recent weeks, it was that she—*and* her lungs—were more than capable of weathering anything. That included the tempest in a teapot that was Lady Dinsmore.

Gray's soft voice at her ear made her jump. "Well done."

"Is Mama very upset?"

"She'll survive," he responded dryly, taking her arm and escorting her down the carpeted hallway. "I am proud of you, sister."

"For what?"

"For fighting for yourself."

Brynn stared up at her brother, her frazzled emotions breaking free of her tenuous hold on them. Her hands shook as she clutched her skirts. Gray was wrong. She hadn't fought for a damned thing, not even when Archer had cancelled the banns. When he, too, had decided what was best for her.

"No," she whispered. "I've done nothing."

Gray stopped at the bottom of the staircase and drew around her to face him. "Why would you say that?" He held her stare, seeing past an excuse she was searching for and failing to find. "Is it because of Hawk's announcement?"

Brynn flushed at the thought of the man who was no longer her betrothed. She had guessed that Archer would make an announcement in the *Times*, but she hadn't expected how much it would hurt. There was nothing between them any longer, nothing left to hold them together now that the imposter had been found.

She hadn't seen him since Eloise's funeral, although he had called upon them briefly before the service. His manner had been distant and preoccupied, which was to be expected, and Brynn had given him the space to grieve. Despite his sister's ultimate treachery, she knew Archer mourned the loss. Now that his name was cleared and the true killer known, Archer was free to live his life. And she hers.

She only wished the idea didn't make her so miserable.

"You are better off without him," Gray said, seeing her expression.

"No, I'm not." Overwhelmed by despair, Brynn's voice broke. "You don't know him like I do. No one does. I'm better when I'm with him. I don't feel weak or useless, and at least he doesn't treat me like a fragile porcelain doll."

"You're not useless," Gray replied. "It's normal to come to…care for someone after sharing a traumatic experience."

"It's more than that, Gray," she said quietly.

His grip tightened on her arms and then relaxed. "You're too—"

"Too what?" she interrupted. "Too young to love? Too sick to live? Too weak to hope for normal things?" Her laugh was empty. "Surely you of all people don't intend to patronize me as Mama does. I know my own mind and the truth of what I feel."

His mouth opened and closed and then, to her surprise, he pulled her close. "You're right. I am sorry for suggesting otherwise. You'll find love again, Brynn. And if you don't, well…rest assured that you can always age into spinsterhood with your interminable bachelor of a brother."

Ignoring the sharp twinge his words elicited, Brynn laughed into his neckcloth. "Not if Mama has her way." Gray groaned, lashing his arms about her and kissing the crown of her head. Brynn couldn't help teasing him more. "Soon she will renew all her efforts to find you a suitable wife, which means I will finally be left in peace."

"Heaven help me." Gray released her and clasped his hand to his chest with an aghast look. "A hellish torture, but one I will gladly endure if only for you."

"You truly are the best brother."

Squeezing Gray's arm with the first real smile she'd had in days, she climbed the stairs to her room where her lady's maid, Lana, was waiting.

"I'm going out for a ride," Brynn announced. It would clear her head. And ease her bruised heart. She hoped.

"A storm is coming," Lana said as she selected a riding habit for her mistress. "Are you sure you want to go out?"

Brynn stood at her window, trailing her fingers along the edge of the cool glass. She pushed a smile to her lips, despite the hollow ache that rested like a stone in her middle.

Brynn studied the band of thunderclouds and sighed—she'd faced worse storms and knew that this one, too, would pass. "Of course. It's a beautiful evening. Those clouds will fade, you'll see."

"It's good to be back, isn't it, my lady?"

Brynn turned, hearing an odd note in Lana's voice. "You didn't enjoy being in London for the season?"

Lana shook her head. "It's too busy, too many people. I prefer the solitude and the quiet of the country."

"But didn't you live in the city while you were in Russia?"

"We spent the winters there," Lana said, nostalgia flashing in her eyes for a moment. "My mother was very busy during those months. With the dressmaking, I mean," she added hastily. "But the rest of the time, we spent in the country."

Brynn shook her head. "You're like Gray, then. My parents usually have to threaten him to attend social events.

Homebodies, the two of you." Lana didn't respond as she helped Brynn take off the gown she had been wearing. "I do love being back," Brynn continued with a wistful smile. "I will miss the balls and the parties, though. I would have enjoyed the spectacle of so many ladies being whisked off their feet by their gallant suitors."

"Like you were?" Lana asked.

She forced a cheerful note into her voice. "Come now, Lana, you and I both know that was a farce, which is thankfully over. It's official now."

"Is it?"

Brynn smiled, pretending to be distracted. "Is it what? Official? See for yourself. It's in the papers on the mantel."

"No, is it *truly* over with the duke?"

As if she were standing on the edge of a precipice that had suddenly given way to the abyss below, Brynn felt her stomach plunge. Trust Lana to ask such a blunt, astute question. Her hands fluttered as she tried to steady herself, drawing a sharp breath into her constricted lungs. It was over. It *had* to be over. Archer had never wanted marriage in the first place. He had called her his love in the mews, and she had thought of that whispered word time and again the last few weeks, but Brynn knew he'd only been overwrought. He didn't love her, and what she felt for him was her burden alone.

She shrugged and forced a smile, even though she knew Lana would see right through it. "I expect so. We concocted the engagement, after all. His Grace does not wish to marry."

"I saw the way he looked at you at Lady Eloise's funeral," Lana said. "And it was not that of a man who wished to escape an unfortunate betrothal."

"He did not look at me once."

He'd been thinking of other, more important things to be sure.

"He could barely take his eyes off you."

Brynn quashed the bloom of hope that unfurled in her chest. "You are an incurable romantic, Lana. I assure you, His Grace has no further interest in me."

"If my lady insists." Lana shook her head, opening her mouth as if she had more to say. She clamped her lips together but then turned around, her eyes flashing. "You English are so blind. When something is right in front of you, you cannot see it, even with your eyes wide open. How can you not see that you and the duke are perfectly suited to each other? In my country, if a man wants to court a woman, he does not give up until she is in his arms."

"And you know this from your vast experience with men?" Brynn said drily, but not unkindly. She and Lana were close enough in age for her to know that Lana was as sheltered as she.

"No, it is because I have two perfectly good eyes."

Brynn grinned at Lana's unexpected display of temper and threw her hands into the air in surrender. Sensing that she wouldn't convince Lana otherwise of Archer's intentions, she changed the subject. "I haven't gotten a chance to thank you properly, by the way, for what you did at the mews. You saved my life, and the duke's." She paused, clearing her throat. "You were right to confide in Gray. It was a stroke of luck that brought you to Hadley Gardens." Brynn shot her maid a circumspect look. "Though I can't imagine telling him was easy, given his temper. He was furious with me for hours afterward. Was he very angry?"

"No, my lady," Lana said, the animation disappearing from her face as she busied herself with removing Brynn's stays and securing her hair into a single braid. "Lord Northridge seemed more concerned with your safety. And it wasn't luck. I've never seen him so deadly focused on anything. Once I told him of your plans with the duke, he was intent on pursuing every possible path. Hadley Gardens was simply the first. He would have left no stone unturned to find you." Lana's voice was soft, holding a strange warm tone as her fingers finished their task, tucking in the last of the combs.

"He was splendid, wasn't he?" Brynn murmured as Lana fussed with her hair. "I thought it was over, and then he showed up like a knight in shining armor. I've never been more pleased to see my brother in all my life."

"Lord Northridge does have his moments."

Brynn glanced up at the odd tone of pride in Lana's voice but couldn't see her face from where she stood braiding her hair.

"There, that should hold," she said, watching as Brynn then donned Gray's old breeches and one of his old shirts. "Shall I put this riding habit away?" she asked, with a resigned look. She knew better than to argue with her mistress's choice of dress.

Brynn grinned at her wry expression. "You know I like to be comfortable." She pulled on her riding boots and secured a lightweight wool cloak over her shoulders. She paused at the door. "Thank you, Lana," she said quietly.

"You are welcome, my lady. I did try my best to secure the braid, but it really is too slippery for the combs."

"No, not for my hair. For everything. For keeping my secrets and going beyond the boundaries of what would be expected of a lady's maid. I hope you know that I consider you a friend, and you may ask me for anything, should you need it."

Something indescribable shone in Lana's eyes but was quickly hidden as a smile shaped her mouth. She fell into a curtsy. "The feeling is quite mutual, my lady. Now go enjoy your ride before the thunderstorm makes an unwelcome appearance."

Brynn shook her head, pointing to the near perfect sky beyond the window. "You are surely imagining things."

But as Brynn raced Apollo across Ferndale's expansive grounds, she realized that Lana's premonition might come true after all. The clouds were rolling in, thick and dark and ominous. She wasn't worried, though. She'd have more than enough time to return to the stables before it started raining.

She stretched forward—her hair long since fallen loose from the braid and its clips—and nudged the stallion into a canter. After a while, she gave Apollo his head and sank low in the saddle, holding fast with her legs. Grinning with delight, she hung over his neck as he soared over the low hedges bordering Archer's property. She knew Archer wouldn't mind. A smile touched her lips as they neared the river, remembering how imperious she had been when she had warned him of trespassing. Now she was guilty of doing the same. It seemed like a lifetime had passed since the boar—a lifetime of stolen moments and false promises.

A lifetime of lies.

She slowed the horse, leading him to the river's edge where the embankment flattened and dismounted. She hadn't been alone since Eloise's death. Hadn't truly wanted to be. She feared the silence and the freedom to think about what had happened that night in the mews. Only she, Archer, Gray, and Lana knew the truth, and they had done their best to preserve Eloise's memory. It all still felt like a nightmare to Brynn. That Eloise, so sweet and friendly and composed, could have been capable of such calculating and cold hatred for so many years was incomprehensible. Then again, love was such a capricious thing—it could lift one to the highest of highs and drag one to the lowest of lows. She stood there, wrapping her arms around her middle, and did the very thing she hadn't allowed herself to do yet—she let the tears come.

The slight rustle of the grass alerted her to someone else's arrival. That, and a sudden deep throb of her heart. It was as if it had recognized him long before she had.

"Lady Briannon," Archer said softly.

She quickly wiped her cheeks on her sleeve. "So formal, Your Grace."

"May I join you?"

"I believe you may do whatever you wish," she said, smiling through the remnants of her tears, her heart trembling in her chest. It was extraordinary how the mere brush of his voice had come to affect her so. "It is your property, after all."

"I do not want to intrude."

Brynn turned then, letting her eyes feast on him as he stood beside his horse. He looked tired. Tired, and heartbreakingly beautiful. She wanted nothing more than to throw herself into his arms, but Brynn kept herself perfectly still. "How are you?" she asked instead.

He frowned and glanced away. "As well as can be expected."

"And Brandt?"

"He is recovering." Archer hesitated before taking the few steps to stand at her side. He clasped his hands behind his back, and she held hers in a death grip. Every part of her body strained toward him, the draw to him magnetic. "He says to convey his gratitude, by the way. He is indebted to you."

"It was nothing."

After a few moments of silence, he lifted his eyes to hers. "Brynn—"

The first clap of thunder rumbled overhead, silencing him. He brushed a hand through his hair as if fighting to find the words, and the tortured look in his eyes made everything inside her crumble.

She swallowed and raised a trembling palm to stop him. "I saw the notice in the *Times*."

He frowned again, but before he could speak, she leaped to continue.

"If you intend to apologize, please—there is no need. I

am only glad things worked out in our favor. Didn't we agree that it would be a ghastly union?" Brynn asked, attempting to smile. Her trembling chin wouldn't support it. "And I know you never wanted to be saddled with a wife."

Her voice broke as the words tumbled out, leaving her empty and aching, but she'd had to say them. Before he did, at any rate. She still had some measure of pride left, and she wouldn't let him strip it from her.

Archer cleared his throat, his gaze sliding across to her. "You're right, I didn't. After what my father did to my mother and to Eloise's mother, I thought I would be just like him. The apple not falling far from the tree, and all that."

She bit the inside of her cheek to steady her quivering lips. He didn't truly believe that, did he?

"You are nothing like him," Brynn replied fiercely. "*Nothing.*"

Archer relented with a small grin. "I realized the same not too long ago. In part, I have you to thank for that."

The gruff and sensual timbre of his voice made her pulse scatter. She could sense him looking at her and felt herself crumbling beneath his gaze. Her battered heart could take only so much, and seeing him now, being with him...sheer will alone was holding her together.

Be strong, Brynn reminded herself. *You have to let him go. It's what he wants.*

But heaven help her—all *she* wanted was to hurl herself at him.

"I'm glad," she blurted out. "You are a far better man than any father could have hoped for. I'm so very sorry about Eloise, but your name has been cleared, and you can finally put this mess behind you. You can move on with your life."

"Brynn."

"And you needn't worry about me," she continued, ignoring the weight of his searching gaze. "In time, the gossip will die down, and people will replace it with the next new scandal that comes along. I will be fine."

"*Brynn*." Archer turned her firmly to face him, but she stared determinedly at his shirtfront. "I don't want you to be fine."

"You…you don't?" He shook his head, and she frowned, looking up at him.

"I want you to be happy. Deliriously happy," he said. "And I want the chance to be the man who makes you so."

Another rumble of thunder cut into his reply. Surely she hadn't heard him correctly. His words didn't make sense. "But you called off the betrothal. You don't want this…me."

"You think I don't want *you*?" A strangled sound erupted from his mouth. He grasped her shoulders, his eyes dark. "Are you mad? You are the only thing I think about. All day. All night. *Especially* at night. I can't get you out of my head. I put that notice in the *Times* because…it turns out, I *am* a coward."

"You're not," she whispered, her heart threatening to erupt from her chest. "You're the most courageous person I know. You save sick orphans and widows and bring hope to the hopeless." She smiled through the rush of emotion threatening to choke her. "Though I do question your methods, it's clear your heart is in the right place."

Archer's thumb grazed her chin as if he were touching something infinitely precious. "I'm not worthy of you, Brynn. But I want so much to be. I…"

With an inarticulate groan, his mouth swooped down on hers as the first drops of rain fell. She gasped at the sweet urgency of his kiss. It reached deep into the very center of her body, Archer's hunger sudden and fierce, matching hers breath for breath. Unwilling to leave a sliver of space between them, he fitted her body against his, his hand rounding her buttocks and pressing his thighs flush against hers. The possessive touch was her undoing. Brynn moaned and clung to him, winding her fingers in his coat, unwilling to let him part from her. She arched against him, her hands climbing up around his neck to draw him closer. She couldn't hold a single thought in her head as his mouth pushed harder against hers, his tongue claiming hers with desperate need. They stood there, devouring each other, as the rain drenched their bodies and lightning cleaved the sky.

Apollo reared up wildly as a peal of thunder shook the earth. The sudden motion drove her and Archer apart, Brynn managing to grab Apollo's reins before he spooked, and Archer doing the same with his horse. Water ran into his face and down his body, making the shirt beneath the open panels of his jacket stick to the muscled planes of his chest. Even in the rapidly falling darkness, the sight of him, illuminated by a streak of lightning, made Brynn quiver with want. Archer stared at her in a similar fashion, his eyes consuming her as greedily as hers devoured him. She gathered her breath, realizing the thin white shirt she wore wouldn't offer much in the way of coverage. Her body burned at Archer's ravenous gaze.

There were two choices open to them: he could go back to Worthington Abbey and she to Ferndale. *Or*…she could throw away every shred of decorum she had left and give in to the demands of her body—and her heart. She wanted him. She'd wanted him for so long, even before their encounter at Bishop House, when his hands and fingers had touched her to her soul. Brynn's chest heaved with the force of the storm brewing inside of her. It surpassed the very real one howling about them. It was a storm only Archer could appease. Brynn closed her eyes and exhaled.

She climbed astride Apollo. "Follow me. My cottage. It's not far."

Chapter Twenty-Five

Archer stoked the fire while Brynn changed behind a screen. He had tied the horses into the attached stall on the far side of the cottage, stocked with fresh hay and water for her horse's use. Apollo didn't seem to mind sharing his bed with a stranger.

The flames lent the inside of the cottage a warm, welcoming glow. He hadn't been inside before, but everything about it felt like her. The cottage itself comprised a single room dominated by a bed on one end and the vestibule on the other. Books were crammed onto the bookshelves along one wall, and whimsical paintings graced the others. A tiny wooden table and a single armchair stood in one snug corner.

He shrugged out of his wet jacket, but kept the rest of his clothes on. Despite her suggestion of using the cottage to weather the storm, Archer didn't want to make any assumptions. He wouldn't touch her unless she invited him to. Because one touch, one taste, and it would be over. He wouldn't be able to resist her, and he knew she, too, would give herself to him. Archer didn't want her to make that decision in the heat of the moment, when her mind and her heart were in tumult. If Brynn wanted him the way he did her, he wanted nothing but her sober, self-possessed permission.

"There should be water in the kettle," Brynn said, emerging from behind the screen. "For some tea."

She had changed into a simple linen shift, a heavy blanket pulled around her shoulders. The sight of her made his breath catch. Like a barefoot duchess, she was fresh and innocent and completely beguiling. She joined him by the fire and combed her fingers through her damp hair. Catching the light, the wet strands gleamed like flame in her hands. Resisting the urge to gather her in his arms and bury his face in her hair, he did as she asked instead, boiling the water for tea while she sat upon a stool before the fire.

"Are you well? How are your lungs?" he asked, handing her a steaming mug. He remembered her draped in his arms, unconscious at the engagement ball, and a frisson of worry shot through him.

"The chill won't take if I am warm and dry."

Archer took another stool and moved to sit behind her. Her eyes flared at his nearness, but he did nothing more than run his fingers through the silky burnished coppery gold waves, holding them out toward the warmth of the fire.

"What are you doing?" she asked.

He smiled. "Drying your hair."

"You don't have to."

"I want to."

They sat in silence, the heat from the fire spreading quickly throughout the small room, and soon, Brynn's hair was dry and soft, falling through his fingers like liquid flame. The sensual feel of it set his body on edge. He wanted to see that glorious hair spilling over her naked shoulders, feel it falling onto his chest as he brought her to the verge and back again. But first, he needed to clear the air.

"Brynn," he began again. "I want to finish what I started to say earlier. What you did for me… No one has ever done anything like that. You put your life on the line to save mine, and to save my friend, with no concern for your own safety. I can never repay you for what you have done."

"You don't have to," she said quickly.

He swallowed and nodded. "You were right when you said that I never intended to marry." The wounded expression on her face had him rushing to continue. "I didn't think I could be happy. And I didn't want the burden of making someone else happy, especially when I saw what that had done to my mother. Until you stormed into my perfectly ordered life wearing naught but a pair of men's breeches, I don't think I knew what true living was. I don't think I even knew what true happiness was."

Archer sat forward on the stool, her hair still twined between his fingers. "I know only that when I am not with you, I am desolate. I know that I want to do everything within my power to make you smile and laugh. To make you come alive in my arms. I cannot imagine a second in my life without you in it."

It was the truth, raw and honest. Every word spoken lifted a weight from his soul, until he felt lighter than he had for as long as he could recall.

Brynn drew a shaking breath. "What are you saying?"

"I went to Ferndale. Your lady's maid told me that you had gone for a ride."

"You came to find me?" she asked in an aching voice.

"Yes," he said. "And to return these."

Releasing her silky hair, Archer reached into his trouser pocket. Her eyes sparkled with tears as his hand appeared again, her grandmother's pearl necklace and matching earbobs filling his palm.

"You didn't sell them," she whispered.

"No, and I realized why only a few days ago. I wanted to keep something that you loved close to me. It was a poor substitute, but my wretched heart couldn't bear to part with them. I wanted your love, you see."

"My love?" she repeated, her gaze sealing itself to his.

"Yes. Haven't you been listening to a word I've been saying?" he teased.

"*You* want *my* love." She stared at him, her lower lip trembling.

"Of course I do. What do you think this is all about?"

"But…I assumed you felt obligated…"

He smiled at her. "No, darling, the only obligation I feel is to love you unconditionally for every last day of my life." His hands rose to her cheeks, cradling them between his palms as he memorized every beloved curve of her face. "And in return, if you give me your love, your anger, your joy, your passion, your hope, your dreams, or any little thing you choose, I would be eternally grateful."

Archer reached for her trembling hands, still clutching her pearls, and pressed his lips to her wrist. His heart nearly burst with the need to make her his in every single way. But he wanted her answer first. Her unclouded acceptance. "Marry me. For real this time."

His fingers brushed away the single tear tracing down the apple of her cheek, his voice catching on his next words. "I am madly and foolishly and unquestionably in love with you, Lady Briannon, and if you don't put me out of my misery by giving me an answer, I—"

"Yes. *Yes*." Brynn pressed a finger to his lips with a tremulous smile, her eyes shining with the force of her emotion. "Will you please kiss me now?"

He groaned as he drew her into his lap and crushed her to him. He kissed her eyes, the slope of her cheek, her nose, before searching for the softness of her mouth. His bride-to-be parted her lips sweetly, offering herself to him completely. This kiss was the opposite of the one by the river, full of promise and love, but no less consuming. This time, Archer held no part of himself back. This brave and courageous woman in his arms was his sole reason for living, and he wanted her to know it as firmly as he did.

She set her pearls on her abandoned stool and turned her hands to his chest, unbuttoning the first button there and then the second. His breath grew shallow as her fingers brushed lower, freeing the next three in quick succession. "Brynn," he groaned at the trail of heat her fingers left behind. "What are you doing?"

She smiled, mischief glinting in her eyes as she pushed the material off his shoulders. "We are engaged, are we not?" she said wickedly, repeating his words from the library in Hadley Gardens. Her palm grazed the naked skin of his chest, flicking past the ridged muscles of his stomach. He stopped its descent with one of his hands, his breathing harsh.

"I want you so desperately, I cannot trust myself to stop," he rasped.

"I don't want you to stop."

Archer stared into eyes the color of clover and warm honey. The world tilted beneath his feet at the explicit invitation in them. The invitation he'd craved. The one he'd waited for, for an eternity it seemed. His hand curled into the lustrous silk of her hair as hers wound around his neck. He lifted her easily and crossed the room to the bed.

The blanket over her shoulders fell away, leaving her in only her thin linen shift. Her dusky areolas pushed against the cloth, already hard and hunting for his touch. Brynn flushed at his hot stare, but Archer wanted her to feel no shame in her body's response to him. He wanted to suckle her and make her moan. He wanted to put his mouth on every inch of her body, just as he'd confessed in her study at Bishop House.

He set her down slowly at the side of the bed, inching her body along his until her toes touched the floor. His arms curved around her to release the string tie at the neck of her shift. The linen fell in a pool around her ankles. Without breaking contact, he lifted her and placed her on the bed. Clad only in sheer drawers, she made no attempt to cover herself from him, even though she blushed furiously as his eyes swept her from top to bottom, devouring every sublime inch of her body.

"God, you are the most beautiful woman I have ever seen," he murmured, watching as the firelight played across her rosy skin. She looked doubtful at the compliment, but Archer meant every word, and he grew determined to prove it.

He had never seen anyone more perfectly formed. She looked like a wanton sprite with her hair fanning over the pillow. *His* sprite. Her breasts, fully bared to him, were as flawless as he remembered, even more perfect than his fevered memories. All the curves and hollows of her body were his to adore. Her long, shapely legs and the soft hourglass contours of her stomach tantalized and fascinated him. He wanted to make her writhe from his touch as she had in her study, see her eyes go dark with passion, feel her body convulse around him, bring her to blissful oblivion again and again.

Archer shrugged out of his shirt and shed his breeches, standing before her in nothing but his smalls. He didn't want to alarm her, and the sight of his erection, already stirring underneath his linen drawers, could very well do just that.

But a slow, secretive smile crept over her lips—and Brynn clapped her hands to her face, smothering a giggle.

"Does something amuse you?" he asked, crossing his arms and waiting for her answer by the side of the bed.

"I have a confession to make," she replied, biting back another grin, this one accompanied by her hands covering her face. "And I fear it may affect your"—her anxious gaze peeked through her fingers—"mood."

Archer had no idea what her confession could be, or why she would choose now of all times to part with it. He was swollen and stiff, and these smalls needed to come off. "Brynn, my love," he growled. "Unless it is a matter of life and death, I forgive you."

She swung her legs over the edge of the bed, and the tantalizing sway of her breasts distracted him wholly as she reached for his leg. Archer remained still, the pad of her finger grazing the healed, shallow gunshot wound on his thigh.

"It's nothing," he said, dismissing the reddish-pink scar tissue.

She glanced up at him, her finger still stroking his thigh, making his body tighten with excitement. "It wasn't nothing. You were shot."

"You've been reading your father's newssheets again," he muttered, recalling once more the article on Lady Emiliah and her report that the bandit had been shot.

She shook her head. "I didn't read them."

He peered down at her. "Then how do you know?"

"Because I'm the one who shot you."

His arms swung loose at his sides, and he caught her hand. "*You?*" He dragged up the murky recollection of the mysterious boy while staring at Brynn. Of course he'd considered the possibility, but at that time, she hadn't known the bandit's identity. He'd figured the Brynn he knew would have taken better aim—and then dragged his corpse off his mount and searched his pockets for her grandmother's pearls.

"Yes, I'm sorry. But I couldn't allow you to rob Lady Emiliah or her chaperone. And I was still furious with the marauder for robbing me." She paused with a wry shrug. "I didn't intend to kill you, just scare you a little."

"You shot me!"

Brynn smiled again, clearly amused, as her fingers continued their exploration up his thigh. "In my defense, I did not know it was *you* at the time."

"Would it have made a difference?" he asked, the soft titillating touches driving him to bloody distraction.

"Perhaps." She leaned forward and pressed her lips to his scar. Her eyes rose to meet his, but they were waylaid by the telling bulge of his smalls.

Archer dimly recalled how the *boy* had shied away from removing his trousers.

"Why, Lady Briannon, how naughty of you," he teased, loving the deep rose coloring of her cheeks. "Had I known it was you there in that cottage, I would have acted far differently."

"What would you have done?" she replied in a breathy tone as he pulled her upward. He fitted her body against his and watched her eyes widen at the indelicate press of his hardened length.

"Why, I would have demanded you do the honorable thing and marry me at once!" He gave an exaggerated flutter of his eyelashes, imitating an artful coquette. "Think of my *reputation*. You lured me into a deserted cottage, manhandled my person; I could have been ruined."

Brynn burst into laughter and threw a pillow at him. "You are a complete charlatan." Tugging her back into his arms, he kissed her, and when they broke apart, she pressed her fingers to his lips. "Although I *am* sorry for hurting you."

He grinned wickedly. "I know a way you can make it up to me."

Taking her with him, he climbed into bed, the mattress sinking beneath their combined weight as he drew the sheet over them. He discarded the last of his clothing, and in a blink, the humor vanished from her face, replaced with apprehension.

"Don't be afraid, love."

"I'm not, but I don't know what to do," she blurted out, and then squeezed her eyes shut with embarrassment.

"Trust me," he said. "Anything you do, I will like."

Brynn peered at him through her lashes. "What if you don't?"

"Do you like it when I touch you?" he asked. She nodded, her bottom lip pinned between her teeth. "Then you can trust that it will be the same for me." He took her hand and placed it against his thudding heart. "Even the mere thought of touching you makes my heart race."

"It makes mine race, too," she admitted. Tentatively, Brynn ran a hand over his shoulder, the flat of her palm skimming down over his nipple and making a surge of raw pleasure spear through him. "Do you like this?"

His body clenched with desire. The woman had no idea what she did to him. "Yes."

"And this?" She leaned over to seal her mouth to his, dragging her teeth across his lower lip. He felt the sleek push of her tongue, and tightened his hands in the sheets, forcing himself to remain still for every moment of her exploration. Her mouth traced a hot path to his ear where she nibbled his lobe, her hands skipping past his ribs to his abdomen. His entire body was on fire at her inexperienced, hesitant caresses. Her fingertips reached lower, brushing against his hips, and Archer couldn't wait any longer.

"My turn," he growled.

He settled his lips to her mouth, his hand sliding along the side of her breast until she arched against him. He kissed her slowly at first, and then with more fervor as her hands came between them to clasp his shoulders. He trailed kisses down her throat, her tiny moans exciting him even more than they had before. Finally, he set his lips to her breast, teasing the peak with his tongue before drawing it into his mouth.

"So incredibly sweet," he said. "So perfect."

This woman is going to be my wife.

This proud, beautiful, irresistible woman. And Archer loved her.

. . .

Awash in sensation, Brynn succumbed to Archer's skillful caresses. Her fingers twined in his hair as he paid homage to her other breast before returning to her lips. He knew exactly how to make her burn for him. His kisses made sharp streaks of pleasure spiral through her as his tongue stroked hers, and his hands flicked down her sides to the waistband of her drawers. His knuckles brushed against the velvety skin of her stomach to slip beneath the thin material. Brynn gasped at the intimate shift of his hands, and a knowing smile touched his lips.

"I've thought of nothing else since, too," he told her. "The way you felt against me, the sweet, unhinged response of your body. I want to see you come apart again."

Her body thrummed an erratic cadence, his seductive words making her weak. Archer kissed her swiftly and began to work his way down her body, his tongue running between her breasts and delving into the sensitive indent of her navel. His hands slid her drawers past her hips and, in one smooth motion, he removed the last piece of her clothing. She lay naked before him, every part of her on display for him to view and appraise. Heat singed her body in a deep blush. Embarrassed, she reached for the sheet, but Archer stalled the movement.

"No, don't. Do you have any idea how beautiful you are? Your ankles, your calves, your knees, your hips, all of you. I could stare at you forever."

Brynn inhaled sharply, seduced by his fevered words as

his fingers caressed the slope of her knee and the curve of her thigh. His mouth and tongue followed the searing path of his hands, his lips tracing the sharp edges of her hip bones. Every touch, every scrape of his teeth, made her skin tingle and burn. Her body felt as if it were melting, transforming from flesh and bone to liquid heat as Archer's hand settled onto the ready, damp core of her. *Oh*. Her hips lanced forward, craving more. Archer circled his finger there with slow, deliberate strokes, her body tightening compulsively at the scorching sensations his touch evoked. His lips grazed across the plane of her belly, closer to the heat of her. She gasped his name as she realized where his mouth was going…what it sought.

"Archer, no."

"I like the word 'yes' more."

His lips followed the hot path of his fingers and, when he finally set his mouth to her core, Brynn's head fell back with a cry of surprise.

The glide of his tongue against her was as electrifying as the storm outside. Brynn almost lost herself in the wild carnal sensation of it as Archer eased his tongue deeper, licking and thrusting, and doing lewd, wicked things that she had never dreamed of. But, *oh sweet lord*, she didn't want him to stop.

Archer settled himself between her thighs and swirled his tongue against her in teasing, flicking motions that drove her daft, his fingers working gently into her passage, stroking forward and retreating. In a mindless daze, her fingers tangled in his hair, and she moaned his name. The exquisite pressure was unbearable. *Searing*. Brynn writhed against his mouth, incoherent sounds escaping her lips. Her body felt possessed, utterly consumed by him, and as he drew her pliant flesh between his teeth, it froze for one terrifyingly bright second—and then shuddered into wild tremors that threatened to break her apart.

"I love the way you taste," he whispered. His erotic words

made her quiver anew at the thought of what he'd just done and how wantonly she'd responded.

With a satisfied smirk, Archer nuzzled her stomach and worked his way back up her body, continuing to stroke her with his hand, sliding it around her hip to hold her flush against him. He caressed the length of her spine, curving around her buttocks and gently molding her flesh. He held her gaze as if needing to measure every moment, every reaction to his every touch. Brynn swallowed hard at the pressure of his arousal pressing so intimately into her, but she didn't pull away as Archer positioned himself at the entrance of her body.

He inched forward, the strain of holding back bunching his muscles as her virginal passage stretched to accommodate him. The insistent press of his blunt tip felt like his fingers had—only much, *much* larger. Her hands found his shoulders, kneading apprehensively. "Archer—"

"Trust me, darling." He pushed as far forward as he could until Brynn felt as if she were going to split apart. He stroked her face, all the love in the world glowing in his eyes. She knew he would never hurt her, not when he looked at her like that with so much aching tenderness. "I love you, Briannon."

The gently offered words were her undoing.

"And I you."

He entered her fully then, and her body arched like a bow against him, a sharp cry wrenching from her mouth. A hot lash of pain tore through her, echoing in waves across her lower abdomen. It felt like she *had* been split apart, her body rebelling against the unfamiliar girth of him. Her eyes smarted as she expelled a shuddering breath.

Archer held himself still, his face above her strained and worried. "Brynn?"

"I'm okay," she assured him, and it wasn't a lie for very long. The pain flattened out until there was only the proud heat of him resting deep within her.

"Are you certain?"

Brynn answered by reaching for his mouth with hers, her tongue curling against his in desperate need. She needed *him*. Archer shifted slightly, and she braced for another bout of pain as he withdrew. Groaning, he sank carefully back into her clinging heat, but this time, there was no pain, just the unfathomable, astonishing slide of his body joining with hers. She gasped at the pressure, and within moments, her body let go, softening underneath him. Receiving him as it was meant to do.

Brynn's hands settled around his waist as he moved, slowly at first and then with more intensity as she clutched at him, her hips rocking instinctively upward to meet his deep, controlled thrusts. Pleasure pulsed through her thighs with every stroke. Instinct took over as she matched his motions, hitching her legs around him as he had taught her and gasping at the deepened friction. Archer growled as if pleased, his movements quickening with the deliberate shift of her hips.

"Archer," she moaned.

"Soon, my love," Archer said, sliding his hand in between their slick bodies and amplifying the tension to impossible heights. His thumb stroked her sensitive bud as his body drove rhythmically into hers. The erotic combination made her senseless. She murmured inaudibly, gripping him with her thighs to bring him closer, to make him more a part of her than he already was. Her nails dug into his back, and Archer responded to her demands, driving deeper, giving her what she asked for.

Brynn matched his hungry rhythm, wanting to please him as much as he wanted to please her. She was reaching for something, but she didn't know what. Deep down, she knew that Archer would give it to her. But she frowned as he slowed his pace, the effort making him grunt as he hoisted his weight to his forearms.

"Am I going too fast?" he asked. "Your lungs. I don't want to push you too hard."

He was worried about her lungs *now*?

"Archer," she gasped, half laughing, half growling. "My lungs will surely burst if you stop."

She wrapped her legs around his waist, making him inhale sharply, and more than conveying what she wanted. He grinned at her boldness and twisted to his back, taking her with him until she was straddling his hips. Brynn cried out in surprise as he pressed intimately up into her and flushed hotly at the brazen position.

"I've always been rather jealous of Apollo," he told her with a knowing wink. Brynn's legs went weak at the overtly erotic suggestion—sitting astride Archer was *nothing* like riding her horse. She hovered over him, her hair a cascade around her shoulders until he pushed it back, allowing him free rein of her breasts once again. He rolled her nipples between his fingers, and she moaned low in her throat.

"What do I do?" she gasped.

He placed his hands on her hips and, with a gentle rocking motion, showed her what he wanted. A smile curved her lips as she followed his instruction, her tentative thrusts soon turning frenzied. Brynn nearly stopped breathing with the sheer torture of it.

"Please," Brynn whimpered, the pressure between her thighs agonizing.

"Almost there," he grunted as his hips ground against hers with desperation. "Come with me, love."

He reached between their bodies to stroke her, and she cried out, her body wracked with spasms as he sent her barreling over the edge. Brynn sunk forward, and he held her close, groaning as the convulsions of her orgasm rippled around his length, still buried deep within her. With a growl of what she could describe only as pure male satisfaction,

Archer surged upward in one powerful thrust, his body bucking beneath hers as he, too, found his release. Brynn felt sated to the center of her bones.

Archer brought her gently back to the mattress beside him. He brushed the damp hair out of her face and frowned. "Darling, is something the matter?" She nodded solemnly, and his hesitant frown turned into something panicked. "What is it?"

Brynn stared at the face of the man she loved and felt everything in her world fall perfectly into place. She smoothed the furrows from his brow.

"I'm afraid, Your Grace, that you have made good on your threat."

"And which threat is that?" he said, his voice wary.

Then she smiled at him, her entire heart lighting up with mischief and love and contentment. "I have been completely and utterly ruined."

Epilogue

Brynn stared at her new husband of barely a month and hid a secret smile as she strolled through the verdant gardens of Worthington Abbey. He stood at the lily pond, one black Hessian propped on the pond's low stone perimeter, in deep conversation with the Earl of Thorndale. The two men were no doubt discussing the new children's hospices they had agreed to build together in London.

Archer had retired the guise of the Masked Marauder for good, instead soliciting charitable donations to improve the situations of the sick and needy in London and in the countryside as well. When Archer had brought her to a handful of the churches, hospitals, and orphanages that the Masked Marauder's repurposed money had benefited, she had been stunned. It had made her and Archer more determined to make a difference…in a legal way, of course.

And so, Archer had founded the Bradburne Trust in memory of his mother, a charitable organization that fed and clothed starving children, provided medicine to the ill, and helped families caught in dire straits. She knew most of the *ton* viewed them and their efforts as eccentric, but she didn't care. She could hardly turn a blind eye to those who were suffering on their doorstep when she had so much and they so little. Brynn was deep in preparations for the Trust's first fundraising gala, one they planned to host every year in honor of Archer's mother, the late Lady Bradburne. It would be an evening of entertainment and dancing and, considering the frenzy of excitement surrounding the duke and his new duchess, not one member of the peerage would dare miss it.

Brynn was inordinately proud of her husband and his burning desire to make the world a better place. He was still Robyn Hode of the old ballads, but now he *asked* for funds instead of stealing them.

Archer was escorting Lord Thorndale to a waiting coach after a lengthy morning meeting. The two were equal in height, though Lord Thorndale was lighter in coloring and far more mild-mannered and approachable than her husband. They did seem to get along well, however. Lady Thorndale had been in attendance at the wedding, and Brynn had taken a liking to her immediately. The wedding seemed like it had happened years ago instead of a few weeks. Archer had reposted the banns a short week before they had been married in Essex in a discreet ceremony in the village church. Archer had asked her whether she wanted a London society wedding, but Brynn had declined. And despite her mother's obvious consternation, Brynn had stood her ground. She'd had enough attention to last her a lifetime.

Their reception ball had been another matter altogether, as the marriage of a duke wasn't one to be ignored. Their friends and acquaintances had traveled in droves to Essex in the midst of the season to toast their nuptials, and the guest rooms at Worthington Abbey and Ferndale had been filled to bursting. It had been a full three days of dancing and celebration with visitors toasting their happiness, all of them misty-eyed at the sight of the handsome, aloof duke smiling in enchanted delight at his young bride.

The wedding had been everything she had imagined and more, even when she said her vows and pledged to obey him, and Archer had promptly crooked an amused eyebrow. She'd stifled a shocked giggle and admonished him later outside the church.

"You terrible wretch!"

"Have to keep you on your toes, now that you are to be my *obedient* wife," he'd teased. "No more midnight escapades attempting to lure dangerous criminals." His voice had lowered a notch. "Unless, of course it is in bed."

Which would explain why her color had been unnaturally high as they entered Archer's splendid ducal coach, enough to provoke a barrage of questions from her mama asking whether she was about to have a spell.

That night Archer had made love to her with a new exquisite tenderness. Only when he had brought her to the heights of pleasure for a third time had he allowed himself release. He had worshipped her with his body, letting her know then and forever that she would always—and only—be his. Brynn trembled at the memory, her body melting as it did when thoughts of him invaded her mind.

Their days were shared with laughter and intelligent, provoking debates, and their nights with passionate lovemaking. He showed her all the ways a man could please a woman and had taken exceptional satisfaction, she was certain, in showing her all the ways a woman could please a man. Some nights he made love to her swiftly and others he took his time, drawing out each blissful second.

A faint blush colored her cheeks as she recalled earlier that morning when she had woken him from slumber, rolling astride him and coaxing his body to life. He loved it when she took charge, and she enjoyed watching him lose himself beneath her. It was a part of him only she would ever know. That underneath his self-possessed and standoffish exterior, there lay a passionate and deeply caring man. When Archer was with her, he had no need for masks or pretenses. He was *him*. And she loved him with an intensity that she could hardly put into words. She couldn't seem to get enough of him, nor he of her.

Which would explain why her monthly flux was late.

Brynn wrapped her hands around her middle and smiled again. Her fingers spread across the flat expanse of her stomach at the thought of the tiny life blooming there. She and Archer had not yet discussed children, though she wanted them desperately. A part of her worried that his own difficult upbringing and his father's innumerable by-blows would have made him resistant to the idea. She didn't want to ask because, in truth, she feared the answer.

She waved as Lord Thorndale's coach ambled past, and then caught the eye of her husband. He strode in her direction, his long legs crossing the distance in a few swift strides. He looked tantalizing in his trousers and linen shirt, his fingers undoing the topmost buttons of his collar now that company had departed. He caught her to him and took her lips in a breathless kiss.

"My lord," she gasped against them even as her body responded the way it always did when he touched her. "The servants!"

"Have been well paid to turn a blind eye to my wife's public displays of wantonness."

"You shameless rogue!" she said, blushing, though relishing the feel of his strong arms about her. "I do no such thing."

He nuzzled her ear, breathing in the scent of her. "Then, my dear duchess, you should stop looking so desirable. The sight of you can incite a man to madness." He glanced up at the clear blue sky and smiled down at her before placing a chaste kiss to her cheek, one that was completely undermined by the leering look in his eye. "Do you fancy a ride before dinner?"

"Not today."

"Is something amiss?" he asked with a frown. "You never say no to taking Apollo out. Is it your health?"

He had taken up Gray's vexing habit of worrying over her breathing once she'd moved to Worthington Abbey, though she found she could better endure it coming from Archer. She didn't enjoy that he worried, but the crease between his eyes whenever he did felt like a small reminder of how much she meant to him. Brynn was quite certain she'd never tire of seeing or hearing how much he loved her.

"No, everything is fine. I…feel like a stroll instead. Walk with me?"

With a concerned look, Archer did as she asked. They ambled through the gardens, the light scent of the flowers rising with the afternoon breeze. He stopped her at a bench out of sight of the house. "Something is in the wind. What is it? Was it the meeting this morning? I am sorry it went so long, but the plans for the hospitals are taking longer than we expected—"

"No, it's not that," she said, drawing him down to sit on the bench with her. She drew a deep calming breath, fighting the rapid cadence of her heart. "I held a baby some days ago at the orphanage, and… I was wondering…if you…wanted children," she finished lamely. A shadow flickered over his eyes as he regarded her in somber silence. "Someday, I mean," she added when his attention lowered to her hand, still splayed across her middle.

"Is there something you wish to tell me?" he asked, gently nudging her chin up to face him.

"I am…past my time."

"You are with child." She nodded, even though his soft words hadn't been a question. Brynn nearly melted at the tender, awestruck look in his eyes. "*My* child," he whispered in reverent wonder. She heard the joy in his hushed tone, saw the cresting light of another dawn in his eyes as they gazed at her stomach again. In that moment, all of Brynn's fears drained away.

"If it's a boy," she said teary-eyed and smiling, "we'll have to make sure he doesn't follow in his marauding father's footsteps."

Archer took her into his arms, his fingers intertwining with hers lying against her stomach. "But if it's a girl, I fear we will have much more to worry about, especially if she is anything like her mother."

"And how is that?" Brynn asked.

"To be beautiful, fearless, and incomparable is to invite great distress upon her father. He will surely have to lock her in a tower and post three guards at all times."

Her breath hitched at the love on his face, and she slid a palm up to his cheek. "And what if she wears her brother's breeches and rides without a saddle and says what she thinks?"

"Then I shall count myself the luckiest father in the world."

Brynn opened her mouth to retort, but her husband leaned down and smothered her words with his lips. And then she forgot everything but him.

Acknowledgments

Amalie Howard

First and foremost, I have nothing but love for my brilliant co-author, Angie Morgan, without whom this series would never have been written. We started writing *My Rogue, My Ruin* out of a shared passion for historical romance, and three books later, I couldn't imagine writing about fearless heroines and dashing rogues with anyone else. One Brain for the win! To our editor, Alethea Spiridon, and publisher, Liz Pelletier, who took on the *Lords of Essex* series, a huge thank you for believing in us and these books—we wouldn't be here without you. To the production and publicity teams at Entangled, thanks for all you do. Thanks to Liza Fleissig who championed this "guilty pleasure" from the start. A heartfelt thank you goes out to all the readers, fans, and friends who continuously advocate for my books. I am so humbled by your enthusiasm and support. Lastly, to my wonderful family— Cameron, Connor, Noah, and Olivia—my Happy Ever After simply wouldn't be possible without you.

Angie Morgan

It's amazing to think that what started out as a funny back and forth on Twitter with Amalie, alliterating all the reasons we loved historical romance ("Dastardly Dukes!"; "Virile Viscounts!"; "Manly Marquesses!"), has become a fully-fledged book baby. I've had so much fun writing the Lords of Essex series with you, Amalie. Thank you for having my back, for pushing me when I needed it, and for always being there. One Brain forever! Thank you to my agent, Ted Malawer, for traveling this new publishing road with me. You've always been so supportive of my writing and my career. I'll say it again: I have the best agent. To the entire team we've worked with so far at Entangled Publishing and Select Historical—Alethea Spiridon, Liz Pelletier, Heidi Stryker, and Holly Simpson—thank you so much for believing in this book and doing everything you have for it. We are thrilled to be Entangled authors! And finally, to my husband, Chad, who is by far the "Duke of my Dreams!" and our daughters, Alex, Joslin, and Willa. I love you!

About the Authors

Amalie Howard's love of romance developed after she started pilfering her grandmother's novels in high school when she should have been studying. She has no regrets. A #1 Amazon bestseller and a national IPPY silver medalist, she is the award-winning author of several young adult novels critically acclaimed by Kirkus, Publishers Weekly, VOYA, and Booklist, including *Waterfell*, *The Almost Girl*, and *Alpha Goddess*, a Kid's IndieNext title. She currently resides in Colorado with her husband and three children. Visit her at www.amaliehoward.com.

Angie Morgan lives in New Hampshire with her husband, their three daughters, a menagerie of pets, and an extensive collection of paperback romance novels. She's the author of several young adult books, including The Dispossessed series written under the name Page Morgan. Critically acclaimed by Booklist, Publisher's Weekly, Kirkus, School Library Journal, VOYA, and The Bulletin, Angie's novels have been an *IndieNext* selection, a *Seventeen Magazine* Summer Book Club Read, and a #1 Amazon bestseller. Visit her at www. AngieMorganBooks.com.

Discover more historical romance…

A FALSE PROPOSAL
by Pamela Mingle

War hero Adam Grey returns home and plans to run for Parliament. But he needs the support of the local baronet, who controls the seat. He learns that his dissolute father has promised him to the baronet's daughter in return for forgiveness of his debts. Adam wants nothing to do with marriage or his father's problems, so he fakes an engagement to Cass Linford—his best friend's sister.

HIGHLAND DECEPTION
a *Highland Pride* novel by Lori Ann Bailey

Scotland, August 1642

Lachlan Cameron is honor bound to see a wounded lass to safety, although the lovely maid harbors a wealth of secrets, some of which, he suspicions, may threaten his clan. Maggie Murray has fled her home to avoid a political marriage to an abusive man, but the honor of the handsome Cameron laird who rescued her will force him to send her home. Despite their growing attraction, she can't disclose her identity and will be safer in a convent. But with each passing day, and Lachlan's gentle urging to trust him, keeping her secrets grows increasingly difficult.

Enticing Her Unexpected Bridegroom
a *Lady Lancaster Garden Society* novel by Catherine Hemmerling

Sarah Jardin is far too outspoken and ungraceful to be a lady… until Lady Lancaster invites her to join the Young Ladies Garden Society. But her new life of high-society intrigue is interrupted when she's discovered in a compromising position with the David Rochester—the man she's always loved. They're forced to marry, even as they are drawn into investigating a dangerous conspiracy. With life and love on the line, their unexpected marriage will either end in rapture…or ruin.

Less Than a Lady
a novel by Eva Devon

Darcy Blake, Earl of Chase, is a soldier, rogue, and a loyal King's man. Commanded to spy on the luscious actress Amelia Fox, Darcy must pretend to be her student for a court theatrical. He is certain he can school her in the art of seduction while discovering if she is a traitor. But to his shock, he finds Mrs. Fox teaching him an entirely different kind of lesson.

CPSIA information can be obtained
at www.ICGtesting.com
Printed in the USA
BVHW030058060720
583037BV00001B/3

9 781682 813522